U ‖‖‖‖‖‖‖‖‖‖‖ D0335606

'It goes without saying that the mo.... child,' said Reed. 'Mother Nature programmed the female of the species that way. But fathers . . . they can be different. Oh, they would say they love their children. But some can be quite indifferent. They'd rather spend their time with their friends, drinking beer, playing squash. But I believe you do love your son very much, Mr Stainforth. You spend time with him, talk to him – not down to him, you treat him as someone very important in your life. Probably far more important than you yourself realise. I see you at Christmas, spending all morning playing on the living-room carpet, putting together toys, laughing and joking together. I truly believe you do that, Mr Stainforth. Ah, now you're wondering why I wanted to establish that belief, and why I am standing here above the North Sea, holding your beloved son's arm. The reason is this, Mr Stainforth. Because I am going to kill your son. And you are going to watch me kill him.'

The power of words.

I AM GOING TO KILL YOUR SON. . .

About the author

Born in 1958, Simon Clark lives in Doncaster, South Yorkshire. His short stories have appeared in several magazines and anthologies, including *Darklands 2*, *Dark Voices 5* and *The Year's Best Horror Stories* (four times.) He has published a collection of short stories, *Blood and Grit*, and his work has been broadcast on BBC Radio 4. *Nailed By the Heart* is his first novel. His second, *Blood Crazy*, is published in hardcover by Hodder and Stoughton and will soon be appearing in paperback from the New English Library.

NAILED BY THE HEART

Simon Clark

NEW ENGLISH LIBRARY
Hodder and Stoughton

Copyright © 1995 by Simon Clark

First published in Great Britain in 1995 by
Hodder and Stoughton
A division of Hodder Headline PLC

First published in paperback in 1995 by
Hodder and Stoughton

A New English Library paperback

The right of Simon Clark to be identified as the Author of
the Work has been asserted by him in accordance with the
Copyright, Designs and Patents Act 1988.

10 9 8 7 6 5 4 3 2

All rights reserved. No part of this publication may be
reproduced, stored in a retrieval system, or transmitted,
in any form or by any means without the prior written
permission of the publisher, nor be otherwise circulated
in any form of binding or cover other than that in which
it is published and without a similar condition being
imposed on the subsequent purchaser.

All characters in this publication are fictitious and any
resemblance to real persons, living or dead, is purely
coincidental.

A CIP catalogue record for this title is available
from the British Library

ISBN 0 340 62573 2

Typeset by Phoenix Typesetting, Ilkley, West Yorkshire

Printed and bound in Great Britain by
Cox & Wyman, Reading, Berkshire

Hodder and Stoughton
A division of Hodder Headline PLC
338 Euston Road
London NW1 3BH

537523
MORAY DISTRICT COUNCIL

DEPARTMENT OF

LEISURE AND LIBRARIES
F

For Janet, my wife.
Her hard work and dedication made this book possible.

Though they sink through the sea they shall rise again;
Though lovers be lost love shall not;
And death shall have no dominion.

– Dylan Thomas

1

'Dad! Look! I'm flying!'

The six-year-old boy came bounding down the beach, kicking up gouts of sand, scattering white shells, the light breeze blowing out the Superman cape behind him like a bright red tablecloth. Every half-dozen steps or so he would make a determined leap.

Chris Stainforth called back to his son: 'If you do take off, don't go too far. Just circle the sea-fort a couple of times then come back.'

David ran along the beach, which lay deserted apart from the pair of them. He turned, almost slipping on some strands of kelp, and came bounding back shouting in a breathless voice. 'That's our sea-fort now . . . isn't it, Dad? We bought it.'

'We sure did, kidda. All ours.' Well, truthfully, thought Chris, they owned around five per cent of the thing outright and the rest was shackled to a gigantic mortgage.

He stood, his feet firmly planted in the sand, and gazed at the nineteenth-century sea-fort. Cut from a stone the colour of butter, it reared up from the sands like a beached battleship. This morning it seemed to shine in the warm April sunlight. Around its flanks the advancing tide swirled and foamed in a shining pool.

There was his castle.

'When can we go in the swimming pool?'

'It hasn't been built yet, David. In fact there's still a lot of work to be done before we can even move in.'

'I want to move in now. It looks ace.'

1

'Me too. But we'll have to be patient.'

David looked up at him, his blue eyes twinkling with that laughing look he had when he was excited. The sun had brought out across his snub nose a spattering of freckles that looked as if they had been sprayed there by aerosol. His grin grew wider.

'Tell me what's going to be in there, Dad.'

Chris Stainforth smiled warmly. 'Well, you know it's an old sea-fort.'

'Like a castle?'

'Yes. It was put there to stop an enemy attacking us from the sea. And you know we're going to convert it into a hotel?'

'Then people pay to stop there?'

'That's right.'

'Even Nan and Grandad?'

'No. They'll come and visit us for free. We'll have our own apartment. Your bedroom window will look out over the sea.'

'And a swimming pool?'

'Yes.'

'Goody!'

David hurled himself at Chris, punching him enthusiastically in the stomach.

Chris clutched his stomach and fell convincingly to the ground.

'Ugh . . . I'm Zorgon the Disagreeable, and Superman is beating me to a bloody pulp. Help! Help! Ouch . . .'

David threw himself on to Chris's back with enough force to drive the air from his lungs and ram his face into the beach.

His little lad wasn't so little any more. Six years old and he could pack quite a punch.

'Can I kick you in the head now, Dad?' asked David politely.

'No, you can't.' He laughed. A long, hearty laugh that had its origins deep inside. He'd not felt this good in years. The plan to convert the old sea-fort into a hotel was a dream come true. From now on he would be his own boss.

Father and son rolled about the beach getting sand in their hair and clothes.

Eventually David collapsed giggling into a sitting position on the beach. Then he asked if his mum was coming down to join them.

'No. She's back at the hotel. She's got to phone some plumbers, some builders and some other people. The sea-fort needs lots of work.'

'Lots and lots?'

'Yes. That's why we're going to see the man in Out-Butterwick about that caravan.'

'When can we look inside the sea-fort? I want to see the gun.'

'Perhaps tomorrow.' Chris smiled until his cheeks ached.

For David the excitement became overpowering and he raced off down the beach once more, leaping from one patch of shells to another, the cape shining a brilliant red in the sunlight.

Chris sat on the beach basking in the warm sunshine. Overhead, gulls hung like scraps of white paper against the sky. Most of them wheeled over the hulking shape of the sea-fort. The mass of masonry, heated by the sun, produced a thermal of warm air on which gulls rose until they were high in the sky. From there they would launch their forays out to sea in search of fish.

He breathed deeply and closed his eyes. The air was fresh and smelt faintly of kelp. Why were people locked away in factories, deafened by machines or offices that reeked of overheated photocopiers, for nine-tenths of their lives? Here he felt truly alive.

'Shells, shells, shells! Here's your bloody shells!' David's sing-song voice cut into his reverie. He opened his eyes to see the boy's impossibly wide grin.

'David, how many times have I told you? Don't swear.'

'I'm not swearing.' David's amused look intensified. 'Bloody hell, I only said here's your bloody shells.'

David slapped a handful of cockleshells into his father's

3

hand. 'These shells are dead, dead funny. They've got pictures of men's faces on them like pennies. But not really like pennies. Because you can see their eyes and mouths and things and — '

'Oh, that's nice,' murmured Chris without listening. He slipped the shells into the pocket of his jeans.

'Can we build a sandcastle now?'

'No, we haven't got — '

'Aw, go on.'

'Oh, all right, a quick one.' Ruth would have disapproved. She always accused him of being too soft on David.

Chris began to pile sand into a mound with his hands. Here above the high-tide mark it was loose and dry. Easy enough to dig with your bare hands.

But then life for the Stainforths had become uncannily easy. Within a week of advertising their old home they had found a cash buyer. The property developer who owned the sea-fort jumped at their offer, which was nearly a quarter below the advertised price. Property conveyancing, usually a tortuously slow process, ran smoothly. Within six weeks he and Ruth were sitting in the solicitor's office signing the transfer deed.

Two days ago, Chris had driven his family out of their old home town, where a dozen generations of Stainforths had lived. It had been raining. The shops, warehouses, and acre upon acre of cheap post-war housing looked dismal – a wasteland of red brick.

On the edge of town they had passed the iron-fenced cemetery where generations of Stainforths lay buried. Chris had acknowledged it with a tiny nod.

As they travelled, the rain eased off, the cloud thinned, and by the time they had covered the seventy miles to the coast the sun was shining brilliantly.

He paused to survey the results of his digging. Without realising it, he'd raised a huge mound of sand nearly to his waist. 'How's that, then?' Chris found himself panting. Hell, he'd have to be fitter than this when it came to working on the sea-fort. He couldn't allow illness or any other distractions if the hotel was going to open in time to avoid instant bankruptcy next spring.

David watched his father at work. The sandcastle was going to be enormous. When it was high enough he would run and dive into it. Maybe with his Superman costume on he'd be able to dive that bit further.

David still hoped that one day he would be able to jump high enough to actually take off. Then he would soar away like that white seagull he now saw skimming over the waves. He would find an old cup – no, a bucket – fly low over the water, scoop up a bucketful and fly – whooooosh! – up the beach and tip it all over his dad.

He'd bet his dad would laugh his head off. He'd laughed a lot lately now they'd come to stop in the hotel. Mum too.

Everything was waiting to be explored. The beach – miles and miles of it. The funny dunes that were like little hills. The marshes behind the dunes. They were all lumpy with lots of long grass and muddy pools.

'Is that big enough for you, then, David?'

Chris rose, wiping his hands on his legs. He breathed heavily; sweat rolled down his forehead.

Once more he found his gaze being drawn back to the sea-fort. His plans ran through his head, as they had done ever since he had seen the place. Cut through the seaward wall, install windows, triple-glazed, giving guests panoramic views of the sea. On the landward side guests would look over the dunes towards the marshes. A bird-watcher's paradise. Ideal, too, for the stressed business executive craving a get-away-from-it-all holiday. The coast here was a slice of ancient wilderness. A gritty no-man's land between dry land and ocean.

Again, he mentally began adding up the cost of the conversion works. It would be expensive. If the venture failed it would mean financial ruin.

'Dad! They're in the water! They're in the water!'

David came running back up the beach in long, leaping strides.

'Who's in the water?' Chris looked back at the incoming tide. 'There's no one there.'

David looked up at him, his blue eyes serious. 'They came up. Then there was one. Then there was two. Then there was three!'

'You saw people? Swimming?'

'Noooo . . . I can see people. With faces. Standing in the water. They are watching *meee*!'

'Everyone has faces.'

'I know-wer. But these men had' – he held his hands within a few centimetres of his face while making a rotating motion with his fingers – 'faces. Funny faces.'

Someone's playing tricks, thought Chris. He glanced along the beach.

No one.

Maybe some kids messing around in the sea?

Unlikely.

Without a wet-suit this time of year you would be half dead of exposure within minutes.

He looked at his son. The expression told him David was not telling tales.

Then again, Chris told himself, David Alistair Stainforth had an uncanny knack of seeing people who were not there.

The River Troll Mark 3, he thought, remembering the time when David had been seeing 'things' in the river that ran near their old house.

Taking his shoulders, he turned David gently away from the sea. His son was shaking slightly. 'It might have been gulls in the water or —'

'Dad, there really was —'

'Or a seal.'

'A seal?' David looked puzzled.

Chris saw the solution and grabbed it. 'Yes, seals. You've seen them on telly. They look a bit like dogs, but with

6

flippers and no fur. And—' Inspiration flashed. 'And when they bob up and down in the sea they look like people with funny faces. Come on, it's time we saw that man about the caravan.'

After ineffectually brushing the sand from his Superman costume, David pushed his fist into Chris's hand. Chris gave the hand a squeeze. It felt hot and gritty.

Hand in hand, father and son walked up the beach to the dunes, which they climbed together. They paused to look back. To Chris this view was nothing less than magic. To his right, the skeleton of a fishing boat lay half buried in the sand, the sun- and salt-bleached spars looking like the bones of a long-dead sea monster left high and dry by the tide.

Chris breathed deeply. Jesus, this air made your skin tingle.

Along the beach to his left, the quickly rising tide had almost surrounded the sea-fort. Already the beach on its flanks was submerged and the first waves were washing over the raised causeway that linked it with dry land. In ten minutes that too would be covered, and for a few hours the sea-fort would be an island.

As he let his gaze run over curling twists of foam which gleamed in the sunshine, his stomach became suddenly tense.

He screwed up his eyes against the dazzling brightness.

What had he seen?

Raising his hand to shield his eyes, he looked hard at an area of sea not far from the sea-fort.

Maybe there really were seals along this stretch of coastline after all. God knows it was remote enough. Yet, just for a moment, he had seen – no, thought he had seen – rising from the deeper water beyond the surf, the dark head and shoulders of a man.

And it seemed, for a second or two, that the man had stared intently back. There had been a sense of intelligence and purpose in that unwavering stare. Inexplicably it had made him feel uneasy.

He looked hard at the area of seawater until his eyes watered, then shrugged. It had gone.

A seal, he told himself. It had to be a seal. Only a lunatic would be swimming in the North Sea so early in the year. He smiled to himself. After living in a town all his life, he would have to get used to all this flora and fauna.

'Come on, David,' he said, squeezing his son's hand. 'Time to go.'

2

After being locked in the ocean freighter's laundry store for three hours, the engineer gave a deep groan and died.

The sixteen-year-old cabin boy sat crouched in a corner, arms tightly wrapped around his knees, his frightened eyes unnaturally wide.

This was hell.

This was pure hell.

Locked in a tiny room with a dead man, his mouth gaping wide where he had tried to chew in his last lungful of air.

His face.

The boy buried his head in his arms and rocked.

Why had they done this?

He had never harmed anyone before in his life.

Everything had been going so well. His first Atlantic crossing from New York had been a cinch. The crew, all American, apart from the Filipino cook, had been like one big matey family. Everyone on first-name terms, apart from the Skipper of course. Well, someone had to be the boss. Just last night he and Tubbs had played checkers while listening to Christmas carols on the radio. They had been able to pick up the American forces radio based in Germany. Even when the DJ played requests from folks back home for the GI Joes stationed in Europe he hadn't felt homesick. Mark Faust had his new family right here on the big freighter, the *Mary-Anne*, shipping frozen beef to Norway.

Tubbs had given him his first beer. First swallow, it tasted like something scraped off the bilges – after the second it hadn't tasted so bad. And everyone in the mess had laughed and slapped him good-naturedly on the back. By the time he'd finished the beer he felt great, all warm inside even though the beer was ice cold.

Mark Faust wondered what his ma and pa would say if they knew. Only at Christmas was wine allowed into the house, and then only sherry in order for the solemn toast to be taken. You just sipped it – you weren't supposed to actually enjoy it.

Not like this. Boy, was this great! Sitting laughing and drinking in the mess, the radio blowing out 'God Rest Ye Merry Gentlemen' until the speaker made the bottles vibrate, and then —

. . . and then it all went bad.

The door opened as if it had been kicked.

In came half a dozen men carrying submachine-guns and shotguns. Tommo Greene had jumped up only to have half his face blown from his skull by a spray of bird-shot.

That's when Christmas became hell.

The attackers seemed physically huge, near-giants, with dark, tanned faces. But their eyes . . .

Their eyes glittered with such cruelty and hate. It was as if fires had been lit behind them. For Mark, their eyes were more terrifying than the weapons they carried in their massive fists. You actually recoiled when they looked at you.

If they had said they were demons from hell he would have believed them.

Within moments he had been thrust into the linen store with Tubbs. The shock had split the fat man's heart.

The *Mary-Anne* rolled gently on the tide. They were at anchor in one of the hundreds of fiords that cut inlets deep into the Norwegian mainland.

He slowly raised his head. Light from the dim bulb reflected from the dead man's dentures. They had slipped halfway from his mouth. One of the teeth was missing. A fight in some port, maybe, or perhaps Tubbs had simply walked into a telegraph pole after one rum too many. Tubbs himself sort of sat, leaning back against the iron wall.

Mark found his gaze pulled to the dead man's face. Eyes closed, the face had turned white as the blood drained from the upper parts of his body to settle in the lower half, turning his hands blue. Then the dead man urinated. Wetness seeped through the denim boiler-suit to roll across the metal floor in a trickle the colour of orange pop.

Something cracked in Mark's head. He was on his feet pounding at the door, screaming to be let out.

He seemed to be screaming for hours before the door opened. A huge figure, as big as a grizzly bear, loomed through the doorway. One look from those eyes silenced Mark.

'He's dead, he's dead,' muttered Mark, only half coherently. 'He's dead. I-I want to come out. I want . . . He's dead. You see, he's dead.'

The man put his fingers to his lips in a shushing gesture, then calmly balled his fist and rammed it forward into Mark's face, knocking him backwards across the dead fat man and into the shelves, scattering sheets and pillowcases in a white avalanche.

Without a word the man removed the light-bulb from the socket and stepped out of the laundry store, locking the door behind him.

Inside, the darkness was absolute. It seemed to creep close.

And softly touch him. A cold, cold touch. As cold as the finger of a dead man.

'Please don't leave me . . . Please . . . Please . . . Please. Don't leave me alone . . .'

Mark Faust's voice fell on dead ears.

3

'David. Stop it. You'll lose your fingers.'

'I'm not doing anything.'

'You're picking your nose again.' Ruth opened the back door of the car to let him out.

She had brought them to visit the closest thing to civilisation near the sea-fort. The tiny coastal village of Out-Butterwick.

Confidently, David headed off by himself towards Out-Butterwick's one and only shop – which was little more than a large, rambling hut of white timbers. He charged through the door as if he were taking part in a police raid and disappeared inside. Chris waited for his wife to lock the doors of the car.

After all those years of running old bangers that broke down with monotonous regularity, this car, a Ford Sierra, was something special to them.

One night he had pulled off the main road on to a farm track. There Chris had made love to Ruth in the back seat of their new car.

They'd not done that since their courting days. And it didn't make Chris regret that those so-called golden days were long gone. It was cramped, uncomfortable; repeatedly they banged naked parts of their bodies on cold plastic.

Any minute someone might have walked by. The astonished pedestrian would have seen a bare backside heaving away in the moonlight.

Afterwards, they had sat in the back seat, their jeans around their ankles, shaking with laughter.

'And what are you smirking at, Mr Stainforth?' asked Ruth, linking arms with him.

'Oh, nothing much. I was just imagining how you'd look after six months mixing cement and humping bricks.'

She laughed. 'We'll have bodies like Arnold Schwarzenegger and swear like how's-your-father.'

'You've no second thoughts?'

She looked back at him, her shoulder-length dark hair fanned across her face by the breeze. 'Any second thoughts?' She pulled the hair away with her fingers. 'Hundreds. And you?'

'Thousands.' When he looked down at her he couldn't help smiling. Not only did she have the same snub nose and freckles as David, she also possessed the same mischievous glint in her eye.

'Come on,' she said, 'let's see what son of Superman is up to.'

When they entered the shop, Chris gazed about the place in wonder. It was one of those places that seemed bigger on the inside than the outside. Shelves lined the walls from ceiling to floor. Hung from the ceiling were string bags full of blue and yellow footballs, fold-away canvas chairs, wax jackets, strings of gloves – a gloriously chaotic mix. The whole place smelt of creosote and oranges.

Chris spotted David. He was talking to a large man who leaned forward across the counter, resting his weight on his elbows. The man, mid-forties, had a head of thick back-combed hair that ran in corrugated waves. Chris noticed that the man's nose had been broken at some time. The bone hadn't been properly set, giving his face an odd, lop-sided look. The man appeared to be enjoying David's company; he was listening intently to what David was saying and nodding every so often.

Chris tried to see where, in this stock-taker's vision of hell, light-bulbs were concealed.

David skipped down the aisle towards them.

Ruth asked, 'Have you been talking nicely to the man?'

'Sure have,' answered David in one of his suddenly loud voices. 'But he's got a funny voice. Like from a film.'

'Shh . . . ' hissed Ruth under her breath. 'You don't say things like that.'

'I only said he talked funny,' protested David equally loudly.

The big man behind the counter light-heartedly waved David's lack of tact away with a huge paddle of a hand. 'Don't be mad at him, folks. The accent throws everybody. They don't expect it in a place like this.'

'He's American!' announced David. 'Like Superman!'

'That's right, I guess I am,' chuckled the big American. 'I've lived here thirty years. Never been away.' Then, grinning broadly, he called to Ruth and Chris. 'How do you do? Need any help? We're a bit of an Aladdin's cave here; things take some finding.'

Chris returned the grin. 'No thanks. We've found your light-bulbs.'

David hopped back to the counter. 'I've got a goldfish,' he told the American jubilantly. 'He's called Clark Kent. Have you ever met Superman?'

'No. But I loved Superman when I was a boy. I collected all the comics. I saw all the movies.' A broad grin split his lop-sided face. ''Course, they were the old ones then. All in black and white.'

'Black and white?'

'Yeah. They were made a long, long time ago. But you know, I used to sit there spellbound, right down at the front, big tub of popcorn in my hands, eyes bugging out at the screen.'

'I think David's found a friend,' murmured Ruth to Chris.

He took the light-bulbs from Ruth. 'Where next? Back to the hotel or the sea-fort?' He itched to have another look round. 'David hasn't been inside yet.'

Ruth hunted for a handful of coins in the pocket of her jeans. 'Actually, Chris, I could do with nipping down to the caravan. I need to measure the windows for the curtains.'

Chris realised his expression must have given him away.

'Don't worry, Scrooge, it won't cost anything. I'll be using the dining-room curtains from the old house.'

Chris saw that David was still talking earnestly to the big American as they walked down the aisle to the counter.

'Got what you want?'

Chris smiled. 'For the time being. But I expect we'll be beating a pathway to your door before long.' As Ruth counted the money out into the man's huge hand, Chris noticed that the American no longer looked so cheerful. Now he avoided eye contact. He even began to talk about the weather in the odd fragmented way that Chris thought was still the strict domain of the English when they were trying to break the ice at parties. Or were trying to pluck up the courage to tell you something important.

Ruth shepherded David out with a goodbye over her shoulder. David shouted, 'See you soon.'

Chris said goodbye. The American said nothing, his lop-sided face now expressionless.

What had David said to upset the man? Chris would have a few words with the boy as soon as they were in the car.

He followed his wife and son back to the Sierra. A breeze drifted sand from the beach across the road in little yellow waves.

He glanced back to see the American standing in the doorway of the shop. He was watching them intently.

As David scrambled into the back seat he gave the man a cheerful wave. Chris saw that the man did not wave back. The lop-sided face was set in an unsmiling mask.

'Misery-guts,' muttered Ruth.

'You noticed too?' Chris climbed in, started the engine, and pulled out. The few cottages lining the empty road looked deserted. Not a soul in sight.

In the rear-view mirror, he could still see the American standing in the shop doorway.

He glanced back at David, sat with the comic on his knee.

'David, what did you say to the man in the shop?'

'Nothing.'

'You must have said something,' said Ruth, looking back. 'He doesn't look very happy at all.'

Without taking his eyes off the comic, David shrugged. 'I only told him we were moving into the old sea-fort.'

Chris watched the man in the rear-view mirror. The American continued to stare after them until they drove out of the village and out of sight.

4

BANG! BANG! BANG!

There's no going back.

This is it.

Mark Faust knew what he must do.

He was in the deepest part of the ship, turning the huge iron wheels that would open the sea-cock valves. Once open the sea would rush into the *Mary-Anne* and sink her within minutes.

Turn the wheel, turn the wheel.

It turned – slowly, too slowly.

'Jesus. Turn! Turn!'

Grease and rust stained his hands red and black. The ship rolled in the swell. Overhead a single light-bulb crusted in dirt swung, illuminating the bilges with a weak yellow light. The piles of old chain, cable, pieces of machinery, and empty boxes cast shadows that swung to the left, then to the right, as if participating in some crazy dance.

BANG! BANG! BANG!

This was crazy, thought Mark ferociously. All crazy. A dream. Perhaps he'd wake soon with the crew shouting Merry Christmas.

Dear God . . . It would be Christmas soon. Turkey. Christmas trees. Paper streamers. Presents. Cards with Santas and sleighs and —

Jesus. Something scuttled by his feet. Another. Dark and fast.

Rats!

The incoming water was driving them up from the bilges.

19

There were dozens of them, running up over the chains and cable, their dark wet bodies glistening in the feeble light. One jumped and bounced off his face. Its thick cold tail hit him on the cheek and its claw scratched his bottom lip.

Overhead the mad banging continued.

Three days ago Mark had been released by the ship's hijackers to cook for them. Once he'd been told to take food to the Skipper's cabin. Was the Skipper dead? He knew most of the crew were.

When he had entered the Skipper's cabin he had stood there, his neck aching with tension. 'Is anyone there?'

Silence – apart from the bass throb of the engine and the wash of waves against the *Mary-Anne*'s iron flanks.

He clutched the tray until the edge of it dug into his stomach. 'Hello?'

Still no reply; but he was sure someone was in the cabin with him. Grey light seeped through the only porthole, revealing the bunk with blankets heaped in an untidy pile at one end. Clothes lay strewn about the cabin. Some had been ripped.

For a moment he stared at the table fixed to one wall. It had been smeared with a rust-coloured liquid; here and there it had congealed into black lumps.

BLOOD.

The word oozed slowly into his mind. He'd seen so much of it over the last few days that the word seemed to be losing its meaning. Blood . . . it gathered in sticky ponds in the walkways, spots covered the wall of the mess in a Dalmatian pattern, your feet stuck to it on the steps. It was as he licked his cracked dry lips that he saw a shape move against the corner of the cabin.

'Who's that?'

The shape became a human figure as the man stood. When Mark saw the face he recoiled as if an electric current had suddenly cracked through his body. The man's eyes were impossibly large; they were round like dinner plates – and black as engine oil.

But then, as the man tottered forward out of the gloom, he saw the face clearly. The man's head had been roughly bandaged so his eyes were covered. Bizarrely, two patches of blood had soaked through the material, making it look as if he had two panda-like eyes, large blurry patches that seemed to watch Mark intently as he stood there clutching his tray.

'Is that you, boy? Faust?'

He managed to half-whisper, 'Yes, Skipper.'

The Skipper lumbered forward, his hand clutching at the air until he caught hold of him; then he gripped him tightly by the shoulders.

'They cut my eyes, boy,' he said, 'because I told the murdering bastards I wouldn't carry them.'

Then the Skipper sat Mark Faust on the bunk and told him what he knew, his gnarled hands shaking. 'They need three or four of us because none of them are sailors. They've murdered the rest, poor devils. We'll be dead too within forty-eight hours.'

'What are we going to do? Jump them?'

The Skipper turned the blurred panda eyes on Mark; he smiled grimly. 'A blinded man and a boy? No . . . But I know they must die, son. I've heard enough of their boasting. Death and torture are meat and drink to these beasts. No, I thought it all through and I see no alternative. We've got to do it.'

'What, Skipper?'

'Son, you've got to scuttle the ship.'

Now, in the greasy pit of the ship, Mark began to heave open the last sea-cock to admit the murky water.

Overhead the clanging did not stop. It sounded like a distant engine with a huge, slow beat. *Bang . . . Bang . . .*

In his mind's eye he could see the blind skipper of the *Mary-Anne* in the freezer store, beating the metal walls with the iron bar, his breath billowing out great white clouds like a steam engine running at full belt.

It would be drawing the men down at a run, the taste of whisky still on their tongues. What the hell was the man doing in there? they would be asking one another. Only

Almighty God knew what was in store for them. By the time they had forced open the door of the freezer store they would be too late to undo what Mark had done.

And the cabin boy? Where the hell is he? We'll split him open with the ship's anchor when we get our hands on the runt!

The thought drove him on. He grabbed the fourteen-pound hammer and hammered at the sea-cock shaft until it jammed tight in its socket. No one could shift it now without stripping the whole mechanism.

Like rats in a trap the hijackers were caught.

When he had finished he followed the fleeing rats upward. He reached a ladder that ran up a steel service well to the forward deck and began to climb.

Once on deck he planned to cut the lifeboat away from its derrick; hopefully he would make shore or be picked up by a passing ship.

Outside it was dark. An icy breeze ripped at his hair and clothes.

As he straightened, he came face to face with a huge figure; a pair of eyes shone unnaturally bright in the dark.

Christ! He never thought he'd encounter one on the deck.

For once one of their number looked almost astonished, seeing Mark outside at night.

Before the man could react, Mark turned and ran. The deck was wet. His feet slipped from under him. As he struggled to his feet he saw the hijacker raise a revolver.

This time when Mark ran he did not slip. And he didn't stop running. He didn't even slow his pace when he heard the crack of the shot. The bullet gouged six inches of paint from the railing to his left.

The guard-rail loomed like a white barred fence out of the dark.

Mark Faust did not hesitate. He vaulted over it . . .

. . . and fell into another world.

5

The bastard, thought Chris Stainforth savagely as he stamped on the accelerator pedal.

'Don't drive so fast, Chris.'

'I'm so bloody angry.' Chris overtook a tractor on a straight length of road. 'What that idiot did to us.'

'Well, it's done now. It's over.'

'But why? We'd agreed everthing. We'd agreed the rent on the caravan; we'd agreed the date we were moving in; we'd even bought the bloody light-bulbs for it.'

'Chris . . .'

'And the brass-faced sod . . . he just stands there, tells us sorry, he's not renting us the caravan. He's expecting his daughter home from Canada and he wants to save the place for her.'

'Chris . . . All right, so we lost the caravan. It's not the end of the world.'

Chris felt the fury burn into him. 'What a lame excuse . . . the daughter. Do you believe him, Ruth? Because I don't.'

In the back, David sat quietly, scared now.

'I've a good mind to —'

'A good mind to what, Chris?' demanded Ruth. 'We have nothing in writing. We can't sue. Or are you going back there to batter the man's brains out?'

Chris shot Ruth a glance. He saw her looking at him, her eyes thick with tears.

He eased off the accelerator and the speed began to drop

until the fields full of black and white cattle were no longer a blur. *And for God's sake at least pretend you're in control of yourself again.*

'No. I know there's nothing we can do,' he said in a deliberately low voice. 'It's my stupid fault. I should have tied Mr Greene down to a written agreement.' He called back to David, 'How you keeping, old son?'

'Not bad, Dad.'

'Shall we have another game of Superman later?'

David grinned broadly. 'Sure can, Dad.'

Although Chris put on a cheerful front, he was worried. The sea-fort's interior remained in a semi-derelict state. Ten years ago, a builder had attempted to convert the place into a hotel. It had new mains services: water, electricity, access road. There were new windows giving panoramic views of the sea. The builder had gone bust, leaving work half done. Mounds of rubble rose from the floor of virtually every room. The place was patently uninhabitable. It would be months before they would have even the most basic accommodation for themselves.

He turned off on to the gravel car park of the country inn that was their temporary base.

'Home!' shouted David gleefully.

'Not for long,' said Chris, then added with a grim smile, 'hopefully.' The plans he and his wife had made were important to him. He would not allow them to fail.

The wheels crunched over the gravel as Chris slowed the car to a stop alongside the gable-end wall of the hotel. A few cars were already there. In six weeks tourists would fill the bars until they overflowed into the beer garden and car parks. Next year at this time, Chris told himself, we'll capture some of that trade.

'Can I play on the slide?' shouted David, taking a heroic leap out of the car.

'All right,' said Ruth. 'Until lunch.'

He ran to the area of lawn where there were swings and

a large fibreglass elephant with a long pink-tongue slide that curved down to the ground.

David liked to climb the steps, sit on the elephant's head and survey his world.

His parents went into the hotel.

'One, two, three, four . . . David counted up the steps. '. . . five, six, seven, eight.' The breeze seemed to be stronger up here. He looked around. It was very high. When his dad stood near the elephant David was higher than his dad's head. David'd call him names, then giggle as his dad growled like a monster and tried to jump up and grab him, his hands grasping like monster claws. It always ended the same way, with his dad climbing the steps and David aiming pretend kicks at the monster's snarling face – just like the films. Bang! His foot would smack into the monster's head. Then it would plummet to the ground below.

To oblivion, he would think with a walloping sense of satisfaction. Then, panting, he would look down, and the sprawling monster would be his dad again, laid flat out on the grass laughing breathlessly, his Adam's apple bouncing in his throat.

David looked up. Big fluffy clouds like mountains of mashed potato hung in the sky. In between, the sky showed through, dark blue.

He sat on the head of the elephant and watched the water flow in the stream that ran by the hotel garden. His dad had told him that the stream ran down to the coast not far from the sea-fort. There it flowed across the beach and into the sea – all that fresh water getting mixed up with the salt. Sometimes they threw sticks into the slow-flowing water and imagined them floating all the way down to the sea like lazy seals.

Sometimes things came up from the sea, his dad had told him. Once a dolphin had swum all the way up-river from the sea to the town where they lived. It had got lost. The police, the council (or was it the fire brigade?) had to catch it and send it safely back.

As he sat in the warm sunshine his attention wandered from the stream to the gulls gliding in big circles high overhead, and he wished he could fly. Up, up, up, high into the sky. As high as the mashed-potato clouds.

'Yes,' answered David, looking round.

His mum – or was it his dad? – had called. It must be time for lunch.

No. No one was in the car park. Just a few empty cars. And there were no windows at this end of the hotel to shout out of. Maybe his dad had sneaked behind the big willow tree down by the stream.

'Da-had!' he shouted, grinning. 'I know you're there-hair!'

He looked hard at the tree, leaning out from the elephant as far as he dared.

No. There was definitely no one there.

It must be someone shouting in the farm over the road. Lots of people are called David.

He sat back down again on the warm fibreglass elephant head. It was nice being there.

'What?' His voice echoed across the car park. 'Where are you?'

He was certain someone had called him again.

Again there was no one there. All he could see moving was a duck in the stream. The duck quacked and flew away, its wings cracking noisily against the water.

Fly . . .

David wanted to fly. Maybe he only had to want hard enough.

And there in the sunshine he felt warm – and light enough to float up and away over the tree-tops like a bubble.

Overhead the sky got bluer and bluer and the clouds bigger and bigger.

I can . . . I can . . . I can . . .

David Stainforth stood on the great grey head of the elephant, arms outstretched like wings; he felt no fear; below him the lawn, as soft as a mattress. Air rolled around his face, making his ears tingle.

He leaned forward into the breeze. It blew lightly over his finger-tips. He was like a big, big bird getting ready to fly. Lean forward. Further . . . Further . . .

And that's when he fell.

6

After leaving David at the slide they went up to their room. Ruth wanted a bath before lunch and left Chris alone in the bedroom.

He decided to change into something a little more respectable for the inn's oak-panelled restaurant . . .

As he kicked off his jeans something fell from the pockets and rolled under the bed. At first he thought it was a few coins and went down on all fours to find them.

What he pulled out were light and ribbed.

He grinned. David's cockleshells.

He would leave them on David's bedside table for him to add to his collection.

On the ribbed outside the shells were a dirty white with the odd yellowy-brown patch.

He turned one over to look at the smooth concave interior.

Then he laughed.

It had to be a practical joke.

He turned the smooth inner side of the shell towards the bedside lamp to get a better view.

There was no doubt about it.

On the inside of the shell was the clear picture of a man's face. Slightly distorted, with his mouth stretching open wide, his eyes shut.

It looked like a still from a film. A particularly nasty film. The man was crying out in terror.

Quickly, Chris examined the other shells.

Each had the picture of a face. Male. Female. Children. Some had their eyes shut, others open wide, shockingly

29

wide, as if they had witnessed some horrible accident.

The pictures, miniature paintings, he surmised, were in a yellowish-brown paint, the colour spilt coffee leaves on paper.

They had to have been deliberately painted.

But by whom?

For a moment he had a mental picture of some barmy old artist living in a hut tucked among the dunes at Manshead, painting miniature portraits on shells before scattering them back on the beach.

Each shell bore the image of a face. Only one stood out from the others. The largest, a monster of its species. Almost the size of an oyster.

The face on this one was different.

All the other shell pictures portrayed victims. This face had narrow, scheming eyes, and the lips were pulled back in the cruellest grin Chris had ever seen.

This one, decided Chris . . . this was the hunter.

'Chris . . .' called Ruth from the bathroom.

'What do you want?'

'Come here a moment.'

'I'm looking at David's shells,' he called, sitting on the bed, his jeans around his ankles. 'There's something bloody odd about them.'

'Bugger the shells, Chris. I need you to scrub my back. And . . .'

He heard more water running into the bath.

'I've been thinking about the sea-fort. And . . .'

'And?'

'I've been working out where we can live.'

'Surprise me.'

'Come here. You can wash my back as I reveal all.'

He smiled. 'So I have to sing for my supper?'

'Of course you do.'

He entered the bathroom which was filled with clouds of steam that rolled around him as he closed the door. In the steamed-up bathroom mirror Ruth had written 'Ruth & Chris: TLFE'.

'True Love For Ever?'

Ruth smiled through the steam. 'Or until my millionaire comes along.'

Moving her bra and pants away from the side of the bath, he knelt down and retrieved the sponge from the water and began to work it into her back.

'Ow . . . You're not polishing the car. This is real skin, you know. Tender, sensitive skin. To be caressed.'

'I know.' He kissed her shoulder. It was warm, wet – and smelt wonderful. 'Mmm . . . Nice enough to eat.' He squeezed warm water down her spine. She arched her back with a deep breath.

'Hot?'

'No . . . Nice. Now, as I was saying . . .'

'Ah . . . Where we live. Don't tell me. We throw ourselves on the mercy of the Church and camp out in the graveyard, with tombstone beds and tombstone tables to eat from? Perfect.'

'No. Let me finish. Keep sponging my back. This is going to cost you. You'll be my slave for a year after this. Mmm . . . Don't stop. I talk better when you're doing that.'

'I hear and obey, mistress. Right, where do we live?'

'It's simple, Chris.' She hugged her knees to her glistening breasts. 'We move in straight away. Brilliant or what?'

'We move into the sea-fort straight away?' Chris sighed. 'But you've forgotten one tiny, tiny point.' He leaned back, wondering if she was mocking him. 'The sea-fort is derelict. The rooms are packed with rubble, and those walls haven't felt the lick of a paint brush in fifty years. So how?'

'And I thought you were the one with the imagination.'

'And I thought you were the practical one. Come on, love. Be serious.'

'Be serious, Ruth,' she mimicked.

She looked up at him through the waves of steam, her eyes misty and huge. That pleased expression told him she had a secret bursting to escape.

'Look. How much was that caravan going to cost for a year?'

'Rent at two-fifty a month. About three thousand.'

'Three thousand? We can get a second-hand caravan for around five. Then we site it in the courtyard of the sea-fort. And when I say caravan I mean a decent one. You know, the kind you get on holiday caravan sites. Bedrooms, kitchen, bathroom, all mod cons. That's it . . .' She wriggled in the bath. 'A bit lower. Ah . . .'

'Five thousand. That's eating into the budget a bit, isn't it?'

'Not a bit. Think of it as an investment. It costs us five thousand now. In twelve months we resell. For what . . . Four thousand?'

'Keep talking. I like what I'm hearing.'

'That way our original budget for accommodation, three thousand pounds, is slashed to one thousand. And there will be no travelling to and from the sea-fort each day. And we will always be on-site if there are any problems. Right, now you can call me Genius.'

'Genius . . . Brilliant . . . Wonderful.' He kissed her – with feeling. 'You are brilliant. You've saved our bloody skins.' Elated, he dried his hands on the towel. 'I'll grab a paper and start looking.'

'Oh no you don't, Chris. You'll finish what you started.' Her look needed no explanation. Her eyes exuded a smoky longing that sent desire tingling through him.

'Which bit of my wife needs washing next, then?'

She lifted a wet strand of hair and flicked a water droplet at him.

'More back. Then you decide.'

First he rubbed her back with long, slow strokes, squeezing out the sponge as he did so, the warm water bubbling through his fingers.

Ruth let her head fall forward until the wet tips of her hair dipped into the water.

'Mmm . . . that's nice.' Water squeezed on to her bare shoulders trickled down her breasts in glistening rivers. He dropped the sponge into the water and firmly began to rub her back with his bare hands.

32

The skin felt smooth to his palms and fingertips – the corrugated contours of her ribs and the slightly curving hollow of her back. He loved the feel of it. His heart began to pump hard.

Gently he began to soap her shoulders, then her stomach. And then her breasts, his fingers gliding over a slippery layer of soap lather, skittering over the hardening tips.

'Oh . . . Chris. I could let you do this for ever.' She smiled, her eyes shut. 'I could *make* you do this for ever.'

He lightly traced a line with his fingertips downward from the tip of her nose, over her lips, her chin, her smooth throat, down through the gap between her breasts which had firmed and risen into soft points that glistened in the light. Down over her stomach until his hand slipped into the hot water. A distinct quiver ran through her body.

After ten years of marriage their love-making could sometimes be almost a chore. Not today though.

Today, he knew, it would be special.

Chris was almost dressed when he heard the knock at the door.

'Hang on.' Ruth, topless, plucked a bra from the dressing-table drawer. With a schoolgirl giggle she ran lightly into the bathroom.

Chris, pulling on his sweatshirt, went to the door and opened it.

'Hello, Mr Stainforth.'

It was the hotelier, a tall man with a white beard.

'Everything okay?'

The hotelier spoke hesitantly. 'Er, I'm afraid there's been an accident. Your son . . . Out in the yard.'

The man's face was expressionless.

A sick feeling began to rise through Chris's stomach.

'Where is he?'

The man's reply was puzzling. 'You mean you can't smell him?'

The hotelier stood to one side. Behind him, tiny and the

33

colour of grey clay, a sullen-looking figure dripped water on to the corridor carpet.

'David?'

Chris pulled a face as the pungent smell of river silt rolled into the room. 'Christ, what happened?'

The white-haired hotelier was struggling to suppress laughter. 'The little fellow said he was on top of the slide when he fell off it into the stream.'

'The slide? That's nowhere near the stream. How could you fall all that way?'

'I didn't fall,' said David in a way that was dignified and angry at the same time. He walked stiffly into the room, his feet squelching inside his shoes.

'I didn't fall at all. I was flying.'

7

The world Mark Faust fell into after he leapt from the ship was one of utter darkness, but full of hissing sounds and rushing air.

Then the ocean swallowed him.

So cold.

He wanted to scream. His eyes snapped wide open with shock, the sheer terror of it, as he went down into liquid darkness.

Jesus . . . Like ice.

If only he had stayed on the ship. If only . . .

What for? To be blinded, castrated then perhaps dropped over the side anyway?

This way he had a chance.

What chance? he asked himself frantically. Here I am maybe a hundred miles from the coast. In the sea. In winter.

I have ten minutes of my life left. What's that the equivalent to?

Two *Tom & Jerry* cartoons. Three Buddy Holly numbers. 'Peggy Sue' . . . 'Heartbeat' . . . 'That'll Be the Day' . . .'

A part of his mind rambled on in a disjointed way as if no longer part of his body.

The other ordered him to kick off his wellington boots.

Then start swimming.

First the left foot.

He reached down. The boot came off easily.

Shouldn't I be breathing?

The right one stuck.

Kick.

35

I need air!

Off!

Kick the mother off! It's pulling you down!

Oh, sweet Jesus, give me air! Abruptly his head broke the surface. Cold winds blasted at him, driving spray in his face. Here at sea level the water roared like thunder. It filled his ears. Angry sounds, constant, unbroken.

Half panting, half choking, he gulped down lungfuls of sweet air. Again, Mark kicked hard, trying to dislodge the right boot.

It wouldn't budge.

The bastard would pull him down as surely as if it were cast in lead.

Holding his breath, he doubled his body, bending down to tug at it.

It shifted slightly.

His heel came partway out.

Breathe . . . Breathe . . . Breathe . . .

His head snapped up; he breathed deeply. One more breath, then try again . . .

Then —

Then his boot was gone. He'd not even touched it.

It felt for all the world as if something had snatched it off.

A simple sharp tug.

Gone.

Shark!

No. No sharks in the North Sea. He panted as he trod water. No sharks . . . No sharks . . .

It must just have slipped off.

Christ, this water is so cold . . .

As his breathing steadied his night vision kicked in. He could see black mounds of water rising and falling all around him. Dark shapes. They bulged upward then smoothly deflated. Almost like the black backs of massive whales breaking the surface in haloes of white foam and froth.

The *Mary-Anne*?

The clouds were being torn apart in the wind, allowing a quarter-moon through. It lit the sea with a thin, silver light.

There she is!

The ship's superstructure and red funnel appeared indistinctly through a mist of spray. A wave came up, blocking his view. The next time he glimpsed her he saw that her nose was dipping deep into the water.

Mark Faust pictured the murdering bastards inside the ship. Surely they knew by now. He imagined their frantic attempts to escape. Running through the corridors, trying to salvage as much as they could before they ran for the lifeboats. If only he could have done something about them. Hacked holes in the bottom maybe. But he couldn't do everything. This way there was a chance most would perish in the sea.

For a moment he lost sight of her. He swam in the direction in which he had last seen the *Mary-Anne*, forgetting that his own life was slipping away in the cold ocean.

He had to see her go.

It would hurt him. He loved that ship and her crew. They had been a second family to him. Still, he knew he must watch her final seconds.

There!

Nose down, stern up. Jesus, she was slipping down like a submarine. The twin screws chewed at air instead of water. Moonlight glinted wetly on the massive keel.

She was going.

Anyone on the ship would no longer be able to stand upright as the floors reared to the vertical. Screaming, they would be sliding forward to the bows.

Mark tried not to picture the captain – or what was left of the *Mary-Anne's* crew. The sea closed men's eyes quickly.

Oh, God, please don't let it hurt them . . .

For ten seconds he was down in the trough of a wave. The next time the sea raised him up she was gone. Already somewhere under his feet, she was falling to the ocean bed like a stone.

All of a sudden it was lonely out there. The cold bit deeply into his skin until he felt his bones would crack.

The waves seemed to take pleasure in battering his face. Breathing became harder and pain worked its way like a sharp-toothed worm into his belly.

He attempted to swim.

As soon as he did so his body slipped underwater as if someone had pulled him from below.

He didn't fight it. He just slipped down, down, down . . .

Shit, the pressure . . . It hurts. Like metal spikes driven through your ears, deep into your brain.

He'd almost lost consciousness before he resurfaced. Drawing a ragged breath, he tried to pull more air into his chest than his lungs could contain. They hurt like – oh for . . . Jesus . . .

God, I want to live, I want to live, I want to live, please, God, let me live . . . I want, I want —

Down.

He was following the *Mary-Anne* once more.

This is it, Mark Faust, seventeen years old, never had a girl, never drank whisky, never smoked a cigarette. Ate too much apple pie . . . Loved apple pie, but —

His mind began to turn, like a stunt car in a film going over and over in slow motion, pieces of it flying off.

Slowly, slowly disintegrating.

He hit the bottom. The shock made him open his eyes. Little bubbles like silver bells rolled away from his face towards the surface.

He wanted to laugh and call after them.

Wait for me! Wait for meeeeeeeeeeeee . . .

But his mouth didn't work any more; his body was nine-tenths dead. Just a few tiny sparks of life had retreated into some part of his brain to cling there as limpets cling to a rock in a storm.

Not long now. I'm going over the edge. I'll be home soon, Mom . . .

Leave a light on in the porch 'cos I'm on my way . . .

There were people.

They stood on the sea-bed looking up at him. Their white faces seemed kind of mournful. Like they wanted him to stay. There were a good nine or ten. All standing in a tight cluster. As if posing in one of those fancy pop posters – all standing tight together looking up. Then they reached up their hands towards him.

They wanted him to stay. Join them there.

Be one of the people standing ankle-deep in the kelp meadow, all rippling brown, brown, brown, standing watching the passing keels of ships go high above their heads.

Were the people nice or nasty?

Kind or mean?

Living or dead?

He stared at the big faces with their wide, surprised eyes.

He couldn't tell. The faces were growing faint. The arms began to move. But they were all blurry. You could not tell them from the fronds of seaweed that drifted to and fro.

Time to sleep. So tired. He didn't need to breathe any more.

His brother John was playing with his plane, the model of the Flying Fortress bomber Uncle Walt had built. He was playing too near Mark's bed. Mark told him not to – it was too close.

Hell. The plane hit him on the forehead. That hurt, you . . .

It happened again.

Spluttering, Mark opened his eyes. He was in the middle of a great wash of white foam. With an effort he remembered where he was. In the middle of the sea.

Jesus.

Why wasn't he dead yet?

End it, for Christsakes, end this torture . . .

The sea battered him. It tugged and pulled and rolled him over and over.

He went under.

This time there was no sense of falling. His head buffeted sharply against something. He thrust his hand out, clutching at it. Shingle. Sand. It felt like . . .

Beach.

A wave hit again and shoved him roughly across a bank of sand.

He tried to stand but once more he was out of his depth.

Wearily, arms and legs feeling as if they were encircled with iron bands, he tried to swim.

In front of him something rose out of the water. A dark silhouette against the silver moonlit clouds.

It was massive. An enormous square block of darkness.

A ship so near to shore?

It looked like one but it had to be enormous. And there were no navigation lights.

He tried to swim towards it but found himself slipping under water.

'We sail our vessels on the sea, we are under power, we steer a deliberate course. But, you know, every so often the sea takes control. And when it does, don't fight it. Go with it. Surrender yourself to its will. Because if you don't, it will destroy you.'

He remembered the Skipper's words. He made a conscious decision to leave himself to the mercy of the sea. If it wanted him, so be it.

The surf pushed and pulled him. All he could do was keep his head above water at least part of the time.

Bitingly cold brine repeatedly flooded his throat or drove into his nostrils.

Then he hit the shore.

This time as each wave receded it left him clear of the water – at least briefly before the next one. Then another roll of surf came roaring up the sand and carried him, this time fairly gently further up the beach.

The water slid back, sucking sand and shingle from beneath his hands.

He wasn't going to drown after all.

Mark stayed there on his hands and knees, wearily shaking his head.

'Safe.'

The word oozed from his lips like something half solid.
'Safe.'

The tide began to retreat. The next wave only licked the soles of his bare feet.

Unable to walk, he moved up the beach on his hands and knees until clear of the surf, his hands crunching on sand and pebbles.

At last he stopped and looked back. The moonlight revealed long lines of surf rolling in with a low continuous roar.

The wind was dropping. But he was bitterly cold.

Rising unsteadily to his feet, he walked to and fro, searching the beach for something to protect him from hypothermia. He knew that wet clothes allowed body heat to bleed away from the body, which would kill as surely as severing a main artery. At last he found a piece of tarpaulin the size of a bed sheet.

His numb fingers were useless things now, like bent sticks that did not belong to his body. It took a full five minutes to wrap the tarpaulin around himself with a piece over his head like a monk's cowl.

There he sat for an hour, perilously close to passing out from exposure. But he had to wait until he could see the ocean properly. The mental picture of the terrorists escaping the *Mary-Anne* by lifeboat still hammered in his brain.

Gradually dawn came, sending streaks of grey edged with red up into the sky.

Two hundred yards to the left he could see that the huge thing he had taken to be a ship was an old sea-fort. It had probably been part of the country's coastal defences for centuries.

Which country? Holland? France? England? He could be anywhere.

As soon as he could he forced himself to his feet. Gathering the tarpaulin round his shoulders like a cloak, he walked down to the water's edge – now at low tide – and looked out.

No ship.

No terrorists. They were all dead. Somehow he was certain of that. The ship had gone down so quickly.

His friends were dead too. But somehow he could feel no sadness. He could think only of the old Skipper, blind, but with the heart of a lion, beating that steady tattoo on the iron wall of the ship as if it were a massive drum.

His clothes were drying and his blood drove its way back painfully into his limbs and face. His nose began to ache where it had been smashed by the terrorist three days ago.

Mark Faust turned his back on the sea and began to walk slowly up the beach. Above the softening roar of the surf he fancied he could hear the distant, distant sound of metal beating against metal. A slow rhythm; almost like the heartbeat of a sleeping giant. He didn't look back.

'Keep beating the drum, Skipper,' he murmured. 'Keep beating the drum.'

The boy carried on, limping up into the dunes. The cold breeze made his eyes water. The slow, regular beat continued, only growing fainter and fainter as he limped slowly inland away from the restless ocean.

After a hundred paces he could hear the massive beat no more. But somehow an echo of it continued in his heart.

8

'You've copped for a cracking black eye there, me old cocker.
Who's tha' been scrapping with?' asked the man as he piled
up the concrete blocks for the caravan.

David hopped towards him, happy he could tell his story
again. 'I wasn't fighting. I was flying. I was sitting on
top of the elephant at the hotel.'

'Elephant?' exclaimed the man. 'They've got a zoo, then?'

'No-wer, an elephant slide.'

The man efficiently wedged more concrete blocks under
the caravan. 'A slide?'

'Ye-ess. Anyway, I got the black eye when I was flying.'

'Flying?'

'Ye-ess!'

The man laughed heartily.

'Nobody believes me. They keep saying I fell in the stream.
But I was flying. Then I banged my face on the tree.'

'You were flying too fast, then?'

'Suppose so.'

Chris leaned forward against the car, elbows resting on the
roof. David had told the story of how he got his black eye
to anyone who would listen to him. By now he was getting
touchy if anyone doubted the truth of the story, so he and
Ruth decided it best to humour him.

Now the six-year-old repeated the flying episode to the
workman. Chris looked over the caravan, feeling pleased
with himself. Within six hours of being told by the old git
in Out-Butterwick that the caravan was no longer for rent,
they had found this one for sale on a caravan site down the

coast. It had two bedrooms, kitchen, bathroom, lounge and dining area. A regular home from home.

Now in its setting, he could have kissed it. They had positioned it on the edge of the sea-fort's courtyard which was big enough to avoid being claustrophobic, even though on three sides of the cobbled square the walls soared up twenty feet. Behind him, the sea-fort rose a good thirty feet in its butter-coloured stone. The dozen or so windows set high in the walls reflected the evening sunshine.

Entrance to the courtyard was through a set of huge double timber gates set in the wall. They were so big you could drive a bus through them. The hinges had corroded badly on one of the gates; it rested uselessly against the wall. Just one more job among the thousands of others to be completed before the sea-fort opened next spring.

In one corner of the courtyard, a narrow flight of stone steps ran up to the walkway that ran around the top of the wall.

'Your lad's got a fair old imagination,' chuckled the caravan man as he walked across to Chris, wiping his oil-black hands on the seat of his overalls. 'Flying? He makes the flipping head spin. Right, you've got the, er . . . doings.'

It's funny how some words in certain situations are taboo, thought Chris. The man obviously considered it vulgar to say the word 'cheque'.

He tore the oblong piece of paper from the stub. 'Thanks for all the help. Now at least we've got a home.'

The man looked around the courtyard. 'Solid-looking place.' He shot Chris a look. 'Don't you reckon you might find it a bit . . . spooky?'

'You won't recognise the place in twelve months. New windows, swimming pool, soft landscaping, a few climbing vines along that wall. And we'll have plenty of company . . . paying company, I hope. This time next year, call in for a drink. It'll be on the house.'

The caravan man leaned forward and shook Chris by the hand. 'I'll hold you to that, me old cocker. Thanks for the . . . doings.' He pocketed the cheque. 'See ya, son,' he said to David. 'Remember, go steady with the flying. No more of them black eyes.' He strode away to his truck parked on the causeway. Already the tide was sliding in to lap at the boulders that raised the roadway above the beach.

'Okay,' said Chris, ruffling David's thick hair. 'Let's see what Mother has to say about the new home.'

Ruth had started to unpack. Boxes of food, cutlery, pans, detergents, toilet rolls, shoes and David's toys covered the floor.

On the dining table stood the fishbowl that contained Clark Kent. The fish swam listlessly, its mouth clamped to the undersurface of the water like an upside-down Hoover. All this moving from house to hotel to caravan hadn't done the poor beggar much good.

Ruth slung a cardboard box through the caravan door on to the courtyard.

'What do you two want?' Her face was pink with exertion. 'There won't be any tea for a long time. And it'll be sandwiches, cake and pop. We haven't got any gas bottles yet.'

'Have we got electricity?' asked David.

'Sure have, kidda.' Chris switched on a light to emphasise the point. 'Just like home.'

David smiled. 'I like it. It'll be like being at home but being on holiday at the same time.'

'That's right. We'll be living at the seaside – for ever and ever.'

'Amen,' added Ruth, then smiled to disguise any cynicism. 'Anything we can do?'

'Yes. Go. Give me an hour to get this place in shape, then you can come back and give me a hand to make tea.'

'You're the boss, Ruth. Come on, David. Let's explore.'

Chris and David walked towards the double timber doors that led into the sea-fort.

'Dad?'

'Yes?'

'I might do some more flying tomorrow.'

Chris groaned inwardly. David was in a happy, prattling mood.

'You know when I was on top of the elephant, Dad? I felt really light like one of those soap bubbles. Then I was flying.'

'David . . .' They had reached the doors to the building.

'. . . the clouds. I wanted to see if you can really stand on them.'

Chris crouched down and took his son's head in his hands so he could look at him face to face. He kissed him on the forehead, just above the bruised eye. 'David, enough of these flying stories now, eh, son?'

'But, Dad, I really did fly.'

Chris looked into those earnest blue eyes. 'Tell me about it later. Now . . . Come on, let's have a look around before it gets too dark. Do you remember the gun?'

'A real gun?'

'A real one, kidda. Come on, let's go find it.'

David ran to the door as Chris fished the key from his pocket. One of the first things the last owner of the place had done was substitute a user-friendly Yale for the old clunking Victorian lock. It opened easily (no Frankenstein castle creak, he thought). Father and son stepped inside into the gloom.

The smell . . . Chris breathed in deeply through his nostrils. A little musty. All the place needed was ventilation. Let the sea breezes blow through the dusty corridors for a day or two and the place would smell almost sweet.

They were standing in a hallway with three corridors running off – one to the left, one to the right; another straight ahead to a staircase. This would be the entrance lobby with the hotel reception desk in one corner. The light from the windows amply revealed the mounds of builder's rubble against the walls. There were rusty iron bed-frames (probably abandoned when the Army moved out), and a neat stack of breeze blocks that must have been abandoned ten years before when the builder quit work on the conversion.

'Come on. Let's explore.'

They began a tour of the long, dusty corridors. Some had been plastered during the conversion attempt ten years ago, but many were still bare stone, the shoe-box-size blocks of rock so expertly cut and fitted together you couldn't have put a knife-blade between them.

The first room they reached must have been used as a rubbish dump. Old drinks cans, bottles (one whisky, most beer – the military certainly knew how to unwind), broken chairs and, along the far wall under the window, a dozen olive-green metal boxes, bearing white stencilled letters. AMMUNITION. They moved on, David at a trot now, wanting to see the gun.

'Hang on, David. Not so fast.' This was still a dangerous place. Cables hung down at intervals; part of the unfinished wiring job. They shouldn't be live, but you never could tell. The other rooms on the ground floor were largely a repeat of the first. Clearing these alone would be like one of the labours of Hercules. Maybe he should hire some help.

They reached another room. Empty apart from an old dining table and three ill-matching chairs.

'I suppose this is where the builders had their rest room.'

'Look, there's some playing cards,' said David, walking across the room, his feet echoing slightly. 'Can I have them?'

'Best leave them.' Chris noticed that they had been dealt out into two hands. Ten years ago the players had been interrupted. There was also a packet of dusty-looking Polo mints. Half were gone. The others looked like circular yellowing bones in the cylinder of crinkled foil. A box of matches. And open on the table, a newspaper. The twentieth of April. Ten years old to the very week.

He shivered. It made him think of the *Marie Celeste*. The builders had simply stopped whatever they were doing and had gone, leaving jobs half done. Bankruptcy hits you like that. It raised a phantom in Chris's mind. What happened if their plan did not come off? They were going to sink every penny they had in the world into this place. If it failed . . .

'David . . . Come on, son, time to move on.'

'I've found something weird,' David replied, looking through a door that Chris had taken to be a cupboard.

'What is it?'

'God knows.'

'Language.' The reprimand came automatically, but he was more interested in what lay behind the wooden door.

David frowned and swung the door backwards. 'Steps, but going down. And we're already on the ground floor.'

Chris laughed. 'It's a cellar. It was probably used for storage.'

But a cellar on an island? The building was only a yard or two above the high-tide level anyway. That meant the cellar was below sea level. That was impossible. Unless it flooded at every high tide.

Chris peered into the black pit of the stairwell but could make nothing out.

'Aren't we going down?'

'Not tonight. We haven't got time. Come on, let's make tracks if we're going to find that gun.'

The idea of the underwater cellar intrigued Chris, but it would have to wait. There could be only a few more minutes of daylight left.

On the next floor they found the big room that looked over the sea. From ceiling to floor, and along the entire length of the far wall, ran the window. Immediately beyond that was the old gundeck; beyond that nothing but sea and blue sky all the way to Holland. After all these years the windows were smeared a blurry white from salt spray, with a random white and black splash here and there. Pure seagull guano.

The room was empty and relatively clean; just a couple of lengths of grey flex added to the evidence of building work abandoned in a hurry. The *Marie Celeste*.

'Where's the gun?' David ran across to the windows. 'Pee-ow! Pee-ow!'

'Over there.' Chris pointed to a shape as big as a car, covered by a tattered tarpaulin. 'A 40mm Bofors. But I don't think we can blow any ships up tonight.'

'Why not?'

'No ammo.' He smiled down at his son. 'Also, I have a feeling the Army might have taken some parts of the gun away so it can't be fired.'

'Isn't that being a vandal?'

'Well, it seems like it. But we wouldn't want any of the guests firing the gun by accident, would we?'

'Suppose not.'

'But you see where those platforms are – near those gaps in the wall? That's where the old-fashioned cannon used to go, before they had modern guns.'

'Breech-loaders.'

'That's right, David,' said Chris, surprised at his son's knowledge. 'How do you know that? I was . . . Blast, what's wrong with this door?' Chris had wrestled with the brass handles for a full thirty seconds. They would not budge. 'I think we've got a little problem here. I can't open the door.'

'Have you got the key?'

'No. There isn't one. There's not even a lock. We're so high up you'd need a helicopter to get on to the gundeck . . . Dear me.' If David hadn't been there the words would have been a little stronger. Chris gave the doors a last rattle. They were shut tight. 'Not to worry, kidda. We'll get the doors fixed then we can have a proper look. We'll just have to see what we can through the windows.'

Even with the windows in a gunked-up state he could tell that the view would be pretty good. Perhaps it would be most striking in winter during a storm. It would have all the spectacular sounds, sights and fury of being on a ship; with the benefit of being firmly rooted in the living rock. He could imagine waves cracking against the wall to send foam and spray gushing up as far as the windows.

He recalled trips to Scarborough when he was David's age. An angry sea would draw crowds of people to the Spa theatre which hung on the edge of the sea. The waves would hurl themselves at the seawall, bursting in geysers of spray that shot perhaps thirty feet high. Showers of brine would drench any spectator who got close enough. And to a young boy's delight, someone always did. The sea always has that power. It creates a spectacular display which radiates a magnetism that draws people to it. Then all they can do is stand and watch.

He didn't know if it was the idea of danger which pulled not only children but grown men and women closer and closer – the feeling you get when you approach the lion's cage at the zoo, and lean over the barrier to see, face to face, the man-eating beast. Perhaps the two were similar. Seeing nature without her clothes on, in the raw, she is more beautiful, more savage, more hypnotic, more fascinating, more powerful, more awe-inspiring, more frightening than you imagined. You just have to get a little closer; see a little more.

As that six-year-old boy, Chris would watch the ocean's antics. Words would run round his head as if the sea were saying, 'Come on, come closer. Watch me. It's fun. Look – a ten-foot wave; look – all this foam boiling up at the foot of the seawall steps. Come down the steps a bit. It's okay. I'll make a little rush at you and you run shrieking and giggling up the steps. Come closer. I want to play with you. Come on . . . Water's soft. I can't hurt you . . .'

'Dad. You said the door wouldn't open.'

He looked down at his hand as if it didn't belong to him. He was gripping the brass handle and rattling the thing, trying to force the door open. He shook his head as if waking from a deep sleep.

He coughed. 'I was just seeing if I could free it. Come on, it'll be dark soon. Let's see a bit more before it gets too late.' They left the big room. 'It's a great place, isn't it, kidda?'

'Sure is, Dad.' David charged along the corridor in the direction of the next flight of stairs up.

Chris followed. Why had those thoughts about the sea run through his head like that? It was almost as if they had originated outside his skull. Even recalling them now gave him an odd sensation. He shivered and licked his dry lips. Do the early stages of insanity feel like this?

'Come on, Dad!'

David had reached the steps. He climbed them, quickly disappearing from sight.

Chris, rubbing his face, followed. The excitement of moving in, he supposed. He was tired.

'What do you want, Dad?'

David's voice drifted down the staircase.

'What do you mean, what do I want?'

David appeared at the top of the steps. He looked fragile against the dark void above him.

'Dad . . .' David assumed the voice that told his parents he was becoming exasperated by their slow wits. 'Da-ad. You shouted at *me*.'

'I never said a word.'

'Did . . . Fibber.' David added the mild insult for emphasis.

'You're imagining things again.'

'Am not.'

'All right, David. It must have been the wind or an echo you heard.'

Or did you call him, Chris? You senile old nutcase. Take two Paracetamol and lie down in a darkened room.

He looked up at the little boy looking down at him. It must have been the perspective or the light or something, but David looked further away than he could possibly have been. And above him was that black cavern – just a whistling great emptiness.

His mind flicked back to those holidays in Scarborough when he would watch children on the seawall steps as the sea, hissing like a great shapeless beast, swelled up against the walls, swallowing the steps in a gush of foam. They would run up screaming with glee, not realising how dangerous their game was. He found himself imagining David playing the same game. Running, chuckling, down towards the shifting mass of dark water, then running back up as the next wave rose up to eat the steps one after another. Of course, David would be too slow. The muscular rush of water would shove him off the stone steps and into the body of the ocean. He would hear David's cry, 'Dad . . . Dad . . . Get me out!'

David's face disappearing beneath foam. Chris's agony at his helplessness.

If the sea pulled David out into deep water he would drown beneath the heaving ocean. If it swept him back to the seawalls, his body would be smashed against the stone blocks.

To jump into the sea there to try to save him would be suicide. No one could swim in those waters.

Would he try? Without hesitation, he knew the answer.

Of course he would.

The inevitable electric trickle of fear prickled across his skin.

'David. Stay there.' He kept his voice calm, but he was climbing the steps quickly. 'Don't wander off.'

'Okay.'

There was nothing particularly alarming about the upper floor after all. Anyway, the sea-fort was strongly built of good Yorkshire stone.

No harm would come to them here.

9

As he had done every evening for the last ten years, the big American, Mark Faust, locked the door of the shop and walked down to Out-Butterwick's seafront.

There were a dozen or more people there. One or two nodded a greeting, but most looked out to sea.

By this time the tide was sliding in over the beach, lifting the few small boats off the sand alongside the jetty.

The Major was there with his dog, a smartly clipped Westie terrier. The man looked every inch the retired officer, dressed in grey slacks and a blazer that bore a regimental patch on the breast pocket. The clothes, like the man, had faded over the years.

Mrs Jarvis had pulled her wheelchair to the edge of the pavement and sat resting one foot on the low wall that separated sand from road. It was common knowledge that she suffered from spinal cancer. She wouldn't make Christmas.

A car passed slowly down the road behind them. That would be the Reverend Reed. He would never stand here with the other Out-Butterwick residents, but Mark knew he would drive his old Austin Maxi up and down the seafront road at least three more times before the sun sank behind the salt marshes. No other vehicles would pass this way tonight.

More people arrived, most middle-aged to elderly. Apart from little Rosie Tamworth. She must have been about thirteen now, but she had the mind of a three-year-old and her hands shook in a palsied way.

He watched. We're all creatures of habit. We come down here at the same time, stand in the same place, and we

53

probably all harbour the same feelings in our guts – that same tense anticipation that draws every muscle in your body taut like a bow string.

Brinley Fox wasn't quite like the rest. With his head down, he paced the beach, ferociously smoking a cigarette. The image of the old-fashioned expectant father with his wife in the delivery room.

Tony Gateman, the little Londoner, arrived panting from the exertion of his hurried walk.

Tony gave the American a brisk nod.

They waited. The sense of anticipation grew.

No one talked at these gatherings. Not yet anyway; not until the waiting was over.

But tonight Mark had something to tell the Londoner; it would have to wait.

The Major's dog gave a little yelp and began to pace backwards and forwards as far as the tartan leather lead would allow. The Major appeared not to notice. He gazed out to sea. As did Mark and his neighbours.

Fox paced faster, kicking up a spurt of sand every time he switched back in the other direction, never raising his eyes from the beach. The sea did not exist for him. It held one object too many.

Chewing his lip, Mark looked out across the sea which caught the last rays of the sun. It looked real, real peaceful.

But the seagulls, he noticed, were deserting the sky to flee inland. There was a bad storm coming.

The dog gave a yelping bark and twisted on its lead.

Mark chewed his lip – harder. Was this it? Was it coming?

All around him there were intakes of breath. They felt it too.

Mark sensed it oozing through the place. A kind of electricity that ran through everything. Right down to the sand crunching beneath his feet. So strong he could almost taste it.

Then it was gone. As quickly as it had come.

It was only an advance wave of the thing they all waited

for. Even little Rosie Tamworth, moving wisps of blonde hair from her little-girl face with a shaking hand.

The sense of anticipation waned. It would not happen tonight. Probably not even tomorrow or next week, but some time – soon.

The Major produced a tennis ball from his pocket and threw it down the beach. The dog, unleashed, leapt after it as if it had been fired from a mortar, the tension in its muscles exploding in a rush of energy.

'Evening, Tony,' said Mark in his deep rumbling voice. 'I've been wanting to catch you.'

'Talk away.'

'Have you heard about the old sea-fort out at Manshead?'

The Londoner shot Mark a startled look. 'No. What about it?'

'Someone's moving in.' Mark watched Tony Gateman's reaction. It was what he expected.

Pure shock. 'Who on earth would do that?'

'A family. Met them a couple of days ago in the shop. They've got a little lad about six years old.'

'They're moving in? Into the s—'

'Sshh. . .' Mark's big tanned paw gripped Tony's forearm. Brinley Fox was heading towards them.

Tony used the pause to light a cigar.

When the Fox brother was safely out of earshot, Tony asked, 'When?'

'Today.'

'You are joking? The place is derelict.'

Mark shook his head. 'Took a walk up there this morning. They've put a static caravan in the courtyard. They'll be living there while they convert the place into a hotel.'

'A hotel? Jesus wept . . . Know anything else about them?'

'Just that they seemed like ordinary folks.' Mark shot Tony Gateman a troubled look. 'Do you think they know?'

10

'Hello . . . Anyone there?'

Henry Blackwood chuckled. 'Come out, come out wherever you are.'

No reply.

Then he never expected one. Using the single oar at the stern, he sculled the boat across the ocean towards the bobbing plastic bottle that marked the position of the next lobster pot.

'You tell me, girl, if you hear it again.'

He listened himself. The sound, three knocks on the bottom of the hull, like someone trying to attract Henry Blackwood's attention, did not repeat itself.

Singing softly to himself, he hoisted the pot up by its line. As he did so he talked.

'Beautiful morning, Suzy. It's going to be a champion summer . . . Now . . . What have we got here? Come out, my beauty, and into the box.'

Taking care not to get crimped by the lobster's massive claws, he placed the creature into his catch-box.

'Seven already, Suzy . . . It looks as if we're going to have a good day . . . A bloody good day . . . There you go.'

There was nothing he liked better. A glass-calm sea, the sun edging up over the horizon, a milky mist softening the line of the coast. And to talk to his beloved Suzy. He'd built her with his own hands fifteen years ago: twenty feet long, she was painted a brilliant white and resembled an overgrown rowing boat. He imagined even God Almighty himself couldn't have been more pleased when He stood back to admire His cosmic handiwork on the Sixth Day.

Suzy never answered back. Always faithful, always reliable. Suzy carried him efficiently away from the noise of his household full of teenage sons who never stopped arguing morning, noon and night, all the way ten miles down the coast, to where he fished the lobster and crab grounds.

'Tea break, Suzy.' He sat on the bench seat and pulled out a thermos. 'Mind if I smoke, old girl? Okay . . . I promise it'll only be the one.'

Smiling, he poured the tea and lit the cigarette. He relaxed with the gentle bob of the boat and looked around, enjoying everything in God's creation. The seagulls scooting low over the water. A formation of geese flying high overhead.

He was all alone. No other boats. Not even a glimpse of a distant cargo ship.

Gradually the mist began to thin and he could make out the houses down the coast at Out-Butterwick.

Half a mile in front of him the lines of the old sea-fort were taking shape in the morning sunlight.

It wasn't always like this, though. The North Sea could be a rough old bastard. When he left school he worked the trawlers. One winter's day the boat had simply filled up with water and gone from under his feet. For twenty hours he hung on to the buoy that marked the deep-water channels.

When at last the lifeboat got him back to dry land a news reporter had gone on and on about Blackwood's superhuman strength; how he'd hung on to the buoy through a force eight gale that smashed boats into matchsticks.

Blackwood had grunted: 'Of course you bloody well get strong, pulling in nets so full of fish that they weigh the same as a family car.'

After that girls he'd never met before would come up to him in pubs and squeeze his muscular arms and giggle.

'You're not a silly giggler are you, old girl?' He patted Suzy's gunwale. 'You're worth your weight in gold.'

It happened again.

'Knock bloody knock – who's there?'

This time four slow knocks beneath his feet – he even felt the vibration through his sea-boots.

'Who do you think it is, Suzy? Mr Neptune? Davy Jones – up from his locker? Captain Bones looking for his booty?'

He chuckled and peered down over the side into the water.

Nothing but smooth green ocean with hardly a ripple to break the surface. Perhaps something had caught underneath the fishing boat. If it was a line or piece of discarded net it could foul the propeller when Blackwood came to start the engine.

'Right, we can't see anything – let's see if we can feel anything on you, old girl.' Rolling up his sleeve, the fisherman knelt down at the side of the boat, leaned forward over the side and ran his hand along the hull below the waterline.

Carefully he worked his way to where the sound had seemed to come through the planking. Leaning so far over he was within an ace of rolling forward into the water, he felt the underside of the boat, fingers tingling with the cold now.

'Nothing . . . You're as clean as a whistle, old girl.'

It was as he began to pull his hand from the water that something touched him.

'Now, what was that?' He reached down under the boat again, his hand clutching at sea water.

Nothing.

Probably just a stalk of sea kelp floating by.

He stood up, flicking the water from his hand, then drying it with a rag.

'Reckon it's Davy Jones up to his old tricks again.'

He reached the next lobster pot, caught the plastic bottle marker floating on the dead-calm surface, and began pulling in the line.

Blackwood returned to his singing again. Then he stopped. The line had snagged. He pulled harder. It still held firm.

He was just about to yank it when the line cracked tight, jerking his hands down towards the water.

'Ach . . . Damn, damn – *damn!*'

He let go of the line and watched as the slack he'd already pulled on board shot over the gunwale and disappeared, taking the bottle marker with it.

He looked over the side. The bottle had disappeared.

The sod had actually sunk like it was made out of stone.

Incredulous, Blackwood shook his head. 'Well, I've never seen that before. Something pulled that bugger straight down . . . Hmm, we've got something bloody peculiar going on here . . . Ach, that's sore.'

He looked at his fingers. A friction burn ran across them in a raw-looking groove. It began to burn like hell-fire.

The fisherman knelt down and reached over the side of the boat again to dip his hand into the water. He stayed there for a moment, letting the cold ocean take the fire out of the burn.

'Suzy . . . What did I say about it being a good day? That sod nearly burnt away my finger . . . But what the hell could snag the line and yank it down like that? Mmm . . . Might be submarine trouble again. Last year old Bob ended up with a periscope through his keel. If the bloody Navy want to —'

Blackwood stopped and stared down at his hand in disbelief. It was below the surface of the water; he could see nothing, but —

'That's odd. You know, old girl, it feels as if someone's holding my – *Christ!*'

It had him.

He tried to pull back his hand.

He couldn't – something held it there beneath the water. For all the world it felt as though another hand were gripping his. Strong fingers around his fingers . . . Shark? Conger eel? It had to be —

Get it out of there! Get it out!

Blackwood wrenched backward until his back muscles creaked.

He couldn't shift it.

He strained harder. He could see nothing, but now the water swirled and boiled under the boat like big fish in a feeding frenzy.

'Let go . . . Let go . . .'

The pull on his hand increased. The boat began to tip sideways. She was going to capsize.

Blackwood shifted his balance so he could pull harder, his mind spinning like fury.

Something was trying to drag him overboard . . . Something wanted him in the water . . . Something . . .

'Let go!'

But the hand only tightened around his. Then pulled harder.

Now his face was nearly in the water that threshed and bubbled to foam.

He felt the boat tipping; now he was lying at an angle so steep his blood ran from his legs to his head. The lobsters slid from the catch-box back into the ocean.

His face was an inch from the churning sea that splashed his head and neck.

'Get off . . . Gerr-off . . . *Groff!*'

He panted and choked as the sea splashed into his mouth. Any second now.

Any second now Suzy would roll over and he'd be trapped beneath her. Alone with her and whatever was in the water, unseen, pulling him down.

He didn't see it come. But suddenly he felt a blow to his face; followed instantly by a pain that pierced his right eye.

'Christ!'

The water churned white. The heavy catch-box rolled over his back and into the sea.

Why could he no longer see out of his right eye? He blinked to try to clear it. Why did it hurt? Why —

He was still blinking when the second blow came. This time to his left eye. Again came the piercing pain as if something sharp had been driven into the eyeball.

Now the foaming white had gone. There was only a throbbing dark, blotched with red.

With a mighty pull, the fisherman freed his hand. With the release the boat slapped back level on to the water.

And then it was still – and silent. The ferocious threshing of the ocean had stopped.

Henry Blackwood shakily pulled himself up on to the bench seat that ran across the middle of the boat.

He lifted his fingers to his face and felt his eyes.

'Blind . . . I'm blind, old girl . . .' His voice was a dry whisper. 'How are we going to get home, girl?'

He sat there for a full three minutes, whispering over and over, 'Who's done this to us, girl? Who's done this to us?'

Then he felt the boat dip beneath him.

He tilted his head to one side, listening. A low splash, then the sound of water dripping on water.

The boat dipped down.

Someone's pulling us down . . .

No . . . No. Someone is climbing into the boat.

He did not move. He did not speak. He did not show any sign that he had heard anything at all.

He just used all his thirty years' experience as a fisherman to sense what was happening – and where.

At the prow, someone was pulling themselves on to his boat. On to his Suzy.

Slowly he let his hand fall to his side.

The oar. His fingers tightened around the timber shaft.

Still pretending he'd noticed nothing, he waited until the time was right.

Then in an explosive moment he was on his feet, picking up the heavy oar and swinging it in a tremendous arc; the oar buzzed through the air.

It hit something wet. Something not hard nor completely soft. Something that felt like —

'A man. A sodding man . . . *I got him, Suzy.*' Blackwood heard the satisfying splash of the man falling back into the water, no doubt with a mess of broken ribs to nurse on his homeward journey.

It happened again. The tilting of the boat as another climbed on. The fisherman swung the oar again, hitting the man. Again the splash.

'If only I could see the bastards. I'd bust their bleeding skulls.' He panted and swung again. The oar cracked against flesh. And yet there were no cries of pain even though the blows were hard enough to snap bones.

'Who are they, Suzy? Why are they doing this to us?'

Drug smugglers. That's it, he told himself. Foreign boats were coming in at night and leaving the drugs in his lobster pots. The next day divers would swim out from the beach, pick up the drugs, and within hours they would be en route to poison the kids in the cities.

Well, they'd cocked up. Blackwood had caught them. He would break their bodies with his bare hands if he had to. He didn't even feel the pain from his punctured eyes now – pumped with adrenalin and anger, he was ready for the fight.

They were coming fast now. The boat dipped at the stern, then on the bow, then the port side. He saw them in his mind's eye, divers in wet-suits, hoisting themselves on to Suzy – catch him when his back was turned then slip a knife through his ribs.

But the stupid bastards had picked the wrong man.

With the Viking blood of his ancestors singing through his veins, the fisherman swung the oar like a warrior's sword, hacking and chopping the men off his beloved boat and back into the water.

'Come on . . . Come on! Get a taste of this!'

Crack!

The oar cracked against a head.

Then another. And another.

For five minutes he batted them off the boat.

Then suddenly they were gone.

Blackwood stood in the centre of the boat, feet apart, and listened.

Beneath his feet a stirring, then a light tap.

That was followed by a series of hard blows that sent tingling shocks up through the man's legs.

Something moved round his ankles.

Bastards.

They'd knocked holes in Suzy's planking. Water swirled up around his knees.

Roaring, like a lion raging at the death of its mate, he fought as the boat settled lower in the water. He struck at the unseen men as they used their body weight to pull his boat down into the sea.

He wouldn't leave his Suzy. Not ever.

Ferociously he fought on. Even when the ocean closed over his head and instead of air in his lungs there was only water.

11

Chris pulled out the drawer in the side of the caravan's sofa and began rooting through the already swiftly accumulating junk.

'Ruth . . . Have you seen the shells?'

She walked in from the bathroom, hurriedly brushing her hair.

'What shells? Have you seen the car keys?'

'On the hook by the door . . . Those seashells David found on the beach last week.'

'Forget the shells, love. We're going to be busy enough today as it is. Do you think this skirt goes with the t-shirt?'

'Perfect. I deliberately put them somewhere safe.'

Chris scratched the bridge of his nose as he squatted over the drawer. 'Remember, I told you about —'

'About how strange they were.' Ruth sighed. 'That you could see faces drawn on them. I know, I remember. Where's that money for the groceries? And I'll need some coins for the phone. Have you got . . . Christ . . .'

'What's the matter?'

'The bloody goldfish has gone and died on us.'

'Jesus. That's just what we need.' He slid the drawer shut. 'Where's David?'

'He's playing outside.'

'Good. I'll flush it down the toilet. You hide the bowl.'

'Reason for Clark Kent's disappearance?'

He kissed her on the forehead. 'You'll think of something.'

The goldfish lay on the surface of the water. Its body

arched so the tail pointed down towards the little plastic pirate ship.

'Hurry up, Chris. I've got to phone the architect at half-past.'

'I was just finding the best way to —'

'Dad!' cried David urgently. 'They're here!'

Chris quickly turned his back on the deceased Clark Kent, using his body to shield it from his son. David leaned in through the door at the far end of the caravan.

'What's the matter, darling?' asked Ruth artificially.

'The lorries are coming. Shall I tell them where to go?'

'No, Dad will tell them. Stand somewhere safe to watch.' She turned back to Chris. 'Do it later. I'll lock the door. Now you two look after one another. Bye.'

Two lorries carrying steel skips came swaying through the gateway into the courtyard. One disconcertingly carried the command PISS OFF in yellow aerosol.

David ran forward to clutch Chris's hand to watch as Chris pointed out where the skips should go.

It had begun.

All the rubble, old timbers, Army boots, boxes, broken furniture that lay heaped throughout the building had to be wheel-barrowed out to the skips. The trucks would be back in four hours to take the loaded skips away then return with two more. He would have to work fast. The tides would dictate his schedules. At high tide the cause-way would be covered by ocean. Then nothing, on wheels anyway, could come in or out.

While David played with his cars in the courtyard, Chris began. He chose the nearest room to the main entrance and began to empty it of old bedsteads, then a mountain of old Army boots.

For two hours he worked furiously, losing all track of time.

He was startled to see Ruth appear. She wore old jeans and a t-shirt bearing a picture of a black cat and the word PURR . . . FECT.

'What are you doing?' he demanded.

'Helping you.'

'You can't, Ruth. This is —'

'Man's work? We're doing this together. I do what you do.'

He looked across at his wife and not for the first time in the last few days he found himself loving her in a way that was new and deeper than ever before. What wouldn't she selflessly sacrifice for him?

They worked together, clearing the next room in half an hour. The dust made Chris's throat paper-dry, and when he sneezed it left a black splotch in his handkerchief.

The next room held all the old internal doors. Drab-green painted things that had warped over the years.

'This is the only room that smells damp,' said Ruth, tugging at the first door. It bore the legend C.O. KNOCK AND WAIT in white letters.

He sniffed. A faint smell of mushrooms. 'It doesn't seem too bad. We'll get the architect to stick the damp meter on the walls.'

'Chris!'

He dropped the door he was carrying. It fell with a painfully loud crash. 'What's wrong!'

'Quick.'

'Jesus, Ruth, I thought you'd hurt yourself.'

Ruth grinned. 'It looks as if we've got a sitting tenant.'

'Christ . . . Not rats.'

'Not animal. Vegetable. See for yourself.'

Behind the door was an ancient ceramic sink. But it was what was in the sink, beneath a single dripping tap, that she had seen. There in the bowl bloomed a mass of green leaves.

'A bush?'

'Not any old bush.' She reached into the green mass that looked as if it was exploding out of the sink and snapped off a thick white shoot. 'Look.' She bit a chunk off and chewed it.

'Ruth?'

She smiled. 'It's celery. Here, have a bit.'

'Celery fits into the palm of your hand.' He ran his hand through the verdant growth. 'This'll fill a wheelbarrow. How the hell did it get here?'

'One of the builders years ago. Probably had a celery fetish and left it in the sink with some water to keep it fresh. And it just grew and grew.' She held out the stalk for him to bite. 'Guess what we'll be having for tea for the next three years.'

He bit. The white flesh was crisp and surprisingly sweet.

The mother of all celery plants took some shifting. The thick bole from where the shoots sprang had swollen over the years to fill the sink. It was like trying to prise a fat man from a too-small bath.

'The sink will have to go anyway.' He smashed the china bowl. 'Shit.' A small rush of water ran over his shoes. 'Now will you look at that.'

Her eyes widened. 'It's filled it.' Like a jelly poured into a mould the celery had grown hard against every contour of the sink. It had even grown around the sink chain which disappeared into the plant. The plug itself must have been surrounded by layer after layer of celery stalks somewhere in the celery heart.

It took another five minutes of prising and swearing before it released its embrace on the sink. With a crisp snapping sound it came loose suddenly, throwing him off balance. 'Jesus . . . That's heavy.' He heaved the monster plant into the wheelbarrow.

'Just a minute.' She snapped some of the smaller stalks from the heart of the plant. 'I'll make lunch.'

'Resourceful. Now if you can knock together a few four-poster beds out of those old doors and ammo boxes, we've got it made.'

He wheeled the barrow out to the skip. Without the sides of the sink holding it tightly in place, the plant had flopped outward in a spray of white rubbery stalks that moved in the breeze. Now, for all the world, it looked like some species of huge albino spider. He covered the monster plant with the doors, then went back to move the last piece of junk from the room – a wooden straight-backed chair. It stood in the damp dirt by the sink. When he tried to move it, it wouldn't budge. When he forced it, it gave with the same crisp crack he had heard earlier when he prised the celery from the sink.

Instinctively, he knew what he would find when he looked more closely at the raw glistening feet of the chair.

It had taken root in the floor. He ran his fingers across the four snapped roots in the dirt which corresponded to where the four legs of the chair had stood. The wood of the chair was alive. The frame had warped, or grown rather, making the leather seat too small for the frame. He felt the arms. They were beginning to bud with new growths. From touch alone he could feel that the legs had swollen. Another ten years and he would have found something between a chair and a tree. Not quite one thing or the other. It would slowly have filled the room, vying for space with the swollen celery plant.

Feeling suddenly cold, he broke the chair against the stone wall, then dropped the pieces into the wheelbarrow. When Ruth called him for lunch he did not mention the chair to her.

12

'Celery boats?'

Chris smiled. 'No thanks, Ruth. I'll stick with the sandwiches. Has David eaten?'

'All he wanted was a Pot Noodle.' She read his expression.
'It's okay. He didn't come into the caravan.'

'Did you get rid of the goldfish?'

'That's your job, loving husband.'

'Thanks a million. Just check your pants drawer tonight.'
He grinned. 'Make sure I haven't slipped it into one of your
stockings.'

'Pig.' Playfully, she kicked him on the shin.

'Ah . . . But I'm your very own loving pig.'

They were sat on chairs on the walkway that ran round
the top of the sea-fort wall. Overhead, spring was doing
a superb new paint-job on the sky, a deep, flawless blue.
Twenty feet beneath him on the beach, David crouched over
a pile of toys. He had drawn huge faces in the sand with a
stick. They had grins and squint eyes.

'Perfect.' Ruth wriggled lower into her chair, resting her
feet on his legs. 'The celery wants eating up before it wilts.'

Below in the courtyard were the two skips, now full and
awaiting collection. In one lay the celery monster spider,
its long white, rubbery legs no doubt splayed out and
crushed beneath thirteen heavy timber doors and five
wheelbarrowsful of concrete rubble.

Get out of that one and I'll call you Houdini, he thought.

'As there's more junk to shift,' said Ruth, 'maybe we should
get help.'

'Any ideas?'

'There's a lad in the village who seems to do odd jobs for people. You've probably seen him. Long, straggly hair and a scruffy beard. Looks like a wild man from the backwoods. I think he's a bit simple.'

'He'll fit in well here, then.'

'Perhaps he could give us a hand.'

'It's an idea. I'll ask him.'

While she shut her eyes and basked in the sun, he settled down to watch David playing on the beach. David had balanced three of his toys on a boulder that rose out of the sand to knee height. The toys were his favourites – a Maddog Bigfoot, a blue stunt car, and a Star Wars stormtrooper figure. He then placed a Superman comic next to those on the boulder. He leaned forward, resting his hands on the smooth boulder and intently studying the toys as if they were about to perform a neat trick.

After that he began to look from the toys to the sea then back again. The sea was creeping in. After a few minutes the first waves hit the boulder. They rolled slowly around it.

David ran a few paces up the beach then turned to watch the boulder with an intensity that made Chris's own neck ache.

Why on earth had he done that? His son had deliberately marooned some of his most precious toys on the boulder. By now the sea had completely encircled the boulder.

When David used a swear word or made some observation on life that would have been impressive coming from an adult's lips, it always caught Chris by surprise. He would shoot David a look, half wondering if some forty-year-old dwarf had switched identities with his son. He felt that way now.

God alone knew why. The boy was only playing what six-year-olds no doubt played. But it had the air of – Chris struggled for the description – a ritual. Or a ceremony.

The waves had swollen in size now. What happened next was inevitable.

One hit the Maddog car and it disappeared into the sea with a splash; the receding wave sucked it away out of sight.

David's reaction was odd.

He slapped his hands over his eyes as if the loss had upset him. But a second later he yanked his hands away.

The boy was forcing himself to watch the toys being washed away by the waves. The comics went next, then the blue car. The Star Wars trooper seemed to hang on the longest, until a splash of water knocked it to the edge of the boulder and it hung over the edge like a drunken diver, arms outstretched.

The next wave claimed it for the sea.

Chris looked back at David. He had retreated up the beach from the incoming tide and sat cross-legged, staring out to sea. He looked drained, as if the act of losing some of his favourite toys had exhausted him.

Losing them?

No. He had given them away.

'Ruth, do you think he's happy here? I mean, moving house, losing his old friends.'

She opened her eyes. 'What makes you ask that?'

He told her what David had done.

'David! Hey, David!'

No reaction.

He hadn't heard. Or, more likely, he pretended not to hear. David seemed to be rolled up in his own personal misery at the moment. He stared at the sea which had taken his favourite toys.

'Don't worry, Chris. I'll go down and talk to him.' Ruth ran lightly down the steps to the courtyard while he watched his son. Something must be troubling the boy.

He turned to go down the steps but was surprised to see Ruth hurrying back up towards him.

'Come on,' she said quickly. 'We've got a visitor.'

13

In the courtyard he found a small man – in his sixties, black-rimmed glasses, white hair combed over a bald patch. He was gazing up at the sea-fort walls as if they had just fallen from the Land of Oz. Ruth and David stood a little way off, watching him. Ruth caught Chris's eye. She gave a puzzled shrug when the little man's back was turned.

'Magic,' the man was saying to himself. 'Just magic.'

Chris coughed. 'Hello? Can I help you?'

The man turned. His most striking feature was his nose. Long, thin and with a bony look to it which managed to seem almost aristocratic without being beaky.

Whoever he was, he could go. And quickly. The trucks were due for the skips.

'Mr Stainforth. Mrs Stainforth. And little David.'

This little man had done his homework.

'I'm Tony Gateman. Good afternoon.' He shook hands with Chris and Ruth. 'The times I've passed this place over the last fifteen years and never once have I seen inside. This courtyard is bloody enormous.' He looked longingly towards the door into the main part of the sea-fort. 'Like a museum in there, I shouldn't wonder.'

'At the moment it's more of a junkyard. Most of the original fittings were ripped out when a builder began to convert it into a hotel. Never got off the ground, though. He went bust.'

'But we don't intend to.' Ruth moved nearer. 'We've a sound financial plan and the bank's backing.'

Tony Gateman peered at her through the thick lenses of his glasses. 'Actually, Fox and Barnett didn't go bust. Barnett had retired by then, but old Jack Fox ran the firm sweet as a nut. It was liquid all right.'

Chris's interest was stirred. 'What happened?'

'Ahh. . .' It was more than an expression of remembering; Mr Gateman was thinking hard. 'He just decided it wasn't really his line of work. Pulled the plug on the project and went back to building semis . . . I'm sorry, Mr and Mrs Stainforth, you'll still be wondering who the hell I am. Poking my nose in.'

Bored, David had drifted back to the caravan.

'I call myself Out-Butterwick's local historian, but that's just a flimsy excuse. The truth is I like sticking my nose into things.' He rubbed the long aristocratic nose. 'So tell me to clear off if you like.' He laughed, and Chris felt himself beginning to like the little man.

He continued: 'A couple of years ago I published a little book, a history of Out-Butterwick. The church, pub, ship-wrecks; the interesting characters of yesteryear, that kind of thing. Trouble is this sea-fort is the most interesting place; up to bloody here in history, and I could never get access.'

'Well, feel free to look around,' said Chris. Ruth shot him a look.

'Oh, I'll snatch your hand off for that invitation. I'll give you notice, though I can see you're up to your ears in crap today. But fascinating place. Manshead here was men-tioned by the Romans in AD 97. A Roman tax collector wrote about it in a letter to his wife in Rome. I managed to get a stat of the thing from the British Museum. It also gets a fair bit of press in ecclesiastical chronicles of the sixth and seventh centuries.'

'Manshead,' said Ruth. 'It's just a lump of rock they built the sea-fort on.'

'Just a piece of rock, my dear? This is a rock and a half. Have you noticed there're no shellfish stuck to it; not a ruddy one. The rock's a freak. Look at the geology round here, it's boulder clay with a few bits of sandstone. Manshead is igneous, probably volcanic. If you could make the sea and sand and stuff round here all invisible, the picture you would get would be of the sea-fort standing on a big black pillar – what? – maybe two, three miles high, a bit like Nelson's Column.'

'But people from centuries ago wouldn't have known that. Why did they make all the fuss about it?' said Ruth.

'Magic, my dear. Place is soaked in it.' He gave a wheezing laugh. 'That's what they believed yonks ago anyway. You know, ley-lines and geomantric forces and that kind of crap. They believed this was one of the focal points. Where they could get closer to their god.'

'We'll put that in the advertisements when the hotel opens.'

'Anything to get the punters in is a good thing,' agreed Tony Gateman. 'Ah . . . must get on.' He glanced at his watch. 'I was just passing so I thought I'd call in. Cheerio.'

Just passing? thought Chris. In those shoes? They were highly polished brogues. And just passing to where? Apart from the beach and the marshes there was nothing for miles.

Tony began to walk across the cobbled yard and then stopped abruptly. 'I'm having a barbecue at my place tomorrow evening. It'd be lovely if you could come.'

To Chris's surprise Ruth said: 'We'd love to.'

'Six o'clock. Make use of the daylight. The name of the house is "The New Bungalow". On Main Street. You can't miss it. See ya, folks.'

Tony hurried away with that amazingly fast stride that only small men seem able to manage.

'A barbecue, eh?' said Chris. 'With the natives. I only hope we're not on the menu.'

'Ungrateful sod,' said Ruth good-naturedly. 'If we're going to become part of the community, we might as well make a start. If we can . . . Chris . . .'

'What's wrong?'

'Look.'

Through the window of the caravan he could see the flicker of the television.

'Jesus . . . I'd forgotten all about the bloody goldfish.'

77

They ran to the caravan.

David stood with his back to them, a drum of fishfood in his hand, while he sprinkled ants' eggs on to the surface of the water.

'Don't worry, kidda. We'll get a new one.'

'A new what, Dad?'

'Well, a new . . .'

His voice dried.

Instead of lying lifeless on the surface, its big eye pressed to the underside of the water like a fishy peeping tom, the fish was racing around the bowl with powerful flicks of its tail.

'A new what, Dad?'

'Oh . . . I . . . just thought a bigger bowl . . . Give Clark Kent a bit more room.'

'Thanks, Dad.'

Chris crouched down beside him so he could see the fish more closely. The shrunken look had gone; its scales blazed with a healthy gold colour.

Shaking his head, he rose and ruffled David's hair. 'Back to work.' As he passed Ruth he kissed her on the back of the neck and whispered, 'I think I'll keep you on the payroll.'

'Why?'

'For quick thinking in the face of adversity.'

'You've lost me, lover.'

'For buying another goldfish and switching it for poor old Clark Kent when we were out.'

'I did nothing of the sort. That *is* Clark Kent.'

'But it was dead.'

'It looked like that.'

'But —'

'But nothing. Let sleeping dogs lie. It's alive. David's happy. Now' – she pecked him on the lips – 'forget all about it.'

The UFO, trailing smoke and flames, crashed into the grey lunar landscape. With a fanfare of thin electronic notes the score on the left-hand corner of the screen flickered up to 1600.

David pressed the button marked START. He had one life left. The next invading UFO began to float down towards his lunar base.

'Are you getting the hang of it now, David?'

'Yes.'

He felt his mum's arm around him tighten into an affectionate squeeze.

They sat side by side on the sand, their legs outstretched in front of them. Down the beach the tide was slipping in over the dry sand; each wave brought the sea a little closer. Above their heads, seagulls floated like scraps of white paper.

'Do you miss your old friends? Chrissie Fawley and Matthew?'

He concentrated on the UFO, his thumb hitting the fire button.

'No, not really.'

'We think it's really nice here, don't we? Living in a caravan by the sea. It's like being on holiday, isn't it?'

'Will I still have to go to school?'

'Yes, you'll go to a new school in Munby – near where we stayed in the hotel.'

'I'll make new friends.'

'Of course you will. There will be lots and lots of children your age. We can invite them across to the sea-fort to play on the beach. And when the building work's all done, Nan and Grandad can come across to stay. It won't be as quiet as it is now; there'll be lots of people about. Look . . . Well done, David.'

The fanfare sounded again. All the UFO army had been despatched to UFO heaven; GAME OVER flashed up with a score of 2000.

'That's the first time you've won, isn't it?'

'Yes.' He gazed at the flashing figures. After months of failed attempts, suddenly it seemed easy. And dull, really.

Now he wanted a – what was the word Dad used to say over and over at the old house?

CHALLENGE.

Yes, he wanted a CHALLENGE.

When he thought of his toys all spoiled by sea water, it still hurt inside. But again David thought of what his dad had said about the sea-fort. He said it would cost a lot of money. That for a while they wouldn't be able to buy many treats. They would have to sacrifice some things they liked. But in the end the sacrifice would be worthwhile.

The loss of his favourite toys still hurt him; he had nearly cried.

. . . but the sacrifice would be worthwhile.

The green numerals of the clock radio glowed 11:11 across the caravan bedroom. Chris lay flat on his back, one hand pillowing his head. By his side Ruth lay sleeping on her stomach. The only sounds were his wife's gentle breathing and the faint hiss of the surf. Shuu-sh-shu-sh . . .

Exhausted from the day's work, his eyelids began to grow heavy in the comfortable darkness of the room. He tried to resist sleep, wanting to enjoy the flow of the day's memories. He would never have believed that hard labour could be so satisfying.

He glossed over memories of David's odd behaviour. Deliberately leaving his precious toys and Superman comics on the rock to be washed away by the waves. Kids do funny things. Hadn't he once taken to swallowing small pebbles when he was five years old? God alone knew why.

Shuu-shh-shuu-sh-sh . . .

Chris's eyes closed.

He dreamed:

The tide had rolled out. This time it had not stopped. It had rolled back somewhere beyond the horizon.

Now there was only a plain that had once been the bottom of the sea. Starfish and shells gleamed like stars in the sand. Here and there, seaweed patches, green and wet-looking, the size of football pitches.

He walked out across the plain.

As he approached an expanse of seaweed he noticed a ship in its centre. How long had it lain at the bottom of the sea?

He ached to take a closer look. This was the kind of mystery that every schoolboy loved. The sunken ship; the anchor hanging from a rusted chain, brown kelp stuck to the funnel. Was there treasure in the hold? Get closer. Read the name painted in white across the stern. See what's inside.

He walked across the sand towards the ship. He was about to climb on to it when, in his dream, he noticed Ruth standing beside him.

'Careful, Chris,' she whispered, 'there are poisonous snakes in there.'

14

They woke up hugging one another tightly; the clock flickered to 12.39.

'I love you, Chris. Hold me.'

'You're not tired?'

'Mmmm,' breathed Ruth. 'But I'm too hungry to sleep.'

'Hungry?'

She kissed him firmly on the lips. 'Hungry for you. Make love to me.'

His heartbeat quickened. Kissing her hard, he pulled her nightie up higher, up over her breasts, which were firming and rising in the cooler air. He kissed each breast, then ran his tongue across the hardening nipples.

'Oh . . .' She pulled his head against her bare breasts. 'Do anything you want to me. Now.'

David sat up in bed rubbing his eyes with his fists and yawning. It must be very late. No television sounds or voices, so his mum and dad were in bed.

He looked across the room, his eyes adjusting to the dark. Oh no. The headless boy was there against the wall again.

He pressed his knuckles into his eyes.

He wanted to shout. But his dad would be mad if he had to get out of bed at this time. He'd come in saying: 'David, how many times have I got to tell you? It's only your dressing gown. Take it down if it frightens you.'

It always did frighten him. The headless boy. A dark humpy-backed shape. He risked a glimpse.

Ye-essss . . .

It was getting closer.

He kicked his way out of the quilt and stood up. Managing to cover both eyes with one hand, he walked forward with the other outstretched.

Headless boy. You won't get me. Headless boy, how did you get that way? Heard a funny joke? And laughed your head off? Ha! Ha!

David kept up the flow of nonsense thoughts to stop his imagination from supplying too many scary pictures.

Headless boys are big asses —

They've got no ears for their glasses . . .

Still shielding his eyes from the figure, David reached out for the dressing gown.

He clutched at something smooth and cold.

Instantly his mind said WET.

A wet, headless boy from the deep blue sea.

Got a kiss for David; if you can find my mouth.

Shouldn't be cold and smooth.

It's the silly wall, he thought, relieved. Caravan walls are plastic.

His hand swept to the left, catching the dressing gown. Roughly he dragged it from the hook. The headless boy just became a naff old dressing gown that he never wore anyway. Screwing it into a ball, he threw it into the corner of the bedroom, then hopped back into bed to lie looking up at the darkened ceiling.

Abruptly, he sat up. He had heard a sound. It seemed to come from the caravan wall just behind his head. He thought hard.

There were no rooms on that side of the wall. The sound came from outside.

He heard it again. A soft grating. Like something sliding across the cobblestones.

Set above his bed was the curtained window. All he had to do was kneel up and look outside.

David knelt up in bed. Then he lifted the curtain.

*. * *

'Oh, Chris . . . I can't believe you're doing that to me. Uh . . .'

He felt her hands round his head pulling him to her tightly.

He could smell her, taste her; his body felt alight. He wanted to hold her so tightly that they fused into a single living being.

'That's beautiful. Oh, harder . . . Don't worry . . . You're not hurting me – ah . . . That's it. Mm-mer . . . Harder . . . Don't . . . Oh, yes.'

His breath came in bursts, his heart a hard pumping engine. *Yes*. He felt enormously powerful, a towering colossus above her, with the power to make this woman cry out or chew her knuckles in ecstasy. She was his; she would do anything.

She panted words breathlessly. 'Oh . . . I love it, I love it . . . You're breaking me . . . Oh, I'm breaking in two . . .'

The pumping engine had taken over. He gripped her, feeling her sobbing gasps hot on his throat. He wasn't in control. That engine inside of him pounded on and on and on. Whatever happened now, it would have nothing to do with him.

The first thing David saw when he lifted the curtain was a face.

His eyes widened.

Its eyes widened.

He opened his mouth.

It opened its mouth too. It had big white teeth with a definite gap at the front.

He smiled. Then tapped the glass. The face smiled back.

'Ree-fleck-shun . . . Ree-fleck-shun.'

He looked out into the courtyard which was flooded with cool moonlight. It lit the skips that his dad would have to fill with rubble tomorrow morning.

Through the open gates he could see the waves all twinkling and foaming across the causeway.

High tide. Now the sea-fort had become a little island once more.

Tonight the sea looked black in places. A bit like black-cherry jelly.

Something broke the surface of the water. Then immediately disappeared again. He leaned forward, pressing his nose to the cold glass. Things were moving about in the water. Maybe they were the seals his dad had told him about. He stared hard, certain they would show themselves again.

'Chris . . .' She breathed a deep, sobbing breath. 'Don't stop, don't stop.'

Her fingernails dug sharply into the back of his neck; her legs were wrapped tightly around him, her heels forcing themselves into his back in a series of spasms.

He had never experienced love-making like this before. Her ferocious passion only excited him more. Their bodies clashed together. She held the two of them together, grinding at him. It was as if she were making that desperate bid to force him so deeply into her body that they would permanently merge into one – like two figures made from moist clay, pressed together to be moulded into a new form. He panted. He kissed her violently; the salt on her breasts bit into his tongue. There was no sea-fort now, no sea, no coast, no Manshead, no nation, no world, no universe. Only the two of them, meshing together, joining into a single pounding being. A huge heartbeat thundered in his ears. Faster and faster.

Now he was no longer conscious of moving his body. He did not own it. It moved faster and faster, like a mechanical hammer, untiring; beating out an ancient rhythm that was as old as life itself.

An explosion was building in his body. She bit hungrily at his neck. An unearthly sweet pain – he desired it; he wanted it to pierce his body from head to toe. The explosion rose inside him.

She panted. 'Do it. Now . . . Break me! Ah!'

*   *   *

David looked out.

There, slap bang in the middle of the causeway, was a —

He jumped, startled. He'd not expected that. Shocked, he covered his face with his hands. For a moment he thought of calling out. But these days he was trying to be a brave boy.

Maybe it was . . . Maybe it was just a . . .

Slowly, so he could just peep through them, he opened his fingers, bit by bit.

On the causeway, just beyond the gates, standing as if it were a sunny day in the park, was a man.

But there was something odd about him.

He did not move. He had a white face. A very, very white face which had startled David.

And the man with the white face stared at David in the window.

Just then he had the strongest feeling that the man wanted David to go to him. It was like being called by your mum or your dad – you just felt you had to do it.

You must.

But David wasn't allowed out of the caravan at night on his own. Too dangerous.

Too scary.

All alone in the dark.

But the man wanted him.

The man did not move. And now the waves were washing round his legs.

Wasn't he wet?

But David couldn't see his feet in the water.

A little boat maybe? A raft?

He felt alarmed.

He had a feeling in his stomach. Like when he had the nasty dream about the wormhole under his bed. This was nastier somehow.

And the man was calling.

Calling him down.

Time to go, David.

Time to see the man on the water.

His sweat-soaked pyjamas were sticking to his skin. They felt cold.

What was he doing here?

He looked around him. The sea-fort walls were like cliffs, shooting up into the moonlit sky. Why was he standing in the courtyard in the middle of the night? The cobbles felt cold and gritty under his bare feet. The caravan lay behind him; the door swayed open in the breeze. Why wasn't he back there nice and snug under his quilt?

Then he remembered. That man had wanted to see him. That was all he knew.

The man with the hard white face stared. He did not move. Even though David was frightened, something inside him wanted to go.

He had something that David wanted. Just what, he didn't know. But he wanted it so badly now.

He wanted . . .

Now . . . Give it to me!

I bought it. It is mine!

David heard his own voice – demanding, demanding, demanding.

He had nearly reached the gates. One swayed, creaking on its rusty hinges. The breeze was fresher here, the hiss of the surf louder over the causeway.

The man's white face shone. It shone brighter than something reflecting mere moonlight.

Would David have to touch that smooth face? Now he could see dark patches where the man's eyes should be.

I've made the swap. I let my toys get washed away into the sea on purpose. We had a deal. I don't have to give any more. That's the rule, you don't have to give any more once you've made the deal. Spit on my palm, shake hands.

Now the face towered above him. Big and round and white and hard. Like the man in the moon.

Too soon, David. Too soon.

David stepped out of the sea-fort and on to the causeway. A wave licked his toes.

*   *   *

'If we hear it again I'll go see what it is.' Chris pulled his wife close. Even though it was dark, somehow he knew she was smiling. She kissed him on the chin.

'If we don't . . .'

'Then it's the same again for you, my dear.'

He chuckled, feeling deliciously relaxed. The sheets were a tangle beneath them but he couldn't care less.

'It's nearly two. We'll have to sleep some time.'

'We will . . . Some time.'

He ran his fingers down her spine.

'Blast,' she murmured. 'Did you hear it?'

'It'll be a seagull.'

'Or a seal. I don't want it raiding the dustbin. I'll just check.' She nipped the end of his nose with her teeth.

She sat up in bed and raised the curtain.

Her sudden yell stabbed his ears.

'David!'

Mark Faust sat on the dunes, watching the sea-fort by moonlight.

Waves rolled in over the beach in a soft roar. He'd watched them creep over the raised causeway, turning the sea-fort into an island. The sea-fort itself loomed against the moonlit sea like a beached battleship. The breeze ruffled his hair and he shivered slightly, feeling the hairs on his arms rising up on end one by one.

The sight of the place always did that to him. He remembered the first time he had seen the sea-fort. And he knew what lay just a few hundred yards beyond it in ten fathoms of ocean.

Through the sea-fort's big double gates he could make out the caravan that the family lived in while they converted the stone heap into a hotel. Jesus . . . A hotel . . .

He shook his head.

As he watched he heard a bang; a light shone from the window of the caravan.

Swiftly, he climbed to his feet. Two figures ran from the caravan towards the gates.

Jesus, one of the figures was as naked as the day they were born. They were too far away for him to be certain, but he got the impression it was the woman. She ran like an athlete across the stone cobbles – in her bare feet.

Why on earth? . . .

Then the American saw what she was running towards.

The little kid. For some reason he stood ankle-deep in the surf on the causeway. Like a little blond statue.

He saw the boy's mother grab hold of him and clutch him to her bare chest. She held him like that for a moment. The husband, wearing a dressing gown, stood a little distance away. Mark saw that they were speaking to one another – at first agitated; he could not tell what they said. They soon appeared calmer. The little boy rubbed his eyes as if he had woken from a deep sleep, yawning.

Then all three returned to the caravan, the naked woman carrying her son. The man shut the door. More lights came on behind curtains.

He waited another ten minutes until it became clear that nothing else was going to happen tonight, then he walked away into the dunes.

15

'David, stop doing that while I'm driving. It's distracting.'

'Okay.'

David didn't seem any the worse for wear after what had happened the night before. Nor did he seem bothered by the experience. They had asked him why he had left the caravan. 'Just a little walk,' he'd replied. They had decided to leave it at that, although Chris still wondered if moving away from his friends might have had a disturbing effect on him. In future the caravan door would get locked at night and the key put where David couldn't reach it.

'Where we going, Mum?'

'I've told you a hundred times. To Mr Gateman's in the village. He's invited us to a barbecue.'

'Why?'

'Because he's a cannibal, David. He's going to eat us for his supper.'

'Chris, you'll give him nightmares.'

'Dad, what's a sacrifice?'

Chris had thought he was going to ask, 'What's a cannibal?' The question tripped him. 'A sacrifice? What makes you ask that?'

'Enough.' Ruth raised her finger – both father and son knew it meant change the subject. 'We're going to have a good time tonight. David, you're having a treat because you're stopping up late. Your dad's having a treat because I'll drive home so that means he can drink beer and get all squinty-eyed.'

Chris turned the car into Main Street.

'Chris, there he is. Quick. Stop.'

He pulled over. 'Who?'

'The man who does odd jobs around the village.'

Chris saw a man chopping at a privet hedge with some shears.

'You said we needed some help at the sea-fort – go ask him.'

'Are you sure? He looks a bit wild.'

'It won't hurt to ask, Chris.'

His arms, legs, and most of his body ached. Some help shifting the rubble mountains, he had to admit, would be welcome.

Stiffly, he walked along the pavement to where the man was cutting the hedge. With every snap of the shears his hair and wild-man-of-the-woods beard shook.

'Excuse me. I'm—'

The man continued cutting.

'Excuse me.'

The words sunk in. The man stopped abruptly and looked up. The face was expressionless but the eyes had an odd cast to them. Chris pressed on. You don't need Einstein to shift concrete slabs.

'Excuse me. My name's Chris Stainforth. I've just moved into the sea-fort up on Manshead.'

No response. Just an empty stare.

'There's a lot of rubbish to shift and I wondered if you'd be interested in some work.'

'Uh . . .' the man held the shears in front of him frozen in mid-cut.

Then understanding hit him like a lump of concrete dropping out of the sky. The empty eyes blinked. Suddenly a fierce look blazed from them.

'Manshead . . . Sea-fort . . .' the wild man shuddered as if he'd found a severed hand in his sandwich box.

'No . . . No. Mans . . . head.' The voice, thin and cracking, sounded as if it hadn't been used for weeks. 'No. I don't go. You don't make me go. I live here. You say . . . you say, go

92

there, go do this, go do that. I'm here, I'm here. You want this, you want that. Go to the sea-fort. Go to Manshead. Do that in that place. That bad place.'

Chris's polite smile dried. 'It's okay. Forget it . . . Don't worry. Just a suggestion.'

The wild man pointed at Chris with the shears. They were stained green with the blood of the privet. 'It's not right. They say: Do this, do that. I wash cutlery, you know. There's so much of the bloody things. Knives, forks, spoons. More than anyone needs. It's just not right . . . No . . . no. I'm not —'

'Easy, there, old son.'

The big American who ran the village store ambled casually along the road, an easy smile on his face. 'You got work to do, Brinley?'

'Cutting this blasted hedge.'

'Hey, watch the language,' said the man soothingly. 'Lady and kid present.'

'I've got lots to do before hometime. Hedge. Watering.'

'Plenty of time, old son. Take it easy. You got your flask? Have a drink.'

It took five whole seconds for the penny to drop.

'I want a cup of tea.'

'Sure . . . No point wearing yourself out. Grab yourself a break.'

The wild man abruptly walked away.

'Thanks,' said Chris. 'I think I upset him.'

'Ah, don't bother yourself. He gets like that. Hey, how's David? Still got the Superman stuff?'

David, leaning out of the car window, beamed shyly and nodded.

'That's great. 'Cos I found some Superman comics in my old magazine store.' He handed a carrier bag full of glossy comics to David.

'That's great. Thank you.'

'That saves on introductions.' Tony Gateman had appeared and was swinging open an iron gate. 'You met my other guest.'

'Sure, we've met before in the shop.'

'This way, folks. The barbecue's lit, the drinks are cold. I don't know if anyone's thirsty, but I am.'

They followed Tony into the back garden.

'There you go, David, old son. I've rigged something up for you.'

'A rope swing!' David ran down to the bottom of the garden where a mature willow stood. From a branch a rope dangled with a piece of wood pushed through a knot at the bottom.

'You shouldn't have gone to all this trouble, Mr Gateman.'

'Tony,' he corrected gently. 'No trouble. The little chap'd be bored with my old-fogey talk anyway.' He led them on to a paved barbecue area. A large purpose-built barbecue smoked in a business-like way. Two tables stood side by side, one laid out with foil-covered plates and bowls; the other with bottles.

'White wine, Ruth? Or am I being a sexist pig?'

'I'm sure you're not, Tony. But I'll have a lager if you've got one.'

'Ah, working up a thirst on that sea-fort of yours, eh? Beer, Chris?'

Mark Faust spoke in his bass rumble. 'Chris and Ruth had a taste of Fox just now. I should have warned them.'

'Ah.' Tony handed Chris a pint topped with a foam as white as ice-cream. 'Every village has a Brinley Fox. Harmless, though. But you'll have met his father?'

'No. Should I have?'

'Fox and Barnett. The builders you bought the sea-fort from. That's old Mr Fox's son.'

'I always dealt with the agent. I never met Mr Fox himself.'

'That's hardly surprising, I suppose.'

Why? Chris was tempted to probe deeper. The excuse that Fox had simply pulled out of converting the sea-fort because he had had a change of heart was pretty light on authenticity in Chris's eyes. And he suspected Tony Gateman knew the real reason.

Tony poured Mark a Guinness and himself a generous Scotch and ginger while effortlessly engaging the three of them in small-talk. Eventually, Mark excused himself, saying he was going to talk to David.

Tony topped up the drinks. 'Smashing place, Out-Butterwick, you're going to love it.'

'What brought you here?' asked Ruth. 'You're not local.'

'Ah, you spotted the lad from the East End accent. A dead give-away. To tell you the truth, my dear, you won't find many true *locals*. As far as I know, only the Hodgson brothers, the chaps who farm all these meadows at the back here, are original Out-Butterwickers. No . . .' Tony leaned forward as if sharing a secret. 'Truth is we're all flaming outsiders. You know Mark Faust is. Came here in '62. I followed in '69. Before that I was a partner in a film production company.' Chuckling, he pulled a cigar from his pocket. He didn't light it but turned it over and over in his long, thin pianist's fingers as he spoke in his soft, eager, secrets-to-be-told manner. 'Film production sounds a bit grand. In fact we made training films and promos for the big corporations. I was the East End lad done good. Flash Jag, apartment in Mayfair, a leggy wife. That's when it got stupid. We had more work than we could handle. I'd find myself in the office at midnight; the night before you've got to present a sure-fire hit to the client. And you know, you've not got a ruddy idea in your head. That's when you reach for the white powders.' He tapped the cigar on the side of his nose.

'With me going flakey on forty fags a day and a lot of white powder up my tubes I came here. We were doing a location shoot for a new lawnmower; up on the dunes. You know, it looks like twenty miles of overgrown lawn.' Anyway, I came. Did the shoot, feeling like a slice of death warmed up, coke up my nose, pains in my arms and chest; God, was I in a mess . . . Then I walked along the beach to Manshead. I just stood there and looked . . . The sea, the fresh air, the dunes, miles of beach, seagulls shooting this way and that . . . And – bang!' He poured himself another drink. 'It hit me.'

He paused. Then smiled. 'God knows what. But something did. It's okay, folks, I'm not going to get religious on you. But I walked out on that causeway. And I chucked my fags and coke into the drink. Gone.' He shrugged. 'I went back to London. And all I did was think about this place. It was like seeing an enchanting woman. I fell in love. That's when I sold my share in the company and came to live up here.' He sipped his drink. 'What do you make of that, then? A dozy old bugger? Mid-life crisis?'

'No,' said Ruth, 'it sounds as though Out-Butterwick saved your life.'

'I think it did, Ruth . . . Ah, enough of me. Tell me your plans. Another beer, Chris?'

'Thanks. Tony . . . You said Fox just pulled out of the sea-fort conversion. To be honest, the idea of someone pulling out after sinking all that money into a project is insane.'

'Look, I'll tell you the truth,' said Tony, leaning forward in his chair. 'If you don't get it from me, you'll get some cock and bull story from one of the villagers. Want a drink, Ruth?'

'Not for me, thanks. I'm driving.'

'Right . . . Old Fox worked on the sea-fort for about six months. His only employees were his two sons. Twin lads in their late teens.'

The penny dropped; Ruth got there first. 'The Fox who cuts hedges was one of the twins, right?'

'Right.'

'The other Fox twin. Was he? . . .'

'A full shilling? He was perfectly normal. As was Brinley Fox in those days. Two bright twin lads all set to follow in old dad's footsteps as master builders.'

'So what happened?'

'So, work went at a cracking rate. No problems. Brinley Fox liked it here. Sometimes he'd camp out on the dunes and go night fishing from Manshead itself – you know, there's a rock ledge that runs around the bottom of the fort. He did that for a couple of weeks. Then packed it in all of a sudden. In fact he got in a fight in the pub with a couple of lads. He accused them of playing tricks on him. Trying to frighten him at the dead of night.'

'And were they?'

'They said they weren't. But lads are lads. Who knows?' He glanced at his watch and then shot a look across at the setting sun. 'Then one day all three Foxes were working on the sea-fort. The tide was coming in, just starting to lap over the causeway, when Jim Fox, Brinley's brother, remembers they've left their sandwiches in the van on the beach. It's a warm day, so he tells his brother he's going to take off his shoes and socks and nip back to the van. He won't be gone two minutes. Anyway, old Fox is doing some work on the doors, young Brinley's sitting by the gate grabbing a nicotine break. By all accounts Jim Fox set off across the causeway in bare feet, ankle-deep in water, and phutt . . .' He shrugged.

'What happened?'

'What happened is, Jim Fox set off on one side to walk the fifty yards across the causeway to the beach; but he never arrived.'

There was a silence. Midges danced above their heads.

Chris rubbed his cheek. 'But Brinley Fox saw what happened?'

'Therein lies the mystery. His sanity disappeared with his brother.'

'It's certainly a good mystery.' Chris took a swallow of beer. 'Good enough for the tabloids. So what happened? Abducted by flying saucers or mermaids?'

'Neither. Old Fox says he saw nothing. He saw his son set off, walking ankle-deep through the surf. He went back to his work. Five seconds later he heard Brinley scream. He turned round to see that Jim had vanished. Brinley yelled, "It's got him, its got him." Then he shut up and said nothing for more than a year. When he started talking again he was just how you see him now.' Tony tapped the side of his head.

'Well, what did happen to Jim Fox?'

'No one knows. He'd disappeared. No body – nothing.'

Logic glared Chris in the face. 'An accident, you'd suppose. I've seen it myself on the causeway. The tide comes in, and although it's only a few inches deep on the roadway you can't see the stones because they're a dark colour. You only need to wander off course a yard or so and you'd fall in the sea.'

'Even so,' said Tony, 'at high tide you would only be about chest-deep if you stood on the beach at the side of the causeway.'

Ruth lifted her eyebrows. 'So, he cracked his head on the side of the causeway when he fell. He wouldn't cry out, and the tide just carried him away. It was an accident.'

'Of course it was.' Tony chuckled, the jolly host again. 'Tell me to shut my trap if I get boring. I just wanted to give you the facts before you heard any half-baked tales. Right, I'm starving. Shall we get started?' He ripped the foil from the plates. 'These burgers I made myself. I like experimenting. Some are plain, those are with barbecue sauce, those with garlic, and I went crazy with those and soaked them in red wine.' Using a metal fish slice, he began arranging the burgers on the barbecue grill; morsels of meat fell into the flames to sizzle against the coals. 'Fancy some celery dip, Chris?'

Chris rose. 'In a minute, thanks. I'll get David.'

He strolled down the rolling lawn. He wrote off Tony Gateman's disappearing Fox twin story as the minor eccentricity of one living alone too long in a place like this. He liked the man; he was just trying perhaps a bit too hard to be friendly – and interesting.

As he sat on the swing, David told Mark everything. About the elephant slide at the hotel the previous week. About the strange feelings and dreams he'd had at the sea-fort.

Grown-ups sometimes treat you like a little kid when you tell them serious things. They laugh like you're telling them a joke or say 'That's interesting.' But Mark listened. He understood when David struggled to tell him that he was making swaps. David couldn't explain it properly. But he did know that if he gave away the toys and comics he liked to the sea, he would be given something back, just as you give money in a shop for a comic.

'You've been making deals, David.'

As the swing came back ready for Mark's next massive push, Mark asked: 'What kind of deals are you making?'

'David . . .' It was his dad's voice. 'Come on. Tony's cooking now.'

'Chow time.' Mark lifted David off the swing, then turned to Chris. 'Tony's not let his tongue run away with him, has he? He's a decent guy but he can talk the legs off a mule.'

'He was telling us how he came to live here. It seems this place has quite a hold on visitors.'

'Sure has.'

'How did you end up here, Mark?'

'Oh, I used to work the North Atlantic merchant freighters, moved into other jobs, then . . . I just sort of drifted in. Looks as though young David's worked up a thirst.'

David was greedily attacking a can of Lilt. A steady stream of green liquid ran down the front of his white t-shirt.

'Reminds me of me when I was a boy.' Tony turned the burgers; puffs of flame leapt up through the grill. 'Coming home from school with gravy stains down my tie. Sent the old man hairless. Everyone got salad? Right, who's for a garlic burger?'

The talk was now purely small-talk. Tony did most of it with Mark underpinning the conversation with a few comments in his rumbling bass voice.

Sunset came, and the sky turned dark blue; a few bats flickered overhead, gorging on insects.

After they had eaten the mood became even more relaxed. Tony settled down into a lounger, while Mark laid more burgers on the barbecue. The smell of sizzling beef filled the garden.

'Tempt you with a brandy, Chris?'

'You certainly can.' Chris leaned luxuriously back into his seat. David was back on the swing; this time with Ruth pushing, a glass of orange juice in her hand.

'Thanks for the barbecue,' said Chris. 'It's been great.'

'My pleasure.' Tony teased the cigar out of his breast pocket. 'Three fresh faces is a treat for me. One day, you'll have to let me show you around the area. We're not snowed under with archaeological sites but we've got a few. You might get a few guests wanting to know where they are. Just to the south of Manshead you've got some Iron Age earthworks and a couple of standing stones. Trouble is you're sitting on the main Neolithic temple.'

Chris looked around him in a brandy haze.

Tony chuckled. 'Not here. Where you live.'

'Up on Manshead,' rumbled Mark. 'Before the sea-fort was built there was a Neolithic stone circle. Five thousand years old.'

'They probably used the standing stones in the fort's construction. You'll probably come across the odd stone lintel, or footing a different colour to the rest.'

'Any time you want a look, just call in. It's a marvellous place. Marvellous.'

Tony refilled the glasses.

'You know,' Chris continued, 'there's actually a cellar under the sea-fort. It's bloody impossible, really. At high tide the water is higher than the cellar.'

Tony slipped the cigar out of its cellophane sleeve. 'Remember, I told you Manshead was a holy place. Do you know how holy?'

'A Neolithic Vatican?'

'Close – damn close. We're talking important. We're talking where the ancients got close to their gods, where they would

ask favours from the big cosmic daddy of them all. But as
I found out as a kid, Chris, if you want something in this
world' – he rubbed his fingers together as if separating
sticky banknotes – 'it bloody well costs. Do you know how
the ancients bankrolled their gods?'

'Rituals? Prayers? Hymns?'

Tony lit the cigar at last and blew a huge cloud of blue
smoke over Chris's head. 'Listen, have you ever made a
sacrifice to supernatural powers?'

'Have I buggery. I've been an atheist since I was nine.'

'Have you ever chucked a few pennies into a wishing-
well?'

'Of course. Everyone's done that at some time, but —'

'Ah, that, Chris, is a sacrifice. Look . . . A wishing-well.
What do you want? A wish to come true. The price? A few
coins in the water. Believe it or not, the wishing-well is a
direct descendant of the art of sacrifice.'

'Everyone chucks a few pennies in a wishing-well at some
time. It's just a fun thing for kids.'

'So you throw in a stone, or maybe an old lollipop stick?'

'No, like I said, pennies.'

'Cash, then. You pay cash for the wish. We're agreed, then.
You give something you value in return for something you
value more.'

'Put it like that, then yes.' Normally Chris would have
wondered what Gateman was driving at but the brandy
mellowed him. 'It's only a pity the bloody wish doesn't
come true. If it worked I'd be visiting a wishing-well every
day.'

'Right . . . You chuck a few pennies into the wishing-
well . . . You want the wish to come true. Now, Chris,
consider this; would you go into a car showroom and try
and buy a new BMW with a handful of pennies?'

''Course I wouldn't. You wouldn't get the keyring for
that.'

'You agree you need to pay a fair price for it?'

'Certainly.'

'Maybe you're not paying enough for the bloody wish, eh? Remember inflation. Everyone's price goes up. Even the water sprite at the bottom of the well.'

'Put like that, I suppose you're right. What's this got to do with Manshead? Was there a wishing-well there or something?'

'Wishing-well isn't far off the mark. It's the place where deals were done between man and his gods. There they paid their price and got what they wanted in return.'

'I take it they were paying more than a few pennies, then?'

'You're not wrong, my friend,' said Tony. 'Because Manshead is the place where they practised their sacrifices.'

'Virgins on altar stones?'

'Whatever the price demanded. A few bushels of corn or a chicken or two for a small purchase, say a safe journey or sick horse to get well again. For victory in battle or something a little more powerful from the god, then . . . Well, a sacrifice of something of greater value. Why do you think the place is called Manshead?'

'I think I know, but you're going to tell me anyway.'

'It's called Manshead because that's where the man's head was placed. Probably on wooden spikes. Think of it as a kind of supernatural stock exchange where the big deals were done.'

'Speaking of sacrifice,' said Chris, 'I think Mark has just made an offering to the gods.'

'Damn.' One of the burgers had slipped through the metal grill and was blazing furiously. Mark grinned. 'One burnt offering.'

Chris raised his glass. 'And you never made a wish.'

There was a significant pause before the other two laughed politely.

After the Stainforths had left, Mark and Tony stood on the pavement, talking in the cool night air.

'The Stainforths,' said Mark, 'what do you think?'

'They're nice people.' Tony dropped the cigar butt on to the floor and ground it beneath his polished shoe. 'But they'll have to go, of course.'

'How are we going to get rid of them?'

'That, Mark, my old friend, is what we're going to have to discuss.'

16

'Are we going to get the guns now?'

'Later. We can't get across the causeway because the tide's in. Go play with your toys for a while.'

David slipped away to the caravan while Chris finished stacking timber he'd salvaged from the sea-fort.

Ruth brought him coffee. 'I've been thinking, Chris. I want to get the main gates repaired as quickly as possible.'

'What's the hurry?'

'There's a lot of building material lying around. The last thing we want is someone walking away with it all.'

'And?'

'And what?'

Chris smiled. 'I know you better than that. It's more than someone waltzing off with the timber and a few stone blocks.'

'I know you're going to tell me I'm silly, but . . .'

'But?'

'But sometimes it's so quiet out here I start thinking. What if someone came here when I was alone with David?'

'Ruth, I don't think you're silly. I'm the stupid one. I should have known you'd feel apprehensive out here by yourself. I'll get the gates repaired by the end of the week.'

He heaved another balk of timber on to the stack. She squeezed his arm. 'Call out a joiner today, Chris. I'll feel safer. Look . . . It might be nothing to worry about, but I saw someone in the dunes yesterday. They just stood there watching the sea-fort.'

'What did they look like?'

'That's the strange part about it. They always—'

'Mu-umer. Da-adder.' The urgent shout echoed around the sea-fort.

Chris grinned. 'Here we go again . . . And don't worry about the gates, love. I'll get someone out to fix them this afternoon.'

'Da-adder!'

'All right . . . Dad to the rescue.'

Chris jumped up into the doorway.

To stand on the goldfish – almost.

Clark Kent flapped wetly against his ankle.

'Okay, the jaunt's over, buster.' He reached down to pick up the goldfish.

'Have you got him?'

It was like trying to catch a cross between a bar of soap and a grasshopper. Each flick of its tail kicked it inches into the air.

Chris grabbed it.

The experience wasn't pleasant.

It was solid muscle – hard, throbbing, occasionally giving a spasmodic jerk.

Ruth had always refused to catch the blessed thing because she said it was like trying to grab a free-floating penis. Now he knew why.

The fish seemed determined to escape. It was far more powerful than he remembered. When it arched its body it prised his fingers apart. Chris dropped the fish back into its water cell. 'And stay there. You cold-blooded monster.'

Cold-blooded.

Chris looked at his hands.

Now that was odd. He had always thought fish were cold-blooded. This one had felt hot to the touch. It had been like carrying, if not a hot potato, at least a very warm one. But then it may have been flapping across the caravan floor for ten minutes before David had spotted it. Chris knelt down to look at the fish, magnified by the distorting effect of water.

'Is Clark Kent okay, Dad?'

'Yeah, 'course he is, kidda. Just look at him swim.'

106

The fish swam round and round the bowl until it was a blur, its big fishy eyes staring fixedly ahead as if it were chasing something no one else could see.

He thought there was something appropriate about a clergyman living in a stable attached to an inn. Even if the stable had been converted into comfortable living accommodation only ten paces from Out-Butterwick's Harbour Tavern.

But Chris saw that the Reverend Horace Reed (retired, yet still wearing a white dog-collar), late fifties, didn't look a happy man. Oh, he smiled constantly. But he'd seen that smile before. Usually on the faces of politicians in a crisis.

'The cannon?' said the Reverend Reed. 'I don't see any real, er, problem. The vicarage is surplus to requirements and the diocese is looking for a buyer.'

'My wife saw the cannon first; that's her outside on the swings with my son.'

A couple of days ago, Ruth had taken a stroll around the village. First to the church, which she wanted to see inside. But sand had drifted against the door. Then she had noticed the vicarage. Outside, a dozen cannon barrels had been set upright in the ground where they served as fence-posts.

'You'd have to agree,' she'd told him, 'cannon would look impressive flanking the entrance to the sea-fort.'

He'd agreed, and here he was in the Reverend's living room.

'Er, you'll appreciate selling the cannon is not a decision I can make.'

Great thought, Chris. No doubt letters in triplicate with justifications *ad nauseam* to the bishop of somewhere a hundred miles away.

'There are, I believe, twelve cannon, Mr Stainforth. Er, how many would you wish to acquire?'

'Three. The two long cannon for the entrance to the sea-fort; plus the short squat one; hopefully that will go inside the bar.'

107

'Ye-es . . . Well, I will, as I, er, mentioned, have to telephone my bishop.'

'Telephone?'

'Shouldn't take long. I don't have a telephone here so I will have to use the one in the inn. Ahm . . . I don't seem to have any change for the pay phone.'

'No problem. Allow me.'

The man's smile was cold. 'Why, thank you. But, er, it is long-distance, I'm afraid.'

'Will this be enough?'

'That will be enough.' For the first time a hint of warmth crept into his voice.

Chris waited in the car park while the Reverend scuttled through the back door into the pub. On the swings, Ruth and David waved to him. He waved back.

Five minutes later: 'Ah, Mr Stainforth . . .'

'Any luck?'

'Yes. Yes indeed. I managed to catch the Bishop before he left for a meeting. Er, he has authorised me to sell on behalf of the diocese. Er . . . Four cannon, wasn't it?'

'Three.'

'Ah, yes – three. Let's see, the Bishop authorised me to sell at one hundred and fifty each.'

The man's dark-ringed eyes watched Chris with anticipation.

Do you haggle with the Church? Chris decided not.

'We've got a deal, Reverend.'

The vicar licked his lips. 'Good . . . good. Now. Removal and delivery. May I suggest I arrange that for you? I'll have Hodgson, the farmer, deliver them to you. He has two muscular teenage sons.'

Chris was about to thank him for his generosity, but he went on:

'I think we should give a little for their troubles, don't you think? An extra fifty?' The grin-cum-snarl didn't falter. 'If you'll make out a cheque. Five hundred pounds . . . please.'

Chris wrote the cheque. 'It'll be payable to—'

'To cash . . . The parish bank account was closed some time ago. Good day.'

He watched the Reverend Reed hurry back to his stable and slam shut the door.

Pleased, he strolled across to Ruth and David, now swaying slowly from side to side on their swings.

'Got them, Dad?' called David.

'Sure have.'

Chris explained that the Reverend Reed had to phone his bishop for permission to sell. Ruth listened, then burst out laughing.

'What's so funny, Mrs Stainforth?'

'He phoned who?'

'The bloody Bishop. I gave him coins for the pay phone in the bar.'

'Chris, David and I watched the Reverend Reed as you waited by the car. We watched him go up to the bar and drink what looked like three neat gins straight off. The phone was right behind him. He never even touched it.'

'The . . . scallywag. You can bet it's not church funds that are being bolstered, it's the Right Reverend's in there. Never mind. We're having the cannon delivered. And we've got them at a bargain price. Right.' He clapped his hands. 'It's back to the ranch. There's work to be done.'

They drove slowly by the white-painted cottages then by Out-Butterwick's village store. Tony Gateman and Mark Faust stood talking outside the front door. When they saw the Stainforths' car, both gave a friendly wave. Chris, Ruth and David waved back.

Chris noticed that the two men, one large, the other small and thin, were still watching as they drove out of the village.

17

Mark heard the thud against the beach. A splash of blood showed dark against the pale sand. He looked up.

Against the moon, the milky-white flash of the owl's wings beat the night air as it carried the mouse back to its nest. He shivered. Did it seem cooler tonight, or was it just him?

The pace of events seemed to be quickening.

It wasn't just the 'feelings'. Everyone in Out-Butterwick had those. They were getting so strong now it was an effort to sit still; you just wanted to jump itchily to your feet and pace around, like poor Brinley Fox.

Not just the 'feelings'. Mark was beginning to see things too.

And hear things. He heard it now.

Mark Faust sat on the dunes, the beach some twenty feet below running out in a long curving arc. In front of him lay the sea-fort. The tide had begun its long roll in.

It looked very different from the first time he had set eyes on it, that stormy night in December. He had been nearly split in two by the piercing cold as he had dragged himself from the surf. He remembered, vividly, the waves that thundered across his body like a locomotive. That night he had been a damn sight closer to death than life. His nose had bled from the re-opened cut from the man's fist. That man, with the rest of his pack, now lay at the bottom of the sea with the *Mary-Anne*. Sent there by a sixteen-year-old Mark Faust.

The sea twinkled, catching the moonlight. Beneath the faint hiss of the surf he could hear it again. That sound he had heard so clearly on that December night all those years ago.

A metal beat. Metal on metal, a deep, deep bass sound –
so deep you felt it in your stomach rather than heard it . . .
. . . Bang . . . bang . . . bang . . . bang.

Keep beating the drum, Skipper, he had thought as he
limped away that night long ago. Keep beating the drum.

Christ knows how. But from the hulk of the *Mary-Anne*
lying rusting on the ocean bed the sound came again. That
beat, deadly slow, rhythmic, like the heartbeat of a sleeping
giant.

His nights were restless now. He dreamt of a dark torso,
water-bloated arms and legs, a head without eyes; long, long,
long white hair floating around the head in the water; the
drowned figure beating the freezer walls with that same iron
bar. Bang . . . Bang . . .

Mark reached down between his legs, picked up a handful
of sand, then rubbed it hard against his face. His skin was
burning; the sand felt cool. He rubbed harder, its coarseness
pushing the nightmare images back into his brain.

The deep pounding continued. Perhaps no one else would
notice it. But he couldn't stop hearing it. It went reverberating
down into his soul, down into the depths of eternity.

'I hear you, Skipper . . . But in God's name what am I going
to do?'

18

For the third time that evening Tony Gateman thought he heard prowlers in his back garden.

He looked up from where he was sitting at the dining-room table to the clock on the wall. Ten o'clock.

'Bloody kids,' he told himself softly. But he knew there were no kids out there.

Shakily, he stood up, walked to the window and looked out.

Nothing but darkness. If he really wanted to check that there was no one there he would have to go out into the back garden.

'Come on, you silly old fool – there's nothing to be afraid of.'

But there is, Tony, old son, said the voice of common sense in the back of his mind. *There is lots and lots to be afraid of. You know it. Don't go out there. The doors are locked, the windows are shut, just draw the curtains and —*

'Oh, God . . . The bloody back door.'

He'd been out earlier to empty the pedal bin and he was sure he hadn't locked it.

Heart thumping, he hurried from the dining room to the kitchen at the back of the bungalow. The door into the back garden was shut but unlocked.

His first impulse was simply to drag the bolts shut and snap on the Yale lock. But a stronger impulse drew him to the door. No. He had to see if anything was out there.

A deadly fascination compelled him. If there was something there, he had to see it. Just as you hear the crash of

113

cars colliding, you have to turn and see, even though the scene might bring you nightmares for years to come.

Fear oozed through him as thick as meat-worms as he slowly pulled back the door.

Nothing immediately outside the door. Just the pale gleam of patio slabs before him on the ground. He stepped out into his garden and walked through the darkness towards the barbecue area, his head twitching left and right at every imagined movement or sound.

Get back inside, Gateman, jabbered pure, naked fear inside his head. *Get inside. Lock the doors. Hide, man, hide!*

No . . . He had to look. If it was *them* he had to see.

Maybe they were no longer dangerous. Maybe whatever it was they had gone through had changed them.

He peered short-sightedly across the lawn. The night had turned everything into shadowy ghosts. The trees, bushes, the fence-posts. They even seemed to creep nearer when he was no longer looking at them.

Get a grip on yourself, you idiot. There's nothing there. They are —

Christ . . .

There's one behind me.

Gateman's heart lurched agonisingly in his chest and he nearly vomited with fear.

He twisted round to see the figure behind him. It stood there, loosely wrapped in a winding-sheet. He backed away, his hands clutched to his mouth, trying to choke out a scream.

It did not move. When the night breeze blew, the winding-sheet flapped gently.

Tony Gateman dragged in a lungful of air.

Idiot . . .

It's only the patio umbrella. He'd folded it up himself that afternoon so the breeze wouldn't yank the thing out of the ground.

Even so, his nerves were shot. He blundered past it back to the bungalow, slammed the door behind him, snapped the bolts across – one, two, three – thumbed on the Yale lock, then, hands shaking crazily, slipped on the security chain.

Better.

Breathing deeply to steady his racing heart, he tottered across to a kitchen drawer, pulled out a tea towel, then mopped the oozing sweat from his face and hands.

After straightening his glasses, he went round every single window, checking they were shut, and carefully closed the curtains.

Now to kill the silence. Still unsteady, he made it back to the dining room. There he switched on the stereo, filling the room with Vivaldi's *Four Seasons.*

Normally the music lifted his spirits and he would conduct invisible orchestras. Not now. It sounded eerily hollow in a home that seemed far too big and far too empty these days.

He returned to the table where his books and files were neatly spread out. Work distracted him from his imagination which could gnaw him like a rat.

First he pasted into a file a newspaper cutting.

CLEETHORPES FISHERMAN MISSING PRESUMED DROWNED SAY COASTGUARD

After a three-day search, coastguards announced that there is little hope of finding the fisherman alive. Henry Blackwood, 49, of Parade Terrace, Cleethorpes, failed to return home from a fishing trip on Thursday. Despite an intensive search along a fifteen-mile stretch of coast, no trace of Mr Blackwood or his twenty-foot cobble boat, the *Suzanne*, has been found.

'Vanished without trace,' whispered Tony Gateman to himself as he dabbed at the cutting with his handkerchief. 'And I believe I know why.'

He turned the pages of his file. They were covered with yet more newspaper cuttings. The ones at the front of the file were now yellowing with age. All basically told the same story.

MISSING AT SEA . . . VANISHED WITHOUT TRACE . . .
ANGLER FAILS TO RETURN TO HOTEL . . . FISHERMAN
WASHED OVERBOARD . . . BODY NEVER FOUND . . .

Some were still heart-rending after all these years:

TRAGIC DEATH OF OUT-BUTTERWICK HOLIDAY MAKER

Eleven-year-old John Stockwell went for a paddle by himself,
after telling his mother he was going to look for the 'funny
shells'. He was never seen again.

That was in broad daylight on a warm summer day.

Tony sighed and closed the file. He picked up a ring binder.
Stark black letters on the first page spelt out:

SAF DAR

He turned to the next page. It was filled with his own neat
handwriting:

Armies throughout history have always utilised their own
particular brand of crack troops or warriors to inflict
mayhem and dismay on the enemy. The Romans employed
black Nubian warriors to terrify the Northern European
foe. The Vikings had their Berserker ceremonies to turn
their wildest warriors into frenzied fighting machines. Nazi
Germany formed the feared Waffen SS.

The Urdu people of the Indian sub-continent created the
Saf Dar. Translated, Saf Dar means simply 'breaker of
the line'.

In those ancient times opposing armies would face one
another in long lines, which can be shown thus:

Army: xxxxxxxxxxxxxxxxxxxxxxxxxxx
Opposing Army: ooooooooooooooooooooooooooooo

The two lines would advance in an orderly way towards each other. Each general's aim would be to force a way through his opponent's line of men to enable his own forces to rush through the gap and attack the line from the back or seek out the opposing army's commanders.

Clearly what is needed is a special force to 'break the line'. Hence the Urdu people's Saf Dar.

The Saf Dar were spectacularly vicious and brutal fighters. One can imagine them dressed in garish clothes, perhaps bright orange, to differentiate them from the common soldier on the field.

The Saf Dar would not be great in number but—

Tony broke off to wipe the sweat dripping down his spectacle lenses.

The Saf Dar would not be great in number but they would target a specific point in the enemy's line of soldiers, which can be simply shown thus:

Enemy line: xxxxxxxxxxxxxxxxxxxxxxxxxxxxxxx

S

Urdu line: ooooooooooooooooooooooooooooooo

The élite warriors of the Saf Dar are represented thus: S

The Saf Dar would charge screaming, brandishing their curving sabres. And even though wounded by arrows and spear thrusts nothing could deflect them from their bloody task: to break the line; which would allow the regular foot soldiers to pour through the breach and annihilate the opposition.

One could imagine that the terrible sight of the Saf Dar rushing towards them would, alone, be sufficient to put the enemy to flight.

He'd written that twenty years ago. Then it had seemed like an academic exercise; purely a hobby to while away Out-Butterwick's quiet winter evenings.

Now he read it and he trembled.

As the centuries rolled by the need for the Saf Dar evaporated.

But in the twentieth century they returned. Or at least a group of men resurrected the name.

Now as Tony thumbed through the file there were more newspaper cuttings, these bearing dates from the late 1940s and 1950s.

CIVILIAN MASSACRE IN KOREA

More than a hundred men, women and children slaughtered in Korean village.

Survivors describe horrific events.

Eight days ago mercenaries of mixed national and racial origins massacred the inhabitants of a farming village twenty miles from the Korean port of Pusan.

A number of villagers had been spared, but not through any sense of clemency. They were blinded and left with the instruction they tell the authorities that a group known as the Saf Dar committed the atrocity. And that the Saf Dar would strike again.

Tony flicked on through the file, reading a fragment of text here and there. Accounts of atrocities, murders, mass blindings. Sometimes this mercenary group that called themselves the Saf Dar would leave no survivors. But they always left their calling card. They would hack the hands and feet from their victims and use them as bloody paint brushes to daub on walls and the sides of buses: **SAF DAR.**

Tony saw the graffiti in his mind's eye in huge wet letters – in the deepest red: SAF DAR . . . SAF DAR . . . SAF DAR . . . The words would drip from a dozen walls.

Saf Dar: The breakers of the line.

After a time a pattern began to emerge. The Saf Dar prowled the trouble spots of South-East Asia, India and

118

Africa during the late forties and fifties. The style was always the same – atrocities, civilian massacres, mass blindings, the same bloody graffiti: SAF DAR daubed wetly on vehicles and buildings.

The Saf Dar's chosen role was simple. They would be employed by revolutionary groups, or even the governments of unstable countries, to break the spirit of the population. Their random massacres created a climate of fear and uncertainty. If the Saf Dar went to work in an area, they created floods of refugees that swamped other areas.

In the late fifties the Saf Dar operated extensively in the Belgian Congo. Thousands of civilians died in their genocidal campaign in the Ruwenzori Mountains in the south-east of the country.

Then they vanished as quickly, and as mysteriously, as they had come. The last recorded encounter was in Norway, north of Bergen, when they were disturbed in their rural hideout.

After a gun battle with the local police they fled.

For a while speculation suggested that the self-styled Saf Dar had been employed by anti-communist groups to enter Russia and destabilise the government as a prelude to a coup.

Wild theories abounded, but the truth of the matter was that the Saf Dar had simply vanished from the surface of the earth.

With the Cuban Missile Crisis and the Vietnam war there was far more to interest the media and intelligence personnel. The world forgot about the Saf Dar.

Tony picked up his pen and on a fresh page he wrote:
THE SAF DAR. WHERE ARE THEY NOW?

A rhetorical question. He already knew.

They were —

His head snapped up. This time he heard the sound distinctly.

The garden gate at the front of his house had swung shut with a thump. Someone had just entered – or just left – the garden.

119

With a cold feeling draining through his stomach, he walked quickly to the back door, still clutching the SAF DAR file in his hands.

'Hello . . . Hello? Who's there?'

Shivering, he listened hard. There was no reply.

With the file clutched in one hand, he used the other to unbolt and unlock the door.

'This is madness, Tony,' he hissed. 'You're out of your friggin' mind.'

But he knew he had to look. Something he could not control compelled him to open that door and come perhaps face to face with —

BANG.

He wrenched open the door, crashing it against the refrigerator.

Then, with his breath croaking noisily through his throat, he looked out.

There was no one there.

Perhaps they're hiding round the corner – or behind a bush, just waiting to . . . Get a grip, old son, get a grip. There's no one there.

From the doorway he strained his eyes into the dark.

He'd nearly given up and was ready to close the door when he happened to glance down.

Tony Gateman stared at what was on the pale flagstones, his eyes bulging.

He swallowed, and electric shocks of fear prickled up his spine, neck and across his scalp.

There, darker than the surrounding flagstones, were a set of footprints.

Tony stepped out, clutching the file to his chest, and looked down. The prints were those of an adult who had walked – barefoot – up to the back door of his house. He could even see the individual toes clearly against the stone.

The prints, Tony saw, were there because the trespasser's feet had been wet. Even as he stared at them they faded as the moisture evaporated.

Without hesitating, Tony followed them along the path to his front gate; once through the gate they crossed Out-Butterwick's main street.

Tony looked to his left and right. The street was deserted. Even at this time most of the houses were in darkness.

'You're an idiot, Gateman, you're an idiot . . .' He whispered it over and over as he followed the drying footprints. What if he turned a corner and they were waiting for him? But he knew he must see where they led.

He followed the footprints as far as Mark Faust's shop. There they turned left to follow a path down towards the beach.

Panting noisily, the file clutched to his chest, he followed the path, then crossed the seafront road to the beach. The prints had vanished now but he knew where they led.

He loped down the soft sand in the dark; ahead the surf showed in a milky line a hundred yards away.

The retreating tide had left a featureless expanse of sand.

Featureless, apart from a set of bare footprints leading in the direction of the night-time ocean. Panting, Tony loped after them.

The prints led to the water's edge and disappeared beneath the surf. Whoever had walked barefoot into the sea had not walked back out again.

Choking in lungfuls of air, Tony dropped to his knees on the wet sand. It was starting. These were the first signs – or should that be: These were the first symptoms?

What next?

Tony shook his head, afraid even to try to guess.

But he knew what the immediate future held for him. He would return to his bungalow, lock the door, take the whisky decanter to his bedroom, and spend the night emptying it down his throat.

19

'Dad! You've missed it!'

Ruth laughed. 'You'll have to start throwing it more gently, David. Your dad's not getting any younger.'

The evening sun shone brilliantly as they played frisbee on the beach. Two hundred yards away, the sea-fort reared out of the beach.

They stood in a triangle, throwing the yellow frisbee from one to the other.

'You're getting too good for me,' laughed Chris, his spirits high. 'Right, I'm ready for some more refreshment.'

'Wimp!' shouted David, and ran giggling back to the picnic they had spread on the blanket.

'I'll second that,' called Ruth mischievously, her dark hair blowing in the breeze. 'Wimp! Wimp!'

'I'm chucking both of you in the sea . . . See who the wimps are then . . .'

'Can't get me!' shouted David.

'Nor me,' Ruth panted.

David picked up the French stick, holding it like a sword. 'We're in our den.'

'Den? It's only a blanket. I can get the pair of you – easy!'

'But it's the den, Dad. You can't be got once you're in a den.'

'Okay.' Chris grinned. 'I'll obey the rules.' He sat down cross-legged on the sand beside the blanket. 'But that doesn't mean you can't pass essential supplies out to me so I don't starve.'

Ruth passed him a glass of Liebfraumilch. 'I'm glad you had the gates repaired.'

'You've not seen that man hanging around the dunes again?'

'No. Perhaps I was letting my imagination run away with me.'

'Anyway, it doesn't really matter now. Believe me, love. Once those gates are locked, they will keep an army out.'

20

Mark looked out to sea. The tide advanced, lifting the few small boats and dinghies off the sand.

All the villagers were there.

The Major with his dog; Mrs Jarvis in her wheelchair, resting one foot on the low wall that separated sand from road.

A car crept down the road behind them. The Reverend Reed would drive up and down the seafront road at least three more times before the sun set.

Apart from Brinley Fox, the beach was deserted. He paced up and down, ravenously smoking a cigarette.

Tony Gateman stood by Mark's side.

As the sun dipped behind the white-painted cottages, Mark found himself thinking of a time long ago. He and his brother were on vacation. Their parents had taken them to a fairground that had a huge rollercoaster ride. His brother was about eleven; Mark would have been a couple of years younger.

They had walked around the fair, going on the usual rides, firing rifles, eating stick-jaw candy. A ride on the rollercoaster would be the climax of the trip. They debated its potential all day – how fast it would go, how high it soared, had anyone ever fallen off, would they scream like the rest? They had enjoyed anticipating the thrill of the ride, with the iron wheels clattering and roaring down the iron track. All day Mark had looked forward to riding the rollercoaster until he had ached inside.

Then he and his brother joined the queue. At last they climbed into the bright red carriages.

It wasn't until the carriage had begun its long clanking climb up the incline that seemed to go for ever up into the sky that he realised the last thing he wanted to do in his life – ever – was go on this thing. Frightened? He was terrified. He gripped the safety bar. This thing wasn't safe. He wanted to get off. He didn't want to ride the damn thing any more.

He remembered those few moments riding upward in that carriage more keenly than he'd remembered anything before.

Because that's how he felt now. Here in Out-Butterwick they were waiting for a terrifying monster rollercoaster of a ride that no one alive had ever experienced. Once again the sense of anticipation and excitement he had felt had been transformed into fear. This was a ride he wanted to get off now. He wanted it to stop. He wanted out.

But he knew, Tony Gateman knew, every damn person here knew, it was far, far too late.

The knots in his stomach grew tighter as the sun hung on, a blob of red fire on the horizon. Then it slipped from sight. The sighs of relief were audible. It would not happen tonight.

The Vicar's car fired into life and he slowly drove back to the Harbour Inn. He had an appointment with a green bottle that promised to wash away his fears for a few sweet hours.

Mark turned to Tony. The little Londoner still stared out to sea, his eyes gleaming behind the thick lenses.

Mark licked his dry lips. 'I've seen them moving about. Under the sea at Manshead. They've found a way out of the ship . . . Tony, they're coming back.'

Tony looked up. 'It's all going wrong, isn't it?

21

After he had left Tony and Mark at the Harbour Tavern, Chris strolled away from the village in the direction of home.

Home? A caravan, parked in the courtyard of a derelict sea-fort? But now it really did begin to feel like home.

He was glad he had made the effort to come to the Tavern tonight. After a day ripping out more pre-war panelling from what had been the sea-fort's lavatories, he'd been tempted to slump in front of the TV, feasting on pepperoni pizza washed down by a couple of cold beers. 'Get yourself out,' Ruth had told him. 'If you're going to be Out-Butterwick's leading businessman you should be mixing with the locals.'

The street lights ended with the last cottage in the village. He struck off on the path that led along the top of the dunes back to Manshead. Even though the moon had started to wane, the thin silver light it cast was bright enough to see by. To his right, the expanse of sand looking misty and pale; beyond that were the brighter bands of surf rolling in towards the shore. To his left the marshes were merely an expanse of dark shapes.

He strolled on, breathing in the warm night air scented by some wild flower, listening to the hushed whisper of the sea. The evening had left him feeling relaxed and amiable; a warm bubble of satisfaction filled him.

The knowledge that in twenty minutes or so he would be sliding into a warm bed beside his wife only seemed to increase his sense of well-being.

After all the beer and brandies he seemed to be almost sleep-walking, lulled by the slow rhythm of his stride, the sandy path crisp beneath his feet. But then this place had a habit of relaxing you at night. After these days of hard work, sleep came over you like the waves of some vast dark ocean, rolling in and out, lulling you, filling you with the most blissful relaxation.

He yawned.

The temptation rolled through him to lie down in some hollow with sand for a comfortable mattress and let himself drift peacefully away to sleep.

He yawned again.

Ahead, a figure stood alone on the dune.

He remembered his policy of positive fraternisation with the natives. He took the right-hand fork in the path which would take him to the figure. The man stood with his back to Chris gazing steadily out to sea.

He'd just say a few words in a neighbourly way then move on. It was coming up to 10.30 and he didn't want to leave Ruth and David alone at the caravan too long.

'Hello . . . Nice evening.'

Chris walked up level with the man and looked into his face.

OH, GOD ALMIGHTY.

Chris's eyes opened wide with shock – so wide the muscles around his eyes hurt.

He stared unblinking at the face. Face? No . . . No face ever looked like that.

The face was round, perfectly white. Shockingly white. As white as a sheet of clean paper, as white as a freshly whitewashed wall; as white as milk; as white as a plate; as white as Christ knows what.

He wanted to lumber blindly away from the thing just an arm's length away. He could not. He was held there. As if a dozen hands had gripped his head, his face, his body; they even seemed to grip his heart, constricting it painfully until he thought it would give one savage leap then stop – for ever.

Something seemed to move beneath the face. As if fingers,

or something sluggishly alive, were wriggling beneath a tightly stretched sheet of rubber, prodding shallow lumps to appear and disappear . . . Slowly.

Nothing else existed in the whole world, only the white disc in front of him. And the eyes.

They were dead-fish eyes. Cold, unmoving.

In the bottom third of the white face a split appeared. The mouth widened like a razor slash. There were things inside it.

Inside, tightly packed, one after another, in two uneven rows, were shellfish. The blue-black mollusc shells glistened in the moonlight. Behind them something moved with a thick coiling and uncoiling motion.

An image of a roll-mop herring squeezed into his head. This had the same dark grey colouring; the same silver underside. It continued curling and uncurling wetly in the cavity of the mouth.

Chris tried to screw his eyes shut. But his body didn't work any more.

The thunder started.

Only it was not thunder. It was a huge thundering voice. Someone bellowed at him in a language he did not understand.

He didn't know if it was in rage. But it seemed to want something from him. Urgent. Demanding.

And it nearly split his bloody head in two.

What do you want from me? he thought desperately. Jesus . . . What do you want? What do you want!

The voice thundered.

Demanding . . . Demanding . . . Demanding . . .

Demanding what, for Christsake?

Christ . . . Go away . . . Please . . .

If only he could understand . . . No!

A raw feeling ripped away all rational thought.

He was conscious only of an intense feeling of revulsion as he looked at the face – his eyes nailed to it.

Then, although the feeling – the sensation he experienced

as he stared at the white face – did not change, his own re-action to it did. From revulsion, a disgust so deep it sickened him, the feeling slipped seamlessly into one of attraction. An attraction so powerful he found himself leaning towards the white face. Closer . . . Closer . . . Touch that smoothly swelling white face with your lips and —

CRACK!

His reaction to the face snapped again: disgust, loathing, revulsion, fear. He wanted to run. Jesus, just run. Please . . .

CRACK!

Back again. The feeling of revulsion switched to a des-perate need to understand what the voice was thundering. It was important. He wanted – no, he needed – to talk to the figure. To communicate.

CRACK!

Once more revulsion swept through him like shit-filled water blasting through a sewer pipe.

Suddenly:

Silence.

The thunderous barrage that had battered his head stopped.

That white face still hung in front of him. The dead-fish eyes looked into his. The slit of the mouth widened. And between the two rows of mussel-shell teeth, the dead-fish tongue rolled to one side, exposing its silver underside, slick with a spunk-like cream.

As he watched, the white face became covered by small lumps that began to swell. There were dozens. He thought of the sea anemones that covered the rocks at low tide in a soft pulpy rash.

Then, like sea anemones immersed in sea water, one by one they opened.

The face was flowering.

Shooting out thousands of waving tendrils of delicate flesh, each one no longer than a matchstick.

As he watched, his body rigid, the thunder voice returned to smash against his skull, a tidal wave of sound that threatened to split his eardrums.

This time something snapped.

He recoiled back from the white face.

Twisting away, he ran across the dunes as fast as he humanly could, the dune grass whipping his legs and arms.

The white disc appeared over his shoulder.

It followed him effortlessly. He ran on, convinced it was riding him, a nightmare jockey, the great white face just inches from his ear.

The voice thundered. Christ, what did it want? What did it want! It was like someone shouting an urgent warning. The edge of the dunes came up to his right with a sheer drop twenty feet down to the beach.

Relentlessly he ploughed through long grass to his left and rejoined the path, his feet kicking up sprays of sand.

The face was still there. Just behind him.

It wasn't going to let him go; not ever.

The thundering voice: it would burst his skull like a paper bag.

He slid down a five-foot tussock on his backside, landing in a crouching position, the momentum ramming his face down into a mound of sand. Instantly he leapt to his feet and ran on.

Each breath felt as if it would split open the lining of his airway, from his throat to his lungs.

Keep going . . . mustn't catch me. If that face touches me . . .

He knew he wouldn't be able to bear it. Embracing a rotting corpse would be preferable. If that face pressed against his, his heart would burst with terror; he would die screaming there on the dunes.

He ran on, shooting pains jabbing from heel to hip.

He looked back. Still following . . . round white face . . . alive with crawling shoots.

He looked forward again.

This time to see the dunes end . . .

. . . and nothing but the night air begin.

He fell forward, then down, his feet higher than his head.

The moon rolled down through the sky until it was beneath him.

He plunged downward.

He didn't even have time to brace himself before his body cracked into the beach twenty feet below.

The beach stopped his falling body instantly, but his mind had jerked free from whatever mounting held it here and it went whirling down . . . down . . .

Down into everlasting dark waters . . .

Of oblivion.

22

'Ready for lunch?'

Ruth slipped her arm around Chris's waist.

'Starving.'

'Come on, then. Where's David?'

He looked along the beach, the brilliant sunshine making him squint. 'He was there a minute ago. Down by the sea. Ruth, do you think David is ... different these days? I mean, different from how he used to be when we lived in the old house?'

Ruth smiled. 'You mean he hasn't mentioned this story about being able to fly for the last few days?'

'But he was obsessed with flying. He told everyone he could fly. Now ... Not a peep. He just seems different lately.'

'And he's not asked to wear his Superman costume for more than a week, and he's not bothered to watch his Superman videos.'

'What do you think it is?'

'Chris, I know exactly what it is.'

He looked at her sharply.

'It's called growing up.'

'But that business with him leaving his favourite toys on a rock to get washed into the sea.'

'It might just be a way of getting rid of his childish toys. You have to realise, Chris, you won't be able to sit on the settee with your arm around him watching *Tom & Jerry* cartoons when he's twenty-three.'

'Point taken. Come on, I'm starving . . . David! We're going home.'

They walked up the beach, Chris enjoying the feel of Ruth's arm around him.

'How is the invalid anyway?' she asked, and rubbed his chest with her free hand.

Chris's mouth suddenly bled dry. He wished she hadn't reminded him. 'Not bad. More stiff than anything. I suppose it serves me bloody well right. I shouldn't wander along the top of the dunes in the dark.'

'With a bellyful of beer.' She giggled softly. 'Next time take a torch.'

Next time? He doubted it. The stiff arm and bruised ribs paled to nothing compared with how he felt inside his skull. Instinctively he had blotted out the worst of it. But occasionally he caught a kind of nimbus of memory, just an echo of what he had come face to face with the night before, and it felt as if his mind was threatening to uproot itself from its moorings and flee into the refuge of insanity. He shook the strange dislocated feeling out of his mind.

He'd told her nothing, of course. Nothing apart from just a manageable portion of the truth. That he'd accidentally taken a header off the dunes to land on the beach twenty feet below. He'd been lucky not to bust his back.

As memories of the previous night began to recede, he began to run through the jobs he'd assigned himself for that afternoon. Clean out Clark Kent's bowl. For some reason the water always felt warm these days. The fish looked different too. It was changing. And he wanted to look in the sea-fort's cellar. He'd still not managed to grab so much as a glimpse of what was down there.

The sand crunched behind them.

'Prepare to die!'

Chris turned.

'Catch the sword, Dad.'

David threw the red sword hard enough to make Chris's hand tingle as he caught it.

'Careful, David. Remember your dad's hurt his arm.'

'It's only plastic.' He swung the sword sharply against Chris's leg.

'Ow! Now for my revenge!' He chased after David who ran giggling breathlessly in the direction of the sea-fort. 'Head him off, Mum,' shouted Chris, trying not to limp. 'We'll make him eat sand and seaweed pie!'

'I'll do no such thing,' she laughed. 'Fight your own battles.'

Swords rattling together, Chris allowed his son to drive him back towards the sea-fort with Ruth shouting encouragement. 'Aim for his knuckles, David.'

'Hey, who's side are you on?' laughed Chris, parrying David's merciless slashes.

'Come on, the tide's coming in. We don't want to be stranded.'

The tide had already flooded the beach around the sea-fort and was creeping along the flanks of the raised causeway. They had plenty of time but it would mean a detour in the direction of dry land before they could climb up the three or four feet to the causeway, then double back to the sea-fort with the waves washing the stone sides.

'Ow! Come here, you monster.' He and David fenced all the way back to the sea-fort, through the open gates and into the sun-filled fort.

Errol Flynn-style, Chris jumped, after two attempts, on to the old wooden table by the caravan where they sometimes ate outdoors. They continued fencing, David gleefully slashing at Chris's ankles. 'David, do you know the meaning of the word sadist?'

'No . . . stand still while I hit you.'

'Chris . . .' Ruth stood looking around her, concerned.

'David . . . Stop.' Chris held up his hand, wondering what Ruth had seen. At that moment nothing seemed unusual. The sea-fort courtyard looked the same as when they had left it an hour before. The table he now stood on, red plastic sword in hand; the caravan, its windows open in the hot sunshine. Everything in its place. He shot a look back at Ruth.

'Chris, can't you smell it?'

He sniffed.

'Petrol?'

'The place reeks of it.'

He climbed off the table. 'There might be a leak in the car's tank.'

He'd barely taken half a dozen paces towards the Ford Sierra when he noticed it was shimmering. The car, wet from end to end, literally dripped petrol; it gathered in puddles beneath the car.

'Jesus Christ.' He looked under the caravan to see a piece of old carpet and half a dozen wooden crates. They too were soaked in petrol.

Heart thumping, mouth dry, he looked around the courtyard. It seemed deserted. Either this was a failed attempt, or they were still in the process of trying to torch the place. He thought of the room on the ground floor of the sea-fort where the half-dozen gas bottles had been stored.

'Mum . . . What's wrong?' David sounded alarmed.

'David, hold your mother's hand. And keep away from that petrol.'

Chris ran round the caravan to pick up an old axe-handle he had propped by the door. 'Ruth, I'm going to check the sea-fort.'

'Chris . . .'

'Someone might be hiding in there . . .' He dropped his voice to a whisper. 'The gas bottles. They'll go up like a bomb if they're burnt.'

'For God's sake be careful.'

'Don't worry. They probably scarpered when they saw us coming back. I'll check inside then we'll put the hose on the car and the caravan . . . Look after this for me, kidda.' He handed the plastic sword to David.

He made a circuit of the courtyard. No one hiding behind the stacks of stone or timber. He ran lightly across the cobbles to the main door to the sea-fort building.

The door had been shut; now it lay open.

On the step a splash of petrol the size of a coin stained the stone. Testing the weight of the axe-handle, he stepped inside.

Standing in the entrance hall, a three-gallon petrol can in his hands, was the person he would least have expected.

Dressed in suit trousers, white shirt, silk tie and polished shoes was Tony Gateman.

For a moment they stood, Chris staring in disbelief, blood thumping through his ears. Tony stared back, his long fingers curled around the handle of the petrol can.

Chris's voice came in a low hiss. 'You miserable bastard.'

'I know . . . I know what you're thinking, Chris. It's not what it looks like. Believe me. It isn't. I stopped him . . . I was walking by . . . up there on the dunes, and I saw . . .'

Chris raised the axe-handle. It felt heavy enough to crack a skull like an eggshell.

'To our faces, my wife, my son, me, you're Mr Nice Guy, then when our backs are turned you pull this bastard stunt.'

'Chris . . . It wasn't me. Look—'

'No, you look. You broke in here; you trespassed on my property with the intention of burning the place down. Jesus Christ, don't you know the work, time, money we've put into this? Over the last two years I've put nine-tenths of my life into it – planning, worrying, sitting in bank managers' offices, talking to architects and piss-stupid planning officers. Now you want to burn the fucking thing down. Jesus . . . Why, Gateman? What have we done to you to deserve this?'

'Chris, listen. I've not done anything. I was walking along the dunes and I saw Fox. You remember Fox? He was throwing petrol around. I managed to talk him out of it – he—'

'Where is he now?'

'I-I . . . I don't know.'

'Leave that petrol and go outside . . . Stay there. Do nothing.'

Tony Gateman nodded so sharply he dislodged his glasses. Straightening them, he hurried outside.

Chris had walked into the first room when he heard a thin cracking cry. He turned to see Fox, as wild-eyed as a demented baboon, running down the corridor and out into the courtyard.

Chris followed.

The man was through the gates before Chris was even through the doorway. Ruth stood in the centre of the courtyard, her arm round David's shoulders.

Chris let the madman go. He knew where to find him when he needed him.

'Chris,' began Tony, 'we've got to talk. I've got to tell you what's happening here.'

Chris swung the axe-handle down; it struck the cobbles so loudly it made Tony jump.

'I know what's happening here,' said Chris.

'You do?'

'Of course I bloody well do. You and that lunatic Fox are trying to drive us out of here. I don't believe for one minute that you just happened . . . just happened to be sauntering along the bloody beach . . . just happened to see him pouring petrol all over the place.'

'Chris, you don't understand . . . his brother died here. He wants to get even. This place —'

'Whatever the motive, I think you're lying. You were helping him.' Chris had never felt this way before – an icy calm, but underneath he could feel some enormous force building, ready to explode. If he snapped . . . if he snapped . . . He gripped the axe-handle tightly.

Tony talked quickly, but Chris did not listen.

'Chris, you don't know what's happening here at Manshead. This place is dangerous. We can't go just yet. Not until the tide drops again. Then you've got to get away from here. Right away. Go and stay with your family for a few weeks. You can —'

'Get out.'

Tony looked out through the gates. 'I can't. Not now. It's too late. The tide's coming over the causeway.'

138

'Afraid of getting your feet wet?'

The smell of evaporating petrol grew more intense.

'I want you off my property.'

'Look . . . I can't. For God's sake's, man, there's something in the sea. We need to lock the gates until low tide then drive out of here. We must get away from the coast altogether.'

'Something in the sea?' That dangerous feeling grew more intense. 'Just what is in the sea, Mr Gateman?'

'Take a look for yourself.' He pointed. 'They're in the water.'

Chris did not even glance in the direction of the gates. 'I don't see anything, Mr Gateman. Now, I'll give you ten seconds to leave my property.'

'Chris, please, you can't make me leave now, I'd —'

'One.'

'Just look for yourself, man. Tell him, Ruth. Make him look —'

'Two.'

Something suddenly occurred to Tony. 'Ruth . . . Can you see Fox? Did you see him make it to the beach?'

'Three. Four.'

'Ruth. Tell me. Can you see him?'

'Five.'

Ruth gave a little shake of her head.

'Oh, Christ. Please. I'm begging you, don't make me go out there.'

'Six . . . Seven.'

'Look. We'll sit down.' Gateman's face ran with sweat. 'We'll talk. I'll tell you everything.'

'Eight.'

'Chris! Your wife, your little boy. They're in danger.'

'Nine.' Chris gripped the handle so tightly his hand turned as white as bone.

'Oh . . . Jesus Christ . . . I'm going, I'm going . . . But just watch me.' Tony ran – the slow jog of an unfit man. At the gates he slowed briefly and looked back. Then he ran as hard as he could.

The pace was slow, that same slow jog. The sea had covered the causeway to ankle deep; sometimes a wave would bring that level up to his knees.

Chris, with an alien calm, watched the little Londoner run through the surf, dragging his feet through the water, the man's arms jerking out like those of an incompetent tightrope walker, fighting to keep his balance on the roadway.

After what seemed a long time, Gateman fell on to the beach at the far side.

Chris walked across to the twin sea-fort gates and watched Tony rise then stagger further up the beach. He was pointing wildly at the surf.

Slowly, Chris closed the massive timber doors, then drew the steel bolts.

Feeling calm, in that detached alien way, he crossed the courtyard and took David by the hand. David relinquished his hold on his mother.

'Chris . . .' Ruth's voice was low. 'That man Fox . . . I didn't see anything, but . . . I didn't see him on the beach.'

He looked at her without emotion.

'Chris, I don't know if he made it to the other side.'

'Come on, Ruth. It's time we had lunch.'

Then, holding David's hand, he walked back to the caravan.

23

At first Brinley Fox thought he had tripped.

The man waving the axe-handle in the sea-fort had terrified him. Brinley was going to hide in one of the rooms – all those rooms squeezed tight full of shadows! – but then he thought of all the petrol he'd gone splash! splash! splash! all over the place and he felt even more frightened.

And those rooms packed full of shadows – not nice, Brinley, not nice . . .

So he'd run out of the sea-fort (seems like the best thing, Brinley); he'd got halfway across the causeway, big boots splashing in the water, and now, oh, silly Brinley, he'd fallen. He was all wet, and cold.

And now he remembered.

The memory had been there all along. Like a frightened puppy waiting to come indoors from the cold.

Now it scampered in.

For the first time in ten years he thought of his brother.

Brinley Fox remembered watching as his brother – Jim, yes, Jim – as his brother ran across this very causeway in his bare feet, the water as deep as this as the tide came rolling in. He remembered.

The arm, dark and strange-looking, flashing up out of the surf, grabbing hold of Jim, then pulling him into the water.

I remember everything now, he thought, the shock driving him sane after ten years wandering in a mental fog full of dreams with a rambling voice that he thought was a ghost. Now at last he realised, the voice had been his own.

Brinley Fox wanted to scream out to Tony Gateman in

141

the sea-fort to help him, but a wave mottled green with mossy pieces of seaweed rushed at his face, filling his gaping mouth.

He tried to climb to his feet.

His foot was stuck hard.

Got stuck in a crevice, or tangled in seaweed.

Half kneeling, he looked down at his foot. No.

A hand held it there. A hand with a wrist that disappeared into the water.

Then a wave hid it.

I've got to get out . . . I've got to get out, he thought, turning back to face the beach. If I can put my head down and just crawl on my hands and knees, just a few inches at a time, I'll make it to dry land. Then he'd be home and safe within five minutes. The door of his caravan locked and bolted. After ten years of insanity he wanted to relish the sensation of being sane again. He did not want his life to end here in the cold North Sea as his brother's had.

He dragged himself forward, jaw clenched, muscles straining.

Again he tried to shout. Again, before he could make even a grunt, he felt a savage tug that brought him whipping face down into the water. No . . .

Suddenly, he felt himself being dragged backwards with tremendous power towards the edge of the causeway. Pain blistered like fire along his legs as his knees were bent against the joint.

He tried to grip the cobbles. There was nothing to cling on to. His nails popped from his fingers as he tried to hook them into the cracks between the stones.

Waves broke over his head as he was dragged further over the edge.

Now his head was under the water more than out of it. Breathing became near impossible; a rising scream in his throat ended in a gurgle.

A hand gripped the waistband of his trousers. The next wrench took him to the edge of the causeway. His legs kicked frantically in deep water, like someone practising the crawl leg-kick while holding on to the edge of a swimming pool.

Panicking, twisting round, he felt his mind slipping back into the dreamworld it had inhabited for the last ten years. No. He wanted to hang on; he wanted to live like a man once more, sane, intelligent, clean, with a mind of his own.

No,

it began

sliding

out of control

again . . . again . . .

. . . Want home. Want to sit . . . eat chocolate, drink cider, smoke cigarettes . . . watch television . . .

Not this . . . Not to be pulled underwater by hands with fingers that looked like raw sausages. Not this . . . don't like it . . . hurting . . . frightened.

He felt another set of fingers gripping his face. A finger and thumb found his eye. Quickly they forced their way into his eye socket.

Agony . . . It felt like a cold chisel being forced through to the back of his skull. Sick, feel sick . . . His trousers filled with shit.

As the fingers tore out his eye.

Briefly he broke the surface. With his good eye screwed shut he saw a world crazy once more through his unsocketed eye. It swung wildly, pendulum-like, blurred images flicking against the twisting retina: ripples on the sea, spray from his flaying arms; a strange red hand gripping; the lady and the boy in the sea-fort; a seagull gliding through the sky . . .

Another hand came up from behind him and gripped his wild bush of hair. It pulled mercilessly.

He managed to stand. Feet braced against an underwater boulder, he held on to a rock in front of him. Two pairs of wetly red hands tried to pull him into the sea but he would not come. He was strong. Probably stronger than any sane man.

The hand gripping his hair tightened its grip then pulled

harder. It pulled until with a splitting crack his scalp gave way. The skin split at the hairline across his forehead. It came away in a solid piece like a wig; hair and skin peeling away in a slow, agonising rip.

The hand released the scalp to leave it dangling by a thin piece of skin from the back of his neck. The skull, denuded of hair and skin, shone like a smooth pink egg in the sunlight.

A hand came up and caught the swinging eye. It parted from the socket with a crack.

Catatonic from shock, Brinley Fox opened his remaining eye. Water swirled round his face. Now, even though his body had become rigid, he did not resist as one of the red hands pulled him back by his shirt collar into the sea.

Above him, he saw the water swirling like a liquid puddle of light. Then the water turned pale green.

His one eye saw little silver bubbles, rising to the surface.

Now he no longer felt or heard, he only saw the sea above him turn from pale green, to green, to dark green.

To black.

24

In the caravan's galley kitchen, Chris scraped two platefuls of burger and salad into the pedal bin. The third, smaller plate had been cleaned of all but streaks of ketchup.

They had not talked much since the incident with Fox and Gateman that morning. Despite Gateman's denials, Chris believed he had been involved in some plot to drive them out of the sea-fort. Why? Jealousy? Did he want the place for himself? Or didn't the villagers want holidaymakers ruining their seclusion?

He squirted washing-up liquid into hot running water. 'Dad, why were you so angry with Tony Gateman?' David sat at the table colouring in a picture with a fat crayon.

'Mr Gateman had done something wrong. He tried to stop us living here.'

'Why?'

'I don't know, David. It's up to the police to sort it out.'

David looked up, interested. 'The police? Are they going to take Tony to prison?'

'We'll have to wait and see. I'm going to drive over to the police station in Munby this afternoon.'

'Where's Mum?'

'She's been hosing the courtyard and the car down.'

'Would that petrol have blown us up?'

'No, of course not. Now you colour in some pictures for me, I'm just going to see your mum.'

He stepped out into the courtyard. It was still wet from the dousing Ruth had given it. The sea-fort's massive gates were shut and locked.

He looked around. No real damage done. But he felt lousy. Tired, and somehow dirty. He just wanted to shower with scalding water. This building, with its high stone walls, had become part of him. It had been violated. Gateman would pay for this.

'Chris.'

Ruth's voice, flat and unemotional, came from above. He looked up. She stood on the walkway that ran around the top of the wall. From the way she stared fixedly out it was obvious she had seen something that held her attention.

Stomach muscles tightening, he ran quickly up the steps.

'What's wrong?'

She nodded down towards the sea. 'Who are they?'

He looked sharply downward. The tide, fully in, swirled waves that sucked at the base of the sea-fort. For a moment he couldn't see what she had noticed. He searched the troughs of the waves. Only dark rocks showed among the surf.

But there should be no rocks where he saw them now.

Leaning forward, gripping the wall's coping stones with both hands, he stared down at the dark shapes in the water.

'People . . . There are people in the water.'

Shivering, he looked at his wife.

'I've been watching them ten minutes. They've not moved. They're just standing there.' She shrugged. 'Waiting.'

He turned and looked down again. There, twenty feet below, shoulder-deep in the rolling sea, waves sometimes breaking over their heads, were six dark shapes.

They looked alike, their dark heads emaciated and hairless.

All six faced out to sea, heads held in the same position, chins slightly up, their eyes shut in a relaxed way that made them look asleep.

Or dead, thought Chris, feeling a tide of cold seep through his body. He recalled the Easter Island statues; they had the same angular heads and impenetrable expressions, all facing in the same direction. And for all that these things moved, they might have been cut from rock.

But they weren't. They were something awful that shouldn't be there.

He felt his wife's hand on his.

'Look. There's another one.'

She was right. He'd not seen it appear, but there it was just like the others. The head above the waves, eyes shut, facing seaward like one of those Easter Island statues.

Chris and Ruth stood transfixed, their attention focused utterly on the heads.

And as they watched, the figures began to move.

Smoothly and slowly. Very, very slowly the heads lifted as they turned their faces up to Chris and Ruth standing on the battlements.

Chris, unable to do anything else, stared back at the upturned faces. Their eyes were still closed in that relaxed sleeper's way. But now their mouths were partly open. Just black holes occasionally catching gobs of white surf.

He turned to his wife. Pulling his gaze from them was like breaking a spell. He guided Ruth gently away from the wall. 'Don't look at them, love,' he said. 'Come on. We're going downstairs.'

Halfway down the stone steps that led to the courtyard, she stopped sharply. 'Who are they, Chris?'

'I don't know, love. And I don't think I want to know.'

She looked at him, her dark eyes frightened. 'I wish they'd connected the telephone, Chris. I want someone to come for us.'

'Don't worry. If they haven't gone by tonight, we'll go to the police.'

'No, Chris. We've got to get away as soon as we can.'

The thought of leaving the sea-fort appalled him. Come what may, he wanted to stay. He lived here. This was his home and his life – everthing rolled into one.

'But we can't just leave. What about the sea-fort?'

Her eyes widened.

'Bugger the sea-fort. Look . . . I think Tony knew something. He was trying to tell us when you forced him out. Chris . . .' She clutched his hand tightly. 'Let's just go. It'll probably be just for a few days, but I want to get away from here . . . Tell me we can go, Chris?'

25

'David!' His mum's voice was urgent. 'Quick, get in the car. Wind that window up. Are the doors locked? Are you sure?'

'Yes.'

He watched unhappily from the back seat of the car. His mum stood, tapping her fingers rapidly on top of the door. The engine was running.

David looked out of the rear window. His dad was running very fast. He was on the battlements on top of the walls, running then stopping to look out over the wall, down at the beach below.

Maybe he was looking for Tony Gateman? Or that man with the loud voice and lots of hair.

Today, his parents' behaviour had puzzled him. His dad had seemed quiet this morning after his fall off the dunes the night before.

Then there was the trouble that morning with Tony Gateman and the funny man, and that petrol all over the place. All that shouting and seeing his dad so angry had scared David. It had made him realise his dad wasn't always the nice person he seemed.

Then after lunch his parents had packed suitcases full of clothes and loaded them into the car. They'd made him stay in the caravan all the time so he couldn't tell what they were saying to one another. But they looked worried.

'Mum?'

'Just a minute, David. We're waiting for Dad.'

'Where we going, Mum?'

'Ah . . . We're just going to your Nan and Grandad's for a few days . . .' She forced a smile. 'That'll be nice, won't it?'

He swallowed a lump in his throat. He didn't like this at all.

His dad had finished looking out over the walls. He now came running down the stone steps into the courtyard, jumping down the last four.

'Okay! It's clear.'

His mum swung herself fast into the driving seat and revved the engine until it deafened David.

His dad opened the sea-fort's twin wooden gates. He leaned cautiously out to look left then right. As David would if there were hungry tigers out there on the beach.

His dad waved. 'Come on!'

The car accelerated savagely out of the sea-fort, front wheels sliding round with a crunching sound. She stopped sharply, throwing David forward against his seatbelt.

His dad ran round to the driving side and shouted, 'I'm locking the gates.'

'Chris . . . Leave it!'

'No. I'm not throwing it all away.' As he talked he kept looking up and down the beach. 'This thing will pass – in a few days. Everything's going to be all right.'

'All right . . . For Christsakes be quick.'

David watched his dad race back the few paces to the sea-fort to drag the doors shut. He fumbled with the lock and the padlock before running back to the car and into the front passenger seat.

'Chris. Your door. Lock it.'

The front tyres squealed as the car lurched forward.

'Slow down, Ruth. It's okay, they won't be up here.'

'You're an expert, then?'

'No, but they never left the water. They came in with the tide; they went out with the tide. Love – we'll end up on the beach.'

The note of the engine dropped; they slowed as they ran off the end of the causeway on to the metalled road that linked with the coast road, tyres swishing through patches of sand.

When they reached the coast road that ran to Out-Butterwick between the dunes and the marshes, she didn't slow the car. The coast road ended there; there would be no traffic.

Seconds later she braked hard again. The car slid to a stop.

'Shit . . .' She punched the wheel. 'Shit, shit, shit.'

'Jesus Christ.'

'What's happening, Mum? Why are we stopping here?'

'Shush, David . . . Just a minute.'

His dad looked at his mum, right into her eyes.

'Ruth . . . We're trapped.'

'We'll leave the car, Chris. We can walk.'

'Normally we could. But . . . I don't think we can risk it. Not now.' His dad took a deep breath. 'Ruth . . . I think our only alternative is to go back. If we go back to the sea-fort, lock the gates, we'll be safe. After all, they built the bloody place to keep out an army.'

David stretched up against the seatbelt to look out. Through the windscreen he could see that the coast road had now come to an abrupt end. Running from the dunes to his left, across the road, to one of the marsh ponds was a mound of beach pebbles. David guessed the mound of pebbles was as high as his head. He could climb it easily. But not the car. It would get stuck. They couldn't pass on either side because of the high dunes and the miles of slimy mud and water.

'The beach. We can drive along the beach.'

'You'd have to cross the stream that runs across the beach. It's fairly deep. If we get the car stuck . . . It means going on by foot . . . And soon the tide'll be on the turn. Someone's gone to a lot of trouble to build that barrier.'

'Those men in the water?'

'Your guess is as good as mine.'

'But what are they? We don't know if they're dangerous. They might be . . . they might be just . . .' She put her face in her hands.   Quickly she recovered. 'You're right . . . You only have to see them . . . You know they're dangerous . . .'

'What's the matter, Dad? Why are we trying to run away?'

'We're not, kidda. We just want to visit Nan and Grandad . . .' A pause. 'Looks as if the council have dug up the road again. We'll just have to wait.'

His mum reversed the car to where the road was widest then turned it round.

David pulled his legs up to his chest, hugging his knees.

This was not nice. This was not nice at all.

That evening they came back in with the tide once more. Seven Easter Island statue heads, the colour of congealed blood. They stood shoulder-deep in the surf and faced out to sea – eyes shut, mouths partly open.

'What are we going to do, Chris?'

Chris and Ruth stood on the battlements looking down at the dark head-shapes in the sea. He put his arm round his wife's shoulders.

He didn't know what they could do.

'We'll just sit and wait. The gates are locked. Nothing can get through them. Whatever they are, they'll go in the end.'

'What about all those people in Out-Butterwick? I'm worried about them.'

'They can look after themselves. It's us, the Stainforths, that are important. We're not leaving the sea-fort until it's all over.'

They stood, arms round one another like frightened children, watching the tide, and the things it carried, roll forward and drown the beach.

26

'What happens next?'

David paused, a chunk of chocolate an inch from his mouth. 'Superman drops the iceberg through the hole into the nuclear reactor.'

'And the fire goes out?'

'It goes out . . . pers-shhh . . .' David pushed the chocolate into his mouth and turned his attention back to the TV.

Chris sat with his arm round David. He'd done it to make the boy feel safe after they had found the road blocked. Now it was Chris who gained more reassurance from hugging another human being. Even one six years old, wearing red pyjamas with a jet fighter on the front. Ruth moved about at the far end of the caravan making coffee and slicing pieces of cake. He could guess what she was thinking.

'Fancy a drink?' he asked David.

'Milk, please. And some cake.'

'You'll burst if you eat any more.'

Chris went to where Ruth was chopping at a slab of Madeira.

'Coffee.'

As she slid the cup across the worktop he took her hand.

'Can you think of another way?'

She shrugged.

He spoke softly. 'We've got to do this for David's sake. It's a pretence, I know. But we've got to act as if everything is normal. That we're just going to stay in the sea-fort a few days. We've got videos, food, drink – all we've got to provide for David is a smiling face and play with him as if nothing . . . is happening.'

'What is happening, Chris?'

'Christ knows . . . But we know this: we know it might not be safe outside the sea-fort. Now we've got those things in the sea.'

'But they're interested in the sea-fort, Chris. Or are they interested in something inside the sea-fort? Us.'

'We don't know that.'

'But we can make a damn good guess. Like we can guess they put the barrier of stones across the coast road. They don't want us to leave. Why?'

'All I can say is don't worry. Look, these walls are over twenty feet high, they're five feet thick, solid stone. The only way in is through the gates – and the timber is that thick.' Chris held his hands ten inches apart. 'I've stacked bricks behind them. You couldn't push through those things with a tank. Believe me, love, what's out there stays out there – nothing, absolutely nothing, can get in.'

'So we stay in here, then; and everything in the garden is lovely.'

'For David's sake – yes. We certainly can't drive anywhere. If we walk, we can't guarantee it won't be straight into one of those things.'

She shook her head sharply. 'I keep thinking about the people in the village. I remember how kind they were when we moved in. Particularly Mark Faust and Tony Gateman. They made us welcome.'

His voice turned to a hiss. 'Welcome. They tried to burn our bloody home down.'

'Who's guessing now, Chris? We don't know that. We do know that Fox was here. And we know he's sick here.' she tapped her temple. 'Don't you believe Tony when he said he was trying to stop him? That he'd taken the petrol can off Fox?'

'Do I hell. I believe he and Fox were in it together. And probably Faust.'

'And the whole of Out-Butterwick as well? Chris, you are paranoid.'

He held the cup with both hands – as if squeezing a throat.

'Look,' she said, 'I appreciate you are doing what you think is best for us. But I'm worried about those people in the village. Okay, nothing might happen to them. But if it does . . . Chris, they are defenceless people living in little wooden cottages; they haven't got a castle to lock themselves up in.'

'What are you suggesting?'

'That we go on foot – if it's safe enough – to the village. We warn the villagers. Also we can phone the police from there.'

'What if those jokers out there have blocked the road out of Out-Butterwick? There's only the one.'

'Then we ask anyone who wants to, to come back to the sea-fort. It would only be for an hour or two before help comes.'

She looked up at him expectantly.

He laughed – a humourless sound. 'You have got to be joking. I'll tell you this: you, David and I are not moving from this sea-fort. That gate is staying locked until it's all over. And I'm sure as hell not going to bring a single one of those people from the village in here. They've been against us from the start.'

He went back to sit next to his son. She stood at the kitchen sink, her back to him.

Before it grew dark, Chris walked once more round the top of the sea-fort's walls. It had grown cold; a cloud-laden sky lumbered overhead. The sea swirled round the flanks of the sea-fort, breaking here and there in a wash of foam. In the gloom, the seven figures were dark shapes against a slightly lighter background of sea. Even so, some deeply disturbing quality shot them through, reminding him of hungry reptiles – watching and waiting.

With an effort he turned his mind to making the place more secure. He decided to use the timbers he'd stacked in the courtyard. He could wedge them behind the gates. He was convinced. Nothing could get in. They would be perfectly safe. All they needed to do then was sit and wait. This thing would sort itself out. By tomorrow, he promised himself, those things would be gone. Life would return to normal and he could return to working on the sea-fort.

He continued his patrol. He climbed the iron ladder from the top of the courtyard walls on to the fort building.

Ruth's suggestion that they bring the villagers from Out-Butterwick to the sea-fort had been ridiculous. What if they were trapped here for days? Where would they sleep? They had ample food for three. But for twenty?

He reached the iron ladder at the far end of the building and descended to the wall on the far side of the court-yard. Every few paces he leaned over the wall to look down into the rolling surf twenty feet below before continuing his patrol.

On the walkway he found a comic. He picked it up. It was one of the old Superman comics Mark Faust had given David on the night of Gateman's barbecue.

As he looked at it he suddenly felt touched by the man's kindness.

He rubbed his jaw. Without his even trying the memory came: Mark pushing David on the swing, the big man's hearty laugh. Chris sitting back enjoying Tony Gateman's beer and smelling the aroma of beefburgers sizzling on the barbecue.

Half an hour before, Ruth had called him paranoid. Maybe he had been hard on Gateman that morning. What if the guy had been totally innocent? Maybe he had just been walking by when he'd seen Fox wildly dousing the car with petrol.

No. He closed off the flow of thoughts. Wild horses wouldn't drag him to the village. He'd concentrate on making the sea-fort safe for himself and his family.

He promised himself he'd make an early start the next morning on strengthening the barricades behind the doors.

As he walked down the steps he stopped, struck by an outlandish idea.

Immediately, he went down to the sea-fort building, opened the doors, and went inside.

'What are you doing, Chris?'

Chris, standing in one of the sea-fort's empty barrack rooms, hadn't heard her approach.

He looked round. 'I had planned on taking out more timber to barricade the gates, but . . .'

'But what?'

'But . . .' He gave a small smile. 'But now I'm trying to work out just where on earth we're going to put twenty unexpected guests.'

27

'Ready?'

'I'm ready.' Chris zipped up his leather jacket. In his hand he carried the axe-handle; as long as his arm, its weight felt reassuring. 'Ruth, close the door after me and lock it.'

'Don't worry. I will.'

'And don't open it again until I get back, not under any circumstances.'

He kissed her. He felt the tension in her face with his lips.

'This goes without saying, Chris. Be careful. If it doesn't look right; if anything's on the beach – *anything* – come straight back. Then we'll do as you wanted in the first place. We'll lock the gates and sit it out.'

He shot a look back at the caravan. David looked through the end window, his face pale and frightened.

'I shouldn't be more than an hour,' he said. 'Fifteen minutes there, fifteen minutes back. That gives me thirty to phone the police and talk to Gateman.'

'Careful, love.' She kissed him.

The closing gate shut off Ruth's worried expression. He didn't move until he heard the bolts ram home, then he jumped off the causeway on to the beach.

Low tide. The sea must have been a good hundred yards from the sea-fort. Even so he felt a growing tension as he walked quickly away.

He kept midway up the beach. It would have been quicker to have crossed the dunes to Out-Butterwick, but there were too many hollows up there that could hide . . . Well, that could hide something unpleasant. The memory of the encounter two nights before still left a ragged memory.

When he looked in the direction of the sea he saw for the first time a mist drawing in. Even so he could make out seven dark heads in the surf. From here they could have been seal-heads poking out of the water.

Could have been.

He shivered and quickened his step. Behind him the sea-fort had become a huge block resting on the beach, its edges growing fuzzy in the thickening mist. For a moment he could see Ruth standing on the seawalls. He saw her arm raised in a slow wave; he waved back.

Then the mist thickened. He could see her no more.

Chris glanced at his watch. Seven o'clock.

He had given no thought to what he would say to the villagers when he arrived. They were in danger. He knew that. The feeling came in invisible waves from the sea. You could almost put your hands into it; a half-solid thing that made the hairs on your neck and body stand on end. But what was the danger? How could he explain it to the villagers? If the village had been cut off from the outside world like Manshead, how would he be able to persuade a mainly ageing population to leave their comfortable homes to go and sleep on the stone floors of the half-derelict sea-fort? They would laugh in his face.

Tightening his grip on the axe-handle, Chris walked faster. Soon the tide would be on the turn. And whatever was in the water would return with the incoming sea.

David climbed the stone steps up to the walkway that ran round the top of the sea-fort walls.

His mum and dad were anxious. He knew that. Like he knew it was something to do with what they had seen in the sea.

When he reached the top, he watched his mother for a moment. She leaned forward on to the wall, chin resting on her hand, looking down the beach in the direction of the sea.

'Mum . . . Where's Dad gone?'

'To the village. To see Tony Gateman.'

'To hit him with the stick?'

'No . . . To talk to him.'

'Why?'

'Go down and play in the caravan. There's a lolly in the breadbin.'

Unhappily, he returned to the caravan below.

Chris had wondered how he would convince the villagers that they were in danger. What he saw when he entered the main village street told him he'd have no problem.

Disembowelled, lying in the middle of the road in a lake of blood that was turning from red to black, was the mutilated body of a horse.

He stopped and stared at it. The tightness in his stomach made breathing difficult; his mouth turned paper-dry.

What else would he find in the village? At that moment he wanted . . . longed to turn and run back to the sea-fort.

Beyond the horse was a car. A door torn from the hinges hung from the branches of a nearby tree. He walked slowly now, axe-handle held across his chest at the ready.

No sign of life.

The houses looked deserted. The doors of some hung open. At his feet a pink bedroom slipper rested on the pavement. As if it had come off as its owner had run down the street.

He looked inside the car. Dark patches moistened the upholstery.

Blood.

He licked his dry lips.

Then from the other end of the village came a commotion. A mixture of noises – snarls, yelping howls, all breathless and high-pitched as if something was in pain.

It was a pack of dogs. They came at him, snarling and howling.

Something had driven them mad. They ran in a tight pack down the street, eyes rolling, whites flashing, pink tongues swinging from mouths that dripped saliva. They were biting one another, ripping off tufts of hair and shredding one another's ears.

He raised the axe-handle. But they did not even notice him and ran on, insanely biting each other, even themselves, as if invisible rats were running across their backs.

Right, he told himself. A quick look round, five minutes at the most; then back to the sea-fort. A glance in a couple of cottages told him the villagers had deserted the place.

Quickly, he walked down the village street. A fistful of banknotes littered the pavement in front of the village store. Another dog lay dead in a front garden, its body on the lawn, its head ten feet away in a rosebed. The teeth shone through parted lips.

What if he saw a man or woman like that? Sweat began to roll down his forehead.

The end of the street was in sight through the thickening mist when Chris heard the voice calling him.

'Chris . . . Hey, Chris. Over here.'

He looked round. In the doorway of the corrugated-iron hut that served as the village hall stood Mark Faust. Gesturing for Chris to approach, the big man looked anxiously up and down the street.

Chris didn't wait for the invitation to be repeated; he sprinted across the road and through the doorway. The door banged shut behind him; the bolts snapped home.

He had seen photographs of scenes like this before, usually accompanying reports about refugees.

In the hall, sitting silently on the orange plastic chairs, were approximately twenty men and women. He knew most of them by sight. Now they wore tired, shell-shocked faces. They stared forward into thin air, seemingly not interested in anything but their own private thoughts. The only movement came from the simple Tamworth girl. She sat heavily in an old armchair, thumbing through a tot's book on animals, mouthing the name of each one in her little-girl voice.

'Ducks . . . Moo-cow . . . Two ducks . . . Mr Rabbit . . .'

At the far end of the hall stood the Major, the Westie at his feet. The only expression of comprehension came when he noticed the dog nervously circling his feet. Gently he'd pat the dog and say in a low voice, 'Good boy . . . Good boy, Mac. Don't worry, we're going home soon, boy.'

As the old soldier straightened, Chris noticed that he wore a leather belt with a holster. The butt of the army revolver gleamed dully. Chris glanced quickly around. A middle-aged man with ginger hair – he recognised him as Hodgson the farmer – sat by a window with a shotgun across his legs. Sitting on the low stage was Tony Gateman, anxiously smoking a cigar.

Chris wondered if the little Londoner thought he had come to finish the job when he saw the axe-handle.

He felt a heavy hand grip his shoulder. Mark's gesture was friendly.

'Come on,' he rumbled, 'let's talk. Tony's got one or two things he'd like to share with you.'

They walked down the aisle between the chairs to the stage. Hardly anyone looked up.

Cautiously, Tony Gateman nodded a greeting; those shrewd eyes studied Chris's face through the thick lenses of his glasses.

Chris nodded back. 'What's happening, Tony?'

'I can tell you that in one sentence.' He drew on the cigar. 'Basically we're in the shit.'

Chris sat beside him on the stage. 'Tony, I know you know more about all this than I do. But I've seen enough and . . . and it sounds bizarre, but I *feel* enough to know this thing is dangerous . . . Look, there are people out at Manshead. They're standing in the water around the sea-fort.'

Mark pulled up a chair and sat astride it. 'Have they done anything? Have they tried to attack you?'

'No . . . nothing like that. Although someone has built a barrier of stones across the coast road. We can't get out by car. As for whoever it is in the water, they just go in and out with the tide. They stand shoulder-deep in the water, their eyes shut. It sounds crazy, but they seem to be watching us.'

'They're watching all right.'

Chris looked at him. 'You know who they are?'

'Let's say', said Tony, 'that friend Mark here had a run-in with them about thirty years ago. And believe me, Chris, those bastards are evil. *Evil.*'

Tony drew on his cigar. 'Ruth and little David all right?'

'Fine. The sea-fort's gates are locked. Nothing'll get in there.' Chris noticed Tony and Mark exchange looks in a way he didn't like at all.

'You know Fox?' Tony spoke in a low, measured voice. 'He never did make it back to the village, you know.'

Chris's mouth stayed dry.

'You know, Chris, I think he's with his brother now.'

'You mean he's dead?'

'I mean, Chris, I believe he is with his brother. Dead is debatable.'

'Look . . . Tony, I don't know what you mean. You're going to have to explain.'

As Tony began to speak there was a bang from the back of the hall. Chris started and jumped to his feet.

'It's only the Hodgson boys,' said Mark. 'They've been out with their uncle. They're collecting sacks.'

Chris watched two boys in their mid-teens pile sacks on the plank floor with more strength than finesse. Both had orange-gingery hair with faces mottled with freckles. And both were obese enough to make Chris wonder if they'd ever make forty-five before a thrombosis cracked their aortas.

'We're sandbagging the place,' Tony explained. 'We'll do the doors and windows.'

Their uncle returned with more sacks under one arm. In his other hand he carried a double-barrelled shotgun.

Chris looked around the fragile tin shack of a place. These people had prepared for invasions before. That time it had been World War II. They were making the same preparations now: stockpiling food, brewing up gallons of tea, sandbagging buildings, and forming a home guard armed with shotguns, old service revolvers, and pitchforks. Again they faced something that threatened to invade their lives – but this time not with amphibious landing craft and carrying rifles with fixed bayonets.

No one knew exactly what the threat was. The only thing every man and woman knew was that this danger – this life-threatening danger – would come.

And it would come soon.

Chris watched the preparations as Tony told him what had happened the night before.

'Woke up at about three. I heard a car engine revving, gears grating, then a crash. That was John Wainwright trying to drive out in a bloody hurry.'

'That was the car in the street? The Ford Fiesta? I saw it.'

Tony nodded to a man sat at the back of the hall. Grey-haired, thin, dried-up-looking; he wore a bandage round the top of his head and had a smear of dried blood down one cheek. Chris recognised him as a partner in a firm of accountants in Munby. The man's face was expressionless.

'For the last few days I've been in the habit of sleeping in my clothes. I managed to reach the front door when the lights went out. The whole of the village blacked out. I tell you, it was pandemonium, fucking pandemonium. I can't really explain it rationally . . . just a lot of people running round not able to see a thing. No screaming or shouting, just running feet, then bang! A window would smash, then dogs'd bark their bloody heads off. Pandemonium, chaos, bedlam – you pick the description. But I tell you this, Chris, I've never been so fucking terrified in all my life. Well, we had some lamps ready and managed to get everyone into the village hall here. Twenty-three of them. Everyone accounted for. Which in itself is a bloody miracle.'

'Who attacked you?'

Chris saw Tony Gateman swallow. 'Too dark to see, really.'

'Those people I've seen in the water at Manshead?'

'No . . . Just people. This time they didn't hurt any of us.'

'Or maybe we were just lucky, Tony. I don't think those things could see too well.'

Things? Chris was going to question Mark further when one of the Hodgson boys came up, breathing hard. 'We're gonna barrow sand up from the beach. Where shall we put it, Mr Gateman?'

'By the door, Ian. You don't want to be far away the next time the tide comes in.'

The boy jogged away down the aisle, his baggy jeans halfway down his massive backside, revealing what seemed like an acre of pink buttock.

Tony's mouth stretched into an artificial smile. 'They're good workers. They'll have the sandbags up against the doors in a couple of hours.'

Chris watched Tony's shrewd eyes as the man looked around the hall, checking the preparations. He realised that the man knew perfectly well that in a few hours they would all be dead. He was merely keeping the active villagers busy to keep their minds off the hopelessness of the situation.

The Major's dog yapped nervously again.

'Tony,' said Chris, 'this is a waste of time. These walls are so brittle I could kick holes through them myself.'

'So?'

'So . . . I'm saying if anyone wants to come back to the sea-fort with me, they're welcome.'

Tony let his shoulders fall. It looked to Chris as if someone had removed a concrete slab from his back. He breathed deeply, then leaned forward and gripped Chris by the forearm and shook it.

'Thanks, Chris. We appreciate it.'

Chris zipped up his jacket. 'Right, Mr Gateman. Lead your people to safety.'

David watched his mother. She still gazed anxiously out across the sands. The mist had come in thickly now. It drifted in thick white rags across the beach. David could hardly see the dunes; or the sea. He could hear it, though. A whoosh-whooshing sound – getting louder and louder as the tide turned.

He wished his dad would come back home.

He ran down the steps to the caravan. Five minutes later he climbed back up with a mugful of diluted orange. He had tried to warm it in the microwave but wasn't sure of the setting, so it was only tepid.

'Here you are,' he said, handing his mother the cup. 'This might make you feel better.'

His mum looked at him in a funny way for a moment, then suddenly hugged him tightly to her. She was on her knees and her face felt wet against the bare skin of his neck.

'Don't cry, Mum,' he said softly. 'I'll look after you.'

It wasn't going to be easy.

Chris watched the straggling group of villagers make their way on to the beach. Some had sticks; one lady was in a wheelchair. A married couple in their fifties both held a handle each and were pushing it determinedly. The Major had to be constantly reminded where they were going. Every few paces he would stop, puzzled, as if unsure why he was there. Mac whined and yelped and sometimes refused to walk at all, splaying his front legs out in the sand.

The Hodgsons were the most able-bodied – the farmer and his wife, their two sons and the uncle. For some reason, Chris didn't know why, the two sons pushed motorbikes laden with sacks of food. The farmer and the uncle carried bulging rucksacks and shotguns. Mark Faust carried a shotgun in his left hand, a PVC holdall in the other, and a rucksack on his back. A few others carried shopping bags, carrier bags and holdalls. Rosie Tamworth skipped along as if on a day trip.

It made a bizarre and pathetic sight. A line of frightened men and women walking along the beach, casting glances in the direction of a sea hidden by mist.

Chris caught up with Tony, who headed the column. 'You were ready for this, weren't you, Tony? You've prepared for it.'

'Mr Stainforth, now isn't the time or place . . . Look . . . I promise. I'll explain fully later . . . I just . . . I just want to get off this fucking beach . . .'

They walked on in silence, apart from the odd yap from the dog. Wainwright's expression was sour beneath his bandage. Wearing a suit and tie, he had declined to carry anything. Unlike the equally miserable-looking Reverend Reed, who carried a leather briefcase in one hand and an overcoat in the other. The briefcase looked heavy. But Chris doubted if it contained holy water and Bibles.

As they neared the mouth of one of the streams that ran along the beach, a dark object rose out of the water.

It was man-shaped.

He gripped the axe-handle tightly.

The Easter Island profile was the same; the same slightly open mouth and the same eyes – closed like those of a deeply relaxed sleeper. But this time the dark granite skin had taken on a different tinge. The balance of red in the red-black colour had shifted to the red.

He slowed down.

Suddenly Mark was at his side. 'Keep walking, Chris. That's one of them. For God's sake, keep walking. Please.'

Chris didn't need any more urging. They forded the stream higher up the beach, the water icy against their legs.

The mist thickened. Chris stared hard into it, half expecting to see shadowy figures blocking their way. Once he imagined he saw a figure standing on the dunes, looking down at them. The figure had a round white face. Shockingly white.

He forced himself to concentrate on the next few yards of visible beach.

As he walked, he found himself thinking about Fox. What in Christ's name had happened to him? And what had Tony Gateman meant when he said that, even though he was somewhere in the sea, whether he was actually dead or not was debatable? He remembered lots of things now. They were all little pieces of a jigsaw falling into place to form a single picture. It produced a shiver that ran from his scalp to the balls of his feet. The monster celery plant in the old sink – its growth had been nothing short of mutant; the wooden chair in the wet dirt – the bottom of the legs had sprouted roots, the carved arms had begun to bud. The goldfish. That had been dead all right. But a few hours later it had been hurtling around the glass bowl like a torpedo. And now it looked as if it was changing. Then a couple of nights ago he had come face to face with something on top of those dunes. It had not touched him physically but it had messed his mind around as easily as a kid twists a plasticine model out of shape. The people in the sea with their sinister Easter Island statue faces?

The questions he had to ask Gateman and Faust were stacking up inside his head.

He glanced at Tony. The little Londoner led the straggling band of villagers. Head bobbing up and down, he plodded determinedly along the beach, thin piano hands gripping the straps of the canvas rucksack on his back. Mark Faust brought up the rear. Walking in a long, easy stride, he wouldn't have looked out of place on a Wild West prairie wearing a stetson, with a pair of six-guns strapped to his sides.

At last Chris could make out the bones of the wrecked fishing boat through the clouds of mist. He quickened his pace, bringing himself level with Tony.

'Tony, I'll go on ahead. If the gates are already open we'll get this lot inside quicker.'

'All right, Chris . . . Be careful. This mist'd hide a bleeding dinosaur.'

Chris's pace turned into a jog. He wanted to see if David and Ruth were all right. They should be. But the surf sounded louder – the tide was coming in; and fast.

His imagination began firing up images of the sea-fort doors flapping open; the place deserted; David crying somewhere, lost in the mist; Ruth lying on her back on the sands, one of those things from the sea on top of her, cutting . . .

He cut off the mental image. But it would come back. Soon, if he didn't see that the pair were all right.

He ran along the causeway, the dark blurred shape hardening into the solid stone building.

'Ruth!' he called up at the sea-fort.

He waited an anxious twenty seconds before a head looked over the wall.

'Ruth, open the gates.'

Seconds later Chris heard the metallic snap of bolts, then the gates juddered open.

'Dad!' David hurled himself at Chris so hard he nearly lost his balance.

'Whoa, hang on, kidda.'

Ruth put her arms round Chris in a fierce hug. 'You seemed to be gone ages.'

Chris smiled. 'Well, I ended up bringing this lot back.' He turned as the group plodded up to the gates. Without a word they continued walking into the courtyard. Last of all, Mark Faust with the shotgun resting over one shoulder.

He nodded solemnly at Chris then walked inside.

Chris took one look along the beach, slowly being engulfed by white mist, then he swung the gate shut and drove the bolts home.

Safe.

For now.

28

Chris swung open the main door to the sea-fort building. The air that rolled out over him felt cool, but dry. He entered, followed by Tony and Mark. This place was going to be home for around twenty people.

'This way.' He led the two men along the corridor and up the staircase.

The caravan would hold eight people. He, Ruth and David could share the double bedroom. Some of the other villagers could sleep in the twin-bedded room David had used with two more on the bed-settee. Those would be the ones who were sick or the most elderly. The rest would have to make themselves comfortable here. He walked into the largest first-floor room.

'We'll get them organised to make up beds out of blankets when they've come round a bit.' Tony's shrewd eyes appraised the room. 'At least we'll be on timber floors. Kipping on stone wouldn't do anyone any good.'

'For how long?'

'At the most a day or two, I expect.'

Mark Faust shrugged. 'This is all new to us, Chris.'

'But you do know something. You certainly know more than I do.'

Tony's smile was half-hearted. 'We thought we knew lots. But events seem to have overtaken our expectations.'

'And what did you expect?'

'What we didn't expect was those things. Not to come back and smash up the place.'

'Something occurred to me,' said Chris, wanting answers. 'Why didn't you just leave? Back in the village you said you were in the shit. You knew something was happening, something that would put you – us – in danger because you've been preparing for it. Supplies of food, the shotguns, sleeping fully dressed.'

'Yes, we were expecting something, but . . .'

Mark finished the sentence. 'But we didn't expect it to be . . . *bad*.'

'You could still have left. When it was first light this morning.'

'I tried,' said Mark. 'The only road out is blocked at the bridge. They've piled rocks across it.'

'You could have walked.'

'We could have,' agreed Tony. 'But you see, Chris, like the ugly old troll in the story, one of those things was sitting in the stream beneath the bridge. And even though I'm ashamed to admit it, I was afraid – bloody afraid – to cross the bridge with that thing an arm's length away.'

Chris sighed. 'So, for a few days anyway, we're trapped. Until when? Monday?'

'Why Monday?'

'Well, it's Saturday today. So barring casual visitors, the first certain visitor is the postman early Monday morning.'

'And God help the poor sod.' Tony removed his glasses and massaged the red pressure marks on the bridge of his nose.

'And God help us,' added Mark quietly.

Chris was about to try to pump more information from the two men when he heard the sound of a shoe scraping across the timbers. It was the Reverend Reed. The expression on his red, blotched face looked suitable for a funeral. He said nothing, didn't even acknowledge the three of them. Slowly, he walked around the perimeter of the large room, looking it over. In his hand he carried the fat leather briefcase, his knuckles white from the pressure of clasping the handle.

With the conscious effort of someone changing the subject, Tony said, 'This is our dormitory, then. We'll get what bedding is available. Then we'll get everybody in here and get them as comfortable as we can.'

Ruth must have caught the last few words as she came through the door. 'And we really need to have some kind of group meeting, Tony.'

'Why?'

'I think everyone has a right to know what is happening.'

'I'm sorry, Ruth. We don't know what is happening. Other than the fact that we are effectively trapped here by those things outside. I think it's clear to everyone that those creatures don't want us to leave.'

The Vicar spoke for the first time: 'And it is abundantly clear that you and your pagan neighbours have no intention of leaving now – just when your sordid little god is about to visit.'

'Excuse me, Reverend Reed,' asked Chris, puzzled. 'What do you mean? I don't understand.'

The Vicar made the snarl that passed for his smile. 'Ask that man, Gateman. He's behind all this.'

The Reverend Reed walked out of the room.

'What did he mean by that?' Ruth asked Tony.

'He says some bloody foolish things . . . He makes it sound like we're a pagan sect. We've done nothing. We just happened to be here. Whatever happens will happen anyway . . . We've done nothing to make it happen.'

'Before we do anything,' said Ruth, 'I think the four of us ought to sit down – then you tell us everything you do know.'

Chris said, 'I agree. Look, Tony, stop holding back. We're not kids. Tell us.'

Mark smiled. 'It's all a question of belief. Will you believe us?'

'We'll believe you all right,' said Chris. 'Now, tell us.'

As Tony unwrapped a cigar, one of the Hodgson boys

blundered in breathlessly, his feet thumping heavily against the boards.

'Mr Gateman! Mr Gateman! My dad says you'd better look at this.' The boy's face burned an excited red. 'They're out, Mr Gateman, they're out!'

29

Chris looked out over the beach.

He saw that they were indeed out. A cold sensation hung heavily in his stomach.

He looked at the others. The villagers stood on top of the sea-fort's walls, gazing silently over the sands, now blurred white with mist.

The tide had begun to retreat. This time the dark figures had not retreated with the water. Those at the top of the beach were now completely free of the sea and sat cross-legged on the beach, looking like ancient Red Indian warriors, their naked bodies a dark red, the colour of ripe cherries.

The things looked brutally strong, their long, powerful arms resting across their knees. Again their hairless heads gave the impression of Easter Island statues with their sharp chiselled profiles. Each had its head turned so it faced the sea-fort, eyes shut.

Eventually the tide slid back, leaving eight figures sat randomly spaced alongside the causeway.

'The Saf Dar,' murmured Tony in awe.

'The what?' asked Chris in a low whisper.

Mark's voice rumbled. 'Saf Dar. It's Urdu. For a special kind of warrior.'

'An extraordinarily violent warrior,' added Tony, staring at the figures. 'Exceptionally violent – the Saf Dar were the breakers of the line. In battles they would hurl themselves at the enemy in a kind of human blitzkrieg.'

Chris heard a sigh that expressed pain as much as anything. He saw the Reverend Reed look away from the figures on the beach, his Adam's apple twitching above the dirty-white dog-collar.

Then Ruth was at Chris's side, her hand finding his.

'Where's David?' he whispered. 'He mustn't see this.'

'He's asleep in the caravan. What's happening to them? They seem to be changing colour.'

'I don't know. But they seem to be acclimatising themselves to the open air. They don't need the sea now.'

Chris glanced around at the villagers. With the exception of the Reverend Reed, no one could take their eyes from the figures.

'Thank God they can't get in here,' said Ruth. 'Hatred. You can feel it, can't you? They're sitting there just hating us.'

An hour passed. The tide slid back, exposing the top of the causeway.

'I'm going home.'

The sudden voice startled everyone. It was Wainwright, the accountant, who had spoken. He still wore the bandage like a white headband.

'I'm afraid you can't, Mr Wainwright,' said Tony. And Chris heard Mark hiss under his breath, 'Pain in the ass.'

'No . . . I've had enough of this.' Wainwright's voice was quick and clipped. 'I'm going home. This – this is obviously some kind of confidence trick. We've been duped. There are probably criminals stripping our homes even as we stand here.'

' 'S not safe out there, old boy,' said the Major. ' 'S dangerous. You wait till we get the er . . . er . . .' He tailed off.

'The Major's right,' said Mark calmly. 'Stay put.'

'Until when? . . . until our homes have been emptied, and – and the crooks are driving away laughing at us?'

Tony Gateman sighed. 'Mr Wainwright, those people, and I use that word loosely, those people out there have ceased to be like us. They are dangerous. You know that, Mr Wainwright. Don't leave the sea-fort.'

'I'm going home. And you'll all come home soon enough. When you realise Gateman is making a fool out of you all.

176

He thinks this place is where some old pagan god has put – has made his den. He's mad. Isn't he mad, Reverend Reed?'

Reed, staring into space, said nothing.

'Don't worry. I'll see myself out.'

Chris followed Tony down the steps as he tried to persuade Wainwright to stay.

He was wasting his breath. Within five minutes they'd had to admit defeat and let the man out through the gate and on to the causeway. Chris locked the gate after him, before he and Tony climbed back up the steps to see what would happen.

Chris noticed that some of the figures had moved. Six still sat on the beach in a line along the side of the causeway, a twenty-yard gap between each one. The furthest sat at the point where the causeway joined the coast road. But the two nearest the sea-fort were now kneeling on the beach, flanking the causeway. Like a pair of statues guarding the entrance to a tomb.

He shivered. The sharp, chiselled faces with the closed eyes were expressionless. Yet he had the feeling that whatever happened, whatever he did, these alien figures would know, and be ready to react.

He wondered what that reaction would be.

He did not have to wait long to find out.

Wainwright stepped out on to the causeway in clear view of everyone. He looked straight ahead at the dunes.

Then, as if he'd consciously blocked out everything but his destination, he began to walk – a quick, stiff pace.

Chris did not like the man. When he looked at Wainwright he remembered his old maths teacher, stiff-necked and grey-skinned like Wainwright, delivering a full-blooded slap across Barry Mitchell's face. And the boy had done nothing wrong.

It had knocked the lad flat against the classroom floor-tiles. He had been ten years old. The memory of that had fuelled Chris's sense of injustice all these long years. Wainwright was a man who evoked those memories of stiff-necked, repressed bastards who make themselves feel good by making people in their power feel bad.

Yet at that moment Chris wanted to shout at Wainwright to get himself back to the sea-fort. But the man would not have listened. He had excluded the possibility from his mind that the things on the beach could pose a threat. For him they simply did not exist.

Wainwright approached the first two figures which closely flanked the causeway. Two sentinels – unmoving, sinister. Not a flicker of movement betrayed that they were even aware of the stiff-necked accountant's approach.

But Chris knew they sensed him.

Wainwright slowed, his feet hardly moving.

He passed between the two sentinel Saf Dar and walked on. Suddenly he stopped and looked back. The two didn't move so much as an inch.

Visibly the man relaxed, his shoulders dropping. He continued walking, now looking as if he was just keeping an appointment at some high-street bank.

Chris heard some of the villagers let out pent-up breath.

It didn't take a Sherlock Holmes to guess what was running through their minds.

Look. If he can walk across there, we all can . . . We can go home . . . No point in roughing it here . . . It's safe . . . We're going home . . .

Wainwright passed another of the Saf Dar. No movement. Not a flicker across the expressionless face that might have been carved from burnt brick.

He walked confidently now. A stiff-legged figure growing fainter in the mist. He was going to make it.

'Way to go, rubber-neck!'

It was one of the Hodgson lads. The other whistled, then both clapped their meaty paws together over their heads.

The spell was broken. Some of the villagers shouted encouragement. The Harbour Tavern's landlord chuckled. 'Home in time for opening time, eh, Tony?'

Conversation rose in an excited buzz. They were going home. They'd woken from the nightmare.

Jesus!

Chris saw it. Most must have seen it, because the sound of their voices cut to a sudden silence that rang in the ears.

As he looked along the line of dark figures on the causeway, they changed, as if an electric current had been jolted through their bodies. Then, one after another, the eyes of the Saf Dar snapped open. Chris's blood turned to ice.

Inexplicably there was something awful about it, merely the sight of eight sets of eyelids snapping back to expose eight pairs of bright staring eyes, the whites gleaming like splinters of glass.

They say the eyes are the windows of the soul. If so, these exposed souls were monstrously twisted and evil.

Two-thirds of the way across the causeway, Wainwright saw the change in the things' faces. And he shuddered when he saw the eyes that looked as large and as shockingly bright as those of a starving man.

Wainwright began to run, arms swinging, bandaged head jerking up and down.

The villagers watched, struck silent, holding their breath, clenched fists resting on top of the walls.

Wainwright had passed the seventh figure; only number eight to go. Then he would reach the road through the dunes which would lead him home.

In his jerking run he approached the eighth and last figure. It still sat staring straight in front of it in the direction of the sea-fort, ignoring the running man.

It knows; Christ, it knows . . . Chris's stomach ached with tension.

Then its head jerked up. It watched as Wainwright approached at a desperate run, arms windmilling, his white shirt now showing beneath his suit jacket.

Then it moved.

The figure on the beach leapt in one explosive movement, catching Wainwright in its red-black arms, sweeping him up, then backward, his feet whipping up higher than his head. Without releasing its grip, it swung the accountant down head-first on to the stone slabs that paved the causeway.

Chris heard the crack of the skull against the stone even at that distance.

Wainwright lay on the causeway stomach down, his head on its side. No movement.

The creature moved a few paces away from the body, then sat down, cross-legged, staring with those bright white eyes at the sea-fort.

The people in the sea-fort watched, stunned into silence, not moving. The scene wouldn't let them go.

The other creatures hadn't moved. They just stared, eyes laser-bright. They made it possible to believe that they could burn holes through granite with a single look. No birds flew overhead; the mist seemed more dense. It grew colder, gloomier, as if the earth lay dying beneath their feet.

Chris muttered that he was going to check on David.

He returned to the caravan to find the boy asleep in the bedroom, his face poking above the duvet.

He felt his son's forehead. It was moist with sweat. Gently he pulled the duvet down to his chest. Then, picking up the binoculars from the dressing table, he tiptoed out.

As soon as he reached the steps he knew something had happened.

He sprinted up to the walkway. The villagers were looking at the causeway, their heads craning forward.

'Look!' cried one of the Hodgson boys. 'He's shifted. The bugger's shifted!'

Chris searched for what had caught their attention. The Saf Dar remained in their positions. Wainwright still lay . . . Chris stiffened. But now he lay on his back, one knee raised in the air.

He saw the man's arm move to wipe his face. Then, painfully, he pulled himself in to a sitting position. It was like watching someone wake with a monstrous hangover.

After three false starts, Wainwright lumbered to his feet, head swinging from side to side.

Chris jerked the binoculars to his eyes.

Wainwright's head swung into view, uncomfortably large in the lenses. The bandage hung round his neck, now stained with fresh crimson. The balding head appeared; slashed across it, a gash in the shape of a smiling mouth, the open wound forming over-red lips with something white showing through. Chris lowered the binoculars and wiped his mouth.

Lurching unsteadily, the accountant looked around him. He needed to stare long and hard at the Saf Dar to pull back the memory of a few minutes before. No nightmare, Mr Wainwright, thought Chris grimly. This is stone-cold reality.

Instead of trying to walk on, away from the sea-fort, away from the Saf Dar, including the one sitting on the causeway just five paces away, Wainwright began to stagger back to the sea-fort.

'Idiot,' whispered Ruth, 'he should be going the other way. Not back. Idiot . . .'

Mark Faust picked up the shotgun. 'I'm going out there. Get the doors for me, Chris, please.'

'Mark, no.' Tony snatched at Mark's arm.

'We can't just stand by this time, Tony. That guy needs help.'

'No one goes out of those gates. It's suicide. No, it's worse than suicide. You of all people have seen what those things can do.'

'Shoot the cunts,' grunted Farmer Hodgson, holding up his shotgun.

'Look,' stammered Tony, 'get ready to open the gates, but only when he makes it back all the way.'

'Tony —'

'Listen, Mark, listen. You saw what one of those things can do to a man. It split his head like a tomato.'

'Come on! Run!'

'You can do it!'

'Move it! Move yourself, man!'

The villagers shouted encouragement.

They were wasting their breath.

181

One of the Saf Dar stepped up on to the causeway and walked towards the accountant. The creature's pace was unhurried. It reached out as the man staggered by and took hold of him. Then it pulled him down. With one red-black hand on the back of Wainwright's neck, it forced the man's bare throat down on to the corner of a stone block that edged the causeway; it dug deeply into his throat.

Watching a man slowly choke was something no one wanted to see; but they couldn't turn away.

Ten minutes later the accountant still struggled and clawed at the beast holding him down. He might as well have tried to scratch at solid iron. The thing merely sat cross-legged beside him and stared with its brothers at the sea-fort; only this one was pressing a man's throat to the edge of the causeway.

Another ten minutes passed and the man still struggled, but now the movements were weaker.

Useless.

The movement had nearly stopped, apart from a few feeble twists of the torso, when Wainwright suddenly moved once more. He kicked frantically, his head jerked wildly.

Then he lay still.

Even though he did not move again the thing didn't release its grip. An hour later people began to drift away to sit huddled against the walls. Still the thing on the causeway didn't move.

Chris could not take his eyes from the creature's muscular fingers rooted to the huge fists.

By the time the tide rolled back in across the causeway, only a few people saw the creature release its grip on Wainwright. The body floated away to disappear in the rolling surf.

Chris moved past those silent villagers who remained.

With a last look at the water, now covering the heads of the Saf Dar, Chris, numb, walked slowly down to the caravan.

The red hands. He couldn't stop himself picturing those brutal red hands.

And David's fragile throat.

30

Bored, David wandered around the sea-fort.

Something had happened earlier in the day. Something that made everyone sad. He didn't know what it was but more than once he'd heard the name Wainwright mentioned. Wasn't he the man with the unfriendly face and all his head bandaged? Maybe he'd got angry about something and gone home. Anyway, he was nowhere about now.

In the big room with lots of glass windows that looked out over the gundeck, people from the village sat on old chairs (some had even been pulled back out of the rubbish skip). Most stared into space. The old Vicar man (he had a miserable face too, and his breath smelt nasty), he walked round and round. He never said anything to anybody.

David mooched on.

Along one of the stone-flagged corridors was a smaller room with a few chairs and a little table. Through the crack in the door he could see his mum, dad, Tony and Mark talking.

His mum said: 'It's not going to last long. Not when we're feeding twenty-plus people, three times a day. You brought what you could carry; we stocked up because its a fifteen-mile round trip to the nearest supermarket, but it's going fast. There's no more fresh bread. We're down to the last carton of milk.'

'So we ration ourselves.' That was Tony Gateman.

'As important' – his dad's voice – 'is the question: are we going to sit and wait or are we going to try and get help from outside?'

Mark: 'All the phones are down. There's no way of getting word out.'

His mum: 'Have you thought what will happen if we don't? Come Monday morning the postman is going to try driving into the village. He's going to stop on the bridge where the road is blocked. Maybe he'll decide to reach the village on foot. You said there was one of those things waiting under the bridge?'

'Ruth's right,' said his dad. 'By not doing anything we're going to let people die. You only have to look at what happened to that poor sod Wainwright to know what's going to happen to anyone trying to get into Out-Butterwick.'

His mum said, 'How many people will die before the employers realise their staff aren't coming back from Out-Butterwick; and how many police will die before the authorities realise something is happening out here?'

'I'm with these two, Tony.' Mark's deep voice made the door vibrate against David's fingers. 'If we sit back and do nothing, we'll have blood on our hands.'

31

This is Chris Stainforth's nightmare:

Night-time.

He had been walking around the sea-fort searching for an axe-head he could fix to the end of the axe-handle he'd chosen for a club. He wanted to upgrade his makeshift weapon. He knew he would need it soon.

His dream search for the axe-head took him on to the sea-fort walls. The dream, unusually vivid, was richly detailed. He saw his surroundings clearly – the car in the courtyard, the timber and bricks piled behind the sea-fort gates to strengthen the barricade, the caravan in darkness. All the good villagers of Out-Butterwick soundly asleep.

He reached the walkway that ran round the top of the walls and looked out. The night-time beach, a vast expanse of sand; the causeway ran ruler-straight towards the dunes.

Tide out, the Saf Dar sat, sentinel-like, dark, brooding, staring at the sea-fort. As he leaned forward, his hands resting on the cold stones of the wall, he saw more things. These were awful.

Lucky it was only a dream. If this were real he didn't know whether he could take it and stay sane.

Approaching through the mist, more figures . . . eleven, twelve, thirteen.

As he watched the figures emerge from the mist, the dream became a nightmare.

They formed a procession. Like the victims of some nightmare weapon that existed only in a diseased mind.

He knew these were people lost to the sea.

They were the recently dead, and the long dead.

Almost straight away he recognised Fox. The beard, matted, hung down in rats'-tails. The wild-man hair had gone, along with the scalp, leaving nude bone gleaming whitely. Only one eye remained. The other socket, a raw split, looked as if it had been roughly packed with raw liver.

One hand lacked fingernails. From the tips of the fingers grew pink cones. As if the force that had thrust its version of life through what had once been dead flesh had also crudely repaired the damaged body. Pink growths sprouted from any break in the skin. These men weren't dead. This was life – some form of life – at its most explosively dynamic.

A larger figure followed Fox, its man-shape being lost beneath the volcanic pressure of growth beneath the skin. How little of the original man remained Chris did not know. But from the resemblance to Fox, Chris instinctively knew it was Fox's brother who had died ten years before. This figure was a bloated copy of his brother. Shellfish grew across its forehead, creating a heavy black crust; barnacles rashed in white speckles over its bloated chest which was bare of any clothing; sea anemones clustered in red and brown lumps around its distended genitals.

A sick feeling bit into the pit of Chris's stomach.

It followed his brother, its oversized feet slapping against the sand.

Behind the Fox twins came more:

A drowned pilot wrapped in a rotting parachute like a funeral shroud.

Then a boy who'd swam too far out twenty summers before, now bulbous-headed with hands the size of footballs.

Following him, a fisherman with a monstrous growth erupting from his throat; as big as a beachball, it was stretched so tight you thought it would burst with every step he took. Then came the accountant, Wainwright, walking a different kind of step now, the white bandage still hanging round his neck; from his smashed mouth a growth the size of a tennis ball and as red as a strawberry budded out.

186

In the nightmare Chris's mind zoomed in on every detail.

Then came more men, with heads that looked as if they had been formed out of beef – red-raw and moist – which shook and quivered with every step.

Behind him, six men who had drowned in the same small boat. They had become welded together by the explosive growth of flesh to form a single creature with bent legs. It moved like a crab scraping a furrow in the beach.

(Thank Christ it's only a dream.)

They reached the causeway and crossed it.

He sensed they had one purpose. One single craving.

They all wanted to go home. Whatever remained of their minds must have mumbled the same word like an incantation:

Home, home, home . . .

They moved like travellers nearing the end of an exhausting journey. Home, home, home . . .

Going home . . .

But then they suddenly stopped.

He noticed that the Saf Dar were no longer watching the sea-fort but had turned to watch the figures crossing the beach. The figures turned; then, as if compelled by a will that defeated their own, they began to walk towards the sea-fort, their eyes fixed on it.

And what eyes. He gripped the top of the stone wall. The eyes were like walnuts, convoluted shapes with ridges and bumps that protruded from their sockets.

They approached.

As he watched, the ones that possessed mouths opened them. They began to cry out, their faces distorting even more grotesquely. The cry, faint, vibrated with their agony. They were being forced to do something they desperately didn't want to do. And it was the Saf Dar who controlled them. He knew they had become their slaves.

Only a dream, he told himself.

Abruptly the force that drove them towards the sea-fort released them. Their old impulse reasserted itself . . .

Home . . . home . . . home . . .

And they moved off once more down the beach and away into the darkness.

The Saf Dar watched them go. Then, as one, their heads turned smoothly back and they stared at the sea-fort.

A movement at his side startled him.

It was Tony.

Tony looked at him for a full moment. Then said: 'No, Chris. You're not dreaming, you know. You're as wide awake as I am.'

Chris leaned forward over the wall, then vomited forcefully on to the sand more than twenty feet below.

32

That morning Mrs Lamb stood on a packing case, tied one end of the washing line round her neck, the other end round an iron hook in the sea-fort store-room ceiling, and stepped off.

Chris was sleeping late after a bad night. David was eating breakfast with the others in the gundeck room. Ruth was sharing out cornflakes.

Shouts from one of the Hodgson boys brought people running to the store room. Mark got there first to find Mrs Lamb hanging. Her face had turned dark, her eyes were open but staring, and she spun like a doll on the end of a string. Mark grabbed her by the waist and lifted her up while Mrs Hodgson cut the string with a penknife.

They laid her on the stone floor, calling her name and shaking her. She urinated where she lay. Mark gave her mouth-to-mouth.

This went on for ten minutes. Until Mrs Lamb kicked out her legs. They put her into David's bed in the caravan.

As Ruth covered her with a blanket she turned her face to the wall. 'Why did you bring me back?'

'Got a bull's-eye, Dad.'

'It's miles from the bull, David.'

'Did.'

'Didn't.' Chris pretended to wrestle with his son but it was an excuse to pull him close and hug him tight.

'Bear-hug!' shouted David breathlessly. 'Cheating.'

Christ, he loved his son; he loved his wife. Why had this

happened to them? He screwed up his eyes and wished everything normal again. Play-fighting on the beach, picnics, sunshine, working on the sea-fort.

That morning he'd taken David up into one of the empty sea-fort rooms to play darts. There he'd put on at least a mask of normality. Not that it fitted particularly well after what had happened over the last forty-eight hours. Wainwright's death. Then, last night, the weird procession of drowned men along the beach. Mrs Lamb with the noose. Maybe they would all be better trying what Mrs Lamb . . .

'Da-ad. I can't breathe.'

Chris relaxed his hug.

'Can I have some sweets, please?'

Chris looked away from those blue eyes. 'As soon as I can get to the shop I'll buy you some.'

'When will that be?'

'Can I play?'

To Chris's relief, Ruth joined them. She performed the happy, carefree trick more convincingly than he could.

They played darts. For a while Chris and Ruth could make David forget that their lives were no longer the same.

Normality.

Then came the sound that shattered it.

'Shhh . . .' Chris held up his hand. 'What's that?'

They listened. Reverberating through the sea-fort came the sound of two hard objects being smashed together. Voices and footsteps passed quickly outside.

'Come on.' Chris picked David up.

'What's wrong, Dad?'

Ruth said, 'It'll be nothing, love. It just sounds like someone knocking at the gate.'

It was.

Chris made David stay at the bottom of the steps that led up to the walkway. Already Mark and Tony were up there with half a dozen villagers. They craned their heads over the walls to see something at the base of the wall.

By the time he reached the top he was panting, not from

exertion but from tension. Now he dreaded looking out there. Each time seemed worse than the last.

Standing at the gate was one of the Saf Dar, its body colour, even its shape, now altering. The dark cherry-red colour and emaciated frame had gone. Now the skin had turned an intense red that made you think of chronic sunburn. But there was still some lingering darkness beneath, as if the blood of the thing was as black as coal.

Beneath the skin its muscle bulk had grown, making the limbs and torso swollen, with hard knots of muscle bulging at the arms and thighs, forcing veins as thick as ropes to the surface.

In its left hand it held a pebble as large as a melon. It used this to pound at the oak gates. Each enormous blow sent white splinters of rock flying outwards. Now and then a bright blue spark would flash when the rock hit one of the iron gate studs.

Even though the force of the blow made the stone floor vibrate, it was hard to believe it could actually get through the gates that way. They were built to withstand cannon-balls. Chris leaned over the castellated wall as far as he could, but he couldn't see the gate.

The thing focused its attention on the gates. It didn't exert itself. The blows were slow, rhythmic.

Chris found himself counting the beats between each blow. Crash – one-two – crash – one-two – crash . . .

The muscular arm would slowly rise, then whip down to smash at the gate at the creature's eye level. It could have been some bastard machine down there. It didn't tire; it didn't get bored; it didn't need a piss. Nothing.

Perhaps its intention was to unsettle the people inside the sea-fort, rather than to break the doors down. If it was, it had succeeded. The villagers flinched with every cracking blow.

The pounding went on and on . . .

After an hour most of the villagers had moved back to the main sea-fort building to try to escape the noise of the hammering.

'Come on,' said Chris to Mark and Tony, 'we've got to talk.'

Chris led the two men into the old mess-room. Half a dozen straight-backed chairs formed a circle where some of the villagers had sat talking earlier. A bare hundred-watt bulb hanging from the ceiling was the main source of light.

He still believed that Tony hadn't told him everything. Even if it didn't help a fig, he wanted to be in the picture.

They sat, Mark with the shotgun across his lap. Chris leaned forward and said: 'Tony . . . Mark. Two questions: one, why is all this happening? Two, what are we going to do about it?

Tony and Mark looked at Chris for a moment, the sound of the distant pounding pulsing through the thick stone walls.

Tony rubbed his jaw. 'Now's the time to bare our chests. You're in this with us. And to be honest I'm to blame for it.' He began to peel the cellophane from one of his cigars. 'When Fox tipped that petrol all over the place I should have put a match to it when I had the chance.'

Chris raised his eyebrows.

'If I'd done that you wouldn't have been in this bloody awful mess. Fox would have been carted away to the nearest psychiatric hospital. And I'd be behind bars in Munby. At least I'd be far enough away from Out-Butterwick.'

Mark's voice rumbled softly. 'You don't believe that, Tony. The other side of the earth won't be far enough away if they break out.'

'Who are they really?'

As Chris asked the question, Ruth slipped in through the door and sat beside him.

Tony shot a look at Mark which said, who's going to talk? You or me?

Mark nodded back. 'You're the one with words, Tony.'

'If you've got time, folks . . .' Tony's smile was forced. 'Then I'll begin at the beginning.' He lit the cigar. 'About six months ago a woman bought a large piece of steak. Big as a plate. Anyway, she cuts it in half. Puts one piece in the fridge on a plate. The other half she grills for her dinner. Later that day she begins to feel ill and goes to bed. Her husband comes home from work and she tells him to get the other half of the steak and cook it for his supper. Anyway, he goes to the fridge and opens the door. The piece of steak not only fills the plate, it's hanging over the side, all the way to the bottom of the fridge. When he comes to look at it more closely he sees it's just – it's just moving. Then he notices some raw sausages. It had touched the sausages and somehow infected them so they had split out of their skins and were swelling up to twice their normal size; a piece of bacon he'd left that morning had become as thick as the Bible. Of course he took the steak to the environmental health office. And what do you think it was?'

Chris and Ruth shrugged.

'Cancer. The steak had been cut from a cancerous cow. What the man's wife had bought was nothing more than a slice of living cancer.'

'Nice little horror story,' said Chris, 'but I don't follow.'

Again during the pause they became conscious of the rhythmic pounding and shifted uncomfortably on the chairs.

'That's just what it is. A modern folk myth that circulates every few years. But I used the idea of the story, the cancer steak infecting the sausages, to illustrate what's happening here. What I'm going to tell you is really about ordinary things being transformed by something extraordinary.'

Tony leaned forward. 'Look. Remember at the barbecue I told you that Manshead, the little island here, on which the sea-fort is built, was believed to be one of those special places that lie on the boundary between our ordinary, run-of-the-mill world and the next world, the supernatural world, heaven, Valhalla, Olympus, home of the gods – give it any bloody name you want. You've probably heard the legends about Sri Lanka, that there is a certain mountaintop, so close to the boundary between this world and the next one that if you listen hard enough you can hear the fountains of bleeding paradise. Manshead is one of those places.' He spoke in a low, even voice, his glasses flashing hypnotically. 'Here on this slab of rock in the sea stands one of those doorways to a world beyond this one. Pagans, mystics, early Christians, even a cynical git like me, Tony Gateman, believes it. This is where, when the times were right, people gathered, carried out their religious rites, and opened the doorway.'

'These were the sacrifices you mentioned? They took place here?'

'That's right, Ruth. If you strip away the fairy stories surrounding sacrificial rites, the bare essence of the ritual is a commercial transaction with the gods. Nothing more than a trade. The sacrificer was saying, "Look, I cut the throat of my valuable ox and give it to you, the god I worship. In return, I trust you will give me the power to defeat my enemies, or ensure that our community enjoys an abundant harvest this year." In all sacrifices it's basically the mortal giving something of value to the god in return for a special wish being granted – good crops, healthy children, a mild winter.'

Chris said, 'I remember you said the more precious the thing you gave, the more you would expect in return.'

'True. Big things cost big prices . . . An arm and a leg for a fast car, as they say. In times of great need such as famine or invasion they would sacrifice what they valued most – a loved member of the community. Or a member of the community they all love or would love if it was theirs: a child. Or even children.'

Ruth shook her head. 'Okay, so it's a way of buying a granted wish from this cosmic shopkeeper, but what on earth is this god going to do with a dead horse or sheep?'

'That troubled me, Ruth. I ruminated on it for many a long month. But then I put myself in the place of the person making the sacrifice. You have a valuable cow, say. It's important to you; it provides food for your family. What do you actually feel when you kill it? You're basically going to be pissed off. You're giving away something precious which you could have put to damned good use yourself. Or, in a more extreme case, how do you feel when you sacrifice your

own child? Cutting your own son's throat . . . Breaking open
his head with a stone axe . . .'

'But why? How does that give this god what it wants?'

'Ancient people understood what was happening. They
weren't being pointlessly savage and cruel when, say, the
Aztecs took a warrior to the top of the mountain, used a
ceremonial flint knife to cut through his chest-wall to expose
the still-beating heart, then yanked it out with their bare
hands. Or when the priests would skin a woman and wear
the skin like a disguise.

'Listen, today modern psychiatrists are only beginning
to understand what was happening. Catharsis: purification,
purging. Catharsis is a way of discharging a build-up of
psychic power inside yourself before it begins to damage
you or affect how you behave. We've all heard of the woman,
say, whose husband has died. Until she cries she can't really
come to terms with what has happened. She may become
withdrawn and reclusive. But when she cries it's an act of
catharsis: the floodgates open and release all that grief that's
built up inside her.'

Ruth nodded. 'So ancient people understood, although it
might have been on an instinctive level, the benefits of
catharsis.'

'The Aztecs had a ceremony where they killed a number
of their own children. This is a horrible, horrible thing to
do. But again they weren't stupid or cruel, or incapable of
feeling grief. On the contrary, they would weep and weep and
weep. Look, to get to the point about sacrifice, what it actually
does is this. One, the Aztecs killed their own children at these
rituals. Two, this would make the people weep uncontrollably.
Three, this would release a huge rush of unconscious mental
energy. You see someone crying, really crying, they weep, cry,
sob, shake uncontrollably, they can't walk. This tidal wave of
grief cripples them. But you see all the emotion come flooding
out. Multiply this by fifty, a hundred, a thousand. It would
be like breaking down a great dam between the conscious
part of the mind and the unconscious.' Tony tapped his

temple with a thin finger. 'All that worry, fear, hate that had been building up there for year after bloody year come out. And we're talking a real gusher; there's lots of pressure built up there. It's like striking oil.'

There was a pause. The distant pounding of rock against wood continued. Muffled, like a heartbeat. Mark, uneasy, shifted the position of the shotgun across his lap.

'So this is what the god wants,' said Chris. 'All this . . . emotion. Why?'

Tony gave a shrug. 'Could you explain to a robot why we need to eat? It's something that the god wants. Needs. We probably can't even comprehend what does happen. But I imagine it nourishes itself on this huge emotional discharge after the sacrifice. Somehow it absorbs it, if you like, drinks it telepathically.'

Chris snorted. 'Well, you've just put us on the level of cattle. Along comes the supernatural farmer, milks us of emotion, slaps us on the rump, and out we go to pasture again until the next time.'

Mark spoke. 'It doesn't sound that pleasant, Chris. But if this thing that is coming through enjoys juicing up on whatever's inside here' – he placed his finger against his head as if it were the barrel of a gun – 'then I'm not over-concerned. Because, like a farmer, he gives something back that his herd wants.'

'And that is?'

'And that is protection from those things out there.'

'But it wasn't always like that.'

'No, Ruth. As I said at the barbecue, this is a healing place. Out-Butterwick draws people to it who are physically or spiritually ill. I was an alcoholic, remember. It draws people to it that suffer from depression, anxiety – people who find everyday life just so plain hard that they can't go on any more. They came here one by one, and one by one, instinctively, they knew what was going to happen. For the last few years we've known that it was coming – the visitation, if you like. That there would be a burst of some miraculous power through this place. And every one of these men and women would have their own personal wish granted.'

'But it would have to be bought by sacrifice?'

Tony nodded, the thick lenses flashing beneath the light. 'Not that I would do anything as insensitive as enquiring what that would entail. But I'm sure everyone was developing their own personal ritual and choosing something they would give. Although it's highly unlikely anyone was planning a blood sacrifice. You might guess my sacrifice, a cynical old capitalist like me. Money.'

Mark rose from his chair restlessly. It was as if he sensed that time was running out. 'And you two fine people will have guessed that all this thing's gone bad. There we were, all waiting for nice miracles. But then those things showed up. And to put it bluntly, they are going to hijack this bit of magic we've all pinned our hopes on. Then . . .' He shook his head, his face grim.

'But who are they?'

'The Saf Dar? From what I can discover they were a gang of psychopaths, different nationalities – American, British, German, African, Indian – who came together shortly after World War II. Dabbled in piracy, arms smuggling, assassinations; they were mercenaries for whoever paid the right money. Later they specialised in destabilising governments in Third World countries. Simply by doing what they loved: killing. Butchering men, women, children. Hence the name Saf Dar – breaker of the line. In 1961 they were en route for England.'

Mark spoke. 'And that's when I met them. I was apprenticed to a merchant ship, the *Mary-Anne*. They hijacked her. Butchered most of the crew and forced the rest to sail for England. God knows what they had been hired to do here.'

'But they never made it,' said Chris.

'Correct.' Mark's dark eyes bled pain. 'I scuttled the *Mary-Anne*. The Saf Dar, my crewmates, they all went to the bottom of the sea not half a mile from here. I was the only survivor.'

Understanding hit Chris.

'Look . . .' Mark's voice was laced with urgency. 'I see it plain and simple. Any time now there's going to be an almighty great chunk of power that no one's seen in five hundred years come whistling into this place . . . Then it's going to be a case of who grabs it first. Us, or those bastards on the beach. Because we're like two teams in a line-out, waiting for that ball of magic that's going to be chucked into Manshead. Whoever catches the ball first is the winner, the other loses. And I'm talking about absolute winners and absolute losers. Chris, Ruth, those things out there are our rivals. They want this power first. If they could, they'd kill us now, then turn us into things like Wainwright, Fox, and the others out there. That way we wouldn't be in competition with them for that power surge when it comes. And believe me, if they get hold of that power they can do anything. These stone walls might as well be made out of paper. We wouldn't even have the choice of dying. We would become their foot soldiers. We would be marched off inland to kill anyone who gets in our way. Those that we killed would become like us. You can imagine it as a cancer spreading, spreading across the country.'

Ruth said to Tony, 'How long have we got? Before this force breaks through?'

'No more than two to three days. You've probably felt it yourself, a kind of tension building. All the signs are there. Already the barrier between this world and that other place is stretched so tight that the magic, supernatural force – manna, cosmic power, whatever you want to call it – is leaking through. It's strongest in these few hundred square yards around Manshead. If you like, we're at ground zero. Living things are being altered or affected by it. It's turned up the life energy already, a bit like increasing the volume of a radio. If you're ill you feel better; if you're tired you feel stronger.'

All at once Chris thought of his tireless work on the

sea-fort, the goldfish, the monster celery plant . . . Christ, those shells David had picked up two weeks ago.

Mark's grip on the shotgun tightened. 'And sometimes things that die . . . they come back. For a while this is going to be the only place on earth where even death has died.'

'The goldfish,' whispered Ruth. 'You remember, Chris?'

Tony leaned forward. 'You've seen things?'

Mark pulled something from his breast pocket and handed it to Chris. 'And you might have seen one of these.'

It was a common cockleshell. He knew what it would have on its concave surface.

'A face,' said Ruth. 'A picture of a face.'

'The beach is littered with them,' said Mark. 'There's probably – *shit* . . .'

Mark stood up quickly, the shotgun in his hands.

Without warning the light-bulb had gone out. Even above the distant pounding on the sea-fort gates, they heard it clicking as the glass cooled. The room, gloomy with only the weak daylight filtering through dirty glass, felt inexplicably cold.

'Could be the fuses . . .'

'Fuses be buggered,' said Tony. 'I'm only surprised they didn't do it earlier. The sea-fort supply comes from a cable strung on pylons along the coast road. It would have been simple enough to bring it down.'

Shit! thought Chris fiercely. Food running low . . . Electricity off. We're down to candles. What could they . . ,

'Water.' Chris looked up sharply. 'Next they cut the water.'

'More difficult. They'd have to dig down through the —'

'No, would they shit . . . There's a stop-cock on the landward side of the causeway. All they need do is flip open the iron cover, reach down and turn a tap. Then . . .'

'Damn. The bastards will soon work that one out.'

Ruth stood up quickly. 'We'll get as many containers together as we can. Pans, buckets, bottles. Fill them full of water.'

Mark walked to the door. 'I'll get some help.'

As he walked to the door, Chris saw a figure move quickly back. He recognised that dried-up profile. The Reverend Reed; he'd been eavesdropping.

When Ruth and Mark had gone, their feet echoing away down the stone corridor, Chris turned to Tony and asked, 'Are we going to make it through this?'

'I hope so, Chris . . . God knows, I hope so.'

33

'Miz-zess Stainforth! Miz-zess Stainforth . . . Toilet won't flush.'

Rosie Tamworth stood in the doorway of the caravan, her little-girl face on top of the lumpy body showing childish concern. Ruth, who was carrying buckets of water across the courtyard with Chris, stopped and looked at him. Her eyes said it all.

He put his buckets down on the cobblestones. 'So the bastards worked it out at last. No electricity. No water.' The mental clock that measured the time they could remain in the sea-fort began to tick more quickly. A human being can last five weeks without food. Without water you are talking days.

He picked up the buckets and carried them to where they were storing half a dozen other buckets, twenty-three bottles of all different kinds, two plastic washing-up bowls, pans, ornamental vases, plastic boxes – all filled to the brim with water. Tony had suggested that they line wooden crates with plastic sheeting to make their own containers; however, they had simply run out of time. Somewhere out on the causeway a hand had reached down into a hole in the road and twisted shut the stop-cock.

Again he thought of those monstrously powerful hands. Again he thought of David's neck. He snapped off the line of thought and went to find Tony.

As Chris climbed the steps after locking the water-store door, the sound of the pounding on the gates connected with his consciousness again. He realised it had never stopped, but in the rush to save as much water as possible he'd successfully shut it out.

Now it came back. It sounded as if death itself was at the gate, pounding, pounding, pounding. And it wanted to come inside.

On the wall walkway stood Mark, carrying the shotgun, and Tony. Both peered over the wall, hypnotised by the sight of the creature, hacking at the timber gates with a rock.

It had used several rocks. Splinters of stone littered the causeway around the gate. The sea, now at high tide, swirled and sucked thickly round the slab of rock that was their island. More Saf Dar sat waist-deep in surf on the causeway. Beyond that, green sea vanished into grey mist.

'I expect you've heard,' said Chris.

Mark continued to stare, brooding, at the figure thumping the timbers with the rock.

Tony turned round, his face as grey as the fog. 'The Hodgson lad told us.'

'What now?'

'Just wait. That's all we can do. Unless you've got any ideas. There's no way we can contact anyone in the outside world. We can't run. Wainwright proved that. We can't fly out.'

'I heard the pub landlord talking to one of the other villagers,' said Chris. 'They thought they might be able to make a raft and paddle out.'

'They were fucking joking, weren't they?'

'They're desperate, Tony. They know there isn't much food and we've only got enough water for a few days and so —'

'And so they thought they might as well kill themselves; get it over with quick. Mark, how many of the Saf Dar were there on the *Mary-Anne* when she went down?'

Mark didn't look round. 'Fifteen.' Those brooding eyes were fixed on the thing battering the door. He gripped the shotgun so tightly the veins in the back of his big hands pressed out against the skin.

'Fifteen . . . The most we've seen on the causeway is eight. That means there's probably another seven scattered around this place. One or two up in the dunes. One guarding the bridge near the village. And maybe a couple sitting under the water out there, ready to reach up and tip anyone into the sea if they are bleeding stupid enough to try and float out on a raft.'

'Tony, do you think the villagers are just going to sit here and starve?' He spaced the words so the machine-like pounding, rock against wood, filled the gaps between his words. 'Mr and Mrs Hodgson have two sons; some men have wives. This instinct to survive, to protect your family from danger, is surfacing. They have to feel as though they're doing something. If we all sit here listening to that thing cracking away at the door we're all going to go mad. If we can't do anything to stop the noise we might as well —'

The tremendous bang came at the wrong time. The thing had changed its rhythm. Chris looked round.

Mark stood on tiptoe leaning forward over the wall, the shotgun up at his shoulder. From one of the barrels a cloud of blue smoke rolled outwards.

For maybe five seconds the pounding stopped. The sudden silence became almost unbearable.

Chris quickly leaned forward over the wall to look down.

The thing with the rock still stood on the causeway immediately outside the twin gates. It had paused. The arm held high, frozen in mid-hammer, still grasped the white pebble in its massive paw. The hairless head still faced the gates, its eyes glittering white in the red face.

Chris stared down until his eyes watered. There was something different about the monster, it had —

That's it!

Running down from the shoulder, down its red back knotted with veins, was a thick liquid, the consistency of rich gravy.

Blood.

Heart beating hard, Chris looked swiftly at Tony to see if he'd grasped the significance of the liquid haemorrhaging from a jagged break in the thing's shoulder.

Then the huge arm came down, cracking the stone against the gate. The mechanical pounding had begun once more. Bang – one-two – bang – one-two . . . A handful of speeding lead shot hadn't stopped it long. But there on Manshead a small miracle had taken place.

'Christ, these things actually bleed,' whispered Chris.

'Sure they do,' said Mark in a low, controlled voice. 'And if they do . . .'

Raising the shotgun to his shoulder, he aimed, every gram of concentration squeezed into his eyes as he looked unblinking down the barrel. His trigger finger tightened.

Again the explosion from the shotgun punched Chris's eardrum – but he never took his eyes off the figure pounding the gates.

This time the shot hit the creature square, knocking it away from the door with enough force to make you believe it had been dynamited away. The momentum carried it back five feet across the causeway, its arms windmilling loosely over its head. Then it fell back into the blanket of foam.

A wave rolled round the sea-fort and the bastard creature was gone.

For a moment they stared down. Gone. The gun smoked. Gone. Mark's eyes glistened with tears, whether from the gunsmoke or what Chris didn't know – but he felt his spirits lifting.

Gone. All that remained was the big white pebble smeared with that black gunge that had oozed from the bastard monster's body.

Jesus. These things bleed. They actually bleed. The words buzzed like lightning through his head.

Now the creature lay at the bottom of the sea with a hole in its chest big enough to plant a tree in.

He looked out at its brothers. Three were visible on the causeway. They sat immobile, expressionless. Sunburn-red bodies splashed by waves from the rising tide. Did they know that one of their kind had just been blown from the surface of God's earth? Did the moronic fuckers care?

From his right came a shrieking sound. It was a Hodgson boy, jumping up and down as high as his lard-arse would allow. He whooped again, his freckled face ecstatic. Then he ran to the steps whooping and shouting: 'Dad! Mr Faust killed one of them things. Dad!'

Tony was grinning and shaking his head as if he'd just seen Father Christmas plop down his chimney.

Chris let out a huge breath. He felt as if he'd been holding it for the last forty-eight hours.

At last they knew. These things bled. They hurt. And they died.

34

Within minutes a dozen or more people crowded on to the walkway to look down at the bloody pebble on the causeway or to slap Mark Faust on the back. At that moment the villagers would have given him everything they owned.

'Looks like you're a bloody hero,' called Tony over the congratulations.

'Should've done it sooner,' Mark replied with one of his broad grins. 'Just never thought a shooter would do a thing against them.'

'Let the dog see the bloody rabbits, then.' Hodgson Senior hoisted his bulk up against the wall, the shotgun in his well-padded hands.

'Make way for a little 'un.' Tom Hodgson joined his brother, rolling his shirt-sleeves up his freckled arms. The two of them leaned forward against the wall, plump elbows resting on the stone, aiming the shotguns. The Saf Dar sat in a group fifty paces away on the causeway.

They fired quickly. The shot at this distance spread enough to hit all four of the things as well as splashing the water around them.

Each shot brought a slight flinch from the figures, but they did not relax their statue-like pose. Nor did they blink their eyes which still glittered like glass in their faces.

As the echoes of gunfire crackled away into the distance, the Hodgsons pulled more shells from their pockets and blasted the creatures again.

Chris knew it would be too much to hope for. But he longed for the bastard creatures to explode into the shit they were and simply be washed away for ever by the tide.

He glanced back into the courtyard. Ruth stood, her arms around David. Chris waved to catch their attention.

She looked up.

He grinned and gave a thumbs-up sign. She nodded and smiled back, relieved. They were going to be all right. He was going to call down, but a deafening battery of crashes came from the Hodgsons' guns as they pounded the figures on the causeway.

He turned to see the figures moving back.

It wasn't exactly a rout. They moved back in an unhurried way like men casually seeking the shade of a bigger tree. But they were moving. And in the right direction.

Tony called out, 'All right, lads. Save your ammo. They're out of range.'

The two farmers stopped firing. 'Pity the cunts weren't a bit nearer. We'd have turned the fuckers into pig-shit.'

'No . . . We didn't even wing 'em, Tom.'

Mark's voice rumbled, excited. 'That doesn't matter. That doesn't matter a shit. What does matter is that we can hurt them.'

Chris realised, feeling the same flash of excitement, that Mark had got the scent of his prey. Now the hunter, not the hunted.

Mark said: 'Whatever those bastards are, they are flesh and blood. We wait till they come back. Then we hit them hard.'

35

'Fill it right to the top?' asked Ruth, slipping the funnel spout into the neck of a bottle.

'Half,' Mark told her. 'It'll be easier to handle. Also we still need to mix in the soap powder.'

'Soap powder? I thought we were going to burn them, not clean them.'

'The soap powder slows down the rate of burn. It also sticks to whatever it touches. A direct hit and those bastards will burn and burn. Chris, will you siphon more petrol out of the car? Half a bucketful'll be fine.'

Chris walked across to the car carrying the zinc bucket together with a length of plastic tubing. Christ, he thought, I came here to open a hotel. Here I am getting ready for a bloody war.

Around the courtyard the villagers were making preparations for the battle to come.

They all knew what had happened. They knew that the Saf Dar, although they weren't mortal, bled and died. Now there was a sense of nervous exhilaration running round the building. They were going to hit back.

Chris watched his son helping Tony line up empty bottles on a table. He felt hope flow back into him again. Soon life should return to normal. (Should he say God willing? Which god willed it anyway? Tony Gateman's pagan god which even now was getting ready to lean over this little rock-slab of an island and slurp up his/her/its fix of human emotion? Christ, there was plenty of that about.) He allowed himself a smile.

He returned to his job, the strong smell of petrol making

his eyes water. He sucked at the pipe, squinting downward to see the clear liquid slide up the tube.

'How we going?' asked Tony, squatting down beside him. There was an unlit cigar in his mouth. 'Don't worry, old son. I'm not going to light it.' He took it out of his mouth and looked at it as if it was a dog turd. 'Disgusting things . . . Funny, isn't it. How stress makes us revert to infantile behaviour. All the Hodgson boys want to do is eat. The Reverend Reed sucks away at his gin bottle like a baby. He must have five bottles in that briefcase of his. This . . .' He put the cigar in his mouth. 'An infantile craving, you know. Something to suck. It's just a substitute for my mother's tit.'

'Tony, if you don't mind me saying so, you're taking a cynical view of what we're doing.'

'Me? Cynical? Whatever gave you that idea?'

'From your own lips, Tony. You said you were the world's greatest cynical bastard.' Chris looked hard at Tony. 'Do you think we've got a chance? After all, Mark blew a hole right through one of those things.'

'You've got every chance, son. I'm not going to pour cold water on all this.'

'But?'

'But . . . But life's all been turned inside out. What we've got here is like running a car on a weak mixture of two-stroke . . . then suddenly we slam in some super-high-octane mixture. We saw what happened to Wainwright. And you and I saw what he became. You mentioned the goldfish. Have you seen it lately? It's changing all right. You can see hard lumps pressing through from under the skin; I think it's really —'

'Tony, I know something weird's happening here. You think this old pagan god thing's going to put in a personal appearance. But do you think it will? And if it does, will it have any effect on us?'

'Chris, you've seen the phenomena. Christ Almighty . . . This thing is so powerful it's made death redundant. You see what it's done? An animal dies. Out goes the old life force, but this thing rams in some of its own high-octane life. This kind of life is what nuclear energy is to a poxy parafin lamp. You saw those things on the beach the other night, Chris. Once they were ordinary people. Wainwright. Fox. A boy. Fishermen. Now they are so full of life they are bursting at the seams.'

'Okay, Tony. I believe you. But look at ordinary, everyday nature. If you stand back and look at that objectively that's as weird as buggery. If someone said a lump of rock two hundred thousand miles away had the power to lift millions of tons of water twenty feet in the air, you'd think they were crackers. But the moon does it twice a day. We don't call it magic, we call it tides. Tons of water are dumped by the sky all over the world. Not a miracle – rain. Invisible forces can slam a door shut. Not ghosts – wind. A natural force can light up the sky at night and blast a tree to smithereens. Lightning. Enormously powerful forces, but they're not supernatural.' He took a deep breath. 'Look, Tony. Whatever's happening is extraordinary. But perhaps we're just encountering some natural phenomenon that nobody's witnessed before.'

'Hey, man. Are you drilling for that gas or what?' called Mark. 'Your wife and I are making napalm over here.'

'Coming.' He climbed to his feet.

Tony said nothing, but Chris noticed the man's expression. Maybe he needed to believe in a pagan god that came to look after its flock.

The Saf Dar would not come.

Had they learnt their lesson? Chris watched them. They squatted on the causeway, the sea rolling round their chests, staring expressionlessly at the sea-fort.

'Do you think they'll get close enough?' asked Ruth, putting her arms around him.

'You sound like a right little bloodthirsty warrior.'

'I just want to get rid of them, Chris. I'm sick of all these people here. I'm sick of being a prisoner in this building.'

'The Saf Dar seem short on common sense. They're like hungry dogs round the back door of a butcher's. They can't keep away. When they do . . .' He shrugged. 'We'll get back to normal.'

Normal? He wondered what Ruth would consider normal. He found himself wondering if she'd want to leave. No. He couldn't believe that. They loved the place. He glanced back at the sea-fort, gloomy in the evening mist. When he looked at the great expanse of building, his mind ran ahead, planning how the place would look when it was completed.

Hugging his wife, he gazed out over the sea. He didn't see the Saf Dar's alien stare; he saw only his dream of the future. And it was a good dream.

'People pile!' shouted David as Ruth and Chris lay on the double bed in the caravan.

'Shh . . .' whispered Ruth. 'Remember there are other people trying to get to sleep.'

Chris smiled. 'Quick people pile, then.'

David jumped on top of Chris, his head lightly butting into Chris's chin. This was one of David's favourite games. People pile. It consisted of Chris at the bottom, Ruth next, then David sitting, kneeling or standing on top of her.

'People pile,' laughed David. 'Come on, Mum. You next. I'll sit on your head.'

'You won't. You weigh a ton these days. Just lie down across your dad's chest and we'll cuddle.'

'All right, then. Can we leave the light on and talk before switching it off?'

'You don't switch off a candle, you blow it out.'

David looked at the candle that lit the caravan bedroom with a yellow light and filled it with odd wavering shadows. 'When are we going to get 'lectric back again?'

'Soon. There's a fault with the power station. When they fix that we'll get the electric back.'

'And the water?'

'Yes.'

'Will all those people go back to their own houses then?'

'They will, David. This is just temporary.'

David snuggled his head against Ruth's face.

'We'll blow out the candle now, David. We've got a lot to do tomorrow.'

David put his arm round his mother's neck and hugged her.

'All right, then . . .' he murmured drowsily. 'I'm going to go to sleep now. Love you.'

'Love you.' She leaned across to the bedside table and blew out the candle.

They would need a good night's sleep. Because tomorrow they were going to fight a war.

Three hours later Chris awoke. He lay for a further forty minutes struggling to sleep again. In the end he slid on his leather jacket and left the caravan, guided by the same kind of urge that drives you to stare at wrecked cars beside motorways.

He climbed the steps to the top of the wall and looked out. Enough moonlight seeped through the mist to reveal them as they arrived. One by one across the beach from the depths of the darkness beyond.

At first they were just fuzzy shapes in the mist. He could almost believe they were just people approaching the sea-fort during some midnight walk. As they grew nearer their outlines hardened, revealing more and more details, until he could no longer con himself into believing they were human.

His mouth dry, he glanced about the beach for the Saf Dar. Although he couldn't see them, he knew they were there somewhere. Probably sat in that weird Red Indian warrior way further up the beach in the mist.

Now, walking slowly towards the sea-fort in a semi-circle, were the pathetic figures he'd seen the night before.

The Fox twins, one grossly fat, the other scarecrow-thin; Wainwright, the dirty rag of a bandage round his neck, dark red growths like bunches of Burgundy grapes hanging loosely from the gash in his face.

Chris zipped his leather jacket up to his throat and hugged himself.

They were changing.

Growing worse.

There were more of them now. Two dozen men and the boy. Drowned or killed at sea anything from a few hours to fifty years ago. Their bodies changing, hour by hour. The massive life force that electrified their once-dead flesh swelled their limbs and distorted their faces. Worse things were happening too.

He chewed his lip. He needed to see this. These bastard sights. They were like razor blades peeling away his outer civilised layer, the nicey-nice Mr Stainforth, who didn't push into queues or swear at old ladies (not to their faces, anyway); peel all that artificial civilised society crap away to expose the primal man. The man who would do anything to anyone, no matter how savage or bestial, to ensure that he and his family survived. Nice men don't kill.

Nice men don't sacrifice what they love. That thought had been planted by Gateman earlier. What would a man two thousand years ago have done, faced with this?

He knew. The man would have gone to his wife and taken the little dark-eyed boy from her arms; he would have dressed him in his best clothes, told him he was special, that he loved him; then he would have laid him across the stone, picked up the bronze axe, and —

He blinked. Coldness trickled down one cheek. Shit, Tony Gateman, I bet you can sell fucking condoms to the Pope.

The figures were closer now. They stood in a long line in front of him, staring at the sea-fort.

Again he saw that these things were not kept alive in some insipid way, like geriatrics on a life-support machine. No, these things were alive with a vibrant, forceful rush of energy.

He watched the figures. Concentrating on every detail of the distorted bodies to rip away the civilised exterior that had encased him like a shell nearly all his life.

He had to turn back the clock to allow that blood of his warrior ancestors to flow through his veins. He had to learn to hate in a full-blooded way. And channel that hate into a force he could use. This would be a battle for survival.

Their swollen bodies looked as if they would rip the skin that tried to contain them. Hugely enlarged hearts pounded ferociously against their chests like engines. Their naked chests shuddered with the concussions. Where a body had been damaged that crude rush of energy had healed it with tumorous growths. Red tomato cancers ballooned from eye sockets where eyes had been torn away. There, a shattered mouth had been repaired by a protruding flesh balloon.

Some of the older corpses had mingled with shellfish and seaweed until you could not tell where the man ended and where the flotsam and jetsam of the sea began.

One, a large barrel-chested man who could have been a ship's captain, stood nearer than the rest.

His chest, as white as milk, was covered with narrow slits in the skin. The slits were probably as long as a thumb. As Chris watched, the slits slowly parted. Pushing through them from inside the man's chest to the outside came twenty or so hard, dark tips.

Chris clenched his jaw until it ached.

The dark objects being forced outward by the internal pressures were mussel shells. Hard. Blue-black. They must have been anchored to the man's rib cage and periodically squeezed through the skin slits, further and further until the shells protruded proud of the skin like rows of long black nipples. A coating of fine mucus gave them an oily gloss that gleamed in the moonlight.

Then the shells would crack open to expose the pale morsels of salty flesh inside. A moment later they closed and withdrew into the man's chest.

Each time the mussel shells protruded through the man's skin, his face split into an agonised grimace as if he were being tortured with hot pieces of metal. But no sound came from the raw mouth.

Chris's face burned. His head rolled. Sometimes he didn't even know if he was standing on the wall watching them, or barefoot in the sand, looking up at the man on the wall, feeling the terror and the pain. And all the time the gnawing need, the naked want . . . to GO HOME.

. . . GO HOME . . .

Just run and run. But the Saf Dar, in their bright red skins, forced us . . .

Chris's mind blurred . . .

. . . the Saf Dar in their bright red skins forced us to come here, to stand on the beach, pain ripping and exploding through our bodies, pain gnawing like rats at our testicles . . . Ohhh, the burning skin, the burning skin on our bodies . . .

They'll let us go

GO HOME

when we smash down the doors of the house on the beach, pull out the people inside, like soft fruit from a tree. Then we give the Saf Dar what they want, the people from the house on the beach, then we —

WE GO HOME.

We need love.

Love us! Love us! Love us! Kiss this burning skin on my body.

Chris dimly recognised blows hitting his body. He struck out with his fists. They smacked against hard stone.

He opened his eyes. He'd blacked out and fallen down on the walkway. His stomach churned; the sweat sliding down his face turned icy. And he felt . . . Christ, he felt like shit.

Legs trembling, he pulled himself to his feet and walked unsteadily down to the caravan.

36

Tense, Mark Faust called down to them: 'Here they come.'

Chris followed Ruth up the stone steps to the top of the wall.

He glanced round at the others. Mark stood looking out over the wall, the loaded shotgun resting over his shoulder, looking every inch the Wild West frontiersman. The two Hodgson boys were in their positions at the far end of the wall. They were armed with .22 rifles which were probably as effective as couple of feather dusters against the Saf Dar, but it kept them occupied. At the section of wall above the main gates stood the two elder Hodgson brothers, their massive freckled hands clamped round the shotguns.

Tony stood leaning back against the wall, his face as white as paper, a cigar between his lips.

'Tony, best not smoke too near those bottles. They're full of gas.'

Tony looked like a man waking from a dream. 'Gas?'

'Gas . . . Petrol.' Mark Faust looked at his old friend. 'You feeling okay?'

'I'll be fine.' He carefully stubbed out the cigar. 'Now, we've got everything.' The business-like tone came back into his voice. 'Enough shells?'

'Should be . . . There's forty in the box on the table.'

Tony turned to Chris. 'You've told everyone to stay in the building until it's over? We don't want people milling about up here; someone'd end up getting hurt.'

Chris nodded. 'And I've filled the buckets with water in case anyone manages to set themselves on fire when we start lobbing those things.' He indicated another table that carried thirteen bottles, filled with petrol and soap powder; wired to the neck of each bottle was a handkerchief-sized piece of cloth.

'Water?'

'Don't worry,' said Ruth. 'Sea water. While the tide was in, Chris and I lowered buckets on string.' She managed a smile. 'I think we did pretty well.'

'Best run through the procedure, folks. Mark, Tom and John are using their shotguns. Chris . . . You and I are chucking the bottles. Be careful. If we drop one, we'll fry.'

'I won't drop them.' Chris had stuffed his fists into the pockets of his jeans so no one would see his hands shake.

'Right. Procedure, folks. When the Saf Dar are close enough, we pour fuel into that pie tin. Chris and I each take a bottle. We dunk it neck-first into the tin to moisten the rag wick. Hold it out to Ruth who lights the rag with the cigarette lighter, then we chuck the bottle at one of the men . . . one of the things down there. Oh, needless to say, pick your target first. You don't want to stand there with a burning bottle in your hand longer than you have to. Right . . . Any questions?'

'Only one.' Ruth looked out across the beach. 'When are they going to come?'

For the first time that morning Chris looked out over the wall. Twenty feet below, the sea washed round the rock on which the sea-fort rested. Great clots of kelp floated in the turbulent water. The tide was dropping, sections of causeway were being exposed between waves. The roar of the surf softened.

Eight figures had advanced halfway across the causeway. The Saf Dar. Standing as they always did, like a line of red dominoes, the sea swirling round their bare legs. Their hairless heads were turned towards the sea-fort and those eyes glared with an unquenchable brutality.

They did not move. They had slipped into their statue mode.

What if they never came near the gates again? Maybe they had learnt after all that those in the sea-fort had the ability to destroy them. The choice then would be did they leave the safety of the sea-fort to attack the Saf Dar on the beach?

He watched Mark put a box containing shotgun shells on the top of the wall beside Tom and John Hodgson. When it came to the showdown they wouldn't want to waste time fumbling in pockets for ammunition. Reloading the guns after two shots would be cumbersome enough anyway.

Tom grunted, 'It looks as if the buggers are in no hurry.'

His brother chuckled heavily. 'You fancy playing bait, Tom? Nip down there and do a fan dance for them on the causeway. It'll bring the fuckers flocking in.'

Chris began to space the bottles out on the table. If he let one of these slip through his fingers when it was lit they'd all be in trouble, with a pool of blazing petrol running along the walkway.

He glanced up at his wife. Her dark eyes were fixed on the Saf Dar. She was willing the bastards to move in close.

Come on. Cluster round the gates then we'll blast you to kingdom come.

'Thought I could help.'

They turned to see the Major standing at the top of the steps, the revolver in his hand. The dog sat at his feet. The old man's hand, knobbly with arthritis, shook, and the weight of the handgun pulled it down.

'Ah . . . Thanks for the offer, Major,' said Tony. 'But we've got the situation under control.'

'Make it quick,' said Mark as calmly as he could. 'We've got some movement out here.'

Tony continued, 'Er, we thought it would be best if you could look after the, er, villagers in the sea-fort.'

'Of course . . . Of course.' The Major sounded puzzled, as if not really sure now why he had come up here. ' 'Course, we should really be getting home. Way past lunchtime.'

'Ye-es. Quite.'

'Tony, they're coming,' Mark warned. 'We're going to need you any minute.'

Tony smiled at the senile old man. 'Major, lunch will be served in the mess in five minutes. Best pop down and have a brush-up first.'

The Major brightened. 'So soon? Good job. I'm starving. Come on, boy.' He quickly went down the steps, the dog following, its claws clicking on the stone slabs.

Ruth shot him a look. 'He'll have a long wait till lunch. It's only half-nine.'

'It doesn't really matter. The old boy will have forgotten every word I said in five minutes.'

'Pick your targets,' said Mark. 'This is it.'

37

'Strategy?' asked Tony.

'Kill them. Burn them.' Mark Faust thumbed off the shotgun's safety catch.

'But what the hell do we do then?' asked Ruth.

'I'm out there with this.' Mark held up the shotgun. 'I'm finishing what we've started.'

Chris felt uncertain. 'What about those two out on the causeway? They're out of range and they'll not come any closer when they see what happens to their cronies in the next ten minutes.'

Tony said, 'Chris's right, Mark. We don't take chances. No heroics. We take our time. No one goes chasing these things across the bloody beach. There're going to be no casualties on our side. We can afford to sit here and pick them off when they get close enough.'

Mark nodded. 'No heroics. Right . . . Tom . . . John. Listen. We want to make sure we hit these bastards hard.'

As Mark spoke Chris looked down at the Saf Dar.

Of the eight that had been standing on the causeway, two had stayed midway, well out of range of the shotguns and petrol bombs.

The other six had moved nicely forward into the slaughter zone. Twenty feet below on the cobbled area outside the sea-fort gates, they stood in two lines of three. The first line must have been six paces from the gates, the other line of three ten paces behind that. Their bald red heads gleamed dully in the misty light. From this high angle he could not see their faces. He was glad.

As he stared down at their massive shoulders, almost bursting with a muscle growth that forced veins and arteries up against the skin so it looked as if living snakes wormed beneath, their heads moved. Smoothly, slowly, they tilted their heads to look directly up at Chris. Their glass-shard eyes glittered coldly, faces expressionless, mouths parted to expose uneven yellow teeth.

It was as if they were silently willing the sea-fort to collapse into dust so they could pick out the fragile human beings from within, like a boy picking out the white flesh of a coconut from its broken shell.

'Let's do it.'

It was time. His heart pumped, sweat prickled like pins on his forehead. For Christsake don't let those bottles of petrol slip through your fingers.

'Looks as though those two out on the causeway don't want to come to the party today . . . Might as well start without them.' Mark, resting his elbows on the wall, brought the shotgun butt to his shoulder. He said to the Hodgsons: 'The three of us will take out the three of them that are farthest from the gates. Tom, you take the one on the left. John . . . the one on the right. I'll hit the one dead centre. Tony . . . Chris. You lob the petrol bombs at the three nearest the gate. At this angle just drop them straight down . . . let gravity do the work for you. And for God's sake burn the bastards to ashes. Get ready. Together on the word go. All right?'

Everyone nodded.

Chris wet the wick of his first petrol bomb. Tony did the same. Ruth stood ready with the lighter.

Mark Faust stood, shotgun snug to his shoulder, squeezing every gram of concentration down the gunsight.

The word came:

'Go.'

All three men fired simultaneously. All three shots struck their targets.

The three Saf Dar jerked back.

Strangely none reacted to the shots, even though one lost

a face in a spattering of shot. A cavity appeared in the chest of Mark's target. The third's stomach split open and something resembling a white bag of minced steak slipped wetly out on to the cobbles at its feet.

The things stood like wounded statues.

The shotguns cracked again. An arm vanished in a spray of cherry red. Mark's shot kicked in the monster's forehead. The thick dark stuff they'd seen before poured down the bodies as if they were melting.

Tom's shot blasted the leg off another. Smoothly, it slipped into a kneeling position, its broken leg at an angle beneath its bare backside.

A wave broke over the causeway and washed round the three, carrying away a dark slick that made the water look unnaturally smooth, like oil.

'Chris . . .'

He looked at his wife. She held out the burning lighter. Carefully he prodded the rag wired round the end of the bottle into the blade of flame.

The petrol-soaked rag flared immediately, spitting blobs of blue flame, scorching the back of his bare hand.

Carefully, he turned, leaned forward over the wall, and released the bottle.

It seemed to take seconds to drop down to the three stationary figures.

Then they vanished in a blossom of white fire. Chris felt the uprush of air hot on his face.

Two seconds later the flare subsided to a burning puddle of petrol on the cobbles.

Another bomb flared brilliantly; Tony had dropped his.

Quickly, Chris dropped another. Then Tony. Then Chris.

They established a rhythm, making sure that the three things below were at the centre of a furnace. Those bastards might not burn in hell but they were burning here on earth. And still too frigging stupid to move.

'One down!' cried Mark. His shot sent one of the Saf Dar toppling back on to the causeway – now a chewed-up rag doll of a thing, with a frayed head; splinters of white bone stuck out through the chest like raw French fries.

The Hodgsons roared out, an ear-vibrating cheer. A wave rolled in, tugging the fallen Saf Dar with it. It vanished into deep water.

'Four to go, lads,' called Tom Hodgson.

Along the wall the two boys also fired their rifles, the small .22 bullets pecking holes in the red skin of the Saf Dar.

The one still kneeling on the causeway had become a chewed-up stump, hardly even approximating a human shape.

Chris lobbed a petrol bomb at it and a rose-coloured flame bloomed around it.

The three Saf Dar directly below who were enduring the fire bombs had sunk into a sitting position, the withering heat eating into the great blocks of muscle in their legs and torsos.

Still they did not react.

They should have been writhing across the ground in agony as the flames turned their bodies to charcoal.

Chris pitched another bottle at the crippled one. This time, burning, it rolled over and dropped off the causeway into the sea. It sank, leaving a slick on the surface.

'Four to go!'

The three gunners concentrated on the remaining figure at the back, the lead shot taking bites out of the creature as if it was being eaten alive by an invisible Pit Bull terrier.

It began to lean back, almost at an impossible angle. Then it toppled, as stiff as a pine tree. The sea swallowed it.

Chris and Tony had not let up with the bottles of fuel on the three nearest the gate. They sat in a lake of flame; the petrol even ran in burning rivulets down the causeway to where the sea washed over it. Smoke climbed into the sky like a ghostly black pillar.

Then, as the final bottle crashed down, splintering, sending flaming pieces of glass across the stone slabs, the three things began at last to move.

They moved like crippled crabs, arms and legs jerking

awkwardly. They crabbed their way slowly, whether on their backs or fronts Chris couldn't tell, as far as the causeway edge, then slipped into the water.

'None to go.'

'You've done it . . .' Tony Gateman sounded as if he didn't believe it himself. 'You've bloody well done it.'

'Thank God,' breathed Ruth with feeling.

Chris reached out and pulled her close, hugging her trembling body.

'That's a total of seven, including the one I took out before,' called Mark, resting the barrel of the shotgun across his shoulder. 'Eight left. Now we sit and wait for them to get close again.'

'If they come,' said Ruth.

'Oh, they'll come back,' said Tony. 'Believe me, they'll come back.'

38

'Tony, what makes them blow up like that?'

David noticed how surprised Tony was when he asked the question.

'Makes what blow up?'

'These coalmines.'

'Oh . . . It's in the book?'

David hadn't been allowed out of the sea-fort building, so he'd sat with the other people from the village (which had been dead boring) and looked at a pile of books he'd brought with him.

That morning he had heard a lot of shooting outside. Also a burning smell had floated through the windows.

But when he'd asked people what was happening they'd replied, 'Nothing.' He'd also asked the old man with the revolver and dog. He was nice, ruffling David's head with one of those old-men hands, bony with brown splotches on the back.

The old man said, 'Damn natives again. Still, the NCO's got it in hand.' Then he'd looked around the big gundeck room full of people as if he'd seen it for the first time. 'Should really be getting off for a spot of lunch.'

After a while David had given up asking. The mist was too thick to see much apart from a bit of grey sea water at the back of the sea-fort, so he'd sat on a chair swinging his legs backwards and forwards while looking at the books. One about coalmines had caught his eye. Inside, a picture showed an explosion, throwing men and machinery and bits of coal and stuff along the tunnel in a big yellow blast.

Tony had come in a lot later, looking dirty and sweaty.

That's when he had reacted oddly to the word 'explosions'.

'That explosion will have been caused by methane,' he explained. There was a big black smudge on one cheek.

'Me-fane.'

Tony smiled, very tired. 'Methane. It's a gas. You know . . . Like air . . .' He moved his hands about him. They were dirty too. 'You can't smell methane, or see it. But it's highly inflammable . . . Inflammable means it burns very easily. A bit like the gas that comes out of gas cookers and gas fires. Sometimes methane builds up in enclosed places like caves —'

'And coalmines.'

'It can be very dangerous. It only needs a little spark, then —'

'Boom . . . Where's it come from then? Me-fane?'

'When things rot they produce methane. Or it occurs naturally in some places underground. Like your coalmine.'

David thought about the cellar beneath the sea-fort. He was about to ask Tony a question when Mark walked into the room.

Tony looked up.

'Any more?'

'No such luck. I don't know if those two on the causeway understood what we did to the others, but they're staying put. John Hodgson popped off a couple of shells at them but they're way out of range. If the tide wasn't in I'd go out and hit them close up.'

Then the big man turned and walked out of the room. Tony followed.

David guessed a lot had happened that morning. Important things. But the grown-ups had all ganged up together. They were keeping secrets from David.

'Coffee, Ruth?'

'Please . . . You couldn't rustle up a couple of fresh croissants too?'

'I'm expecting the delivery boy any moment.' Chris handed her the mug. 'You're entitled to one digestive biscuit now.

228

Or you can save up your ration and orgy on three biscuits tonight with a cup of hot chocolate.'

'Oh, I'll have it now. I'm starving.'

At least they could treat the rationing a little more flippantly now. After the success that morning, wiping out six Saf Dar in the space of a few minutes, the outlook looked brighter.

They joined Tony. The little Londoner sat on one of the cannon that Chris had bought from the Vicar. The Vicar himself walked unsteadily in the direction of the sea-fort building. Pissed again.

Tony had half finished his coffee and was smoking a cigar in nervous pulls.

'Went the day well?' Chris grinned. 'At this rate we'll have the lot in a day or two.'

'I hope so, Chris. I hope so.'

Ruth told Tony about the state of the food and water. There were adequate supplies for up to four days. Surely long before then the Saf Dar would be wiped from the surface of the earth and life could return to normal. Chris decided that as soon as it was over they would all drive over to Lincoln and feast on Big Macs as a special treat. Also he could call in on the architect and gee the man up to get the plans completed. This place had to be transformed into a thriving hotel within ten months. The days were beginning to slip by, bringing that deadline remorselessly closer.

He looked around the courtyard. Nothing, but nothing, could get in the way of his dream.

Mark looked over the wall at the two heads protruding from the water. He said to John Hodgson, 'I reckon I could wade out that far and blow their heads clean off at point-blank.'

'You'd be a dead fucker if you did. You can see those two sods plain enough; but what about them you can't? There'll be a couple more sat underwater waiting to grab any silly chuff's legs who tried to get across there.'

'I want to get out there. I want this place rid of them.'

'Aye, all in good time. It's when you take risks you start

losing people. They'll come back up to them gates. It pulls them like a bitch on heat pulls dogs from miles around. They can't stop themselves. And when they come it'll be like shooting rats in a tub.'

Mark Faust knew the farmer was right.

But for some reason he couldn't explain, he felt that time was running out.

39

Chris had fallen asleep where he sat on the courtyard floor, his back to the wall. The attack on the Saf Dar that morning had exhausted him. And when he woke he had that drugged feeling as if he and reality were still out of synch.

Tony stood looking down at him. A pair of binoculars dangled from one hand.

In a flattened way, Tony said, 'Come on.'

Chris pulled himself up, yawning into his hand, and followed Tony up the stone steps to the top of the wall. They were alone.

Without a lick of emotion, Tony said, 'Look.'

Chris looked out over the beach. The tide had retreated.

Then he saw what Tony had been scrutinising through the binoculars.

On the causeway, now high and dry, stood a dozen figures.

They stood in a domino-straight line, stretching back along the causeway, staring impassively at the sea-fort gates.

Saf Dar.

He looked at them in silence for a full two minutes before leaning forward, his elbow resting on the wall, his face nestled in the palm of his hand.

'Jesus . . . We've been wasting our time, haven't we?'

Tony nodded.

Chris stared at the figures. Of the twelve, five appeared as before. Naked bodies swollen tight with muscle, veins pushing through the skin; the skin that sunburn-red colour.

The other seven differed.

Different shades of red mottled their skin, anything from

231

small spots to large patches that covered half their bodies. This colouring possessed a shiny, fresh quality. The way skin looks when you pick off a scab too soon.

These seven were the seven they had 'killed'.

They had come back. And they didn't appear weakened by the furious blasting from shotguns or burning by petrol bombs. In fact, the latest growth of flesh that had infilled their wounds stood proud of the surrounding areas as if the new flesh had been infused with more power than the old.

And it had taken six hours.

Now they were back: fresh, strong, murderous.

'What does not kill me makes me stronger . . .' murmured Tony. 'Want these?' He offered the binoculars.

Chris shook his head. Whatever strength remained oozed from his body, leaving him empty.

'We failed, Tony.'

'We did our best. But there's something stronger behind all this. Can you sense it? That power I told you about? It's leaking through into this place now. You can feel it running through the stones. You know, like when you touch a water pipe with water rushing through it. You can feel the vibration.'

'What's it going to take to get rid of those things?'

'I'll tell you what we have to do. We'll have to drop this civilised pretence. This twentieth-century-man pose. We're going to have to do what our ancestors did.'

'Sacrifice?' Chris shook his head. The man was mad. 'Pick someone out? Then what? Knock out their brains? Skin them alive?'

'Chris, it's not as insane as it sounds. Look at every culture from the time that human beings stopped crapping in their own nests. Independently of each other, cultures have developed their own rites of sacrifice. Remember what I said. It was a trade, a barter. They were saying to their gods we give you food, or – or the life of my child. In return you give me something. A good harvest, success in war.'

Chris shut out the words. He could only stare with a

hypnotic intensity at the twelve figures strung out like red beads along the causeway. They, in turn, glared with chiselled Easter Island statue faces at the sea-fort gates as if willing them to crumble to dust.

As he watched, the others joined him and Tony on the wall. They watched the Saf Dar silently. Each of them must have realised that the ones with the sticky red patches were the ones burnt and shot to shreds that morning.

Then he heard a cry. The kind of cry someone would make if they had walked barefoot on broken glass.

Mark Faust. He lunged forward to the wall, his eyes bulging as he glared at the figures.

'No! No! No!' The violence in his voice shocked Chris. 'I won't let the bastards beat us! I won't.'

Jerking up the shotgun, he fired two shots as fast as his finger could snatch at the trigger. At this range the shot shredded a few scraps of seaweed on the causeway but not much else. Mark thrust the gun out for Chris to hold, then snatched another gun from John Hodgson to blaze off another two rounds.

The Saf Dar showed no reaction, even though some of the shot had struck them. From the bare shin of one a trickle of black ran down to pool on the causeway.

'Bastards . . . Bastards. They weren't stupid after all. They knew we could do nothing – not one little thing – to hurt them.'

For one terrifying moment Chris thought that Mark would throw open the gates and run out on to the causeway to attack them with his bare hands. His body shook with rage, his teeth were bared in a snarl, his eyes blazed.

But the moment passed as quickly as it had come. With a coughing cry he turned his back on them and sat down on the stone walkway, arms clutching his knees to his chest like a baby in its mother's womb.

Chris looked round at the drawn faces of the villagers as they watched the big man reduced to this.

Impotent. He had seen the word a million times before.

Now he knew what it really meant. It's the feeling that breaks you in two when something is going to happen and you know there's nothing in the world you can do to prevent it. Like a mother watching her baby dying of cancer. You can hold the baby in your arms; you can shout and swear at a heartless bastard of a god who let this happen. But there's nothing you can do to stop that tiny life slipping away through your fingers.

Watching Mark seemed somehow shameful. He turned back to watch the living statues who now ruled their lives. And tried not to listen to the sounds that Mark Faust was making.

40

Depression.

Hopelessness.

The villagers retreated into themselves. Most went back to the gun-deck room to stare into space.

Chris watched Ruth help David colour in a drawing.

He found it hard to think of anything else but water. What would they do when that ran out? He glanced out through the window at millions of tons of the stuff sliding backwards and forwards across the sands.

He purposefully turned his back on the window.

Just an hour before there had been a real mood of optimism. The things bled, they seemed to die. But their hopes had all been smashed to buggery. The things were immortal. We can make more petrol bombs, blast them with shotguns, stone them, but they'll keep coming back.

The one hope now was that someone from the outside would come.

From OUTSIDE.

Chris suddenly realised how odd that word sounded. Outside. The rest of the world – with streets, cafés, graffiti, crowded buses, parks; it all seemed so remote now. As if this bit of the world had somehow cracked away from Planet Earth.

Manshead had now become a borderland lying between the common-or-garden world they all knew and that place Tony had talked about. Where some . . . thing that the ancients had worshipped as a god stalked.

The mental video in his head played footage of a hungry

tiger restlessly pacing backward, forward, backward, behind the bars of a cage. The bars were all that separated it from its small territory of the cage and the sunny walkways of the zoo, filled with soft and tasty *Homo sapiens*. Easy meat. The bars of the cage were growing flimsy now.

'Dad, when are we going down the cellar?'

'Not now, David. Some time soon, eh?'

'Dad . . .'

'Don't worry, kidda. We'll go down and have a good explore when we get the chance.'

'But I've been down there tons of times. I want to show you something. It's dead interesting.'

'You've been down before? When?'

Ooops! David realised he shouldn't have told him. After all, he wasn't allowed down in the cellar.

'Just a few times. It's great down there.'

His dad was definitely not smiling. 'What's down there, David?'

'Come on, I'll show you.'

David grabbed him by the hand and pulled him to the door.

In the corridor they met Tony. His face was red and he was panting.

'Another one, Chris.'

'What?'

'Mrs Christopher. She tried to . . .' He noticed David. 'She tried to end things.' Tony turned and spoke in a low voice that David wasn't supposed to hear – but he did. 'In the toilet. Plastic bag over the head, tied a ribbon round her neck to seal it.'

'Suffocated?'

'Damn well nearly succeeded, too. Ruth found her just in time.'

'Go play, David, there's a good lad. We'll go down later, eh?'

Then his dad and Tony hurried away.

* * *

Life went on.

In a slow, half-hearted kind of way.

That evening the LPG bottle that fuelled the caravan's gas cooker ran dry. Tony helped Chris to change it. They manhandled the empty bottle through the doors into the sea-fort building, along the stone-flagged corridor and into one of the store rooms. In here were another five of the blue metal cylinders, all full and each almost the size of Tony Gateman.

Five full cylinders, thought Chris. A lot of gas. Enough to last well into the summer. If we live that long.

A lot of gas. He turned an idea over in his mind like an archaeologist examining a new artefact. A lot of gas.

'You know, Tony, before the fresh water runs out we could rig up something to distil sea water. That way we'd have an unlimited supply. We're already bringing it up by the bucketful on a line when the tide's in.'

'It's an idea.' Tony's lack of enthusiasm was hardly subtle. He wasn't interested in turning sea water into drinking water.

What was wrong with the man? Didn't he want to survive?

'I'll start looking round for some tubing. See if I can rig something up.'

Tony simply nodded as he helped him hoist one of the full gas cylinders upright.

As they got ready to drag the cylinder to the caravan, Tony looked up at Chris and asked, 'Did you hear a sound?'

'A sound? What kind of sound?'

'It doesn't matter. It's nothing . . . Come on.'

In silence they pulled the full cylinder out through the doorway, the metal base making a rasping sound that rumbled down through the corridor, like the respiration of some great animal waking from a deep sleep.

Mark Faust pulled the blanket over his shoulders. Only half-past seven in the evening, but nonetheless he tried to sleep.

He lay on his side on the stone floor in the gundeck room, one arm pillowing his head.

237

Outside, the mist imperceptibly shifted down from white to grey as, unseen, the sun slipped below the horizon.

Inside, the Reverend Reed snored thickly in the corner, his face red from the gin. Maybe he had the right idea. Sweet oblivion.

Mark now appreciated the attraction of killing yourself. Dead, you feel no more pain, or distress or misery.

The Christopher woman, when they had brought her round after tearing the plastic bag from her head, had given such a groan of disappointment at having life thrust back at her that it made him wonder if they had done the right thing. Maybe they should have just turned away and left her.

Then again, maybe if he had never left the States everything would have been different. MAYBE. The world was full of maybes. Maybe if Hitler had died in that gas attack in World War I; maybe if Charlie Manson had stopped a Vietcong bullet with his face; maybe if it rained for a year in Ethiopia and turned the deserts green; maybe if he had stayed at home in Boston, USA, he would be sitting in front of the TV now with a beer. A wife cooking him supper. A daughter on a date. A son practising power chords on an electric guitar in the garage with a couple of friends. MAYBE . . . Those kind of maybes were as hard as the nails going through Christ's hands and feet into the solid God-given wood.

He rolled over on to his back, trying to sleep.

He felt like the condemned criminal, lying caged in his cell, waiting for the last walk down to old Sparky. This was a post mortem existence. Waiting, waiting, waiting.

When would the end come?

Problem: remember Wainwright and Fox?

Death would be no ending, no finality.

It would be the beginning of something else.

They would wake up on the beach. With new companions.

The radio should have been an ear to the outside. News reports, music, weather bulletins, time checks. The sounds of a normal world.

After five minutes, Ruth switched it off. She had scanned every wavelength from AM to FM. All that came from the speakers was the hiss of static. Which sounded very much like the surf that beat upon the beach.

Chris had been shifting junk in one of the store rooms, looking for an axe-head to hammer on to the shaft he had armed himself with. That's when he saw the thing on the wall.

Despite his exhaustion he had shot backwards from a crouching position like an athlete.

'Jesus Christ.'

With an involuntary movement of disgust he covered his face with his hands. Then, swallowing down the unpleasant taste in his mouth, he looked again.

There, stuck to the wall, was a cluster of growths the colour and texture of white cheese, the largest the size of a dinner plate.

What the growths actually were he did not know. But he knew what they looked like.

Clinging there, to the stone wall, just inches away from him, was a human face.

Later, he sat on the caravan steps, tapping nails into the end of the axe-handle. He'd not been able to find an axe-head but he'd found a huge hammer-head caked in rust and mould. Its solid cast-iron weight, as big as two fists side by side, felt reassuring. Ruth leaned against the caravan wall, a cardigan round her shoulders against the chill night air. They talked in half-whispers.

'What are we going to do, Chris? David's six years old. He's just a baby.'

He said nothing; he tapped another nail into the end of the shaft to secure the hammer-head.

'Chris, we can't go on like this. Have you seen how much water is left in —'

'I know, Ruth. I know . . . I've tried to talk to Mark and

239

Tony. I said we needed to rig up some apparatus so we can distil fresh water from sea water.'

'And what did they say?'

'Sod all. Mark's retreated into himself – depressed. He blames himself for not being able to kill those things out there. Gateman seems content to sit and wait for some kind of supernatural cavalry to come charging across the sand.'

'And what do you think, Chris?'

'As Mark said when – if – it comes, this supernatural power, the first to grab it is going to be the winner.'

'But we don't know how to do that.'

'By sacrifice, according to Tony. We give something so we can get something in return. In this case that bucketful of miracles Gateman goes on about.'

'What do we sacrifice?'

'Search me.'

'Has Tony said any more about this sacrifice thing, Chris?'

Chris turned round to look at her, standing there in the near-dark. He could no longer see her face, but he sensed something immense troubling her. She wasn't asking him these questions because she didn't know what Tony had said; she knew well enough. He realised that his wife was using the questions to direct his train of thought.

Sacrifice.

It always came back to that. As if sacrifice was the only solution. Sacrifice. It was unthinkable. He could not even accept the idea of it. It was as if his mind were a computer into which someone was struggling to insert a new programme. It refused the reprogramming. This mind would not load that barbaric concept. It belonged in the tomb with those long-dead men and women who had practised it.

Chris changed the subject.

'Is David asleep?'

'He should be. I left him looking at a comic, but he's exhausted.'

His wife pulled the cardigan closer around her shoulders and shivered. 'Perhaps someone will come, Chris. It's Monday

240

tomorrow. There have to be deliveries to the village. It's not as if we're on an island.'

No, we're not an island, thought Chris, but for all the contact we have with the outside world we might as well be on the dark side of the fucking moon.

He tapped the final nail into the wood.

41

'Oh God! Get it away, get it away!'

Screaming.

'God! Oh God, oh God, oh God, God, God, God . . . Please . . .Oh – oh . . .'

Ruth was first to reach the screaming woman as she ran from the sea-fort building. Immediately she stopped screaming but clutched the side of her head and sobbed breathlessly.

Chris didn't know the woman's name; she was in her mid-fifties, very thin, with tied-back grey hair.

A couple of the other villagers came to see the cause of the commotion, but significantly most didn't bother to rouse themselves from their apathetic slumbers.

Tony Gateman, who had been standing on top of the wall, came puffing down the steps, his face red beneath the thickening stubble on his cheeks.

'What happened?'

'I'm not sure,' said Ruth, holding the sobbing woman.

Chris immediately thought the woman had found someone who had succeeded in committing suicide, but all she could pant out was that she'd seen something.

'Get her into the caravan.' Ruth sounded in control. 'We'll get her a drink . . . She's calming down now.'

Ten minutes later, a blanket round her shoulders, cupping a steaming mug of tea in her hands, she was able to talk.

She had been to the toilet, one of the old ones in the sea-fort building. When she had finished she had looked down into the bowl as she got ready to pour down a jug of sea-water to flush it. The waste from the toilets simply discharged via a wide-bore pipe straight into the sea.

What she had seen there had nearly paralysed her heart.

Squeezing up around the U-bend as tightly as a rat squeezing through a piece of hose had been a human face. Chris imagined a flat, expressionless face squeezing up through the hole through three pints of water and urine in the bottom of the bowl.

It had been the strange, flattened face of a girl, its eyes as dull as those of a dead fish on a slab.

She hadn't remembered much after that.

Later, Tony had muttered, 'Hysterical. Seen her reflection in her own piss.'

Chris knew that Tony had himself been unconvinced by this explanation. The woman had seen something. And he remembered what he had seen in the old store room. The face glued there to the wall.

He had bitten back the foul taste of bile in his mouth and pulled together enough resolve to examine it. The white stuff (he guessed it to be a fungus) had grown in the shape of a human face. A smooth white man's forehead, two eyes – lightly closed like a sleeper's – smoothly sculpted nose, two even lips. He recalled the marble heads of Greek gods.

Surrounding it was a constellation of other white blobs, each one a clone-line copy of the large face, right down to the ones the size of a little fingernail. High white forehead, eyes, nose, lips. A dozen perfect white faces.

As he watched, he had noticed a faint shiver. They were alive.

When Mrs Hodgson came to sit with the woman, Ruth and Chris went up to the toilet the woman had used. He carried the massive hammer in one hand.

The white-washed room, bare apart from the old china high-flush toilet, looked normal. In one corner lay the plastic jug and a pool of sea water was spreading across the stone slabs.

But no face.

A prickle of goosebumps rashed across his skin. He thought about the pathetic bastard on the beach; a mixture of shellfish and human, crushed together then fired into an agonising kind of life. Maybe out there under the sea near the outflow pipe someone had drowned by the lair of an eel. One of those thick-bodied congers. He imagined a human head mashed together with the conger body, thicker than a man's neck. He thought about the long snake-like body worming up through the sewage pipe.

Quickly he picked up a bucket of sea-water and dumped it on to the piss in the white bowl. On top of that he poured half a bottle of bleach. Then he and his wife walked quickly away without looking back.

Midday. Chris restlessly paced the walkway running around the top of the wall when he heard the noise.

He immediately ran to the point where the wall passed over the gates and peered into the mist. The tide had begun its inward roll once more. Waves frothed around the base of the sea-fort and along the flanks of the causeway, but the causeway itself was still dry.

The sound went as quickly as it had begun. He couldn't be sure what it was, muffled as it had been by the banks of dunes. He leaned forward. Below, on the ledge of rock that extended a yard or so beyond the walls, stood eight reddish figures. They were doing nothing – just following the old statue routine.

He looked back down into the courtyard. No one about. Everyone it seemed had slipped back into their navel-contemplating mode after a lunch that was getting smaller each day.

The sound came again, a high wailing, swelling then falling across the dunes, growing louder. It was . . .

It was a motor. A car. He leaned forward, craning his head to one side to scoop more of the thin sound into his ear.

A car. A bloody car! He gripped the wall hard.

No siren, though. Not police. Maybe the Army. Christ, someone was coming to get them out of this hell. He willed into his mind the image of massive armoured personnel carriers lumbering round the coast road and through the gap in the dunes on to the beach.

He listened hard. The sound of the engine sounded too high-pitched. As if being driven frantically at too high a speed in too low a gear. Surely whoever it was would have to stop at the barrier of pebbles that blocked the coast road.

No. It got closer. Louder. Someone was coming.

The mental video clicked on and Chris pictured some terrified postman racing his van along the coast road after coming across Out-Butterwick – deserted, *Marie-Celeste*-like, doors flapping open in the sea breeze.

No. Not this way. Go back. Bring help.

The car's engine howled as it powered through the gap in the dunes then skidded sidewards off the road and on to the sand.

From this distance, the mist fuzzed the lines of the car. But he could see that the passenger door was missing.

That it was a white Ford Fiesta.

Shit.

A weight dropped into his stomach.

Shit, no.

The car was Wainwright's. The one that had been abandoned in the village's main street. He couldn't see the driver. But he could guess who was at the wheel.

The sound of the engine being revved ragged rolled down the beach, howling like a beast of burden being flogged until it bled.

The white car lurched forward, engine shrieking, then stopped again, still on the beach, just feet away from the road that linked the causeway to the coast road.

'Go away.' Understanding began to seep into his mind. 'Go away.'

Again the engine howled as the driver crushed the pedal to the carpet. The car pulled to the right then moved slowly forward in a juddering motion. The front wheels, spinning like fury in the loose sand, sent spurts back over the car like the plume from a whale.

For some reason the yellow hazard lights began to blink on and off like the slow wink of some nightmare lizard, pulsing a blurred yellow through the mist.

The car juddered across the sand, then, savagely, jerked forward as the front tyres bumped up on to the raised roadway.

For a second he thought the car had stuck there, front wheels screaming in a craze of blue smoke and sand, dragging the car sideways in a useless crab motion.

'Bog down, you bastard,' he hissed, leaning forward, gripping the top of the wall, willing whatever drove the thing to fail. 'Bog down!'

No gods listened to Chris that day.

With an explosive jerk the rear wheels bumped up on to the roadway. The one-litre engine howled in a painfully high-pitched whine.

Then the car was moving.

Really moving this time.

Horrified, he watched as it blasted along the road, then on to the causeway, yellow hazards flashing, weaving from side to side, bumping across the cobbles like a racing car across a rutted track.

His mouth dried.

He stared, unable to move or take his eyes from the ton of steel and rubber and fuel barrelling along the causeway at sixty miles an hour. Blue smoke spurted from the ruptured exhaust. The thing, unsilenced, sounded more like a motorbike wound up to a frenzy of clattering pistons and howling transmission.

Chris now knew what the Saf Dar intended.

They had turned Wainwright's car into a battering ram. In ten seconds it would hit the sea-fort gates like a guided missile.

The Saf Dar waited on the fringe of rock below.

This was it. Chris chewed his lip. Events were rushing to a climax. He could do nothing. The Saf Dar would flood into the sea-fort grinding the life out of every man, woman and —

His eyes locked on to the car as it weaved at seventy along the slippery cobbles, the slipstream blasting away clumps of black kelp.

Oh death, sweet death, where are you now?

End it . . . end it . . . Surely they can't keep even you away for ever.

But the grim reaper had been booted out by something a million times more powerful. Death's a has-been, death's a loser, death's on the dole . . .

These swollen red men are going to rule . . . They won't let us die.

He watched in a trance, his brain icing.

There was Wainwright at the wheel of the swaying car, one hand casually on the steering wheel as if driving down to the bank to count money; head rolling loosely from side to side, crimson growths mushrooming from the split in his head, his mouth hanging open as if he'd seen something that had surprised him.

Then, thank Christ . . . God . . . or some age-crusted god from beyond the beyond.

The car hit a blanket of seaweed and slid, howling madly, to one side.

Dead Wainwright compensated.

Over-compensated.

The car veered to the right across the causeway, clean off the roadway.

For seconds, whole seconds, the fucking machine flew, tail-end flipping up, lights winking yellow, then splash —

— it hit the sea, dug down through the skin of salt water, slamming into the sand below. It cartwheeled in a fury of foam and spray; ninety pounds of gouged-up sand and seashells splattered high into the air like a depth-charge explosion; spinning rubber, then —

— then silence. It lay belly-up in the sea. Cold water steamed from the hot metal; the back wheels still turned but the front wheels had gone, along with most of the engine, radiator and front wings.

The silence caused by the suddenly killed motor hurt Chris's ears.

The car had come to a rest alongside the causeway, just twenty paces from the gates.

Christ, if it had hit . . . We would have been lucky to last ten minutes.

He noticed a shape slide away from the wrecked car. And caught a glimpse of white bandage trailing slowly through the surf. However broken up he must be, the Saf Dar weren't letting Wainwright die.

He'd be back. Along with the rest of them. And the swollen red man-monsters still stood on the rock below.

'Look,' Chris told the half-dozen or so villagers who were peering down at the wrecked car now being washed by the surf. 'We need someone up here at all times. Armed.' Oil leaking from the cracked motor painted a rainbow sheen on the surface of the water. 'If the car had hit those gates, it would have bust them wide open, and . . . and to put it bluntly we wouldn't be standing here talking now. Those things down there would have been in to slaughter the rest of us.'

Without much interest Tony Gateman asked, 'What do you propose?'

'I propose, Tony, a rota. Someone up here with a shotgun. Also I propose to reinforce the gates with the pile of bricks in the courtyard. Thirdly, I propose we have a fall-back position in case those things break through the gates. Christ, Tony, they only have to get lucky once. How many cars are there left in the village for them to try this trick again?'

Chris forced himself to stay calm. But it was getting tough. After the attempted gate-ram he had gone round trying to get everyone to come up and see what had happened. Hardly anyone had bothered. The villagers wanted only to stare into space.

Mark Faust had been worse. The big man lay beneath his blanket in the gundeck room, eyes shut, eating nothing, saying nothing.

It had taken Ruth five minutes of solid persuasion to get Tony Gateman up here.

Tony sniffed and gazed down at the car as the surf rolled over it with a roar. The man looked divorced from reality.

'Tony,' prodded Chris, 'we need to make plans in case the gates are broken down and those things get inside. We need to barricade the lower windows of the sea-fort. There has to be some way of defending the doors of the building.'

Ruth added, 'Also we need a barrier up here so they can't get on to the roof of the sea-fort.'

'The sea-fort gates are that thick.' Tony held up a finger and thumb with a gap wide enough to accommodate a hefty dictionary. 'The doors of the building are less than a quarter of that. If the Saf Dar took a rock to them, I imagine they'd hold out two or three hours.'

'So what do you suggest, Tony?'

'Chris, I suggest we don't bother.'

'What? Not bother to try and survive? Are you serious?'

'Chris, I don't know if you've noticed, but . . . Can't you feel it? Can't you feel the tension building in the air? Oppressive, like a thunderstorm?'

'So?'

'So the time's almost come. That entity, the old god, it's going to be here in a matter of hours.'

'What good will that do us if we're like Wainwright, Fox and the rest? Zombies?'

Tony began to walk towards the steps. 'We need to make preparations. All the villagers know what they have to do.'

Chris hissed, 'We're back to sacrifice again – that primitive crap.'

'Primitive yes, crap no. These people know what they have to do. Yes, sacrifice. No, Chris, not because I told them, but because they know instinctively what to do. It's born inside of us. Like a baby's born with the inbred ability to mimic its parents, so it can learn to talk and hold a spoon. We're born knowing about the need to sacrifice. Don't fight it, Chris. Allow it to flow up from your unconscious.

Ask David. He'll know. Children do. Ask him if he's destroyed any of his favourite toys lately and not known why. Ask him, Chris. Ask him, Ruth.'

Chris remembered David leaving his favourite comics and toys on a rock for the sea.

'You're talking crap, Tony. Look, we need to keep this place safe.' He turned to the elder Hodgson men. They were farmers. Down to earth. Pigs and muck were their lives. Chris appealed to them.

'You'll help keep guard, won't you?'

Their eyes shied away. He realised they had swallowed Tony Gateman's get-ready-for-the-coming-of-the-olde-worlde-pagan-god sales talk.

'You'll help, won't you?'

'Oh, aye.' John Hodgson glanced at his brother. 'Aye, we'll help.'

Chris turned back to Tony to ask him again, but the little Londoner was walking down the steps as quickly as he could.

But Tony was right about the growing tension.

Chris heard raised voices coming from one of the sea-fort rooms. Arguments were springing up among the villagers like fires spontaneously igniting on a dry moor.

He passed the Major pacing restlessly about the courtyard with Mac. The dog turned in circles, pawed the cobbles, its claws scratching noisily, coughing out high-pitched yelps.

One of the Hodgson boys sat astride his motorbike. Chris watched him start it, then sit there pointlessly revving it. The dog yelped louder. The sound of the revving motor would provoke more arguments.

Chris, tense, tapped the long shaft of the hammer against his leg.

The pressure was building. There was no safety valve. Something would have to burst soon.

That night the dead who should have stayed dead came back. Chris watched them emerge from the dense blanket of mist, to stalk the sands. Wainwright looked crooked now. Fox was beginning to swell like his brother. The little drowned boy ran ahead of them.

Dotted here and there, kneeling on the beach, the Saf Dar stared at the sea-fort, milk-white eyes gleaming unnaturally bright in the dark.

He had told himself over and over that the Saf Dar were stupid, animal-like things, following some residual craving for death and mutilation.

Now he wasn't so sure.

Yes, they still hated. But their eyes seemed to glint with a sinister intelligence.

Yes, they had stood and allowed themselves to be burnt and blasted by shotguns. But it hadn't hurt them. No, they were not stupid; just confident.

All they needed to do was sit there patiently on the sands.

When the time was ready to kill . . .

Then they would kill.

And no fucker on earth would get in their way.

He walked round the top of the sea-fort walls. John Hodgson, shotgun in hand, nodded a greeting, then turned back to watch the figures walking through the mist.

This time Wainwright, the Foxes and their kind did not stop and cry in agonised voices; they walked right up to the gates.

Then they battered at them with their bare hands. Close up he could see the tumorous growths that erupted from their flesh.

He ran down to the courtyard, to watch as the gates rattled and shook as they were battered and shoved by more than twenty dead/alive men from the other side.

Bolts and padlock shivered as the gates swung inward an inch then sprang back. If the gates should give way, thought Chris, there's nothing between those things and my wife and son but me.

Just what the hell could I do?

I wouldn't even be able to die a martyr. I would end up like

Wainwright or one of those raw bastard things that were a mess of human flesh and shellfish.

He walked towards the trembling gates. If he reached out to push them back it would be a futile gesture. But anything was better than this morbid impotence.

He stood there, feeling the shocks transmitted through the wood shiver up his arms like a series of rapid electric shocks. He pictured the bare fists, palms, swollen knuckles cracking against the thick timbers. Did they feel anything? Did they want to turn and run for a home that might no longer even exist? They were held there only by the will of the Saf Dar. Forced to do things they did not want to do.

Once more Chris felt his mind slipping.

Was he inside, an ordinary man, with a wife, and one son, holding the doors, knowing he had no chance of keeping them shut if the bolts should snap?

Or was he outside, bare feet on cold stone, beating with his bare hands (look, look, they are changing every day now, bigger and bigger, tighter and tighter, veins bulging out like knotted ropes through the backs), beating the gates with bare hands, wanting to get in, to drag out those soft-bodied people, with their cool, cool skins; throw them at the red men on the beach who rule . . .

Making our minds turn and turn faster and faster so we don't know where to run. One minute wanting to run home; the next to grab and beat and kill the men and women in the stone house on the beach . . .

Kill, kill, kill, kill, kill . . . We want to force our fingers inside your bodies . . . kill . . . kill . . .

Home . . . go home . . . want to go home . . .

Chris blinked the sweat from his eyes. Why was he pushing the sea-fort gates? There was nothing there.

Then he remembered. The dead had been there trying to force their way in.

He dropped his aching arms and shook his head. It felt as if he had woken from a dream.

Flexing his stiff fingers, he went back to the caravan and to bed, beside his sleeping wife and son.

Even though Chris was not sure whether he was fully awake or not, a vivid dream streamed through his head.

'They're in . . . they're in . . . They're in . . .'

Someone shouted, their voice echoing off the walls of the sea-fort.

The Saf Dar moved as smoothly and silently as panthers through the open gates.

For what seemed hours he ran around the sea-fort looking for David and Ruth. Anger burned into him like splashes of molten metal on bare skin. Why hadn't he planned a hiding place in the sea-fort?

The Saf Dar breaking in . . . It was inevitable. He should have known. He should have made some kind of bolt-hole in the cellar. David would have shown him where.

But why had David gone down there?

'David . . . David, where are you?'

David knew all about what lay in the mysterious cellar beneath the sea-fort. For some reason Chris had never been able to go down there. He should have.

He was running in his pyjamas through the labyrinth of passages. Then he was out in the open air, mist rolling like surf through the open gates.

The car. In the car sat David and Ruth. Just as they would when they were going to the shops. David in the back reading a comic, Ruth patiently wearing the seatbelt.

He tried to shout but he couldn't.

He ran to the car, started the engine.

The tide was out as he drove the car furiously out through the gates and along the causeway. No. The coast road is blocked.

All he could do was drive up and down the beach, skidding the car into tight turns before he reached the boulders that blocked the northern end of the beach. Then south towards Out-Butterwick where the stream cut through the sand. Too deep for the car to cross. He would drive back.

While he drove, they were safe. The Saf Dar would not catch them. He glanced back at David, still reading the comic; then across to Ruth at his side, combing her hair.

Chris ached inside. He wanted to tell them how much danger they were in; and how much he loved them. But he had to focus all his concentration on the expanse of sand in front of him – avoid the rocks, avoid the deep pools of sea water; avoid the men standing on the beach.

The needle on the gauge dropped lower and lower into the red. The engine choked away, leaving the car to coast, its tyres rumbling across hard ridges of sand. Slower, slower . . .

Slower . . .

Stop.

Lock the doors . . . Close the windows . . . They're coming . . .

No escape now.

They're crowding around the car. Red, bulging faces pressed to the windows, pressing harder. Harder until stars appear in the glass as it cracks beneath their pushing faces. Those thick red hands reaching into where . . .

'Chris . . . Wake up.'

Chris jerked up, his heart cracking into his ribs like a power hammer.

'You all right?'

'He saw his wife's silhouette in the gloom, dark hair falling forward; her fingers stroked his forehead.

'Yes . . . Just a dream. I'll be all right. Lie down and get some sleep.'

Chris lay back, the sweat turning chilly on his face.

Only a dream . . .

It seemed more like a premonition.

42

'Now . . . Listen to me. Every one of you. There's no reason for anyone to get hurt, if we're all careful; don't do anything stupid. We will all get out of here safely.'

The Major held up his finger to emphasise the point. Then he continued with a story of some jungle campaign in Asia.

They were standing on the walkway that ran round the seawall.

Tom and John Hodgson were there, with Tony Gateman (he was a reluctant participant) and Ruth. Chris had been explaining how they would lower buckets on lines to fill them with sea water. Then the Major had ambled up, holster belt still around his thin waist, the dog bringing up the rear. The old man looked tired and more confused than ever. You could hardly blame the poor sod, thought Chris, sleeping on stone floors, and with dwindling rations of food, some of which he must have shared with the dog.

'We need to mount the machine-guns. Here and here.' The old soldier pointed. 'I'll see that the quartermaster issues each man with hand grenades.'

This was largely a replay of what the Major had said to Chris a couple of days before.

Chris wanted to say there were no machine-guns, no hand grenades, no flame-throwers, no platoon of highly trained commandos. There were three shotguns, the Major's old revolver, which might not even work, three ancient cannon that had been used for fence-posts for a hundred years, and twenty frightened villagers. Most over fifty. Some sick. And certainly one senile old soldier.

'Now what you civilians have got to do is keep your heads down. Those beggars are damn good with a rifle. They'll be sniping at us from the dunes yonder. Now if I can find Corporal White, I'll have him whistle up the artillery and they can put down a pattern of twenty-pounders. That'll spoil their aim a bit, eh?'

Chris noticed the Reverend Reed waiting conspicuously at the end of the walkway. Odd, because he rarely made it up on to the wall. Usually too pissed.

Even more unusually the man carried a large black book that could only have been the Bible.

Chris wondered if the man was working up to a sermon against the villagers' pagan leanings.

As the Major talked, Chris watched the Vicar sliding along the wall towards them.

The old priest looked ill. From his face flared two red-rimmed eyes; the man's lips were cracked and dry, covered with flaking pieces of skin.

'Padre,' acknowledged the Major with a nod, and walked away to rally his imaginary troops.

The Reverend Reed hugged the Bible to his chest and glared at them. His voice was a dry-throat whisper:

'Why have you ignored me?'

Chris, Ruth and Tony exchanged puzzled glances.

'We haven't,' said Ruth gently.

'Oh . . . You have, you know, my dear. The times I've watched you all. Huddled away as thick as thieves, whispering away.'

The Vicar caught Chris's expression. 'No, I'm not mad. Or even drunk this time . . . wish I was. No. Listen to me.' Tony had begun to turn away. 'Listen to me, Mr Gateman. I've had to be content to stand by and allow you to treat me like some innocent virgin while you gossiped about sex . . . Now isn't that true, Mr Gateman? Mr and Mrs Stainforth? You've not once asked me to contribute to your secret little meetings. Why? Because I am what they call a man of the cloth? Because I would be shocked by what you had to say about the nature of this place? About that man's beliefs.' He used the Bible to point at Tony.

Chris spoke. 'Look, Reverend . . . We haven't questioned your beliefs. All I'm interested in is keeping us alive. You know we are low on food and fresh water. What I'm —'

'Listen . . .' Tony interrupted. 'The times, Reverend Reed, I have tried to tell you what was happening here at Manshead. That there was some . . . force building. That this was a pagan holy place. But you closed your mind to it. You fucking well didn't want to know. Now it's coming. And there's nothing you, your Bible, your candles, your fucking holy water can do about it. Now if you want to hide your head in the sand, be my guest.'

'Good heavens. I am not saying I do not believe you, Mr Gateman. That is just the point. Look at me.' He held out his trembling hands, the Bible almost slipping from his fingers. 'Look at me. Gateman, I am admitting I am wrong.' He held up the Bible above his head. 'How many times have I read this? How many years have I believed? Since I was a tiny child! How many years did I study at theological college? How many sermons have I written? How many baptisms, weddings, funerals, harvest festivals? Christian ritual after Christian ritual. And now at last I stand on top of this wall and say here in this place I have been wasting my life. Because I know this' – he slapped his palm down on to the Bible. – 'I know this does not matter here. It is irrelevant. It may as well be written in Chinese. Because time and time again here I've had my nose rubbed in the truth. And that truth is that my Christ, my saviour, my God has no jurisdiction in this place. The father, the son and the Holy Ghost are not here. They never have been here! What rules absolutely is Gateman's ugly old god. The foul pagan thing that has made this place its own garden.' He paused, his eyes watering. 'And yes, I admit it, we belong to that ugly, ugly old god.'

Suddenly, with a ferocious swing of his arm, he hurled the Bible over the wall. It hung for a second in the misty air, its pages flicking through from Genesis to Revelation. Then it dropped down to the sea.

The man leant back against the wall, his arms wrapped around his body as if trying to comfort the frightened child that must still be there inside him. He breathed deeply. 'Listen to me . . . I believe in the power of this pagan . . . beast. Maybe my God is dead, Mr Gateman. But I know yours is very much alive. I can feel it here.' He tapped his chest. 'It is coming here. Soon. And I know what must be done. You must make that sacrifice. You have to sacrifice as our forefathers did. You have to pay the price to the old god: render unto Caesar that which is Caesar's.' The old man looked steadily at Chris for a moment with raw eyes that bled pure pain.

Then the old priest said simply: 'You have to give the thing what it wants.'

43

Edgy.

Very edgy.

Like a bunch of kids before Christmas Day.

They found it hard to sit still now. They paced the floor
of the gun-room or stared expectantly out of the panoramic
window over the mist-shrouded sea.

Chris had been trying to persuade Mark to help them with
his plan to distil sea water into fresh water, but the big
man had not replied. He lay on the stone floor under his
blanket, not eating, not drinking.

Chris looked round at the twenty or so villagers restlessly
pacing away the hours until . . .

Until what?

He wasn't sure whether or not he preferred their silent
apathy. At least when they were like stuffed dummies they
didn't make him edgy. Why stare out of the window like
that? There was nothing to see. Just a few acres of lumpish
salt water. The mist effectively sealed them within a great
white-walled box. Now, it seemed, nothing lay beyond it.

The Major stood peering out, his dog walking around him,
its bright eyes looking up at his master's face.

He felt a stab of sudden irrational anger towards the
villagers. No, it wasn't irrational, it was rational. Here he and
Ruth were, flogging their guts out to keep these ungrateful
bastards alive. This is our home. Our food. No one offers to
help.

He shot an angry look around the roomful of people. Faust
pining away beneath his blanket; the mad Major with his

261

fucking useless dog; the idiot Tamworth girl playing with a grubby doll; the landlord of the Harbour Tavern, arms folded over his massive gut, mist-watching with half a dozen others.

As he turned and walked from the room, his face burning with repressed fury, the thought occurred to him that maybe he should turf the bastards out on to the beach and let them fend for themselves.

Outside, Gateman sat on one of the cannon, smoking one of his panatella cigars. Got a nice little supply, hasn't he? Couldn't the selfish little sod have brought something useful? Chris snatched up the huge hammer he'd left by the sea-fort doors; his eyes raked the courtyard. Soon they would have to do something to protect themselves. If not they would all die here.

Christ, why did I let Ruth talk me into bringing the worthless bunch of peasants back here? Some small voice at the back of his head questioned whether this anger was really justified. Or was the thing that drove the others to endlessly pace the room or fire their tempers now beginning to have the same effect on him?

Repressing the voice, he walked across to the caravan. He owed himself a coffee.

'You've got to help us.'

The figure Chris crouched beside did not move. Mark's eyes were shut as he lay on his side, one arm pillowing his head.

'It's no use,' whispered Ruth. 'Don't push him.'

'But we've got to do something. We're running short of food and water.'

'Why do you think Tony isn't making any suggestions? You know he'll have thought it all through. There's nothing we can do.'

It was as if they were parents arguing in whispers over their sleeping baby, although Chris knew that Mark Faust wasn't asleep. He knew everything that was going on around them – the villagers eating their little puddle of baked beans and sausage on paper plates; Ruth and Chris's hissed conversation above him.

'We can't kill them.' Ruth sounded exhausted. 'We've tried and tried and we can't.'

'I know, but—'

'But we can do nothing, Chris. Just wait. Perhaps someone will come from the outside and raise the alarm. Then, yes, thank God, we can leave that lot out there for someone else to deal with. Until then—'

'No . . . We've got to do something. We ought to be sitting down thinking how to get a message out. We need to bring help . . .'

'You sit down, Chris. You work it out. I'm going to sit down before I fall down.'

There was the sound of tired feet plodding away. Then the grate of heavier feet turning on the gritty floor. And slowly walking away.

From the top of the sea-fort building, Chris watched the dark figures on the beach in the evening gloom. Streaming great clouds of fog rolled in from the ocean like a more nebulous surf.

He chewed the knuckle of his index finger. There had to be a way out of this. There had to be a way.

Think, you stupid bastard – think . . .

You've got to find a way to save your home and your wife and your son.

Think . . . think . . . think . . .

Early evening.

In the gundeck room, six-year-old David was having a one-sided conversation with the big figure beneath the blanket.

'Why don't grown-ups tell children what's going on?' David crouched, his hands resting on his knees. 'I know something's happened. Bad people won't let us out of here, will they?'

The big shape under the blanket didn't move.

Behind David the Major's dog yelped. The people stood looking out of the big windows over the gundeck. But you couldn't see anything. David had looked. There was only a bit of sea water and mist. Anyone would think that the most interesting thing in the world was going to jump up out of the water.

'I wish Tony would have a barbecue again. It was brilliant. All that pop and crisps and burgers. And you pushed me on that swing. Is it still there, Mark?'

The only bit of Mark that showed was the black hair sticking out of the blanket and one hand, fingers half curled.

'Because someone's not letting us out, we can't go to the shops, can we? So we can't buy any food. I'm hungry a lot now. But I'm not telling Mum, because she'll worry. You see, there's not much left in the pantry. I know it's not my mum or dad's fault. It's those bad men outside. So I'm going to go to bed now. I won't feel hungry if I'm asleep.' He stood up. ' 'Night, Mark.'

David left the gundeck and walked out into the evening gloom. It was quiet. His dad sat alone on the stone steps. Thinking.

In the caravan bedroom David pulled off his sweatshirt and jeans and put on his pyjamas. Out of habit he went into the lounge and tried the television. It didn't work, of course. No electricity.

He wished he could watch one of his Superman videos. It might make him feel better. The meals were so small; he felt hungry all the time. And he'd heard his mum making a noise last night. At first he hadn't been able to tell what it was. But it had gone on and on and on.

Then he had recognised the sound.

She was crying.

Chris had been sitting for a good half-hour on the stone steps, trying to hammer out an idea that would get them away from the sea-fort. It could only be a matter of time now before the Saf Dar managed to get inside.

As he thought, he allowed his eyes to travel up from the cobbled yard towards the doors into the sea-fort building. As he looked, a massive figure moved out from the shadows, swaying weirdly as if walking was something new and strange.

He jerked to his feet in a single spasmodic movement.

Jesus, they're inside! The thought cracked through his head like an executioner's bullet.

Then the towering figure moved slowly into the foggy evening light.

Mark Faust. The figure walked with a swaying motion; life was only just returning to its limbs. Chris looked across to where Tony Gateman sat huddled on one of the cannon. He too had noticed his old friend . . . the big man had come back to life. Now he moved with a purpose in mind.

Mark headed straight for the caravan, where Ruth was boiling water for an ever-weaker coffee.

Chris followed the big man inside.

Mark looked around the caravan slowly, his face drawn, the stubble now a beard.

'I reckon I'm owed some coffee,' he rumbled, 'and some food.'

His face was stony.

Ruth handed him a mugful of black coffee. 'We're low on food. But I put aside the biscuits you're owed. In the plastic box behind you.'

Stiffly he turned, nearly filling the kitchen area of the caravan. David watched from the sofa, his eyes wide.

Mark pulled out a handful of biscuits.

Then he held them out to David. His face broke into such a broad grin it felt as if a light had shone into the caravan.

'Here you are, son. When I was your age I always hated going to bed on an empty stomach. And yes, as far as I know the rope swing is still there hanging from that tree. Waiting for you to play on it again.'

David delightedly took the biscuits. 'Thanks, Mark.'

'Pleasure.' Mark, taking his coffee, stepped out into the courtyard where he stretched his stiffened arms into the air.

Chris followed.

'It's time to do something,' Mark said. 'I reckon there isn't much time left.'

'We've done what we can. Tony says we can do nothing but wait.'

'Tony Gateman is full of shit.' Mark grinned. 'There is something we can do. Hey, Gateman, can we have the pleasure of your ugly face, please?'

The little Londoner walked cautiously across the courtyard, maybe wondering if his friend's sanity hadn't leaked away under that old blanket. Mark looked almost cheerful. Like a man who knew there was work to be done and was itching to do it.

Ruth joined them as they stood there in the growing gloom.

Tony asked, 'What now?'

Mark took a deep swallow of the scalding coffee. He relished the rush of burning liquid down his throat. 'I've decided I'm going for help.'

'In God's name how?'

Mark nodded at the Hodgson boys' motorbikes leaning against the sea-fort wall. 'I'm riding out.'

'That's suicide, Mark. You know that.'

'It's suicide to stay here, old pal.'

Chris shook his head. 'But you saw what happened to Wainwright. Even for someone on a motorbike those things move bloody fast.'

'And you'd never get past the ones outside the main gate. There are always four of the monsters blocking the causeway now.'

'If you ask me,' said Tony, 'this is what they're expecting now – us to panic, and make a run for it, right into their arms.'

Mark wouldn't be discouraged. 'No problem. We blast the causeway clear with shotguns. We did it before and we put the bastards out of action for six hours. All I need is six minutes. I'll be long gone.'

'A problem.' Tony held up a finger. 'They are learning. They stand about twenty yards from the gates which puts them beyond effective range now.'

'And if you do get past them,' said Ruth quickly, 'there are more up the beach. They've put a barrier across the road. I know they must have opened it up to let Wainwright drive through, but no one can guarantee the road has been left clear.'

Mark swallowed another mouthful of burning coffee. 'With the Saf Dar on the beach, I'll have to take the chance that the bike can shift faster than them. I used to be pretty good on cross-country trials bikes. If the barrier of stones is still there I can lug the bike over even if I can't ride it over. Or maybe cut up through the dunes. Then if I get a clear run I can be in Munby within twenty minutes. A couple of hours after that the choppers will be lifting you off the roof.'

The man's enthusiasm was infectious. A straw for a drowning man to catch. Chris felt his spirits rising.

But Tony poured on the cold water. 'But how are you going to shift the Saf Dar from the causeway? You can't simply ride at them and hope you'll get through. They'd yank you off that motorbike as easily as if you were a child on a tricycle.'

Mark smiled. 'I haven't a clue. But I know someone who's got the answer.'

Tony stared back at him through his thick-lensed glasses. 'Who?'

'My old friend Tony Gateman. That's who.'

Tony blinked.

'Chris, Ruth, can I prevail upon you to get Mr Gateman a coffee? He's got some thinking to do. If this cunning old fox can't come up with a solution, no one on earth can.'

Tony shook his head. 'You've over-estimated me this time, old son.'

Mark smiled. 'We'll see about that.'

*   *   *

Chris sat with his arm around Ruth on the caravan sofa. It was 8 p.m. Dark outside.

She rested her head against his cheek. 'I'll check David in a minute.'

'Oh . . . No rush. He's all right. He'll be fast asleep by now.' He smiled. 'You'd think Mark Faust had given him the world when he gave him those biscuits. You know, I'm sure David knows more than what we've told him.'

'He's an intelligent boy. You can't hide the truth for ever.'

'But what effect is it going to have on him psychologically?'

Ruth kissed the back of his hand. 'Don't worry. He's safe in here. We're still able to give him attention. It's not as though he's been separated from us. That'd be traumatic for a six-year-old. At most all he's experiencing is inconvenience. No sweets. No videos.'

Tony tapped lightly on the caravan door. 'Sorry to bother you, folks. But I thought you ought to know something.'

He pushed his glasses up the bridge of his nose. 'And that is I've completely lost my ruddy sanity.'

'You've come up with an idea?'

'Yes. I've come up with an idea. But it is utterly insane. Come on, I'll explain.'

Chris and Ruth followed. Tony, carrying a camping-gas light that hissed loudly, walked across to where Mark waited at the far side of the courtyard. One of the Hodgson boys was standing with his prized motorbike, its fuel tank brush-painted banana-yellow. Mark inspected the engine closely, his big fingers caressing cables and wires as he looked, his face fixed in concentration.

'Right, Mark.' Tony sounded brisk. 'I've told these good people I'm mad. And I've come up with a mad plan.'

'Don't believe that shit. The little guy is a genius. Right, Tony. Spill the beans.'

'Well . . . this is it. Mark's going for help. We have been kindly allowed use of the motorcycle. The bike is fast and the tank is more than half full. More than adequate for

Mark's requirements. The immediate problem is that lately the Saf Dar have, when the tide is out, posted a guard across the causeway. This is beyond the reach of the shotguns. So . . .' Tony gently kicked one of the ancient cannon lying against the wall. 'We clean two of these babies up and use them to blast the Saf Dar off the causeway. 'Course, it won't kill them. But it'll give Mark time to ride out across the causeway and on to the road.'

'You are joking.' Chris's hopes sagged. 'Tony, those things have been used as fence-posts for the last hundred years. Look at the rust. You could no more fire those things than you could sit on them and fly rings round the bloody moon.'

Ruth shot him a look. 'Listen to what he has to say, Chris.'

'Thanks, Ruth . . . I know they're old. But I'm gambling on the fact that they've not rotted through. Look, Chris, desperate times call for desperate measures. And this isn't pie in the sky. I've thought it through. In theory it should work.'

'All right. But these cannon are two hundred years old. What do we use for ammunition? How do you fire them?'

'Basically, all cannon are metal cylinders open at one end. Down through the open end you stuff explosive, then you pack wadding, cotton wool or shredded rags; after that you put in your shot, a cannonball, or any chunks of metal – nuts, bolts, nails. Pack in more wadding. Then you point the cannon at your target and light the fuse at the breech. That could be a piece of string soaked in petrol or rubbed with gun powder.'

Mark rubbed his oily hands on the seat of his trousers. 'We've got everything we need. Tony suggests the two long cannon. You've got piles of old bolts in the sea-fort. They'd make good shot.'

'For the explosive we'd use shotgun shells. We'd have to cut open maybe forty or so for the explosive charge.' Tony smiled grimly. 'Don't forget . . .' He prodded one of the cannon with his toe. 'These were formidable brutes in their day. Loaded with grapeshot they could turn men into piles of mincemeat at fifty paces.'

'But how are we going to lug these things up on to the walls?'

'We're not. We'll aim them at the gates. When we're ready, we swing the gates back. Fire the cannon through the gateway. They'll blast away anything on the causeway – including the Saf Dar. When that happens Mark rides across the causeway and disappears in the direction of Munby like greased lightning.'

'We open the gates?' Chris chewed his lip. 'It'll take split-second timing.'

'It will. We'll have to get everything right first time. Gates swinging open together, cannon firing first time, Mark riding away like the clappers, then getting the gates shut before those red monsters either come back to their senses or whistle up reinforcements.'

'When do you propose to do it?'

'Tomorrow. Tide will be low enough by 8 a.m.'

Chris rubbed his jaw and thought of Ruth and David. This was their chance to make it out of here. 'Let's do it. What do you want me to do?'

Tony pushed up his sleeves. 'You, Mark and I will clean the cannon. Ruth, we need you to cut up shotgun shells. Carefully. Get Mrs Hodgson to help. We'll need plenty of explosive.' He smiled. 'I want to make sure that when we fire these things someone hears the bang in paradise.'

The early stages were easy enough. By lamplight they rolled the cannon across the courtyard. With help from the Hodgsons they upended the cannon, muzzle down. A dried plug of earth dropped out on to the cobbles like a massive crumbling dog turd. Then Tony, using a mop and sea water, carefully cleaned the inside of the barrel.

'Shit,' he panted over one of the long cannon. 'This one's fucked.'

'How?' Mark leaned forward, his eyes burning intensely.

'The barrel's split. If we fired the thing it would kill anyone standing within ten feet of it. The barrel would explode like a bomb. We'll use the other.'

The third cannon was a short, squat thing with a massive bore that would have taken a cannonball the size of a football.

'Chris, nip over and tell Ruth to cut the charges out of another thirty shotgun shells.' Tony rubbed his jaw. 'I'd hate to be stood at the wrong side of this when it goes off.'

Hardly speaking, they worked for another two hours, carefully cleaning the barrels of the cannon, then rolling the things, crunching heavily across the cobbles towards the gates. There they were heaved on to stacks of timber and aimed at where the opening would be when the gates were swung back. Then Tony and Chris spent a further hour sorting through piles of rusting bolts the size of a man's thumb. Fired from the mouth of a cannon at three hundred miles an hour, the shrapnel effect of these would be devastating.

As Chris worked he couldn't help but recall the villagers' pathetic attempt to barricade the pea-green village hall. Then, as an outsider, he had been able to recognise immediately that this was just a device to take people's minds off what was happening.

Now he was an insider. He was working on what might turn out to be a crackpot scheme. Maybe it was just Tony's way of taking their minds off what would happen in the next few hours.

Tony believed that the old god that once every few centuries stalked this gritty divide between dry land and ocean, demanding a blood sacrifice, was about to show.

He scooped handfuls of bolts into a plastic bowl.

The old pagan god. Ha, ha, that's a good one, Tony.

That's what Chris would force himself to say. But deep down he believed it was true.

It was coming.

Slowly.

He could feel it.

Like the old man with a beaky nose and staring eyes from your nightmares, leaning in through your bedroom window at the dead of night. He was there. Just outside. But he was beginning that strange lean forward.

Just a little more.

Then he would be inside. On this bit of earth, this beach, this crummy old building Chris dreamed of turning into a hotel.

He would be coming soon and he would expect something from the people here.

He wanted something special. Something valuable. Or the prize would go to those red man-shaped things on the sands. Then his, David's, Ruth's, the lives of everyone here would be ended in this world.

If Mark's escape failed, he knew he would have no alternative.

Sacrifice.

The word came back like an iron clapper against the body of a bell.

Sacrifice.

He would have to give up – sacrifice – what meant the most in the world to him. He wouldn't even let himself think what that might be.

44

'Eight o'clock!' shouted Tony.

It would happen at 8.15 a.m.

Mark nodded as he sat astride the 500cc Honda, motor idling with a smooth ticking sound as it warmed through. To stall the thing on the causeway would spell disaster.

Tony, shirt-sleeves rolled up his thin forearms, bustled round the two cannon now strapped to two stacks of timber.

'Chris, nearly forgot to tell you. When you light the fuse, don't be alarmed if nothing happens.'

'Alarmed? I'll shit myself.'

'After you've lit the fuse it'll take maybe two seconds to burn through to the explosive charge in the cannon.'

'And in a situation like this,' called Mark from the bike, 'two seconds can seem a hell of a long time . . .'

Once more (probably for the twentieth time that morning) Tony checked the arrangements.

The time: four minutes past eight.

On the walkway that ran round the top of the walls stood the senior Hodgsons – John and Tom, their faces looking white against their caps of ginger hair. They gripped the shotguns in their beefsteak hands.

Chris had run up earlier to watch the Saf Dar on the causeway.

Five of them sat in a loose group thirty paces from the gates. Out of range of the shotguns; but not the cannon. If what Tony had said was true, the three-hundred-mile-an-hour rush of timber bolts would sweep them away like autumn leaves before a stiff broom.

Of course, it wouldn't kill the red bastards. But it would disable them and give Mark the chance to ride the motorbike out of the sea-fort; then off this cursed bit of coast back to civilisation where he could bring help.

He glanced at his watch. Five minutes past eight.

His mouth was dry and his heart began to beat like a high-powered pump.

He glanced around the courtyard. Cleared of villagers, it looked huge, empty, and slightly unreal. It was as if the laws of space and time were not laws now but only suggestions, which could be accepted or ignored. He licked his dry lips. It's the tension . . . it's only the tension . . .

But he couldn't help thinking of Tony's ancient god of this borderland between dry land and sea. Now approaching.

Suppressing this line of thought, he pumped new thoughts through his head. Tide out. Causeway dry. Misty; not too dense. No more Saf Dar to be seen on the beach.

Might be some in the dunes . . . No. Don't think that. Mark will do it this time. Christ, the man was so psyched up he could junk the bike and do it on will-power alone.

The time crawled over the ridge of another minute. Six minutes past eight.

The Hodgson boys paced restlessly near the gates. At 8.15 they would swing them open – as wide as they could. Like curtains opening in a theatre to reveal what lay beyond. Beach, causeway, and those five red monsters that looked like pieces of raw meat forced into the shape of men.

Ruth would stand at the back with Mark's shotgun. He'd leave this place armed only with an iron bar. The shotgun, he told them, would be more use here. Anyway (he insisted) he wouldn't need the thing (big face breaking into one of those mighty grins); he added that if he made good time he might call into the Happy Eater first for bacon and eggs.

'Nearly ten past!' Tony's voice sounded high with adrenalin. 'Places everyone, please. We go in five minutes.'

Christ, it sounded as if he were making a TV commercial.

Chris returned to his cannon. He would fire *Short & Stumpy* while Tony fired *Long John*.

A gap of perhaps five paces separated the two cannon which lay parallel to one another. Through this gap, Mark would ride the bike after the blast of shrapnel, out through the sea-fort gates.

'Now, Chris . . . The fire.'

Mark lightly revved the bike.

Ruth closed up the shotgun and slipped off the safety catch.

Using Tony's lighter, Chris touched off the wood shavings and barbecue firelighters he'd piled on a tin tray. A little distance from that lay a glass bowl in which rags tied to two six-foot bamboo poles were soaking in lighter fuel. When the time came he and Tony would take a cane each, light the fuel-wet rags, then, as the Hodgson boys heaved the gates wide open, touch the fuses that protruded from the back of the cannon.

He noticed the Vicar watching like some damned ghost from the far side of the courtyard. Nothing he could do would stop this now.

Twelve past eight.

He stooped to pick up the long bamboo stick, heavy with dripping rags.

Tony called out, 'Okay, boys. Open the gates.'

'Wait!'

Tom Hodgson. The man leaned over the walkway, looking down into the courtyard.

'Shit . . .' Mark exploded. 'What's wrong? We've got to go. We can't wait. Open the gates. Get those things open!'

'No . . .' Tony ran in front of the bike, holding up his hands. 'Give me a minute.' He laboured up the stone steps.

Tom Hodgson talked earnestly, pointing at something over the wall. The two men talked for almost five minutes before Tony returned.

'Problems . . . We can't do it.'

'Shit we can't.' Mark Faust sat defiantly astride the bike, his hands on his hips.

'I don't know if the Saf Dar can . . . see in here somehow. We know they stare at the sea-fort as if they can. But two more have come up from nowhere. One is this far from the gates.' Tony held his hand at arm's length from his face. 'And it's just standing there, staring at the gate. The other is on the beach about twenty yards from the sea-fort and a dozen yards from the causeway.' Tony looked from Mark to Chris. 'It's beyond the angle of fire. The cannon shot won't hit it.'

'Fine,' said Mark. 'Blast the one on the beach with shot-guns, then open the gates and blast the rest with the cannon. The one nearest the gate gets more than his fair share of hot iron – but I'm not complaining.'

'Mark . . . You know as well as I do that the one on the beach is out of range of the shotguns. You might wing it, give it a bit of a slap, but that's all. And the one outside the gate is too near. Tom can't get a clean shot at it from the top of the wall. And remember what I said about the cannon. It might take a good two seconds for the fuses to burn through to the charge. In that time the thing could be inside the sea-fort. It's strong, it'll move fast. It could kill us all before we even get a shot at it.'

Mark studied Tony's face, then he said: 'So the odds are getting shittier by the minute. But we still go through with it. Stay here.' Mark climbed off the bike, leaving it, motor still ticking, huffing soft balls of blue smoke from the exhaust; then he ran up the steps to the waiting Hodgsons.

Twenty-four minutes past eight. Time wasn't just running out, time was haemorrhaging from them. Chris knew it. There was a sense of a tremendous weight shifting somewhere beyond the fabric of the walls. Its balance was shifting in favour of the Saf Dar. If the living people here in the sea-fort did not act soon, then the Saf Dar would be masters of this place. And very soon they would be masters of much more. They wanted the world.

Twenty-five minutes past eight.

Up on the walls Mark was explaining something to

the Hodgsons, pointing beyond the walls and gesturing vigorously.

Chris waited, his muscles so tense he felt as if something was holding him tight in an enormous fist. He wanted to shout, fight, run – anything. Do something. Just to get rid of this build-up of energy inside his body.

At last Mark ran down the steps.

He looked like a man with his own internal motor set in gear. Nothing would get in his way now.

'We can do it.' Mark climbed astride the bike. 'Chris . . . Ruth . . . Tony. The plan stays the same . . . More or less. Only we're going to have to do it fast.' He punched a fist into his palm. 'Gates open. Bang. Fire cannon.' Fist into palm again. 'Then I'm on my way. I've talked to John and Tom. We reckon that if that thing on the beach comes after me they can at least knock some wind out of it with the shotguns. That will give me enough space to get clear. Then I'll be travelling so fast it'll never catch up with me.'

Tony shook his head. 'You're insane . . . What about the one directly outside the gates?'

'That's where I need Ruth. If she stands a little to the front of Chris she can blast it with both barrels – if it begins to move.'

But – but Ruth has—'

'But Ruth nothing,' broke in Ruth. 'I can fire one of these.' She pulled the shotgun up across her breasts. 'And you know as well as I do you don't have to aim. You just point and shoot.'

'Too risky. We can't be sure—'

Chris spoke. 'Tony . . . Tony, listen to me. Time's running out. Those things don't even have to break in here, and you know it. They only have to wait and grab that power as it comes through. Like Mark says, it'll be just like catching a ball. They will be the winners – absolutely. We'll be the losers – absolutely. Okay, so this is a risk, a bloody enormous risk; we've got to take it.' He paused, watching for the little

Londoner's reaction. None. 'Look . . . Tony. I don't want to see my six-year-old son like Wainwright. That's what we'll become. The Saf Dar's foot soldiers; marched across country to the next village. To kill everyone we can lay our hands on. Then to the next town. We'll be like a virus, infecting the next person, then the next.'

Tony shrugged. 'Okay. We do it.' He called out to the waiting Hodgsons on the wall and the two youths by the gates. 'In your positions, please.'

Ruth moved past Chris until she was almost level with the muzzle of the cannon he would fire.

'Ruth . . .' he called. 'Back here against me. You're too close.'

Reluctantly she stepped back to his side and gave a tiny smile. 'Get ready to duck, love.'

Mark revved the motor, slipped the bike into first gear; it moved forward an inch, then he held it back, waiting, his eyes bulging as he nailed his attention to the gates ahead.

'Now, Tony! Now!'

Tony nodded. 'Chris . . . Light the torches.'

Chris picked up the bamboo sticks and held them over the yellow flames. Instantly the fuel-soaked rags caught with an *ooomph* sound.

He passed one to Tony, then held the other out in front of him away from Ruth and the cannon. It burned with a brilliant blue flame, looking like a fiery chrysanthemum head, a perfect globe of blue that spat red sparks of flame with a faint crackling sound.

Tony called to the Hodgson boys. 'Open the gates . . . Now!'

They snapped back the final bolts, then yanked back the gates. They pulled them back as far as they could, using the massive timbers to shield themselves from any stray shrapnel from the cannon blasts.

Time ran slow like a freezing stream and almost stopped. Chris saw everything. With unnatural clarity.

Beyond the gate, the nearest figure stood framed by the

gateway. The red skin gleamed; the power that leaked through from that other place had pumped up the arms, legs, and neck muscles until they bulged manically, forcing the veins outward like coils of string beneath plastic shrinkwrap.

Blazing like white balls of glass from the expressionless face were the eyes, staring with a bulging intensity at something above Chris's head.

Thirty yards beyond that man-shaped chunk of cancer were six more of them, staring at the sea-fort. Beyond that, only causeway. Sand. Dunes.

'Chris! Now!'

He slapped the burning head of the torch down on to the fuse threaded into the cannon's breach.

Hell . . .

Nothing happened.

He looked down at the feeble trail of smoke from the fuse. He could not believe it. Christ . . .

The thing wasn't going to fire.

Gateman, the idiot, had ballsed it up.

He had killed everyone in the sea-fort.

Movement swirled at his side. Ruth stepped level with the cannon's muzzle, bringing up the barrels of her shotgun.

No, Ruth! Back.

You're too . . .

Jesus Christ . . .

He jerked his head round to look at the figure in the gateway. Abruptly, it tilted its red, hairless head down in a single, fluid movement. Then those eyes were nailed to him.

He felt his body jerk back as if hit by an electric shock. The hate radiating from its eyes punched the breath from his body. They burned with a ferocious power that seared his soul.

Then came a sense of darkness. It rushed into him, filling him, like someone's home being inundated by flood waters boiling with mud and shit from the sewers, sweeping over clean carpets, swirling away armchairs and sofa and tables and cushions. Its force hosed out Chris's memories and polluted them. He glimpsed fragments as they spun past, caught by the inrush of darkness:

On the beach with David. He runs in his Superman costume, laughs happily. David runs kicking up gouts of sand.

But it becomes blackened, dirty, this lovely memory:

David . . .

Kill the little bastard. Now. Thin little neck. Easily broken. My son's a piece of shit. No loss to anyone. Kill the whining little bastard now.

The figure in the gateway took a single step forward. Already it seemed to fill the courtyard, like a train plunging into a tunnel.

Then it –

CRACK!

The explosion was so loud he thought a chunk of hot iron had gone whirling through his skull.

The cannon had fired.

His bastard two-hundred-year-old cannon had actually fired! Sending a bucketful of timber bolts cracking through the gateway at three hundred miles an hour.

He blinked.

The figure had gone.

Just gone.

Yet he retained a subliminal image of a gush of smoke, a spray of yellow flame.

Then the figure, still upright, simply shrank. The almighty blow of metal hammered the thing with explosive force backward along the causeway.

Then Tony's cannon fired, a sharper crack.

The Saf Dar, twenty yards away on the causeway, jerked backward like dry leaves before a gust of wind, spinning and turning over and over across the causeway, some of them tumbling off on to the sand. Liquid sprayed up into the air as if their bodies had become aerosols. It hung there, briefly darkening the white mist to crimson before falling like spring rain to the earth.

A rapid movement to Chris's left.

Mark Faust.

Twisting the hand throttle, he bulleted across the courtyard and through the gates.

A second later he scorched through the mess of body fluid on the stones, avoiding the twisted men that littered the causeway.

Chris saw movement on the sands themselves.

The one who had been beyond the angle of cannon fire moved after the motorbike like a big cat, huge legs blurring with speed, the red body thrusting forward, reaching out to grab at Mark.

Chris heard nothing but saw sand spurt at its feet.

The Hodgsons were firing at the thing.

One of its legs suddenly rashed with black spots; it stumbled forward, arm outstretched like a sportsman lunging after a ball; its hands brushed the spinning back tyre.

But it fell short, sliding face down across the stone slabs of the causeway.

Mark was clear. Already a shrinking dot, accelerating away into the mist in the direction of the dunes.

The red monster jerked itself to its feet.

Then it loped along the causeway. This time towards the sea-fort, long arms pumping backwards and forwards.

Chris moved forward. At his side Ruth was shouting. He could hear nothing. The thunder of cannon had deafened him.

The Hodgson boys struggled to swing the heavy gates shut. On one side Tony helped. Chris threw himself against the timbers of the other, winding himself. He pushed hard and it swung shut.

He threw the first of the huge bolts as the thing cracked into the other side. Although his deafened ears heard nothing, he felt the solid concussion shiver the timbers.

Quickly he shot the bolts across, expecting to feel the fury of the monster on the other side trying to batter its way in.

It never came.

For now, they were safe.

Ears buzzing, he followed the others up the stone steps to the top of the wall to see if Mark had made it.

But Mark had disappeared into the mist.

If Chris had been able to hear, he might have picked up the whine of the high-revving bike powering away along the coast road behind the dunes. He heard only a buzzing with a constant ghost echo of the cannon explosions.

He glanced back into the courtyard. Smoke filled it, almost liquid-looking; lying on the stone floor, spluttering torches still burned, casting a flickering violet light that flashed against the suspended sheets of gunsmoke and the metallic surfaces of the car and the caravan, like images from a silent movie.

There was Ruth, moving across the courtyard in the direction of the sea-fort building – she would be going to check on David – her movements jerky in the flickering light.

Tony's cannon had snapped free from its cradle with the force of the explosion and was pointing vertically upwards, a piece of metal the size of Chris's fist torn from the end.

The Hodgsons leaned forward over the top of the wall to stare down at what lay on the causeway.

From the sound and the fury and the pandemonium of five minutes before, the scene on the causeway below was now one of stillness.

As if some sick artist had been using finely minced raw beef as modelling clay, six man-shaped figures lay sprawled across the causeway in a pool of what looked like thick red oil. Not one moved. Most lay on their backs where they had been thrown by the hammer blow of the cannon blast. The one that had been standing in the gateway had caught the worst of it and had been batted back almost twenty yards. It was little more than a wet skeleton.

Even though the couple of hundred timber bolts flying outwards at three hundred miles an hour had done an effective flesh-shredding job, it wouldn't last long. Already the force that had driven these things from the wreck of the *Mary-Anne* to lay siege to the sea-fort would be repairing the mutilated bodies. The growth of cancer flesh would start to fill in the holes made by the iron bolts; arteries would worm through the bloody mess to reconnect to whatever heart pumped those fluids through their bodies; new skin would slide over torn muscles; new eyes would bud in their sockets.

Even as they watched, the one on the causeway heaved its ripped body on to the sands; then, on all fours, moving like a seal ruptured by a ship's propeller, it began to drag itself down to the sea. In a few hours it would be back. Stronger than before.

Like the one that now sat ten yards from the gate. After its charge at the gates it had simply knelt down on the causeway. It stared at the sea-fort like some sinister but wise Red Indian warrior, its heavy-lidded eyes blinking with a slowness that was not human.

These things were in no hurry. Down there on the causeway the creature broadcast through its body language alone:
We will win . . .

We have only to wait . . .

45

'Careful, Mark, old son, careful.'

He spoke the words aloud as he eased the throttle down.

'No rush now. Slow down . . . Take it easy, old son.'

The back tyre slid as he turned from the causeway on to the coast road.

Don't spoil everything now by falling off the blasted bike. Easy does it.

He throttled down further. The speedo needle slid back to forty-five.

He breathed deeply, refreshing himself with the cool misty air blowing across his face. It left the taste of sea salt on his lips. And, God, the air smelt sweet here away from the sea-fort. The sudden sense of freedom was immense.

He shook his head to try to dislodge the aching pressure from the cannon blast on his ears. What he had seen would take longer to fade. The strawberry mash of twisted bodies he had driven through – and over. Bits of the red grue still clung to the front tyre.

The manic hammering of his heart began to slow; he felt cooler, in control. His eyes scanned ahead as far as the mist would allow.

No Saf Dar. Maybe they were haunting somewhere else with their red statue faces. The dunes looked deserted. Ahead, as far as he could see in this damn mist, the road was empty. Same as the flat expanse of sea marsh to his right.

Mark rode, keeping the bike at around forty-five, actually enjoying the feel of it as it ticked confidently across the tarmac. At this rate he would be in Munby in twenty-five minutes.

The time was 8.29.

David stopped, his stomach hurting with the shock.

The room was full of strangers.

He stared for a moment until his vision blurred, the gold-fish bowl clamped in his fists.

How did strangers get inside the sea-fort? Tall. Strange colour. Stood up straight. Not moving.

Shout for his dad?

No . . .

Suddenly he gave a little chuckle.

No.

'Bottles . . . Bottles full of gas.' He said the words aloud to dispel the scary feeling.

In this room it wasn't easy to see that well. The window was small and really, really dirty. And there was no electricity. It had gone somewhere. He wasn't sure where, but he hoped it would come back soon.

He crossed the room, walking by the six big gas bottles that stood there on end. They looked like ghost soldiers all in a line, with blue uniforms, standing stiff and straight.

He placed the goldfish bowl on the windowsill. It was covered with fluffy bits of old cobweb and an ashtray with dusty cigarette ends piled up in it. Not that anyone would be allowed to smoke in here now with the gas bottles.

'Flammable,' his dad had said. 'We have to keep these away from fire, kidda. They can go up like bombs if we're not careful.'

He positioned the goldfish bowl, then peered in through the plastic.

'Take fish thing away . . . Nathty.' That's what that big silly girl had kept saying. 'Nathty fish thing. Ah – ah don't like it. Don't like it, not one little bit.' The girl was as big as a grown-up; but she had a little white face and a little kid's voice. 'That fish thing . . . Take it away, David . . .

or . . . or I won't marry you.' Then she had made that silly grin.

He knew only vaguely about the word 'marry'. That's when two people lived together.

Me and Rosie Tamworth, he thought with disgust. No way.

Even so. He'd carried the goldfish out of the caravan. Across the courtyard with the big guns near the gates, smelling of smoke (something had happened but the grown-ups were keeping secrets; so could he).

He'd moved the goldfish partly because he was fed up with Rosie moaning all the time, and partly because he no longer liked the look of it.

He pressed his fingers lightly against the plastic bowlful of water. It felt warm. Like a cupful of warm milk.

He looked more closely but he couldn't see much. The room was half full of light and half full of darkness.

'Gloomy,' he mouthed as he stared, the blue-soldier gas bottles standing to attention behind him. It was very quiet. No one about.

The water in the fishbowl had gone green. The colour of water in toilets when you wee in it. Inside there were pebbles covering the bottom. Once they had been white and pink; now they had gone a slippery green colour. The little wrecked pirate ship and then the —

He started back. He'd not noticed what it had been doing. The eye . . .

He'd not liked that . . . the eye had shocked him.

The goldfish had been staring at him with that big round eye. No . . . He didn't like his fish at all now. It had changed.

When they had won Clark Kent on the hook-a-duck at the fair it had been little and cute (his mum had said). Now it wasn't cute at all.

In the last few days it had changed.

It had become a big, lumpy thing now. So long it couldn't straighten its body in the bowl. Mostly it moved in fast jerks round and round the bowl.

And it reminded him of one of those cartoon snakes that had swallowed lots of buns, their long bodies going all bumpy from the big lumps inside pushing against the skin as if wanting to burst out. Maybe that would —

'David!'

'Mum?'

'What on earth are you doing in here?'

'I was just —'

'You know it's dangerous with those things in here.' She nodded at the soldier gas bottles in their blue uniforms. 'Come on.' She wasn't smiling. 'Let's see if we can find anything to eat.'

Without looking back at the staring goldfish, he went to his mum as she stood in the dark doorway, her hand outstretched.

On the coast road he rode the bike into a fog that rolled in a swollen white cloud down from the dunes.

Easy, Mark. He throttled down to thirty.

He had still not seen a single Saf Dar.

He had covered a mile along the road, the scenery unchanging. Dunes rising to the left of him. Swamp to the right.

The mist thickened. He dropped the speed to twenty.

The engine ticked smoothly, the vibration making his feet, buttocks and hands tremble.

Then something took shape out of the fog in front of him.

A dark line.

They had replaced the barrier of rocks and pebbles in the road. He had gambled that they had left the road clear when they had created a gap to allow poor dead Wainwright through in his car to drive at the sea-fort gates.

But the Saf Dar had been too smart for that. They had probably directed their corpse-slaves to replace the stones.

He braked, slowing the bike to a walking pace. Not wanting to stop, just in case . . .

He shook away the mental pictures coming into his mind.

You've got three options, Mark, old son. Up into the dunes. Risky. One of those things might be lurking in one of the hollows.

Next option: ride round the causeway the other way. That means going into the marsh. Risky again. Too easy to get bogged down and drown the motor in marsh slime.

Option three: straight over the top of the mound. The temptation burned simply to charge the mounded barrier and hope that like a ramp it carried him over in a mighty leap. He chose caution. He would ride up to it, then simply lug the bike over.

The barrier was little higher than his waist. He should be able to do it.

The edges of the barrier became more defined as he neared it. Fifty yards away he saw a large rock rising up from its middle.

Ten yards later he realised that the big rock was in fact one of the Saf Dar, squatting Red Indian-like on the mound. It faced Mark, watching him approach through the mist, those large eyes lasering through the fog as if it wasn't there. It had watched him approach. It knew.

Half turning in the road, front tyre pointing to the marsh, he stopped. What now?

The red thing on the stones could as easily hammer the life out of him as he could that of a fly. Feet planted on the road on either side of the bike, the big man raised himself from the saddle. In the fog beyond the barrier he could make out another shadow shape rising out of the mist. Up on the dunes, another. Like ghost statues. Waiting.

No way out that way.

He revved the bike gently.

This couldn't be the end of the road – literally. He bit his lip. He had to go on. The people in the sea-fort, hungry and exhausted now, clung desperately to the idea that he was going to get help. They needed him to do it.

Mark turned his head in jerks, looking ahead along the

road to where the barrier and the Saf Dar blocked his route; he looked up at the dunes, across at the marsh, then back along the road the way he came.

And he wondered in God's name what he should do.

'Not long now.' Chris, Ruth and David had the caravan to themselves as they ate their small helpings of chips, tinned tomatoes and one beefburger. The rest of the villagers ate the same meal in the gundeck room.

'How long, do you think?' asked Ruth, half anxious, half excited.

'A couple of hours – not much more. As soon as Mark gets through he'll tell them —'

'The truth?'

'Some plausible cock-and-bull story . . . half true anyway.'

'What's Mark telling who?' asked David, confused but sounding happy because his parents were.

'Listen, kidda,' said Chris, 'Mark's going to arrange a surprise. We'll be going for a little trip somewhere and guess how we'll be going?'

'By boat?'

'Nope.'

'By car?'

'Nope . . . Give in? By helicopter.'

'Helicopter?'

'Chris . . .' Ruth signalled to him with her eyebrows – *Cool it, Chris.* 'We don't know for sure yet.'

'It's a good bet, though.' Chris felt good. 'That way they can get us out safely. We can leave all this for someone else to clear up.'

Ruth's smile paled. 'Just hope he can get through.'

'Don't worry, love. He'll get through. This time I'm optimistic.'

Mark was far from optimistic.

There was no way he could continue with the bike. Although the red man on the barrier of stones had not moved so much as a millimetre, he knew it would pounce the moment he got near.

Still astride the bike, he walked it backwards until the back tyre left the road and hit the first slope up to the dunes.

'Hell . . .'

He hissed the word through clenched teeth.

Slipping the bike into first gear, he revved the engine until it roared with a fury that matched his own. He let out the clutch.

The rear wheel buzzed like a chainsaw on the rough grass and sand, sliding the bike sideways; then the tyre bit into the tarmac, rocketing the bike forward across the road and out on to the swamp.

More through wild, shot-in-the-dark luck than anything else, the bike ran out across a long spit of tussocks which penetrated deep into the marsh in a long bumpy pier. Behind him the road, dunes and the Saf Dar on the barrier disappeared into the fog.

He slowed the bike to a crawl, thinking fast.

For Christsakes, the marsh might not be the impassable stretch of mud and shitty water he had first thought it. Working from tussock to tussock (they were firm enough to support the bike) he might be able to cross this miserable swamp.

The marsh was some two miles wide. Then it began to rise imperceptibly to form a rather soggy pasture populated by a few wet-foot cows. Beyond that it became cultivated fields. His hopes rose. Fields wouldn't present much of a barrier. Another four miles or so and he would hit another road into Munby. With even more luck there might be an isolated farmhouse, maybe even a pay phone. Then a single telephone call and all this shit would be at an end.

He pushed the bike on across the lumpy turf. At little more than walking pace, he steered carefully, avoiding the pools of water – most no larger than table-tops. Worst were the expanses of near-liquid mud, punctuated here and there by tussocks that looked like the flattened heads of drowned men partly breaking the surface.

He nailed his attention on the wall of fog that seemed as solid as concrete.

He had moved perhaps a quarter of a mile along the narrow ridge of tussocks, little wider than a footpath, mudflats to his left and right, when he saw the shape solidify out of the mist.

There was no way back. Only on. He rode towards the shape that reared out of the marshy ground like a rotten tree stump.

It was a human figure.

Or at least it had been.

Once.

Tony said, 'You know, Chris, I think when they invented electric light it killed off all the ghosts. Now we've lost the electricity the bloody ghosts are coming back again.' He glanced up the gloomy stairwell. 'There's a lot more shadows lately . . . You noticed?' He said it with a smile, but Chris realised that the man wasn't joking.

Chris leaned against the corridor wall drinking a pale yellow liquid he'd told everyone was tea (two teabags between twenty-five people). At least it was hot.

Tony sat on the stone steps. A cigar he'd half-heartedly crushed under his muddy shoes sent out a trail of blue smoke.

'I never used to believe in ghosts,' said Tony. 'When people used to tell you a *real* ghost story . . . Laugh? I used to piss myself . . . Rubbish. Now . . . a bloody old cynic like me . . . Over the last three years everything I believed in turned upside down.'

Chris nodded in a way he intended to be reassuring. Tony was exhausted. He could be allowed his half-coherent ramble.

'Tony, remember the night we met in the pub? Me, you and Mark?'

'Jesus . . . Do I . . . Seems like half a bloody lifetime ago now.'

'Afterwards, when I walked home along the top of the dunes . . . To put it simply – I met something.'

'Something? What? One of the Saf Dar? Or one of the poor bastards they've got dangling on the end of their strings?'

'Neither. It's hard to put into . . . No, to be honest I can't put it into words. Only I met something. I thought I was hallucinating. Later. But it had an enormously powerful effect on me. The equivalent of some kind of psychic loco-motive slamming into your mind.'

Tony sat up straight now. 'Tell me about it.'

Chris did. Or at least as much as he could remember. Even in the retelling his hands began to sweat; the saliva in his mouth bled away, leaving his tongue paper-dry.

He fumbled for words, trying to say how even though the white-faced thing looked disgusting and repelled him he had felt it exert a kind of magnetic pull on him. He had wanted actually to go forward, closer and closer . . . to embrace it. The idea revolted him again as the memory suddenly squeezed up into his mind as warm and as fresh as the night it happened.

The tea in his mouth burned his tongue. Sweating, he looked down into the cup, not realising he'd even taken a drink.

'Even telling you now, Tony, makes me . . . Shit . . . It brings it all back. It's actually hard for me to describe it.'

'You know, Chris, what you are describing is a numinous experience.'

Chris's bewilderment must have shown.

'Numinous. Rudolf Otto, a nineteenth-century theologian, identified the primal religious experience: the numinous ex-perience. This is religion in the raw, stripped of all rituals, prayers, hymns, words, even rational thought.' As Tony's talk became more and more animated, Chris understood less and less. 'What you felt, Chris, when you encountered that apparition, is fundamental to all religions, the *mysterium tremendum.*'

'The what?'

'*Mysterium Tremendum*. Translated, the tremendous mystery. Such an encounter provokes this response.' Tony flicked his fingers, ticking off the words: 'Shuddering revulsion . . . Irresistible attraction. That's the creature feeling people experience in such an encounter.'

'What are you talking about, Tony? What did I encounter?'

Tony looked at Chris with an expression that seemed like awe. 'Chris . . . What I'm trying to say is that on that night you came face to face with the old god.'

The figure that he approached across the rough grass, the bike's motor ticking lightly, had died a long time ago.

Drowned.

Perhaps a sailor washed overboard, hauling up lobster pots from the North Sea.

It stood upright, rags of clothes wrapped in bands around its distorted body, almost like the bandages around an Egyptian mummy. Barnacles rashed across its face and one eye like a hard white leprosy; seaweed sprouted from a vertical crack in its bare chest in a horse's mane gone green.

Mark rode a little closer. It did not move. Its arms hung by its side; its remaining eye was shut.

Fifteen yards away. The thing twitched. The mouth dropped open. It was full of sea anemones.

Ten yards away. Mark walked the bike forward.

Eight yards.

Its remaining eye snapped open.

It bulged out, an inflamed red, like a hard-boiled egg filled with blood.

The expression also altered with a snap. To one of shocked pain.

It tilted its head abruptly to fix the blood-red eye on Mark.

Without thinking, he twisted the hand throttle; the motor revved with a sound like metal sheets being torn in two. The bike lurched, almost throwing him like a bucking stallion.

Then the bike was screaming across the tussock grass, the front wheel barely kissing the turf.

The agonised face with its crust of barnacles flicked by a yard from his shoulder as he hurtled by.

The buffeting of the bike became a smooth rushing motion. He glanced down. He'd ridden the bike off the raised tussocks and on to the mudflat.

For what seemed an impossibly long time the momentum carried him forward. As if he were driving a powerboat, the mud sprayed up ten feet into the air on either side of him in a great black V.

Then the momentum went. The bike slowed, to settle into the deep black soup of mud. The engine choked and cut instantly. Hot metal hissed against wet sludge; white steam boiled around his legs.

Managing to keep upright, he clumsily climbed off the useless bike, leaving it to gurgle in the mud. He made for the nearest raised tussock of grass. The mud made walking as difficult as wading through treacle. He reached the tussock, dropped forward on to his hands, and began to pull himself out. One leg came easily. The next stuck. It seemed as if his foot had become stuck on some —

Christ!

Suddenly panicky, he wrenched forward, hands winding round the marsh grass. For all the world it felt as if a hand had gripped his toes beneath the mud's surface. With a tremendous wrench he pulled it free.

He pulled himself to his feet, panting. As he straightened, a pain speared up his calf where he had yanked the muscle.

An ancient timber fence-post leaned at an angle in the middle of the tussock. A hole had been bored near the top for a non-existent rail. He stretched out his hand, using the post as support as he checked his ragged breathing. God, his leg hurt. He felt for the iron bar that he'd tucked through his belt. It had vanished somewhere into the swamp.

At last he straightened and wiped the sweat from his forehead. Where his mud-slimed hand had rested against the timber post it had left a large dark palm-print, the fingers outstretched.

He breathed deeply, trying to ignore the pain in his leg.

No doubt about it. He would have to go on. It would

take longer, but he could make it, jumping from tussock to tussock as if in some holiday-camp game. Keep out of the water; and get to a phone. The prize?

Survival.

For him and the others back at the sea-fort, waiting for him to bring help.

He thought about the Stainforths – 'nice folks', he had told Tony. The thought of them ending up like Wainwright and the Fox twins sent him leaping from mound to mound across the mud.

He had to do it.

He didn't even pause when a misshapen hand thrust up from the mud at his leaping feet, the fingers snapping shut – a clumsy grab. But Mark heard the crack of fingers against palm.

He ran on.

'That's the first time you've kissed me in days,' said Ruth with a smile.

Chris kissed her again. 'When all this is sorted out we've a few things to catch up on.'

They had snatched a few minutes alone together in the room where the gas bottles were stored. Alone apart from David's goldfish which still torpedoed round its bowl, churning the greenish water until it frothed.

'Jesus . . . That thing will have to go. We can tell David it—'

'Forget the goldfish for a moment, Chris.' She pulled lightly at his t-shirt. He felt the electric trickle of a desire he'd not felt for a long time. For the last few days they had simply ticked over as if in hibernation. Mark's break-out that morning had brought everyone back to life. They talked, moved about the place. He had even heard the sound of laughter echoing down from the gundeck room. The big man would bring help. They would be going home soon.

He kissed Ruth on the soft skin of her throat, pushing her hair away with his face, enjoying its cool wash across his skin. Her hand stroked down his spine and she tucked her fingers into the back of his jeans.

He bound her to his chest with his arms, holding her tightly. God, he'd missed this. The physical closeness. It was as if his senses were coming back to life. Even though they were existing on smaller and smaller portions of food, today was the first day he had felt really hungry. He wanted to eat a huge piece of sirloin steak. The desire burnt so strongly he could almost taste the meat on his tongue, hot and savoury; he could imagine his teeth working through the meat, devouring it.

'Chris, I want you to make love to me.'

Waves of hot blood surged up through his body. He'd never felt so excited . . . Or alive.

It was as if the volume control of his senses had been turned up full. With the heat flooding his body, his sense of smell and taste heightened, he could taste her saliva, the sharp tang of salt on her skin. His sense of touch, somehow amplified, transmitted the delicious silk feel of her bare arms up through his fingertips. This felt good. His body-motor revs were high; something was pressing his accelerator hard.

Her hands worked at him through his jeans. Christ . . . He'd never felt like this before. He felt as if he were going to explode right there in her hungry hands.

Rabbits shit here, he thought as he ran doggedly on.

Like handfuls of dried currants it littered the marsh grass. Rabbits had found a route through the stagnant pools and expanse of liquid mud. If only to shit.

With a grunt he jumped to the next tussock.

Christ, how long now? Soon the ground should dry out as it rose into meadow. Then an easy jog to the nearest road. A phone or house shouldn't be far away after that.

If only he could see further. The fog thickened. Visibility dropped to a dozen yards. All around him at the edge of the thick white muck he imagined (hoped he imagined) that he saw shadows; the shades of dead men or worse following him, waiting for him to fall exhausted so they could move in – and make him one of their own.

He made a terrific leap across a pool of liquid mud.

Surely he must be nearly there. The marsh didn't go on for ever.

The pounding of his running feet juddered up through his torso and neck; his eyes blurred; his forehead bled sweat; his breath was torn from his lungs in panting gasps. Soon, Mark, he promised himself. Soon.

Here comes another mud channel; jump to the next tussock and —

Oh, Jesus, sweet Jesus!

He'd nearly run into it. He twisted to avoid the dark shape rearing out of the turf and slid to his knees.

Arms up to defend himself, he slithered back, blinking the sweat from his eyes. The dark shape towered above him.

Shit.

He shook his head, a choking laugh rising in his burning throat.

A post. Just a stupid old fence-post.

A thought slid into his brain with all the menace of a poisonous snake.

No. Don't believe it, Mark . . . Jesus. The fence-post. The rotten post sticking up in the middle of this bastard swamp.

Panting, he rose slowly to his feet and limped forward to look at the timber post.

The post, old, rotting at the base, leaned slightly towards him. Near the top of the post a round female hole which long ago took the male fence-rail. Just below the hole a muddy palm-print, fingers splayed out. Trembling, Mark held out his hand and covered the handprint perfectly.

For the last hour and a half he had been running in one huge circle.

Tony looked up into the sky. Is that the colour of real cloud? Or is it changing? Has it begun?

'More evidence of your god, Gateman?' the Reverend Reed's

voice was a rasp. 'He's coming, isn't he? He's on his way. Following his well-worn track down here to Manshead.'

'What do you think, Reverend?'

'Down he comes, Gateman. What footprints does he leave on his garden path? Are there toes, a heel? Or are they the hoofprints of a goat? Does he have a fine head of hair like a Greek god? Or does he have horns . . . here and here?' Reed pressed his fingers to either side of his head. As if they were horns.

46

To the rhythm of his running feet words thudded through his brain. 'Move in a straight line . . . a straight line . . . move in a straight line . . .'

He ran on, leaping from tussock to tussock rising like islands from the marsh. Most were within leaping distance from one another across the pools of mud. Some were not. Mark would leap as far as he could before sploshing down into the swamp mud and water. Its wet-earth stink oozed up through his nostrils. It squelched through his clothes, splashing his face with what looked like cold diarrhoea; it coated his teeth and tongue with a gritty paste.

And he bled sweat.

'Keep that straight line . . .' he muttered to himself, glancing back to judge whether his crater-like footprints through the mud were straight.

Damn . . . No sun. No landmarks. Nothing to guide him.

But the thought kept him going.

Get help. He liked the Stainforths. Nice folks . . . Nice folks. The words echoed around his brain like a chant.

If he'd ever married and had a family he would have wanted it to have been like them. He had never got close to marrying. He'd had some good relationships with women, but they always became platonic friendships. He could never establish a deeper involvement. He knew why. Part of him had died that night thirty-odd years ago when he killed the *Mary-Anne* and all on board her.

Not much further now, then he would be pounding up the meadows. He imagined himself gratefully falling down into the meadow grass, then lying there hungrily sucking at the cool air. He would grab five minutes' delicious rest before moving on. Not running. A steady jog. Get to the road. Maybe flag down a passing car. A police car would be like Christmas come early. Then help would be on its way. As he ran he nourished himself with this mental picture.

He took a huge leap over the next stretch of liquid mud. He fell short of the tussock, his hands grabbed at the rough grass; his legs sank knee-deep into slop.

Hell.

Heaving himself out, he moved on, panting until his ribs ached.

When he reached the next expanse of mud he noticed something moving in the centre of the channel. Like a seal. It turned slowly over and over with a heavy squelching sound. Although too far away for him to tell exactly what it was, Mark had a damn good idea.

He swallowed. Perhaps it really was a seal – sick, lost . . .

Was it hell. It was one of them. Not Saf Dar. Perhaps it was Wainwright, or Fox, or one of the long-dead encrusted with barnacles or seaweed or sea anemones spreading across its naked body like a disgusting disease.

Mark dropped forward, supporting the weight of his body with outstretched arms against his knees, panting noisily and shaking his head. A thread of silver snot slid from his nose to stretch down to the grass.

He would have to work round the thing rolling manically over and over in mud in post-mortem ecstasy.

He turned left. Soon the splashing seal-shaped thing was out of sight, and he turned in what he judged to be a half-circle before moving forward – again in a straight line.

'Come on, old son. Nearly there.' Soon the level of the land would rise up from this squelching muck. There would be fields, a few trees and —

The post.

He stopped.

Standing out like a lone ghost sentinel guarding the swamp was the post.

Near the top, the round hole.

Below that, a muddy handprint. Fingers splayed out.

Shit!

Back where he started. He dropped to his knees and punched the turf. He punched again and again, his mind a boiling mess of confusion, frustration, anger.

Shit . . .

Which way now?

The time was ten minutes to two.

Chris glanced at his watch. Ten minutes to two.

He stood in the courtyard, watching what seemed the full complement of villagers moving restlessly to and fro. An exception was the Reverend Horace Reed, who sat on one of the cannon that had been fired that morning. The man himself, lost in a gin-sodden haze.

The villagers, excited by the idea that rescue might be on its way, chattered and laughed in overloud voices. Help was coming. Nothing else mattered – just the idea of that first hot bath in days, a square meal then a comfortable bed.

Chris walked quickly round the perimeter of the walls, looking down on to the beach.

Already the tide was sliding in, gobbling up acres of sand. Soon the first waves would be licking the flanks of the causeway. Within minutes Manshead would be an island again.

A hundred yards along the beach three Saf Dar stood, the surf tonguing at their bare ankles, their tomato-red bodies vivid against the sand.

He passed John Hodgson keeping watch over the beach, and went down the steps to the courtyard full of villagers.

The excitement. You could almost reach out and run your fingers through it. His pulse raced, like an electric motor whirring away in his wrist. His legs ached, the muscles tensed into hard cords. This was like all the Christmas Eves and last days of school term rolled into one. He knew that nearly everyone felt that way. That sizzling sense of expectancy. Any minute now . . . Any minute now . . . It's going to happen soon . . . This is it . . . this is it . . . It's coming now . . . Any minute now. A sense that something immense was straining at a barrier that would give way with a crack and a roar.

He joined Ruth. She was throwing a tennis ball for David to catch. He missed it and it rolled under the front of the car.

'I'll get it,' called Chris.

'Are you playing, Dad?'

'Of course.' He threw the ball harder than he meant to, and felt a burst of surprise and pleasure when his son leapt up to catch the ball easily.

'Good catch.'

'You feel it too.' Ruth's brown eyes darted with excitement.

'I feel relieved that we'll soon be getting out. I'm ready for a bath and a decent meal.'

'It's more than that.'

'Mum . . . catch.'

She caught it. '*Uph*. Well done.'

'His throwing's improved these last couple of weeks.'

'He's changed in lots of ways, Chris. Or haven't you noticed?'

'Changed? How?'

'I'll tell you later. What I was talking about is the change in the villagers. Just look at them. Chatting, laughing, moving about. They're different people. It's as if they're high on something.'

'Like someone spiked their tea with cocaine.'

'Exactly. I feel it too. It's hard to explain. I feel good. Look in a mirror. You'll see your pupils are dilated – everything seems brighter. I'm happy. I shouldn't be. With those things out on the beach. But —'

'Mum! Throw the ball.'

She threw it. David caught it easily.

'I take it you're subscribing to Tony Gateman's theory of the second coming of the—' He held his hands to his head, poking his fingers out as if they were horns. '. . . the horny old god who feeds on the souls of sacrificed virgins.'

'See, it's affecting you, Chris. You wouldn't normally talk so flippantly.'

'Maybe.'

'Listen, Chris, this is important.'

Chris caught the ball his six-year-old son had thrown at him, so hard it made his palm tingle. 'Wow! I'll need gloves soon.' He returned the ball. David snapped it out of the air with one hand.

'Chris . . . Listen. You're forgetting what Tony told us, when he talked about sacrifice – that we had to give something precious – precious to us – so we'd receive something in return.'

'This bloody enormous chunk of energy, this magic power, that's supposed to gush in.' Chris laughed, feeling almost drunk.

'Yes . . . Chris, I'm serious. Tony's been right about everything else. Maybe we should work something out with him. To make sure we get this power when it comes through – and not let it fall into the hands of those things on the beach.'

'You mean make a sacrifice.'

'Yes.'

'But what would you sacrifice?'

'Something that is very important to us, Chris.'

'Ruth, be sensible, love. What on earth can we sacrifice that means so much to us? David's goldfish? Your collection of U2 tapes? If you look around you'll notice we don't have many fatted calves or goats kicking around the place . . . Or maybe we could find some suitable virgin for the sacrificial altar.'

'Don't close your mind to this. We've got to accept something is happening. The evidence it is beginning is out there on the beach. Those red men. You feel the tension in the air.

The sheer excitement. It's happening, Chris. It's happening here. Now.'

'Ruth, tell me what we can give – sacrifice – to Gateman's bloody god.' He looked across at David. 'Are you suggesting that . . . Christ, what's that now?'

Suddenly the courtyard was filled with the sound of a pounding that rolled from wall to wall as if a salvo of thunder had dropped from the sky.

Something was knocking furiously on the sea-fort gates.

47

Chris shouted up to John Hodgson: 'John! What is it?'

No reply. John Hodgson, feet barely touching the walkway, leaned forward over the top of the wall as far as he could, his big stomach squashed over the coping stones, so he could see what was battering the gates with enough force to shiver the timbers like a power hammer.

'John?'

The farmer beckoned to his son to carry on watching as he heaved himself off his belly and ran down the steps to the courtyard, the shotgun gripped in one beefsteak hand.

'It's Mark!' His gruff voice was boosted to a higher note by adrenaline. 'He's back . . .'

'Jesus . . .' Chris felt his mind draw back sharply, deeper into his skull, like a snail retreating into its shell. He'd failed.

The pounding on the gates stopped abruptly. The only sound was the hiss of the advancing tide outside.

'Open the gates . . . Get them open,' Tony was shouting, frantic. 'He's not armed.' He began pulling at the timbers propped against the gate.

'No!' bellowed John Hodgson. 'They're out there. The bastards have got him trapped.'

'Open the gates!' Tony's eyes flashed wildly behind the glasses. 'You've got the gun. Blast them.'

Tony pulled the remaining timber away and reached for the bolts.

'Mr Gateman . . .' The big farmer pulled Tony's hand from the bolts. 'It's not that simple. He's trapped out there.'

Chris said, 'Listen to what he's got to say. We can't rush this, Tony.'

'Chris, Mark will—'

'Shut up, Tony. John, where is he?'

'He's stuck on the ledge to the left of the gates. The sea's round the base of the rock. There's a couple of those Saf Dar bastards in the sea. They're no real problem. The real problem is there's two outside the gates. And there's one at the far end of the ledge. Left-hand side.'

Chris nodded. 'So Mark's stuck between two of them on the ledge. Can you get a shot at them from the top of the wall.'

'Angle's too tight.'

Tony's nerve was snapping. 'Fuck . . . I don't believe I'm fucking hearing this. Stood chatting while Mark's out there. They'll tear his fucking head off.'

'Tony . . . You heard John. We can't open the gates. The Saf Dar are right outside. They'll . . .'

'Mark's risked his life to get help. You're going to fucking well leave him out there?'

'Do you think I want to? Jesus Christ, Tony. What happens when we open the gates? Those two will be in here in one second flat.'

John spoke. 'Look, for the moment they're not trying to harm him. They're just standing there.'

Tony rubbed his forehead. Chris realised that the idea of leaving his friend of fifteen years out there to be battered to raw meat was breaking the man in two.

'Dad . . . They've moved.' The Hodgson boy ran heavily down the steps to join them. 'Them things have moved.'

'Where?' Tony's eyes sharpened.

For a moment the boy looked as if he couldn't speak, then with a flash of inspiration he bent down and picked up a white pebble. 'Like this.' He drew on the wall:

O   X   O   O

-------------------/----/------------

'The dotted line's the wall, them slash marks are the gates, right?'

'Keep going, son.'

'The O's are Saf Dar. The X is Mark. They're on the rocky ledge that runs round the bottom of the walls. And – and there's a couple of the things in the sea. But not close.'

'We'll do it,' Chris said quickly.

'Best get everyone into the building,' rumbled John.

'There's not time.' He waved to Ruth to get back. 'We open the gates. John . . . shoot the monster between Mark and the gates. He can run for it.' He turned to Hodgson's son and nodded at the shotgun leaning against the wall. 'Know how to use that?'

'Yessir.'

'Cover your father's back. There's still the one to the right of the gates. Don't fire unless you have to.'

'Yessir.'

Tony slipped one of the three bolts back. His fingers shook.

'Might I be of any assistance?'

Chris looked round.

Shit. No.

The Major stood there, the dog sitting beside him; he had pulled the revolver from its holster.

'Move back from the gates.' This wasn't the time to be polite to senile old soldiers. And Chris hoped that the museum exhibit of a revolver wasn't loaded. 'Right, Tony. Open the gate.'

Tony dragged back the other two bolts then heaved the gate back.

The causeway beyond the gates was empty.

Cautiously, John, his son at his side, stepped through the gates. Chris and Tony followed to stand between father to the left and son to the right.

John raised his shotgun but did not fire.

Chris glanced first to his right. One of the Saf Dar stood like a red statue at the far end of the rocky narrow ledge. The sea was washing in a milk-white froth all around the little island now.

To his left he saw why the farmer had not fired.

Mark Faust, smeared with black mud, stood with his back to the sea-fort wall. Like an animal's prey he had frozen up with fear.

There the ledge was at its narrowest. Beyond Mark stood a Saf Dar.

But between Mark and the safety of the gateway in a half-crouching position was another of the red man-shaped things. It didn't even glance back at Chris and the others standing outside the gates. Every shred of its concentration was focused on Mark. It was hunched, great slabs of muscle on its back tensing in corrugated ridges. Chris knew it was ready to leap forward, then probably batter Mark against the wall like a cheap doll.

'Shift, you bastard, shift . . .' John stood, the shotgun to his shoulder. Sweating, he stared down the barrel, his eyes bulging.

'I can't get a clean shot. Fucker's too close to Mark.'

'Do it,' hissed Tony. 'Fucking do it.'

'I can't . . . This fires shot. I'll hit Mark as well.'

'Well, do something . . . Quick. They're coming thick and fast.'

Twenty yards along the causeway one of the red beasts had half pulled itself out of the surf on to the roadway. Like some hungry alligator, it paused half in and half out of the water, outstretched arms taking the weight of its top half. Smoothly, its head turned to look at the men in the gateway. The cruel eyes glittered hungrily.

In the surf, almost at Chris's feet, two more Saf Dar stood waist-deep, the water washing around them in wave after hissing wave. Even the water was repelled by the skin of the things. It rolled off in glistening white beads like rainwater off a freshly waxed car.

'I can't . . .' The farmer's plump face shook. 'If I fucking well fire I kill Mark as well.'

Chris's head spun. Answer this one, Stainforth.

No answer.

Mark was trapped. He couldn't go backwards along the yard-wide strip of bedrock; he couldn't go forwards; he couldn't jump in the sea. Whichever way he moved put him into the hands of the red monsters.

A voice ran through his head. Get back inside and shut the gates. You can't save Mark. You've got to leave him there. Soon Mark would become like Wainwright. Like the Fox twins. Like the others. Standing on the beach, crying out, gripped by alternating waves of mind-warped terror-pain and fury.

As the realisation sped through his mind he noticed a figure behind him. Before he could turn round a crack split the surf's hiss. Instantly the red man between Chris and Mark rolled sidewards into the sea.

Chris twisted round.

The Major stood, one arm stretched out, the revolver bleeding blue gunsmoke.

'Didn't know I still had it. Was a gold-medal-winner, you know. New Delhi handgun league. Top of fifty-six contestants, when the —'

Chris recovered. 'Move!' he yelled at Mark. 'Come on!'

Mark snapped out of the spell. He ran towards them.

Behind him the thing on the rock ledge suddenly began to run after him. Mark was fifteen yards from the gates.

'Mark! Down!' bellowed John.

Mark threw himself down on to his stomach as John let rip with both barrels. The force of the blast sliced away the creature's face, punching it backwards. The monster bounced off the rock ledge and into the sea.

Mark, powered by pure fear, punched himself to his feet to run at the gates. Chris urged the Major, still talking, through into the courtyard, followed by Tony, Mark, the Hodgson boy, then John.

Within three seconds they had crashed the gates shut and snapped the bolts home.

Chris left John to lean the timbers against the gate, jamming them tight shut. He knew that Mark brought bad news but he wanted to hear it from the man's own mouth.

Three o'clock. Middle of the afternoon.

Mark, still coated in cracking scales of marsh mud, swallowed what was left of the coffee. He sat exhausted in the caravan's doorway, the cup held tightly in both hands. Ruth, Tony and Chris watched him. In a voice barely above a whisper he told them what had happened.

'Sorry . . . Jesus Christ, I'm sorry . . . I just couldn't get through the marsh. Whichever way I went I always returned to the same place . . . Going in circles . . . Just going round and round. I couldn't get through.'

'The mist disorientated you,' said Chris, feeling as if nothing now stood between them and the fires of hell.

'No . . . It was more than that. Something weird . . .'

Tony nodded. 'I suspected as much. We've been quarantined here. No one gets out. No one gets in. Not until this is over.'

'The Saf Dar?'

'No. Not them. I'm talking big power now. Big, big power. The thing that's visited here every few centuries. It wants this trade – through sacrifice – to be very private. For a little while it divides this place off from the rest of the world. No interruptions, no outsiders. Just the local people and . . .' He shrugged. 'It. One of the old gods – not one that people can discuss or say little rhyming prayers to. This is one of the ancient gods. You don't have to make an effort to believe in this one; when it gets close to you, the animal part of you feels it. It would be like standing next to a huge bonfire; even before you can begin to put a name to it, its presence burns into you; you can't ignore it. Any more than you can ignore the bonfire; you feel it burning into your mind. It paces back and forth behind your modern religions, without a name, without a face, without any gospels or churches. Without Bibles. It doesn't need them. But it's there still. Still powerful, and still hungry for trade.'

'Shit . . . Sacrifice, sacrifice, sacrifice . . .' Chris spat out the words. 'It always comes back to that. If it's so fucking powerful, why does it need a sacrifice?'

'Sacrifice is a commercial transaction, remember? Between gods and men. When you buy, it's to acquire something you haven't got but you need, whether it's food, a box of cigars, a magazine. This old, old god craves that thing we possess.'

'Our emotions,' said Ruth. 'It milks them from us when we grieve at losing something that's precious to us.'

'That's right. It can't get that thing – the human rush of emotion – from anywhere else. It needs it badly. Maybe like a dope addict needs a fix of heroin. So here it comes. To Manshead. It's friendly downtown emotion store. It takes what's offered – say the agony of a father sacrificing his own beloved daughter – and it pays something back in return. A chunk of its own supernatural powers.'

'David . . . Have you seen him recently, Ruth?' Chris, suddenly uncomfortable, looked around the courtyard.

'I'll check,' she said. 'He might be with the Hodgson boys.'

Chris shivered. For some reason the sound of the surf washing round the sea-fort sounded far louder than usual. He glanced around the courtyard as Ruth went to hunt for David. It was deserted. The villagers, depressed by Mark's failure to get help, had drifted back indoors.

Mark rubbed his eyes. 'What now?'

Chris shrugged. 'What can we do? We've tried everything short of sprouting wings and flying out. Any suggestions, Tony?'

'I don't know. My problem is, Chris, I think too much. It's all up here. I'm a hard-headed cynic. Too cerebral. My grandmother would have said you should think more with your heart, not with your head. A psychologist would say you should let the unconscious part of your mind supply the answer, rather than the conscious mind. Don't think your way forward to a solution, feel your way forward; in an animal way. As they did ten thousand years ago when the first men knocked a few branches together here and called it home. You know, inspiration. Don't let the civilised man get in the way of the primitive chunk of brain you've got in there.'

'I reckon what he's saying, Chris, is think like a child. Do what *feels* right – not what you *think* is right.'

'Right now I don't think or feel anything.' Chris leant back against the caravan. 'I feel shell-shocked.'

Tony's face was stony. 'Believe me, the best – or the worst – is yet to come. I think that thing, the old god, is on its way. By tonight, probably, it will all be over.'

'Chris!' Ruth ran across the courtyard so fast her arms windmilled to keep her balance.

'Chris! He's gone . . .' Terror deformed her voice. 'David's gone. Someone's opened the gates . . . he's outside.'

Chris ran round the caravan and past the car. The timbers once propped behind the gates lay on the ground, the bolts were back.

The gates lay half open. Beyond, the causeway, now feeling the first lick of a new tide, was deserted.

48

He didn't stop to think about it.

The Saf Dar could have been waiting outside to welcome him with open arms, then crack the life from his body as easily as snapping a biscuit.

With no weapon, Chris ran out through the gates on to the head of the causeway before stopping to look round.

By chance there were no Saf Dar in sight. Nor was there any sign of his son.

'David!'

Nothing.

With a triumphant hiss, the sea creamed around the rocks, sending the first sheets of foam sliding across the causeway.

Where on earth was he? Chris stared hard at the beach, blurred with mist. A couple of Saf Dar stood at the far end of the causeway. But no sign of David.

No, not this. They couldn't lose David. Christ felt something bleeding inside him. This was pain he'd never felt before.

'David!'

Then Mark Faust was by his side, gripping the shotgun in his two huge hands. 'Any sign of him?'

'No. Christ, why on earth would he come out here?'

Ruth ran up and gripped Chris by the arm. 'Find him, Chris.'

'Look, he can't have gone far.' He was lying through his teeth. He could have gone far. His son might be at the bottom of the sea.

He looked back at the rocky ledge that ran round the

bottom of the sea-fort walls. Just half an hour before, Mark Faust had been trapped there.

At first Chris did not see them there.

His eyes searched the ocean boiling around the slab of rock on which the sea-fort was built, half imagining he saw David struggling in the surf that was streaked brown by strips of kelp.

The realisation of what his mind had subconsciously registered came in a slow burn of understanding. His head snapped back.

Almost at the far corner, standing on the narrow ledge of rock, four feet above the sea, was the Reverend Reed, white tufts of hair stuck out, his raincoat hanging off his thin body like a grey blanket.

Behind him a smaller figure, blond-haired, twisting and turning as if moving in a strange kind of dance.

'David!' The relief he felt was short-lived. Something was wrong.

The old man had one bony hand clamped around David's upper arm.

'Dad . . .'

Even though the rumble of the surf almost submerged David's voice, he knew the little boy was frightened.

He reached the ledge first, Mark behind him, Ruth last. The ledge was narrow enough to make it feel as if they were walking along a plank, the massive wall of the sea-fort behind them and five feet of seething North Sea beneath their feet.

Moving as quickly as he could, Chris reached a point a dozen paces from Reed. Here the ledge, as flat as a pavement, broadened to four or five feet.

'Stop!' Reed watched them through a pair of eyes that were frightening. They blazed with a manic intensity. All civilisation, culture, education had been stripped from that blazing stare. This was animal. Something trapped in a corner – terrified, but more dangerous than it had ever been before.

'Dad . . . Make him let go . . . I don't like it . . .'

Chris took a deep breath. 'Mr Reed. Mr Reed . . .'

'Reverend Reed, please . . . Don't forget I am a holy man. The link between mortal men and God.'

'Reverend Reed, look, it's dangerous out here. We should go inside where it's safe.'

'Safe? Ask Gateman whether it's safe or not.'

'If you're concerned about something we'll talk about it. But inside.'

'No.'

'Reverend Reed . . . Let my son go . . . please.' All at once he knew that Reed had planned something. Unpleasant.

He couldn't rush at the old man because all Reed had to do was push David over the ledge into the sea. The sea was dangerous enough. But likely as not there would be things waiting there. Already he'd noticed shadows swimming beneath the surface. The Saf Dar probably, drawn like sharks to a chunk of bloody meat.

'Reverend, please come inside. My son's done nothing to you. Can't we talk about it?'

'Yes. We can talk until the cows come home. Go ask Gateman. The time for talking is over. It's time we acted. Boy . . . stand still, will you!' Shocked, David stopped trying to twist himself free.

'Reverend Reed . . . Look, please let my son go. He's only six years old. You're frightening him.'

The old man looked keenly at Chris and asked: 'What are your feelings now? When I twist the boy's arm like this does it distress you?'

'Yes . . . you know it does. Don't do it. Please . . . You're hurting him . . .'

'Mummy . . .'

'Don't hurt him, Reverend. He's just a little boy.'

'You love your son, Mr Stainforth?'

'Yes. Of course. Now —'

'Listen to me, then. What did you buy him for his birthday this year?'

'Just let him go.'

'Answer the question.'

'A video . . . Books . . . And – and a computer game.'

'You love him a lot, then?'

'Yes! But why—'

'It goes without saying that the mother loves her child. Nature programmed the female of the species that way. But fathers . . . They can be different. They say they love their children. But some can be quite indifferent. They'd rather spend their free time with their own friends, drinking beer, playing squash . . . football. But I believe you do love your son very much, Mr Stainforth. You spend time with him, talk to him, not down to him, you treat him as someone very important in your life. Probably far more important then you yourself realise. I see you at Christmas spending the morning playing on the living-room carpet with him, putting together the toys, laughing and joking together. I truly believe you do that, Mr Stainforth. Ah, now you're wondering why I wanted to establish that belief, and why I am standing out here above the North Sea, holding on to your beloved son's arm. The reason is this, Mr Stainforth. Because I am going to kill your son. And you are going to watch me kill him.'

The power of the words:

I AM GOING TO KILL YOUR SON.

Chris stood locked in the same position, trying to draw breath.

'Dad . . .' David sounded weaker.

The Reverend Reed manoeuvred David closer to the edge of the rock. The sea churned fiercely beneath him. Chris glanced back at Mark's grim face; behind him Ruth looked as if she was in shock.

In the surf a head broke the surface. Red, grotesquely hairless, the eyes like two splinters of white glass staring at what was happening on the ledge.

'Sacrifice,' said Reed. 'Gateman was right. He should be here to witness this. Oh, and there he is.'

Tony stood a little beyond the gates, watching.

'You were right, Gateman. I was wrong. I understand now. We have to sacrifice the boy. Just as you wanted,

Gateman. The most powerful sacrifice is when you give what is most valuable. And what is more valuable than the life of a young child? If an old woman is terminally ill you hear nothing about it. But a sick child . . . Then you hear about it day after day. You see it on the television, in the newspapers. Charitable people raise money to send it for the finest treatment. As the saying goes: you see a sick child and your heart goes out to the child. When I kill this handsome little boy, whom we all like, everyone will feel the grief. More importantly, the child's parents will feel it most powerfully. They will watch as he dies. Their grief will be like a hurricane.' Reed reached into his pocket, groped there for a moment, then pulled out a screwdriver.

The long steel shaft glinted in the misty light. Years of use had worn the tip as sharp as a blade.

'The parents' outpouring of grief is what Gateman's dirty old god wants so badly. In return it gives us the power to remove those monsters that imprison us here so we can return to our homes, and to our lives. And we will forget this ever happened.'

Mark rumbled, 'After you have murdered a six-year-old boy? Man, you're crazy.'

Chris felt oddly calm. More than that, it was as if all his emotion had been locked away in the heart of an iceberg. The feeling was dangerous. As if that emotion could not be contained for long. Any more than you could freeze a nuclear reactor.

'Let him go.' Chris breathed ice. 'Let him go now, Reed.'

'Hurt him,' rasped Mark, 'and I swear I will personally — '

'Who said this would be easy? Not me. Ask your new holy man, Gateman. This is not easy at all.' Reed angled the screwdriver so that he could force the glittering shaft into David's eye.

'Mummy . . . Daddy . . .'

Chris bled inside.

'Listen to me,' cracked Reed's voice. 'I admit it. We obey different rules here. My God, my redeemer, cannot enter this place. I know . . . for some reason he is excluded. So: we sacrifice the boy. Then we are free.'

'Oh no you're not, Reed.' Tony spoke for the first time.

'We have to make the sacrifice, Gateman. We have to give something precious.'

'Yes, we do. We must give something precious – something so precious it hurts us to part with it. But what are you giving?'

'The boy. That mother and father's only child.'

'But he's not yours to give. He's theirs. The sacrifice will only work if the mother or father gives the child.'

The wild look returned when Reed understood this. 'But they're not going to do it, are they?' He moved his arm back with the screwdriver's point a foot from David's eye.

'Well then, Gateman. It's a gamble. Maybe you're right. Maybe I'm wrong. But we will have to see which one – ah . . .'

How David did it Chris didn't know, but he kicked out with both feet. Reed was still hanging on to the six-year-old boy but it threw him off balance. He had to use the hand holding the screwdriver to steady himself against the sea-fort wall.

Chris ran.

He threw himself forward, grabbing the old man's thin arm, pushing the screwdriver upward away from David.

It was the right thing to do.

And it was the wrong thing to do.

He smelt the gin stench on his face as Reed spat, 'Fool . . . Fool.'

With a single shove of his arm, the old man pushed David off the ledge and into the sea four feet below. The foam swallowed him without a splash.

'No!'

Chris threw himself down, eyes searching the surf. David didn't come up.

Just five yards away there was a semi-circle of four Saf Dar, the waves breaking over their shoulders.

Behind him Mark picked up Reed, swung him out over the

sea, past Ruth, then threw him along the ledge, bouncing him off the sea-fort wall. The old man squawked like a wounded crow.

'Get him inside.'

Dangerously, the villagers were spilling out through the gates and on to the dry section of the causeway.

Tom Hodgson strode forward, shotgun in one hand. He grabbed Reed by the dog-collar and hauled the old man inside.

Chris looked down at the shifting mass of water. It looked alive, sucking at the rock, slapping the sides of the causeway with a cracking sound that sent spray shooting six feet into the air.

'I'm going in!' he shouted to Mark.

'No. Not yet. Those things are in the water.'

'It's my boy in there. He can't swim. He's —'

'He'll come up. He's got to. Wait until he does, then grab him. They'll kill you if you go in there.'

Chris threw himself on to his chest, not even noticing the Saf Dar surfacing one by one just yards away. Five . . . Six. Another broke the surface below the ledge ten yards to his left. Seven.

Thrusting his hands into the water, he blindly felt for David beneath the surf. Spray fired up into his face.

Water, only water. His fingers swam through it, touching nothing solid; he didn't even acknowledge the possibility that a larger hand might grab his and drag him forward into the sea.

Beside him Mark did the same, the shotgun on the ledge by his side. Behind him Ruth stood staring at the surf in numb horror. Her son was somewhere beneath it all, battered by the whirling surf, unable to breathe, the little air that remained in his lungs turning into pockets of fire in his chest. Wanting to breathe . . . Needing to breathe . . . No air . . . Only a roaring darkness . . .

Barely twenty seconds had passed, but to Chris it seemed like an age. His little boy was drowning in here. Or maybe he was already in the big red paws of the Saf Dar.

He had to get him out of there.

His hand caught something.

He pulled. Up came a handful of leathery seaweed.

Ten yards along the ledge, a red figure was pulling itself out of the water with a reptilian smoothness.

Tony shouted, 'They're coming out of the water. We're going to have to get back inside.'

Chris didn't answer; his world consisted of an area of hissing sea-water the size of a table-top beneath his face. He searched through it with his hands.

It's no good, he's gone. I'm going to go in myself. Even if those things take me. It's better than admitting defeat. He dug his hands deeper into the sea, ignoring the pains shooting through his shoulders as he stretched his arms out. His face nearly touched the water as the waves swelled up towards him, the water now rising up to within an inch of his face.

God, if only —

There!

'Got him!'

Mark knelt beside him, ready to help.

Chris felt his fingers round the thin arm. Never let go, never let go . . . The words sped round his mind.

He pulled. At first nothing happened, then he saw the shape of a head just under the water, a blurred pale shape, then —

'Jesus Christ!'

A head of matted hair.

It was the dead boy.

The boy he had seen on the beach. With that procession of long-drowned men. The Fox twins; the dead pilot; the drowned fishermen. And there had been this boy. A skeletal figure with enormous eyes and black hair.

That was the face he looked into now.

The face must have mirrored Chris's in a surreal way. It wore an expression of shock, mouth wide open, a silver-sided tongue looking like a tinned sardine.

One eye stared up into his. It bulged hugely; the boy was torn by some colossal agony.

The force that had brought it to life had been so powerful it had ruptured the other eye, the explosive cancer replacing it with a red growth that swelled from the socket like a ripe tomato, its skin so tight it looked ready to split once again.

The boy opened and closed his dead mouth, trying to speak. Chris knew it was pleading to be lifted out of the sea and carried inside. After all these cold and lonely years, to be held tight and consoled. He wanted Mummy to kiss away his pain and make him better.

The vast red cancer eye began to crack open, exposing spiky fibres like the antennae of a shrimp.

Chris released his grip on the arm, which was as thin as an African famine victim's.

The face with its beseeching expression slipped away.

David had been under the waves for forty seconds.

'Hold my legs!'

Even before Mark had a chance to grip properly, he launched himself forward, his head beneath the surface of the water. Eyes open, he saw only distorted silver bubbles and rags of dark weed. His arms snaked away into the darkness beneath, searching desperately. No David.

Chris yanked his head up. Mark was still hanging on to his legs.

'Chris . . . They're moving in.'

The Saf Dar were half a dozen yards away, wading forwards.

Soon they would be able to snatch Chris into the sea.

'We've got to get into the sea-fort!'

Gasping in cold air, Chris shook his head. He plunged his face into the water again, arms shooting out.

Hit.

He grabbed, hands gripping fabric.

Chris pulled. A blond head emerged from the swirl of bubbles.

Then Chris's head was clear of the water.

'Mark . . . Got him. . . Pull!'

Chris hoisted himself partly back on to the ledge.

Mark, kneeling, heaved, but the angle was too awkward for him to get proper leverage. Together they hauled David by his sweatshirt. They got his head and part of his upper chest clear of the waves. He was conscious, sobbing with shock and fear.

'I can't lift him any further,' shouted Mark. 'Something's got hold of him! From underneath.'

Chris pulled but, still lying on his stomach, his leverage was worse than Mark's.

'Quick . . .' called Mark. 'They're coming.'

The Saf Dar were almost within arm's length. Their red faces were expressionless above the water; but their eyes blazed with menace. They sensed new victims.

'Dad . . . My legs . . .'

Chris cried, 'They've got him . . .'

This close. Christ. They might have to let David go after all.

No. Not ever.

As Chris hung on, another arm reached over his head.

It grasped David by the back of his sweatshirt.

When the arm pulled it seemed effortless. David came cleanly out of the water like a baby lifted from the bath. The force was enormous. As the arm raised David up, it lifted both Chris and Mark's upper bodies clear of the rock ledge.

Chris twisted to see who had lifted David from the water with such superhuman strength.

'Ruth.'

She completed the single-armed lift, her face blazing with concentration.

Around her bare arm, muscles knotted into bullet-hard lumps beneath her skin, the tendons looked like steel rods raising the skin into ridges. It took three seconds. As soon as David was clear, the expression melted from her face and she collapsed back against the wall.

Mark panted, 'Get David inside!'

The Saf Dar reached up their long red arms towards them, fingers as thick as raw beef sausages.

'Don't worry about Ruth, I'll get her.'

Chris picked David up then ran along the ledge to the gates. John Hodgson was standing on the small area of causeway that was still dry, his son by his side. Both held their shotguns raised to their shoulders.

Chris ducked in through the gates. Mark, carrying Ruth, followed them. Then the Hodgsons were inside, slanting the balks of timber against the locked gates.

Mark set Ruth down on the floor against the wall. The arm she had used to lift David in a single mother-love-fuelled pull had gone into spasm. Uncontrollably, it stretched out, rigid, as if it didn't belong to her; the muscles still bulged like clusters of walnuts beneath her forearm. She looked in agony, but she was more concerned about David. She made Mark sit the little boy on her lap. With her good arm she hugged him to her breasts and stroked his forehead with her fingers, rocking him and whispering softly.

Mark looked at her in wonder. 'You . . . you hear about things like this. Mothers lifting up cars to free trapped children, and beating off bears attacking their kids to . . .' He broke off embarrassed and moved away, dripping a trail of sea water, to sit next to Tony on one of the cannon.

Chris watched mother and son, closer together than any man could understand.

Then he walked into the centre of the courtyard and looked up into the sky.

The mist moved like smoke. Now it was flushed with a rose-pink tint.

Around the walls the villagers watched. They were waiting to see what he would do next. Because they knew he would do something. Even before he knew he would. His body language sang out a message as old as humankind itself.

The message rolled out from deep inside his mind. Some part of him that he shared with the first men on earth as they gazed in awe at a thunderstorm or painted animal-men on cave walls was telling him what he should do. It was not thought in words, it was a primeval, wordless understanding.

A knowing.

When you are hungry, you find food.

When you are thirsty, water.

When the old god that normally stands in the shadows of your soul steps into the light to be recognised, you know what you must do.

Chris's lips, after the fourth attempt, clumsily shaped the word:

'Sacrifice.'

49

Wrapped in a large blue-striped bath towel, cuddled by his mother as she sat on a straight-backed chair in the court-yard, David looked three years old.

More than anything, Mark wanted to pick them both up and carry them away from this nightmare.

David allowed his head to be hugged against his mother's breast; the still-dripping fringe partly concealed a bad graze above his left eyebrow. Already it was swelling, speckles of blood seeping through the scraped skin.

The graze would be the least of their worries.

She moved her arm to hold David more securely. She winced. The muscles still stood out through the skin in a painful cramp.

'Ruth, you should get some ice on that arm,' Mark told her gently. 'A bag of frozen peas would do it.'

'There's nothing left.' Ruth forced a weak smile. 'Anyway, it's feeling better . . . Thanks, Mark. For all your help.'

Mark couldn't manage a reply. He felt like shit. He'd let them all down. They had depended on him to get help. All he had to do was get through a miserable half-mile-wide strip of marsh.

'You might need this, lad.' John Hodgson walked up, a shot-gun in his hand. 'It's loaded, and here's two more shells.'

Mark looked around the courtyard. All the villagers were there. Waiting expectantly. They'd fed their hopes of escape from this place. Now they hung around unwilling to accept the idea that they were still trapped here, the food all gone.

What next? They had discussed sacrifice – why not slip back further into the mire. Cannibalism. In a couple of days it would be an option.

And he wondered about Chris. As he walked across the courtyard, he'd worn an expression that he'd never seen before. Fear wriggled inside him like a bellyful of cold worms.

Tony was sitting on the floor, his back to the wall. He seemed absorbed in some problem.

What the hell was he thinking? Another idea to get them out?

Shit . . . They'd finally run into the brick wall at the end of the road. There were no more ideas. No more hope. All they could do now was wait. What for? Mark no longer believed in miracles.

Body aching, he walked across to Tony and squatted beside him. Behind the glasses the man's eyes twitched quickly from side to side. Mark shivered. It was like looking into the eyes of a man who had been struck blind.

'Tony . . . You okay?'

Tony did not answer.

'Tony. Hey, Tony. Anything I can get you?'

Tony suddenly snapped out of it. He looked up at Mark, his face bright like a kid who'd just been shown the world's biggest Christmas tree. Surprised – and almost frightened by its stupendous size.

'Mark . . . It's happening . . .'

'Now?'

'Yes . . . Oh, yes. Now. Can't you feel it? I never thought it would be like this. . . I didn't think I would feel things . . . Or see things. But it's inside my head. Sort of . . . Ideas – images mental. No, er, I – I mean . . . Mental images. It hurts in a way . . . Something I don't want. Frightening. Hurting. Then I do want it, badly. Feels like . . . Or should I . . . Feels like I should reach out and pull it to me. Hold it to me. Tight.'

Mark listened to the low babble of words.

''S always been there, you know. Always. I think it . . . You – remember Williams? Ralph Vaughan Williams. What

328

he said when he first discovered folklore, folk music. He . . . he said: "I had a sense of recognition . . . here was something which I had known all my life, only I didn't know it . . ." It's like that. Known it. But didn't know it. Know it deep down . . . Like babies knowing how to suckle. Instinct. Born down the . . . eggs waiting to hatch. Eggs . . . small eggs . . .'

Speaking in tongues? To Mark it made no sense. But he knew Tony was trying to communicate something of enormous importance.

'You know, you feel as if your mind is a single thing inside your head. It's not, you know. Not at all. It has different parts. Now . . . I feel as if part of it is becoming separate . . . Sort of moving away from the other parts. Like two people who've danced together so closely, for so long, you think it's one person . . . But ent . . . ent-uh . . . but it isn't.' His speech was disintegrating.

'They're hanging apart now. And you realise that's how it was long ago. When we were covered in black bristles and lived in the forests. You know . . . you know, that's what makes us human. For us the separate minds inside our head dance so closely together, they seem like one. Always in the same step . . . you know, like a waltz. Two dancers – one young, one very old. Both following the same step so closely you think it really is one entity.' His eyes darted up at Mark. 'Don't you feel it?'

Mark shook his head. His old friend had not been able to keep a tight enough grip on his sanity. Now it was slipping from him.

'Weird . . . 'S weird . . . Like it just shouldn't happen. Like holding a radio battery in your hand and watching it grow in size; to as big as a brick . . . fills the room. The battery keeps growing and growing until it's bigger than all the aeroplanes in the world put together . . . And they sort of melt into one that's so big . . . Only it's inside your brain . . . growing and growing until it wants to split your head apart. Ha, a pregnant brain. That could be it. Your brain's pregnant and it's growing and growing . . . only the skull's too small, too tight . . .'

The grip on Mark's forearm tightened. He looked down. Tony's eyes had suddenly cleared.

'Mark . . . You'd better warn everyone. It's coming through. Warn them things are going to start happening. We're – we're going to see things, hear things . . . probably experience things, physically.'

'Look, Tony . . . Take it easy. You need —'

'Listen, Mark, listen.' Tony Gateman's voice was crisp now. 'Everything we've seen in the last few days will be nothing compared to what will happen in the next few minutes. All that with the Saf Dar, Wainwright, the Fox twins . . . Forget it. It's nothing.' Tony watched the walls as if expecting the stone blocks to bud eyes, noses, mouths and call strangely down to him.

'All that's happened is trivial,' whispered Tony, his thin fingers digging painfully into Mark's arm. 'The events of the last few days. Those things the Saf Dar did, killing Wainwright, resurrecting those dead men from the sea and dancing them across the beach; they were just like a few dry leaves that the breeze can slide across the street. What's coming now is the real force of the gale. The kind of wind that can lift the roof of your house or blow a car into a river. Mark, it's coming. That old, old, old god is going to enter this place . . . And Mark . . .' He pulled Mark's arm towards him. 'We're not ready. He will expect to make the trade; we have nothing. We have no sacrifice.'

Tony Gateman crouched against the wall, looking almost fetal.

Mark turned away, not wanting to see his friend like this.

As he did so his hand brushed the wall.

He stopped and stared at the wall. A buzzing filled his ears. He reached out and pressed his palm to the stone blocks.

They felt warm.

As if, impossibly, hot-water pipes ran beneath this two-hundred-year-old fortress wall. He took his hand away.

It left a palm-print.

Not dirt or sweat. The pressure of his hand had actually deformed the wall. As if he had pressed his hand against a block of soft plasticine. The print stayed.

Instinctively, shotgun in hand, he moved back to the mother and child. Instinct, yes. Back to the tribal pack. Males protect females and children.

Ruth looked up at him, trustingly. David stirred briefly to touch his grazed forehead with his little fingers.

But who are you protecting them from, Mark? he asked himself.

Who?

The Saf Dar? They were still beyond the locked gates. But for how long?

From the Reverend Horace Reed? An old man, a drunk, unarmed. Hardly. But as Mark looked across the courtyard at him, sitting on the caravan steps, his broken dog-collar sticking out, he noticed seven or eight villagers standing around him; an impromptu congregation listening carefully to the words peeling from those dry lips. After all, the man had been parish priest for thirteen years. He still carried some authority. Even now he might be telling them that the easy way out was to make the sacrifice. Kill David.

The villagers were dividing into two camps. If the Hodgsons chose to go under the black wing of the Reverend Reed, then life would get very difficult very quickly.

Or was he protecting mother and child from Tony's god of this little island, the boundary post between ocean and prehistoric swamp? What could he do? Without his trying, the image oozed into his mind of that ancient time-bleached spirit or god or whatever you wanted to call it stepping into this world as easily as a psychotic killer steps into a bedroom full of sleeping children.

Or – the thought sneaked into his mind – or was he really protecting the child from Chris Stainforth? The man's face

331

had suddenly become terrible – and terrifying – before he had walked determinedly towards the building and disappeared inside.

What was he planning?

Stainforth's face had completely altered. Was he gripped by the same contagious madness that infected Tony? Now that madness seemed to be infecting Mark. Because he could believe that Chris had been possessed by the spirit of an old man. No, not an old man, but a man from long ago, so long ago that the eyes that blazed from the face occupied some place between human being and beast.

Tony had told Chris about the old ways – fathers sacrificing their children. The most potent sacrifice of all. Releasing a torrent of emotion for the god to feed on.

Would he have to protect the son from his father? He looked up into the sky.

It had changed.

The colour was pink, like blood-flushed skin.

He wished he could believe in a benevolent god, who would gather them up and take them away from this.

He hated seeing this skin of civilisation torn from every man and woman here. It was ugly. Even more ugly was knowing that the primitive man-beast had been there all along, inside them all. That as soon as the civilising forces were removed it rose up through the depths, like an ugly ape emerging from the undergrowth – to take control again.

'Mum . . . I'm cold.'

David was looking up at his mother, shivering. She wrapped the towel round him more snugly and whispered something to him; David nodded. Ruth looked up at Mark.

'I need to get David some dry clothes. And a warm drink.'

Mark looked across at the Vicar and his flock congregating around the caravan.

'I'll get him some. It might be best if we went into the sea-fort, though. Can you manage with David?'

'I'll manage, Mark. If you could just —'

Bang.

The sea-fort doors crashed open and Chris strode out.

Mark watched him stride purposefully across the courtyard towards Ruth and David. In his hands he held the huge hammer.

He did not like the look in the man's eye.

He looked as if he had made the most difficult decision of his life. One that he was determined to see through to the bloody end.

Mark thumbed the safety catch of the shotgun and, holding it at hip height, raised the barrels until they pointed at Chris Stainforth's knees.

This was shit. Mark hoped the feeling he was getting from Chris was wrong. He liked the man. Christ, if it came to blasting his legs . . .

Chris approached them, his eyes frozen into an ominous stare, the face set, a rigid mask of tensed muscle.

Mark Faust put himself between Chris and Ruth.

'Ruth.'

Mark heard the icy calm in Chris's voice.

'Ruth. Bring David.'

Chris held the hammer with two hands across his chest as if he were holding an executioner's sword.

'Chris . . .' Ruth began, but Chris turned and walked purposefully to the gates. With the hammer he knocked away all but two of the timber props.

Then he turned and said:

'Come on. Bring David. We're leaving.'

50

'Come on. Bring David. We're leaving.'

It felt as if the words that spilt from his lips had been spoken by another person.

He hammered away the two remaining props. Even though the force of the hammer blows was enough to explode yellow wood splinters from the timber, he felt in control. No. More than that. He felt over-controlled; the kind of deadly calm before the volcano erupts.

He slid back the gate bolts.

Then he turned and spoke to everyone in the courtyard. Not a shout. His voice was calm, even, amplified by the explosive force growing inside him.

'Everybody out.'

'What!' Mark stared at him.

'Get out. You. Everyone. Move.'

'Chris . . .' Holding David wrapped in the towel, Ruth grabbed his arm.

'Chris! You can't send everyone out there.'

'You're mad,' cracked Reed, limping forward. 'Those things out there will kill us.'

'He's right,' said Ruth. 'It's murder, Chris.'

'You can't . . .' Reed took another step forward.

Chris raised the hammer to head height. 'Get any closer, Reed, and I'll crack your skull.' He heaved open the gate. 'Now . . . Walk. That goes for everyone,' he called. 'Everyone out. Now . . .'

'Chris,' pleaded Ruth, 'you can't do this. You can't!'

He smiled grimly. 'If they don't run, then they will burn.'

'Chris, what have you done? What —'

A muffled roar rolled from the direction of the sea-fort building. Smoke spurted from a broken window on an upper floor.

'Oh, God, Chris . . . Don't tell me you've done this.'

He turned to the crowd. 'Get out. Now. There are six gas bottles in there. They're full. When they go this place will be blown to kingdom come.'

'Chris, you're out of your mind . . .' Mark's eyes bulged. 'Where will we go?'

'Up to the dunes.'

'Why? They can still reach us.'

'Why?' Chris looked up at the bulk of the sea-fort, smoke bleeding from the windows in white streamers. 'Why? . . . Because I want to see this place burn. I want to see everything I've worked for, everything I've sweated over, cut my hands to shreds for, I want to see it go up in smoke and turn to rubble and shit.'

A violent hissing was followed by a sharp crack and a yellow glow that shone through the windows.

Feeling that unnatural calm freeze him inside, he said, 'Move.'

He stood by the gate, the hammer in his hands, watching the villagers file by; the Hodgsons led the way without protest.

There were no Saf Dar on the causeway now, but six formed a line to the beach in the sea, their heads above the water like blood-red islands set with two glittering eyes that watched the ragged procession of frightened villagers. There were more Saf Dar in the dunes. Four stood across the coast road.

They were massing. The hunted were walking as meekly as lambs to the hunters.

Mr and Mrs Smith pushed Mrs Jarvis in her wheelchair.

The rest followed.

No one looked him in the eye. They all stared zombie-like

in front of them. Not running, just walking. They crossed the causeway, the sea swirling round their feet, while on either side of them the bigger breakers rumbled shorewards, splashing over the watchful heads of the things in the ocean.

The Reverend Horace Reed passed out through the gates, dog-collar splayed outwards. The man was afraid.

Chris looked up at the sky. The mist glowed a hot red.

It was nearly here.

Soon man and god would meet. On this spur of sand and rock. It had been six hundred years since the last encounter. A long time for flesh and bone to wait. How long for the thing that lived before the existence of life itself?

It didn't have a name now. Chris breathed deeply. It just *was*. It was everything. Everything you could see, feel, breathe, taste, hear. It was everything you could be and do. Chris knew it had always been there. It was part of him. It was merely stepping from shadow to light.

A mental image flowed into Chris's mind. Two dancers. Dancing close. So close you think they are one person, moving in a perfect synchronised rhythm. Now they begin to separate . . .

Two dancers . . . moving slowly apart. Now you can see their faces.

One has your face.

The other's face – you see it clearly for the first time. You feel the cold points of spider legs running down your back.

The other dancer has a face that is shockingly familiar.

It has your face. But your face is altered somehow.

Mark helped Tony past Chris.

The big man's face expressed reproach. Tony's eyes belonged to the mind of a man that was lost and mad somewhere inside his head.

They passed by.

Then came the idiot girl with her mother. Then the Major carrying Mac. He patted its head, his eyes staring straight

337

ahead. He went outside.

Last of all, Ruth, still carrying David. She'd hooded the blue-striped towel over his head as if it would protect him from what waited patiently outside.

'Why, Chris?'

He looked into her eyes. Even though they were frightened they were strong. She would fight for her son's survival until her heart beat no more.

He wanted to answer her, but a barrier formed between his mind and his voice. He looked back at the sea-fort.

The scene left a photographic image in his mind as he turned and walked out through the gates one last time.

Even as he followed his wife and child across the causeway, oblivious to the cold water sucking at his ankles, he held that image. The car they had bought just the month before; the caravan they had moved into as happy as children going on holiday; the cannon he had bought from Reverend Reed, which would have formed an impressive entrance to the sea-fort; the sea-fort itself, built from butter-coloured stone. In its two-hundred-year history, it had never had to weather a siege. Until last week. Its builders would have been proud that it had fulfilled its purpose.

Now its destruction would come from inside – not outside.

Chris's feet were sure across the causeway stones. He followed Ruth and the others by the rusting mass of metal that had been Wainwright's car. Waves rocked it back and forth.

He passed the Saf Dar. Five yards away in the sea, their heads turned smoothly to watch him pass.

The Stainforths joined the rest of the villagers on the beach above the high-tide mark. They clustered there looking like an Old Testament tribe waiting for the end of the world.

Ahead stood a line of Saf Dar, like statues. No hurry for them now. The villagers were helpless. It would be as easy as harvesting plums from a tree.

Between them they had three shotguns with barely a dozen shells, the Major his revolver with two rounds.

There were now fifteen Saf Dar either in the dunes, on the beach, or in the sea.

Ruth sat on the beach with David in her arms. Other villagers sat down too. They were waiting for this cold, cold dream to finish.

'What now, Chris?' hissed Mark. 'We can't get any further. In God's name what do you propose we do?'

'I know what I'm going to do. I'm going to watch my property burn.'

He walked to the edge of the group as the Saf Dar slowly formed a widely spaced ring around them. From the dunes walked another procession. Wainwright, the Fox twins, the drowned little boy. The dead fisherman. The pilot. They were moving in for the kill, their minds cruelly dominated by the Saf Dar.

The sea-fort stood in the surf. From it smoke streamed up, making the thing look like the cooling tower of a power station.

Sacrifice.

This was Chris's sacrifice.

After entering the sea-fort building, he had first collected his hammer; then he found the jerry can of petrol. A petrol bomb remained from the earlier attack on the Saf Dar. He took that too. With the jerry can slowly swinging in one hand, the bottle of petrol in the other, and the hammer tucked beneath one arm, he moved purposefully to the room in which were stored the liquid petroleum gas bottles, standing there in a line like blue soldiers. Against one side of the room was a stack of wooden boards. On the window David's goldfish continued its manic circling of the bowl.

With alien calm, he removed the top from the jerry can and tipped petrol over the wooden boards, then the gas bottles. Above, the ceiling was timber. Two hundred years old and dry as a wafer.

The stench of petrol bit into his nostrils. He retraced his steps to the corridor; rested the hammer against the wall; lit the rag wick around the neck of the bottle then tossed it into the room with the gas bottles. The flare of heat scorched his face.

Still calm, he had picked up the hammer and walked outside. The gas bottles would have to heat up inside the inferno for a good five to ten minutes before they burst. Then they would go up like a bomb.

Now he watched the sea-fort from the beach. The villagers watched too.

This was his sacrifice; his dream about to erupt into flame. He had loved the place. Nothing in his life had ever been so important to him. Now he was giving it up. He was sacrificing his most precious possession.

Tony and Reed had been right. The ancient god had a contract with everyone who came to live on this stretch of coast. Even though the inhabitants might not know it, that contract was still valid.

This old god expected it to be fulfilled. It demanded the sacrifice. In return it would trade something of its own.

And this was no gentle god, meek and mild, it was a god of muscle, sinew, blood, life and death. If the deal wasn't fulfilled, then there would be only the full force of its fury. He knew the Saf Dar would become the vehicle of that fury. The human race would have more than just its fingers burned.

In the sea-fort he had realised that their survival depended on him now. No one else could help. He had to act.

This was his trade, then. The grief he would feel at the destruction of the sea-fort. His dream for the future.

He knew that in a few hours the Saf Dar would have been inside the sea-fort. They would hound the villagers through the building, breaking them apart with their bare hands. He saw himself frantically trying to barricade Ruth, David and himself into a room; the red things swelling through the passages to rip down the flimsy doors. Then what would those monsters subject them to? He imagined them snatching David, crying, from his mother's hands and dragging him away to the beach . . . playing with him for a while first.

What would they do to Ruth? Those things had been men

once. Now they were inflated with a supernatural life force that might have inflated their other appetites too.

Then later they would be like Wainwright and Fox. They would become the Saf Dar's puppets, marching across the countryside to the next town, their bodies driven on by the sheer power of the life force that would bloat them with its cancerous vitality.

He watched the sea-fort.

Concentrated everything on it. This was his dream. All the stomach-twisting endeavour to buy the place. The work; all the money they had poured into it. This place was going to be his future. His family would grow up there.

Then, as he watched, the white smoke streaming from the building turned yellow. A flash swelled up from the well of the courtyard in a burst of flame.

Later came the thunder rumble. Fire poured upward through the rising smoke.

He waited.

This was it. His home, his business, his future had just become a bonfire.

What did he feel?

Come on, Chris, what do you feel?

Everything you've worked for is burning.

Where's the bitter grief at losing it all?

What do you feel?

I feel nothing.

The realisation thudded home.

Nothing. I feel nothing.

He rocked on his feet.

The sacrifice had not worked. He was supposed to feel the pain of the loss. He didn't. The sea-fort had been just a pile of stone. The loss just wasn't that important. He had no outburst of emotion to give to the god. He would receive nothing in return. Now there was nothing he could do to save his family or neighbours.

Above, the sky was turning a brighter red; the sand beneath his feet began to steam.

341

In the sea-fort the bottled gas must have burned itself out. The building, still intact, was just pouring out smoke to that living red sky.

Feeling a cold emptiness, Chris turned to the villagers who were watching him.

'Sorry . . . I thought . . .' The emptiness inside robbed him of speech.

Mark and the Hodgson brothers had raised their shotguns. They turned to face the red men as they took another step towards the villagers.

Confused, the Major took a shaking step away from the group. 'I want to go home,' he muttered, bewildered. One of the red men moved towards him, its long arms swinging by its side in a way that seemed so relaxed it was sinister. Like a professional mugger strolling towards another victim.

Snarling, the old man's dog leapt at the man-shaped monster. It tore at the thing's shins with its small teeth. For a second the thing did not react. Then one of its long arms swept down.

Mac screamed like a child.

His spine broken, the dog dragged itself frantically along the beach by its forelegs, its back legs dragging a moist furrow through the sand.

'Mac, come here, boy. Come back, boy. Come back . . .' From somewhere in the mist came a sudden crack. The dog stopped squealing.

The Saf Dar took another slow step forward. The circle tightened around the villagers.

David opened his eyes and pulled the towel from his head. The graze above his forehead tingled. For a while he had been frightened. He had closed his eyes. Everything had seemed dark and cloudy inside his head. Then in his mind he had seen two people dancing. Very, very, very, close. In fact he thought at first it had been one person. A boy, like him. Then they had moved apart. There were two people.

Then the dark clouds inside his head had broken apart

and a brightness like sunshine had come flooding down. The other dancer spoke to him.

David looked around at the people on the beach: Tony Gateman sitting down, looking sad; Mark with the gun to his shoulder. The nasty red men were there. His mum was looking at his dad in a funny way, her eyes watery and silvery.

Tears.

'Don't cry, Mum. I know what to do. To make it all better.' She shushed him gently. She had not understood.

But he understood what had to be done. He knew a secret grown-ups didn't.

'I want to stand up, Mum.'

She let him go.

The towel slipped on to the sand. He knew what to do. And he had to do it now.

It was time.

His dad was not looking his way. He was staring at the red men. David waited until his mum looked the other way.

Then he ran.

'Chris!' Ruth's voice pierced his ears. 'Get him!'

Chris looked round.

David had run down the beach in the direction of the causeway. He ran between two Saf Dar who made no effort to catch him.

Plenty of time for that . . .

Plenty of time to play with the little boy in our own special way . . .

Chris bounded down the beach, the hammer gripped tightly in his hand.

By the time he reached the causeway, David was a third of the way across.

'David! Come back . . . You can't go back there.'

David didn't, or pretended not to, hear him. He ran on; a small blond-haired figure in a red sweatshirt and jeans, bare feet splashing through the surf.

Chris struggled through the waves. Now they were above knee-deep, making running nearly impossible.

By some fluke, David must have been running between waves. He ran easily and fast.

He prayed that a wave would not knock David into the sea. Flanking the causeway were Saf Dar. Waiting.

He moved as quickly as he could, not knowing what he would do when he caught up with David. The sea-fort was alight. Maybe not all the gas bottles had exploded. The smoke would be choking. How could they return to the shore?

If they did, they would only meet the Saf Dar. Time . . . life was running out.

Something twisted round his ankle. He pitched forward, sliding along the cobbles on the palms of his hands and knees. Picking up the hammer, he kicked free the long strand of seaweed that had bound itself around his ankle.

Then on his knees he suddenly stopped.

He knew he would chase after David no longer.

He watched his little boy leave the causeway and run through the open gates of the sea-fort. Smoke rolled through them and up into the flame-coloured sky.

He should save his son. His inner voice begged him to go on, to bring his son out of the burning building.

But another voice, the voice of the other dancer, said *No*.

The voice, clear and overpowering his, rang through his mind: *It's time to leave David now.*

As Chris Stainforth knelt there, the water curling round his legs, the final blast came.

This time the explosion was titanic.

The sound tore open the sky with a tremendous crack. A fountain of flame shot up from the courtyard, turning the sea the colour of liquid gold. He screwed his eyes to slits.

But he had to keep watching. He knew he had to.

The top half of the building – the windows, the balcony – split from the rest. In a single piece it rose into the sky, flames spurting from the bottom, cracking like thunder.

Like some stone rocket it rose higher and higher towards the rose-coloured sky.

Then, with horrible slowness, it tore itself in two. Bleeding fire and smoke, it dropped piece by piece into the sea.

Chris's eyes opened wide. Fragments of burning wood were raining down from the sky all around him, to fall into the sea with a sharp sizzling sound. A burning tyre from the car dropped like a meteor on to the causeway ten feet in front of him and rolled into the sea.

The sea-fort was a mound of blazing rubble.

David.

Chris, the father, had knelt there and let his son run into the building. Now David lay crushed beneath that inferno.

As if a handful of skin had been torn from his face, he howled.

His only son.

An avalanche of memories swept everything from his mind.

It was more than grief; it knocked the breath from his body.

David. He remembered how three days after he was born they had brought him home from hospital wrapped in a white shawl. The time he had fallen from his bike and cut his chin. He was three years old; Chris had been nearly mindless with worry. Driving him to hospital, David in Ruth's arms in the back. And two years ago, when David had woken in the middle of the night crying and holding his head, saying it hurt him. Chris had convinced himself it was meningitis.

When David had first started school a bigger boy began bullying him. How can someone punch a four-year-old child? David, his eyes large, had calmly catalogued how the boy had hurt him: punches, kicks, bending fingers back, jabbing a thumb into his spine. All the times Chris had taken his son to school then walked away. David had watched him with those big frightened eyes, giving him a little wave and a forced smile, knowing that the bully would be waiting for him round the corner.

God . . . You try to protect your children. There are so

many cruel things waiting to hurt them: a car travelling too fast; a dormant cancer waking in their bones to kill them by inches; or choking to death on a piece of apple.

You're afraid some pervert's going to snatch your son or daughter off the pavement. Even from the garden. You see it over and over in your mind. Some faceless man, gripping your child by the hand, pulling them along crying and frightened. Then doing what to them?

You've read enough newspaper reports to know. The remembered fragments of text, odd sentences, stream up in a poisonous flow through your mind: little girls, little boys, abducted, tortured, killed.

The little details haunt you. The little girl murdered and left in a deep-freeze. Police find a single tear, frozen to her cheek. Perverts forcing whisky down the throat of the five-year-old boy. They hold him by the throat too hard. He is asphyxiated. The little boy had only gone to the canal to watch the swans.

For years and years he had read these reports. He had wished over and over that he could have surprised one of these perverts just as they abducted a child. He would have broken every bastard bone in their body.

Those thoughts had sifted through his mind for years. He had tried as hard as humanly possible to keep David safe from harm.

He had failed.

A change took place inside him.

The icy calm broke. A fury began to run through him, bitter, and burning like fire.

'Bastards!'

Chris stood up, the huge hammer gripped in his two hands.

'Bastards!'

Those red men had caused this. The Saf Dar. They had destroyed Chris's life. They had taken away his son. They had robbed him of the reason to live.

Bastards.

Fucking bastards.

What have I done to you?

He walked back towards the beach, fury pumping his legs, forcing him through the surf like a man-of-war.

The hammer seemed to quiver in his hand.

The Saf Dar's circle was tightening around the people on the beach.

Chris didn't give a shit now.

He wasn't walking away from this one.

Those bastards killed my son.

Revenge.

The word had a beautiful power. Revenge. It resonated inside his skull. REVENGE.

The monsters would pull him apart like roast chicken, but he wouldn't run away from this. No. This was where he stood and fought.

Fury thundered through him, bursting inside, lighting up his arms and legs in a rush of blazing power.

The first red man turned to face him, glass-splinter eyes gleaming hungrily. The lips parted in a vicious grin. It lifted its gorilla arms, muscles bunching, distorting the skin and veins.

'Bastard!'

Fury ripped a scream from his throat; he swung the hammer at the flat red face.

He had not expected it.

The impossible happened.

The massive iron head of the hammer swung down into the face – dead centre. And it kept on going, the fury-driven swing sending it down through the spade-like forehead, down between the eyes, splitting open the nose to wreck the jaw, driving out teeth to punch through the skin.

The red man crashed back on to the sand, flat out, arms and legs outstretched as if he had fallen from a tower block.

One to Chris's left lurched forward furiously, its arms reaching out, the fingers flexing to snap his neck.

The anger blazing through Chris powered him into something more than human. Arms straight out, he swung

347

the hammer towards the side of the monster's head.

The head exploded like a paint-filled balloon; splinters of bone, cancered brain, and a gobful of black shit hung through the gaping hole the hammer had made.

The thing's knees bent and it folded dead on the sand.

Shouting, he twisted round to face the next one. He was howling, swearing, the fury blasting through his whole being like a high-pressure hose; its intensity hurt, but there was a sweetness too, a sweet pain like pulling a deeply embedded thorn from your finger.

'Kill me!' he roared at the red man. 'Do it. Do it!'

He wanted the thing to rip him apart and end his life. He didn't want to live knowing he had failed his son.

'Come on! What are you waiting for? Kill me!' he bellowed furiously. The fire blazed in him, from his balls to his brain; it torched the core of his being.

'Kill me! Come on, I want you to kill me!'

He walked forward, body burning, the hammer above his head.

Then he saw it.

The realisation stopped him dead.

He had looked into the monster's face and seen for the first time an expression of the emotion it felt.

On that great flat face there was . . . fear.

This lump of man-shaped shit was actually frightened of him.

He moved forward, hammer swinging over his head.

The creature groaned.

Fear. He scared that great bulging block of muscle.

The knowledge uplifted him. He felt strength flowing through him. He felt a new power. His fury met with it; fused with it and —

The hammer tore off the monster's face.

Faceless, terrified, it turned and tried to run.

The next hammer blow snapped its spine. It fell to the sand, face down.

He didn't stop to finish it off. He walked over it, his feet stamping down, cracking the ribs like wishbones, rupturing its internal organs.

The remaining Saf Dar were backing away now, looking from one to the other.

They didn't look so big now. Their arms looked thinner. The look of evil had been replaced by one of fear.

This shouldn't be happening . . . Chris knew what they were thinking. *This wasn't what was supposed to happen. These people from the sea-fort were sheep.*

Well, one sheep had turned into their nemesis. The avenging angel.

He moved among them. He moved fast. The hammer became an extension of his arms; it had no weight, it sliced through the air like a blade, pounding a skull to red mush here, separating an arm from a torso there.

The Saf Dar howled and ran in terror.

And he exulted in their destruction.

For a few days the Saf Dar had soaked up the power from this chunk of coast. That force had animated them, driving them on to fulfil their own warped passions. But now the power was leaving them. No, not quite that. Something was taking away that power – and redirecting it through Chris Stainforth.

Even as he cracked open another face he saw that they were weakening.

Their skin was wrinkling, like a tomato left too long on a shelf. Inside they were withering, muscles shrinking. Their skin was turning grey – bloodless. They stumbled across the beach and died as the massive block of iron hammered them to mush.

Within minutes he faced the last one. It trembled.

He looked into that grey face. The eyes were sticky white drops, weak, barely focused. The face twisted into an expression of utter, bottomless fear.

It raised its thin white hands to its face.

He raised the hammer high, ready to swing it down on top of its hairless grey head.

But he did not bring the hammer down.

Welling up from deep inside him was a huge swelling of absolute power; it rocketed up through the core of his body, up through his throat, to his mouth.

Then he roared out an ear-bruising cry. The sound rolled over the beach and away, to reverberate down and down and down to another sea, which belonged to a different world.

For ever and ever, world without end.

Amen.

Before him, the last Saf Dar crumbled without being touched. Its skin peeled away from its head, exposing shrivelled eyes that looked bleakly back at Chris. As if moulded from ice-cream, the body melted, dribbling down to form pools of grey on the beach.

Seconds later it flopped on to the sand with a wet smacking sound.

As he walked slowly back to Ruth and the villagers, the sea slid in to wipe away the melting remains of the dead men.

He knew. They would not come back this time.

The villagers watched him in silence.

Chris looked down towards the surf. A line of figures – Wainwright, the Fox twins, Hodgson, the drowned boy and the others – was filing into the sea. They walked calmly, like sleepwalkers. Now a greater voice was calling. They obeyed. Their nightmare was over too.

He dropped the hammer to the sand, put his arm round his wife, and they crossed the causeway together, back to the sea-fort.

They stood together in what was left of the courtyard, the car a crumpled metal box beneath the masonry. What was left of the caravan blazed.

Hardly one stone stood above another; there was just a heap of rubble rising from the sea. Here and there, like a scattering of yellow daffodils, small flames flickered through the rubble.

I killed our son. Chris wanted to say the words, but nothing came.

He had his arm around Ruth. She said nothing. She seemed somehow inert, as if part of her life had left her.

A car tyre hissed as air escaped from the burning rubber.

He felt empty now. The huge reservoir of bitterness, frustration, rage had been spent.

Ruth. I sacrificed our son. The words would have to come out soon. *I let him run in here. I waited. Knowing it would blow and that our only son would be killed.*

I sacrificed our six-year-old boy.

The contract is fulfilled.

That old god that resides behind our shadows milked me dry of the grief and rage I felt. And took them away to use for its own purposes, whatever they are.

And it gave me the strength in return to destroy the Saf Dar utterly and completely.

Something touched his foot. Something soft. For a second he was afraid to look down, guessing it might be —

He forced his eyes to travel downward, down from the sky now clearing, the blue of early evening showing through, down over the mounds of rubble with their scattering of fires, past the wrecked car, the caravan, with its scorched curtains trailing across the ground, and down to —

— a flattened, scorched ball. The one David had played with that morning.

He moved it with his foot.

The feeling that came over him now was one of enormous sadness. David would never leap on to their bed in the morning, laughing, pulling him out of bed. Asking if he could go and watch a Superman video as they ate their cornflakes together.

All that had gone.

He stared down at the punctured ball. Its edges blurred as Chris felt his eyes prickle, as if little needle-points were touching the skin around his eyes.

'Dad . . .'

No . . . He wanted to shut off the mind video now. No more.

'Dad . . . I want to go now.'

'David?'

Ruth's voice.

Chris looked up. On a mound of stones a figure stood, looking smoky and indistinct against the sun now pushing through the mist.

'David!' Ruth's voice rose into a piercing squeal.

The smoky figure jumped down into the courtyard. And became solid.

David flew towards them.

'I hid in the cellar, Mum. I went down inside . . . and bang! Then I got out again.'

Chris crouched down and threw his arms round his son, hugging him tightly. Ruth wrapped her arms round both of them.

Chris whispered, 'David, I . . . I'm sorry . . . I'm crying . . . I'm actually crying. I'm sorry . . . stupid . . .'

'It's not stupid,' said Ruth, kissing her husband and son. 'It's not stupid to cry.'

He held on to his wife and son and wept. The sound that came from his throat was not sobbing. He felt it rather than heard it, as it flowed from him in sweet notes, like the sound of some delicate, mystic music.

Something inside him had been made new again.

He held his wife and son close, feeling the animal warmth of their bodies.

Meanwhile, the sound of the ocean gradually changed.

The tide had turned.

51

'Afternoon, Chris. Running to schedule?'

Chris looked down from the top of the ladder to where the Major stood with two West Highland terrier puppies which pulled enthusiastically at their leads. The Major shielded his eyes against the brilliant October sunshine.

'Just about.'

'When you opening?'

'A week on Friday.'

He chatted to the Major who watched him at work with his keen blue eyes while the white puppies nipped at the laces of his highly polished brogues.

He found it hard to picture the Major as he had first seen him six months before. Then the old soldier had wandered around the village in crumpled clothes, his eyes sliding out of focus as senility ate at his mind. The old Major had vanished like an exorcised ghost.

Like everyone else who returned from the sea-fort, he had changed. The Major could pass for a man in his fifties.

He laughed. 'These two are a handful. Nearly called them Donner and Blitzen. You know, Thunder and Lightning. But we're almost house-trained, aren't we, boys?' the Major waved an enthusiastic cheerio and allowed himself to be pulled on down the street by the dogs.

Grinning, Chris returned to the job.

'Want me to hold the ladder for you, Dad?'

David stood astride his new bike, one foot resting on the bottom rung.

'No thanks, kidda. Nearly done.'

The ladder juddered again as David used it to push himself off, pedalling hard along the curving drive in the direction of the village street.

Chris's dream was coming true at last. The insurance company had paid up without a murmur for the loss of their car, the caravan, and the sea-fort itself.

With the money they had bought the redundant vicarage in Out-Butterwick. The builders had carried out the conversion work superbly. Soon the Vicarage Hotel would be open for business.

'Magic, isn't it?' he'd say to Ruth.

'Magic it is.'

But then life had been nothing short of magic these last six months.

The awkward questions they had expected from the police – two people missing, an old fortress torn apart by a colossal explosion – never arose. They took photographs of the wrecked buildings, made notes, and swallowed everything he told them. Not that they were stupid. It was something about Out-Butterwick and Manshead which altered the way they thought.

David came pedalling down the gravel drive.

'When are we going down to the beach?'

'In about twenty minutes. When I've finished this.'

'Is Mum coming?'

'If she feels up to it.'

'I'm up to it.' Ruth leaned out of the window at his side, smiling. 'This doesn't make you an invalid, you know.'

'Mum . . . How did you get that baby in your stomach?'

'Your dad'll explain later.' She grinned at Chris mischievously. 'Won't you, Dad?'

'A lot later.'

'Coffee?'

'Love one, thanks.'

Ruth shut the window.

They had not planned another baby just yet, but . . . it had happened.

The memory of the day he had set fire to the sea-fort was now oddly flattened. Almost dream-like. After they had stood on the beach to watch the sticky mess, what was left of the Saf Dar, being washed clean away from the beach by the surf, they had walked back to the village. There someone had suggested a beach barbecue. But it was more than that. A wild celebration – euphoric; an ancient exultation.

Odd images flitted through his mind. The feasting on mounds of steak. The blazing timber on the beach. People had even burnt their furniture.

And he remembered running with Ruth through the dunes, their bare feet flicking across grass and sand. They were running and laughing. The next image: both naked, rolling over and over in the rough grass. They had never made love like that before. Their bodies had collided like exploding stars.

Then it was over.

He had been conscious of a long period of peace, and a sense of quiet satisfaction, which remained with him. And when they learnt that Ruth was pregnant they both accepted it as a natural part of the sequence of events.

A sequence, a magical sequence, that was continuing.

He looked to his left. The trees that screened off the church were turning gold, those in the orchard bent under the massive weight of apples.

The village looked a more affluent place than it had done for years, with new cars in the drives. Beyond the cottages the sea, as blue as the sky it mirrored, rolled in over the sandy beach.

Odd fragments of recent memory ran through his mind. John Hodgson, smiling proudly, leaning over his farm gate, plump fingers knitted together, saying: 'Bleeding milk yield's gone through the roof. We're going to do our own cheese with it. Y' can't pour the stuff away, can you? It's not right.'

Rosie Tamworth, the retarded girl, had always called Chris *Mifter Th-tainfer*. Yesterday, she had sung out, 'Hello, Chris', her voice as bright as a silver bell.

Mark Faust had talked a lot about the *Mary-Anne* and the

loss of his crewmates. Chris guessed that the big American was going through a period of healing. Recently, Mark had been promising to take a boat out, for the first time, to where the ship and crew he loved lay on the sea-bed. It was time to say goodbye to them.

Mrs Jarvis, who should have been crippled with spinal cancer, walked along the street in the direction of Mark's shop, a basket over her arm. She gave a cheerful wave. Chris waved back.

'I've never seen a whole community like this,' Ruth had said. 'I can't believe it. Everyone's so happy.'

'Don't knock it. That's because we live in an enchanted village.' Chris had said it lightly. But he believed it. Magical. Enchanted. Yes. A happy enchantment.

He found it hard to describe. The nearest he could get to putting it into words was to suggest that these couple of miles or so of coast had become sexy. Like the sexy girl who works in the newsagent's. You find yourself going to buy a magazine you don't really want because you know she'll be there. When you see her you get a warm buzz of sexual electricity goosing through you. Compared with the rest of the world the very molecules of the place seemed to dance to a richer rhythm.

David pedalled down the drive as Tony Gateman strolled towards the house.

'Hi, David. How's school?'

'Fine, thanks. How's the pub?'

Tony laughed heartily.

Chris came down the ladder. He'd slipped into this relaxed custom of chatting to neighbours. Time was a plentiful commodity in Out-Butterwick.

They chatted for a while. Then he began to suspect that Tony had come for more than small-talk. There was something on the man's mind.

After five minutes it came out.

'Chris, I haven't told you this, but for the last few weeks I've been attempting to put down on paper what happened to us at Manshead over those few days in April.'

'You're not going public?'

'No, perish the thought. Everyone in the village agreed to keep it secret. I'm certainly going to abide by that. No, it's . . . it's just that I want to get this thing straight in my mind. Call it intellectual conceit, but I want to work out what happened up there.'

'Perhaps there's no need. Any more than you really need to know why the sun rises each morning. It happens. It's beautiful. That's all we need to know.'

Tony smiled. 'Humour me, Chris. What happened on that final day?'

'In a nutshell, some kind of sacrifice took place. Whatever came here – god, cosmic spirit – took what was offered and paid us in return.'

'And the result was that the Saf Dar were destroyed for ever. And there was enough left of that payment, that burst of supernatural power, to heal everyone that was sick in the village and leave us with an uncannily happy and prosperous community.'

'True.'

'But what was sacrificed?' Tony smiled. 'You know I keep recalling what I read in my history books. That in ancient times the greatest, most valuable sacrifice was self-sacrifice. In some cultures, the men and women who sacrificed themselves in times of acute danger became gods themselves. Or so the legends ran.' Tony looked hard at Chris. 'Chris, what happened to David that afternoon, when he ran back to the burning sea-fort?'

'Tony, I don't want to think about it. Really I don't.'

'Humour me, Chris. Let me put this into words for you. Then stick it in the back of your mind and get on with your life.' Tony Gateman pressed his hands together. 'David did this. He knew what he had to do. Even if he wasn't completely aware of it consciously. He had to make you believe he had died. So that it would release within you that tremendous outflow of emotion – not just grief, hatred, anger, but an emotion so deep, probably so primal, that it has no name.

357

He knew he had to break that barrier between your higher mind and that reservoir of emotion that burned deep down inside you.'

'So . . . out it all came,' Chris whispered. 'This eruption of pure emotion. Whatever it was took it. And paid us with some of its own power.' He stood up, rolling the words around his mind. He looked out to sea. Moving away from the jetty across the ocean, shining in the October sunlight, was a rowing boat. Chris knew who the giant figure at the oars was. With each slow pull of the oars, Mark Faust moved further away from the shore.

'But how could David know all this? He was only six years old.'

'David's special. You know that. The things he tells you. Tell me this, Chris. Do you ever go out to Manshead?'

'Sometimes.'

'Notice anything?'

'Yes. And I think I know what you're going to say.'

'David told us that when he ran into the burning building he hid in the cellar. And that the cellar protected him from the explosion that demolished the sea-fort.'

'Yes.'

'But you know that's not possible, Chris. It wasn't exploding gas bottles which destroyed the sea-fort. The detonation came from within the cellar itself. Perhaps a natural build-up of methane gas – who knows. Anyway . . . The building collapsed into the hole created by the detonation. The cellar is full of rubble. No one could have survived in there.'

Chris nodded slowly, trying not to allow his imagination to show him pictures of what might lie beneath that mound of butter-coloured stone.

As they talked, David came pedalling towards them.

'You know what happened now, Chris, don't you? To David?'

'Yes.'

'Right. I'm ready, Chris. Oh . . . hello, Tony.'

Ruth walked as quickly as the new bulge in her stomach would let her. She smiled. 'Someone tells me they saw you out walking with Elizabeth again.'

For the first time ever, Chris saw Tony blush. 'Ah . . . that'll be Mark. The old gossip . . . Yes. It's true.'

Chris grinned. 'Something you're not telling us, Tony?'

'Time for the beach, Dad? called David, catching hold of Chris's leg to steady himself on the bike.

'Sure is, kidda. Coming, Tony?'

Tony laughed. 'Love to. But I have . . . er . . .'

'An appointment with Elizabeth?' Ruth's smile broadened.

Tony coloured again. 'I'll, er, walk part of the way with you.'

'Can I go down on my bike, Mum?'

'I expect so. Come on.' In the warm sunshine, mother and son walked ahead, Ruth waddling slightly, David on the bike wobbling a lot.

Chris did not bother to lock the door. There was no need to be security-conscious in Out-Butterwick.

'So . . . Chris.' Tony spoke in a low voice as they followed. 'You know what happened to David, don't you?'

'Yes, I do, Tony.'

I do know. I know that on that afternoon in April my six-year-old son returned from that place to which we all ultimately travel. And now I know he will grow into a man the world has not seen in centuries, if not thousands of years.

'Chris?'

They had reached the crossroads.

'Yes, I know what happened, Tony.' Chris smiled. 'And I know things are going to happen to David in the future – wonderful things. But that's in the future. For now, I've made up my mind not to think about it too closely.'

Tony smiled back, understanding. 'You're right. Enjoy your lovely family, Chris. You're a lucky man.' Tony straightened his tie. 'Presentable?'

'Presentable, old son.'

'Right . . . Wish me luck. Cheerio.'

Tony walked quickly away along the street.

At the crossroads, Chris paused for a moment, looking round at the village he called home, the handful of cottages, Mark Faust's store, the pea-green village hall, the tip of the church tower almost hidden by autumn trees. He nodded with a quiet satisfaction – then he followed his family down to the sea.